Smoke and Adders

Jennie Finch

First published 2016
by Impress Books Ltd

Innovation Centre, Rennes Drive, University of Exeter Campus,
Exeter EX4 4RN

British Library Cataloguing in Publication Data
A catalogue record for this book is available from the British Library

ISBN 13: 978–1–907605–89–5 (pbk)
ISBN 13: 978–1–907605–90–1 (ebk)

Typeset in Sabon by Swales & Willis Ltd, Exeter, Devon, UK

Printed and bound in England
by imprintdigital.net

Acknowledgements

As I come to the end of this series of novels I am more aware than ever that every writer is part of a loose but vital network of people without whom the whole enterprise is doomed.

I have been so lucky with my friends who have shared their stories with me and patiently listened as I talked through ideas and scenarios.

None of the books would have succeeded without the help and support of everyone at Impress Books who took a chance on an unknown writer in an unfamiliar genre. Thank you.

The series began when I took an extra module at Teesside University in Detective Fiction. This course, led by the wonderful Carol Clewlow, set me on a new path and has been an inspiration for the last five years.

Thank you once more to all at Southside Broadcasting, especially Alex Lewczuk, for all the support and encouragement.

And last, but never least, thank you to Jackie who has an eagle eye for typos, a fine sense of my dodgy timelines and the patience of Job in the long, dark writing months. You started this and you're still with me every step of the way. These are your books too.

Smoke and Adders is dedicated to everyone who stood up to be counted during the hard years. Those thousand small kindnesses are not forgotten for without you all we would not be here today.

Prologue

The afternoon was hot and Steve wriggled as the heat from the paving stones struck up through his worn shorts, burning the backs of his unprotected legs. Leaning against the yard wall, he screwed up his eyes, admiring the red flashes as they sparked across his vision. He opened his eyes with a sigh. Stockwell was baking and it was too hot to do anything interesting. All his friends were out at the Rec' but he was confined to the back yard by his mother on account of yesterday's 'incident'. Steve was bored.

As he flung himself back once more, seeking the tiny ribbon of afternoon shade cast by the brick wall surrounding the yard, his glasses slipped and almost fell off his face. The boy grabbed at them, catching them in his damp hand before they could hit the flagstones. He had already broken one pair and was reduced to wearing the hated black plastic National Health frames. 'Gimp glasses', his class-mates called them. All they could afford and damn lucky to get them according to his mother.

He stared at the heavy glasses, twisting them back and forth, squinting as he struggled to focus. As he turned them

1

in his hands a bright spot appeared on the stones in front of him, flickering and then vanishing again. Steve stopped and turned the glasses back until the spot reappeared, staring in fascination as the tiny dot grew larger, then smaller and even brighter in response to his movements. He reached out to touch it, only to jerk his hand back as the tightly focussed light burned his fingers. His glasses clattered to the ground and he peered at them anxiously but they were unharmed. One lens was warm and he touched it gingerly, lifting it up to peer through it before holding the spectacles out in front of him once more.

This time he concentrated the light on a patch of grass, already dry and fading in the hot sun. For a few moments nothing happened and then a tiny trickle of smoke began to rise from the crack in the stones. Steve grinned with delight, moving the lens so the little dot slid along the floor, extending its range of destruction. More smoke rose in front of him, drifting in the still air to surround him. Steve sniffed, savouring the strange peaty smell that was so different from the acrid fumes of the kitchen stove. Totally absorbed in his new game, he failed to see his mother until it was too late.

'What do you think you're doing?' she shrieked as she flew out of the back door and seized him by his collar. 'You stupid little fool. You'll burn us all alive!'

She stamped on the smouldering grass, still keeping a firm grip on her wayward son. When she was sure the fire was extinguished she dragged her son inside by his ear. Soundly slapped, Steve was sent to his room for the rest of the day. Lying on his metal-framed bed, he listened through the narrow window as his mother chatted to Mrs Stimpson over the adjoining wall.

'I really don't know what I'm going to do with him,' she said, her hands busy untangling the washing line and coiling it neatly. 'I've tried reasoning with him, explaining how dangerous all this stuff is. One time we called the bobby in – you know, him over the road. He come in, all official in his uniform, and give our Steve a good talking to but it don't seem to do no good. In one ear and out the other – don't touch nothing on the way, neither. So what's left 'cept a good belting? And even that don't do no good. Seems he's getting worse and I don't know what to do. Find himself in one of them approved schools soon, I reckon, and then what'll his dad say when he gets back, eh?'

Steve tuned out to the so-familiar complaints and closed his eyes, imagining the beautiful shining dot as it glowed brighter, that tantalizing ribbon of smoke rising from the grass. When he sniffed he could still detect the sweet smell that rose from his shirt, seductive and fascinating. Whatever punishment his mother devised, it had been worth it.

Chapter One

Ada shot through the kitchen door and out into her garden, alerted by the barking of the dogs, the coal shovel in her hand ready to ward off intruders.

'Oh bloody hell,' she said as she spotted the smoke rising from the verge just beyond her gate. Wielding the shovel she beat out the smouldering foliage, stamped down on the blackened earth with her feet and finally dowsed the whole patch with water from her sink. Feeling through the charred area with her foot, she pushed an empty beer bottle out into the road. She lifted it gingerly with the edge of her apron before stowing it in the rubbish bin, rinsing her hands under the tap when she was done. In the unseasonably hot weather something like that could cause a major fire, she thought. Stupid kids probably – a passing motorist or some little fool on one of them new bikes, just chucking stuff everywhere with no thought for anyone else.

She went back out to praise the dogs, stopping to offer Pongo, her big goat, a handful of twigs from the back hedge. Pongo took the offering surprisingly gently, chewing thoughtfully as he gazed at her with his strange amber eyes. He'd almost cleared the second patch of land she and Tom had fenced off, Ada noted. Be time to start setting out some beds for planting in a few days. Pongo was only on loan, a scrub-and-rough-ground clearing machine of awesome efficiency and Ada was very grateful for his efforts that had opened up her crowded garden, making it possible for her to plant and grow more crops than ever before. His task was over, however, and he would soon be on his way back to his owner. Ada stroked the goat's nose gently. Despite her initial misgivings she had grown fond of him and she would miss him when he was gone.

A car drew up outside and Ada hastily rubbed her hands on her apron. Tom was early, she thought. There was a pause and then a rather tentative knock on the gate. No-one knocked way out here, she thought, so who was this calling?

'Ent locked,' she shouted and the gate opened to reveal the slightly harassed face of Alex Hastings, her son Kevin's probation officer.

'Good morning, Ada,' Alex began, before being overcome by a fit of choking. Ada chuckled and waved her guest towards the kitchen.

'Come on through,' she said. 'Takes a bit of getting used to, does goat smell. I don't hardly notice now.' She busied herself at the stove, setting the kettle to boil and putting cups and saucers out on the table. Alex slid into a space at the back after closing the door, and the smell diminished slightly.

'Sorry,' she said when she caught her breath. 'It was just – well, a bit of a shock.'

Ada nodded, smiling at her visitor. She liked Alex. The probation officer had saved her wayward son from being charged with murder and helped him find a job with the travelling fair. Kevin was away from home a lot of the time but seemed to be doing well and was behaving himself, so it was with some trepidation Ada sat down and waited to see what Alex wanted. Mindful of local etiquette, Alex sipped her tea and complimented Ada on her garden before moving on to the reason for her visit.

'It was good to see Kevin last month,' she said, setting her cup down carefully. Ada had served her the best china but Alex, while mindful of the honour, would have preferred something a little more robust. She did not have a good record with delicate things. 'I think he's doing really well and he's still reporting in to all the offices on the fair's route. It won't be long before he's finished and a free man again.'

'Don't know as that's a good thing,' said Ada. 'Been the making of him, that probation has. Don't suppose you could keep an eye on him a bit longer?'

Alex suppressed a groan of frustration. There had been a time, not so long ago either, when a probation officer had a bit of discretion. A client like Kevin, new to the ways of honest living and still vulnerable to outside influence, could be given a little unofficial help, the odd nudge in the right direction for a few months. Now it was about control, setting standard objectives and forcing the probationers to conform to a series of rules designed to ensure they behaved – at least whilst subject to an order of the court. There was no room for young men like Kevin once they had finished their time. There was a big push on to clear away 'dead' cases, often at the expense of preventative work. He would just have to get on with it on his own.

Ada interpreted Alex's expression correctly and shrugged her shoulders.

'Well, was worth asking, eh?' There was the sound of a van drawing up outside followed by the slamming of doors. 'Should be Tom,' said Ada. 'An' young Brian too.'

'It was Brian I was hoping to see,' said Alex, glad to get away from the topic of Kevin. 'He said I could always catch him here during the day. I understand he's not living at home any more?'

Ada pulled a face as she rose to her feet.

'Wouldn't call it much of a home,' she said. 'Never seemed to do no looking after him, and when his dad's back seems to spend most of'n his time using the lad as a punch-bag.'

Alex nodded her understanding. 'Still, he is supposed to reside where the court put him.' Seeing the look on Ada's face she hurried on. 'We can always change that on our records but I do need to have a valid address. Technically he's in breach of his order and I really do not want to send him back to court, especially as he's actually making some progress at last.'

The kitchen door burst open and the object of their discussion burst into the room, a wide grin on his face that faded slightly when he saw Alex.

'Oh, right ...' he said, stopping in the doorway. The entrance of Tom Monarch cut across the slightly uncomfortable silence.

'Now then, lad, move yerself.' He nodded to Alex before sliding round the table and dropping into a chair. 'Any tea left in that pot, Ada?' he asked hopefully. Ada reached behind him and pulled down two beakers, motioning Brian to sit down as Tom glanced from his mug to Alex's cup and saucer.

'Bit of favouritism here I think,' he said with a grin.

'You'd be complaining if you got a cup,' said Ada sharply. ''Sides, you's not a guest no more.'

Tom looked at her over the rim of his beaker and she smiled at him. 'You's just Tom,' she finished.

'So, Alex,' said Ada, 'you was asking about Brian. Well, he's with Tom at the moment, 'til we can see how this college idea goes. How's the studyin', by the way?' she added, turning her attention to Brian who was wriggling uncomfortably on his chair.

'Alright, I s'pose,' he mumbled, staring at the table.

'We's doin' some work of an evening,' said Tom cheerfully. 'Reckon he's coming on now. Don't suppose you got any idea what they likely to be wanting in the way of writing or 'rithmetic?' he asked, eyeing Alex hopefully.

'The college does ask for at least a CSE in English and preferably one in science and maths as well. They have a paper Brian can take instead though. I'm guessing you don't have any qualifications, by the way,' she added.

7

Brian kept his eyes firmly on the table, shaking his head.

'So, I'll ask if they have any past papers you can look over, if you're happy to help out, Tom.'

Tom nodded. 'That's great,' he said. 'Now, you'd better have my address for him, for the time bein' anyway. Is Corner Cottage in Sutton Mallet.'

Brian looked up for the first time. 'I thought was called "Caravan Cottage",' he said.

Ada snorted in disgust. 'No, that's just what some ignorant locals call it, on account of Tom being *Rom*. Proper name is Corner Cottage. 'Cos is on the corner by the crossroads, see?'

Life did get very complicated very quickly, thought Alex as she wrestled her decrepit Citroën over the ruts and dips of the Levels. A simple query about a client's address turned into a soap opera as soon as other people got involved. Alex still struggled with other people a bit and sometimes wondered whether she was in the right line of work, but as soon as she was faced with a client needing her help all her misgivings faded away. If only, she thought, if only she could be left alone to deal with the criminals, delinquents and little hooligans on her case load. That was what she'd signed up for, not all the politics and paperwork.

The rest of the day was taken up with home visits, trips to the homes of clients (or future clients) to interview, encourage, admonish or cajole, and meetings to prepare the reports needed for their pending court appearances. She stopped off in Nether Stowey for a quick sandwich and sat on a bench opposite Coleridge Cottage, home to the poet for three years and a source of great local pride ever since. Alex eyed the building with mixed feelings. Coleridge had written some of his greatest works in the village but having suffered through *The Rime of the Ancient Mariner* at school she was not of a mind to pop over and bask in his literary glory. Instead she turned her attention to the view of the Quantock Hills, their patchwork sides rising in the distance, framed by a pale blue sky. Alex wasn't a great outdoors person but she had a soft spot for the Quantocks and had spent many happy weekend afternoons rambling through the ferns and scrub, admiring the views across the Bristol Channel.

For an instant she toyed with the idea of calling in sick from the phone box outside the pub and heading for the calm of the hills but she was due back at the office in Highpoint to hand in her notes and to check nothing new had come up in the day centre. Besides, it was hard enough arranging the home visits with so many clients scattered over the area and so few having their own telephone. Reluctantly she put her sandwich papers in the rubbish bin, brushed the crumbs off her clothes and climbed back into her car.

It was gone five in the afternoon when she arrived back at the main office in Highpoint, having covered more than seventy miles between appointments. Seventy miles of hard driving, much of it along narrow, twisting lanes with cracked tarmac and patches of gravel that slid from under her wheels and rattled on the aging undercarriage. She was very fond of her eccentric old car but it was unlikely to last another winter and the worry over how she was going to replace it kept her awake at night sometimes.

Tired, fretful and with a head full of other people's problems, she almost walked past an unexpected visitor seated in the corner of the waiting area.

'Samuel,' she said as he stood up and walked towards her. The last person she wanted to see at this point. Samuel Burton, hostel resident and two-year client, convicted of a string of minor but persistent offences. Samuel nodded politely.

'I'm sorry to just drop in,' he said. 'I hoped you might spare me a few minutes but if you're too busy …?'

He waited, perfectly still. There was nothing in the least threatening about his demeanour yet he managed to look like a giant cat about to pounce.

Alex forced a smile.

'Of course,' she said. 'Come through to my office.' She

pushed open the door to the day centre, which should have been deserted as there were no groups scheduled in her absence. Instead there was a four-man pool match going on with several other clients hovering around the table. They fell silent at her appearance, all apart from one young man Alex had never seen before who was wielding his cue with considerable skill and a lot of showmanship.

'Eight ball, centre back,' he called and flipped the ball into the air. It rolled across the worn table, bounced off three cushions and dropped into the target.

'And thank you,' finished the player as he dropped the cue on to the baize, spinning round and holding out his hand towards one of the young men standing at the head of the table – Charlie Dodds – one of hers, Alex noted. Charlie slipped his hands into his pockets, trying to hide the fact they were full of money. He gave a surreptitious shake of his head as he stepped away, glancing at Alex. Finally alerted to his situation, the pool hustler turned to face her.

'Right – you must be Alex then,' he said with exaggerated cheerfulness.

'And you are ...?' Alex asked.

'Steve. Well, it's Stephen actually, of course, but everyone calls me Steve.'

'Do you have a second name?' Alex enquired rather icily. She found herself taking an instant dislike to this cocky stranger who was making free with her day centre. Behind Steve, the rest of the lads began to drift slowly towards the door.

'Don't any of you move,' she warned. They all froze, staring down at the floor, each one of them hoping she picked out someone else. Alex was deceptively small and slight but her anger sent grown men running for cover.

'Well – do you?' she said turning her attention back to Steve.

He tried another cheeky grin. 'Steve Wilson,' he said holding out his right hand, which Alex ignored.

'So what exactly are you doing in my day centre, Mr Wilson?'

Steve's face fell a little and he withdrew the proffered handshake.

'Just called in and these lads were good enough to invite us for a game. No harm in that, eh?'

Alex looked at him for a few seconds, just long enough for Steve to shift slightly from one foot to another.

'This is a probation day centre, Mr Wilson, not a social club. Any facilities here are for the use of clients only. As far as I know you are not one of my clients at present. Now, do you have an appointment with one of the officers?'

Steve swallowed before replying.

'I got a letter at the hostel,' he said. 'To come 'ere for five thirty and meet you about some report.'

Great, thought Alex, this day is just getting better by the minute. Nothing of this showed on her face, however, and she fixed Steve with her best hard stare.

'If you could please be so good as to wait in reception, I will send for you at half past,' she said before turning her attention to the rest of the group.

'You all know better. The pool table may only be used under supervision and after a formal session. Tidy up here and go home – Charlie?'

Charlie Dodds stopped on the way towards the door.

'If you could return the money you are holding to its rightful owners? And if I *ever* catch *anyone* betting in this room again they will be back in court the next day. Have I made myself clear?'

There was a great deal of foot-shuffling from the assembled company as they cleared away the pool cues and posted the balls back into the table pockets. When everything was tidied away to her satisfaction, Alex nodded to dismiss the group and turned back to meet Samuel's amused stare.

'This way,' she said, leading him through into her tiny cupboard of an office. Despite the sunshine outside, the cramped space was cool – almost cold due to its tiny window and thick walls. Partly below ground level, it was necessary to have the lights on all year and Alex generally preferred to work in the day centre or at home. It was quiet, however, and offered privacy for interviews and talks with the clients.

She slid behind her desk and gestured Samuel towards the one remaining chair. When she first interviewed him she had used the secure room in the main building. There was something deeply unsettling about Samuel and she suspected he was a dangerous and cunning stalker – if not worse. He was openly hostile to just about everyone around him, showed contempt for the hostel staff and was so unpleasant the other residents refused to share a room with him. The only exception to his dislike seemed to be Alex herself. Her he treated as – well, as a human being rather than an object. Alex wasn't sure what she had done to deserve this honour but she wasn't going to renew his hostility by using the secure room with its safety glass and panic button. That would be showing weakness and she knew that could destroy the fragile connection she had developed with this man.

'How can I help you?' she asked.

Samuel tilted his head slightly to one side, fixing her with a bright, hard gaze. She was relieved to see his eyes were a dark grey this afternoon. When he was angered, or aroused in some way, they changed colour to a bright, electric blue. It was a startling phenomenon, one Alex had witnessed on several occasions but not one she wished to see directed at herself.

'I'm attending that workshop, out there.' He flipped one hand dismissively in the direction of the yard.

Alex nodded, waiting for him to continue.

'I've been there for months. It's getting a bit tedious and I don't feel I'm learning anything. To be honest, it's not exactly demanding, just some basic woodwork and a side line in repairing the rejected bicycles *so* kindly donated by the local constabulary.'

'I offered to move you to another group a few weeks ago,' said Alex, hurt by his dismissal of her hard-won programme though she tried not to show it.

Samuel shrugged his shoulders.

'Well, let's face it,' he said, examining his sleeve and flicking at a microscopic speck of dust, 'most of them …' Again there was a nod towards the window. 'Most of *them* hardly try at all. The only reason for even bothering is the chance to be in the raft race.'

'And the fact you're ordered to attend by the court,' Alex murmured, her eyes on his open file. She sneaked a glance at him and was gratified to see a faint flush spread across his face. It was petty and as dangerous as poking a lion with a stick and she gave herself a mental shake before continuing.

'Of course, we can look at modifying the programme to ensure you get the maximum benefit from your time with us. Is there something you would prefer?'

'I certainly deserve a place on the race crew,' said Samuel, leaning over the desk. 'I've done everything they've asked of me. I've not missed a week and I'm the only one there with any idea how to row properly.'

Alex sat up straighter, moving a short distance away from Samuel who was suddenly uncomfortably close.

'So you want to stay in the workshop?' she said.

'They say I have to if I want to be in the race,' said Samuel with a scowl. 'It's still two months away – two more months of those lazy, smelly idiots …' He broke off abruptly, keeping his gaze fixed on the desk in front of him.

'If the foreman says that's the rule I can't interfere,' said Alex. 'Still, the next few weeks should be a bit more – demanding. The raft has to be built. In fact, it needs to be designed first. Is that the type of thing you think you could take on?'

Samuel lifted his head and his eyes turned blue as he gazed at the tiny office window for a moment.

'It would be more of a challenge,' she added. 'I could suggest it if you like?' She watched his face relax a little.

'I suppose it would make a bit of a change,' he conceded.

'Good. Well, I'll talk to them tomorrow.'

Alex stood to indicate the meeting was over and after a brief hesitation Samuel rose, nodded to her and moved swiftly to the door. He disappeared out into the corridor without a sound and Alex repressed a shudder. Probably the smartest of all her clients, he was also undoubtedly the fittest and strongest. For an instant she regretted her snide remark. It had been petty and stupid – and in some circumstances might have been a big mistake.

With a sigh she put it out of her mind and turned her attention to Steve Wilson. A quick phone call to the front desk established he was still waiting but no-one seemed to have any paperwork for him. It might have been sent to the hostel, someone suggested, in which case there was little chance it would be forwarded to them very soon. Alex was inclined to agree with this assessment but was too professional to say so, at least in the office.

'Send him down,' she said wearily.

There was a minute's delay before a tap on the door. It opened before she could say anything and Steve peered in at her.

'Alright,' he said and strutted over to the newly vacated chair. His eyes took in the clutter, the cramped space and gloomy atmosphere. If the accommodation offered was any indication of status then Alex was a very long way down the field. Slightly below the evening handyman's cat, Alex thought grimly as she watched a look of ill-disguised contempt slide across his face, replaced in an instant by one of amusement.

'Seems they shoved you in a cupboard,' he said with a smirk.

Never at her best when tired, Alex struggled to keep her temper in check. Ignoring his remark, she pulled out her notepad and rummaged under a large pile of files to locate her diary.

'You said you're at the hostel?' she said, looking through the pages for the next week.

'Yeah. Bit of a dump, innit,' said Steve.

Alex glared at him over the desk.

'It would appear most of what we can offer you falls somewhat short of your expectations,' she said.

Steve opened his mouth but the expression on Alex's face caused him to hesitate and he made do with a soft grunt in response.

'You are currently residing at the hostel, on bail pending a court appearance?' Alex continued. God, I sound pompous, she thought. It was a coping strategy, a way of keeping her real feelings hidden and under control. Still, it acted as a warning for those clients who knew her and confounded those that did not. Steve, for example, was sitting up straight and eyeing her more warily, waiting to see what she was going to say next.

'Perhaps we should begin again,' she said softly. 'You're at the hostel on bail, right?'

Steve nodded.

'Do you have a date for your next appearance?' she asked.

Steve cleared his throat nervously. 'Couple of weeks,' he said. 'Think it's on a Thursday.'

That told Alex he had been up in front of the magistrates and had drawn the sternest of the benches. More referrals to Crown Court came from the Thursday session than any other. It also meant she did not have much time to prepare the report and it would need to be one of her best as they tended to sentence to the limits of their powers.

'You're from out of the county,' she said. 'How did you end up here?'

'Just passing through,' said Steve. 'Stopped for a bite to eat and there was a bit of a misunderstanding, that's all.'

Alex waited. There was a strained silence and Steve took a deep breath, glancing at her to see how well this approach had gone down. Finally he cleared his throat again.

'Left me money in me jacket pocket, out in the car park so I was just going over to find it. Stupid old bastard behind the counter said I was going to skip and he grabbed hold of me. I just gave a bit of a push, trying to get 'im off. He was hurtin' and that's out order. Not my fault he fell an' sort of knocked his head on the bar now is it? All an accident, nothing meant

– honest. Next thing I know I'm banged up and they start on about charging us an' stuff. Load of fuss about nothing. Wasn't even much of a meal either. Too much salad an' rubbish cluttering up me plate. And the beer weren't even cold.'

Alex's heart sank as she listened. Bilking – trying to run without paying – was one thing but an assault resulting in injury was at least ABH and that could easily have been bumped up to the Crown Court for sentence. The courts took a bleak view of this sort of behaviour, especially when perpetrated by smart-mouthed young men, and Steve was not the most plausible of clients. His whole demeanour radiated juvenile arrogance and the fact he came from London made it even worse.

London, in the minds of many in Somerset, was the source of everything evil. No-one from there could possibly be believed or trusted. Alex, who grew up in Essex, had fought this prejudice for almost three years and she suspected either she or Steve was likely to be tainted by association if she did the report for the court. It would be better for everyone if she could get someone else to cover this one but the chances of that were half-way between fat and slim.

'I will call in to the hostel tomorrow morning,' she said with a swift glance at her overcrowded diary. 'I'll phone and let the staff know you have an appointment with me so you'll be able to stay in for the morning.'

Most clients would have been pleased with this. The hostel policy of locking their doors to anyone not on the cleaning rota or taking a class was deeply unpopular, though Alex could see the reasoning behind it. The hostel was supposed to be a supportive and rehabilitative environment and clients were expected to do their bit and either work or study. If they had no work then they were put out like stray cats to walk the streets and find some. It was not a policy of which Alex approved but the hostel was run by a warden who was not a trained probation officer and she had no say in how he did things.

Steve shrugged and glanced up at the grubby window.

'Okay,' he said. 'See you then.'

He rose from the chair and headed for the office door before Alex could finish. She almost called him back but a wave of fatigue swept her good intentions away and she leaned back in her chair, closing her eyes briefly. After a moment she roused herself and picked up her briefcase. She needed to get back home before her housemate, Sue, began preparing the evening meal. Sue was a good friend and Alex was very fond of her but she was a disaster in the kitchen. Alex was feeling too tired and frail to face any of Sue's culinary creations – the memory of last week's sprout omelette popped into her mind and she headed for the door, hurrying to lock up and get home.

Chapter Two

Samuel did not eat at the hostel. The food was plentiful but of poor quality and often cooked with the dubious assistance of the residents. He had tried a few breakfasts and once ventured into the dining room for the Sunday lunch. The meal was adequate – roast chicken, vegetables, potatoes and rather sorry looking Yorkshire puddings – but it was cold, served on cold plates and swamped in gravy. To make matters worse, the vegetables had been cooked to a flavourless mush, carrots only distinguishable from sprouts by their colour.

On that first Sunday Samuel took his plate and found a small table at the side of the room where he sat with his back to the rest of the residents, picking through the contents with his fork in the hope he might find something worth eating. When he pushed it aside and rose in disgust two residents, Petey and Charlie, descended on the remains, squabbling over the chicken leg. Charlie proved the quicker of the two, seizing the drumstick and wrapping the whole thing in a slice of bread. Samuel watched, nauseated, as he gobbled it down, the gravy dripping on to his clothes.

Glancing around, he saw most of the other residents with slices of bread and margarine, padding out the meal by eating everything in a sandwich. He'd seen the same behaviour in prison, where inadequate rations were stretched by the addition of a handful of cheap, white, sliced bread. Samuel never ate like that. In his opinion it marked you as an ex-con, quite apart from being a disgusting way to behave.

Chafing at the requirement to log in at the main office, he reported his presence and left within five minutes, his pockets full of fruit and whole grain crackers. Although he never ate there he only received a proportion of a full benefit allowance as the rent and board went to the hostel, and he had to feed himself on what was left. The nagging hunger he was beginning to suffer did nothing to improve his mood and he brooded on what he was going to do about the situation as he walked round the hostel to the tow path beside the old canal. Breaking into a trot, he allowed the rhythm of the exercise to take over, soothing him as he ran past the road bridge and turned right onto the edge of the Levels.

It was a beautiful evening, warm and bright from the evening sun. Insects buzzed lazily over the reeds and streams and a gentle breeze caused the willows to rustle. Soon the willow branches would be lopped, taken for making baskets and wicker fences, but in the summer they bowed over the landscape, trailing their leaves in the water and offering much-needed shade to the many small creatures living around them.

All of this was lost on Samuel. Moving in an exercise-induced haze, he was concentrating on much darker thoughts. Samuel was driven by deep, ugly desires, a perpetrator of monstrous acts of violence against women. He was also very clever and very, very careful, which had helped him to avoid detection for many years. Whenever it looked as if he might be caught he offered himself up for a petty crime, something stupid and minor carrying at most a few months' jail time.

His willingness to add a string of equally stupid and minor offences to his confession, 'taken into consideration', played well with hard-pressed police forces eager to up their success rate and frequently resulted in a more lenient sentence. It also tended to make him invisible as far as his real actions were concerned. Dumb, petty little criminal was how the authorities saw him. Never considered in their major enquiries. In fact, on one occasion the 'taken into consideration' offences had given him an alibi for a particularly enjoyable evening he had spent with one young woman. Well, Samuel had enjoyed it anyway. By the time they found his companion it was too late to ask her.

Samuel stopped near Kings Sedgemoor, the huge drain running through the centre of the Levels. His breath was coming in tight gasps and he was sweating in the heat. The lack of decent food was beginning to tell on his superior and carefully nurtured physique and he was forced to stop for a few minutes, alarmed by the slight trembling in his legs. Leaning against a tree, he ate his inadequate supper, chewing each bite carefully to extract every scrap of nutrition from it.

The apple cores went in the canal but the cracker papers were folded and zipped into his back pocket. Indifferent to the beauties of nature, Samuel was not too concerned about littering. He was, however, too careful to leave any sign of his movements. With a soft grunt he levered himself off the tree, brushed the dust from his clothes and set off down the path beside the drain. The main sluice gate glittered in the golden sunlight ahead of him, marking the turning onto a smaller track. Samuel hoped he would find a new hiding place somewhere out there in the thickets. Somewhere to gather his things, to plan and to dream of his next little adventure.

Alex was doing something creative with some sausages, an onion, the slightly soft half of a red pepper, a couple of tomatoes and a selection of spices. Sue lounged on the high stool beside the counter, smiling appreciatively.

'It's my turn to cook,' she said. 'This is really good of you. I know you've had a long day.'

Alex gave her a little smile and shrugged off the compliment.

'We've both had a long day,' she said. 'Besides, I find cooking rather relaxing, especially after dealing with the likes of Samuel Burton.'

A frown crossed Sue's face at the mention of Samuel. 'There's something not quite right about him,' she said. 'He's always polite when I see him at the office but he gives me a creepy feeling. Can't explain it – I just don't like being around him. I don't know how you manage. I wouldn't like to be in a room alone with him.'

Alex gave a non-committal grunt as she turned the sausages in the thickening sauce. Privately she agreed with her friend but professional etiquette prevented her airing her suspicions, especially as they were only that. She had no proof of his actions – nothing she could take to the police anyway. She was sure he had been behind an attack on her admin assistant, Alison, a few weeks ago. Whoever it was had broken into Alison's home and threatened her with a straight-edged razor but had been chased off by Alison's husband before he could do worse than frighten her. The intruder had escaped over the tracks of the Levels, outrunning and outsmarting the police before vanishing without a trace. Alison was unable to give any useful description apart from the fact he wore a ski mask over his face and her husband had only got a glimpse of the intruder as he fled.

A tin containing the clothes worn by this mysterious predator had been unearthed a week later but there was nothing to help identify the owner. Alex was sure it had been Samuel, but sure without evidence was worthless. She could only watch him very carefully and hope he made a mistake before someone got hurt.

'Fancy rice with this?' she said, giving the pan a final stir.

'Sounds good,' said Sue, slipping off the stool and grabbing a couple of plates from the side.

'I wish we had some wine,' she called from the other room. 'I could just murder a glass of wine tonight.'

Alex smiled to herself. They couldn't afford wine every night. In fact, they were struggling to afford wine for their Friday get-togethers. It didn't bother Alex much – she could get drunk on the smell of a cork according to her friends – but she did wish the household budget wasn't quite so tight.

'Tomorrow,' she said. 'Everyone's coming round tomorrow evening. Something to look forward to at the end of the week.'

They sat at the table, Sue lacing into the meal with enthusiasm.

'You're a pleasure to cook for,' said Alex with a grin.

Sue nodded, her mouth full of sausage casserole.

'Meant to ask you,' she said after swallowing. 'When's the last alcohol education session? I thought it was supposed to be on a Thursday evening.'

'We've postponed it,' said Alex. 'It's been so busy lately and we're *still* short-staffed so we decided to wait a couple of weeks. Means I can get some other stuff done this week and line it up properly.'

Sue put down her fork and fixed Alex with a hard stare. 'Are you still planning on running the session you worked out?' she asked. 'You'll be in so much trouble if anyone finds out you know.'

Alex was acutely aware of how much trouble she would be in if anyone apart from Sue found out about the final session. It had seemed a stroke of genius when she dreamt it up in the cold winter months but now she felt her courage begin to slip away. She had already broken the rules by giving the group small measured drinks whilst they played a driving game on her little computer. The results had been enlightening – none of them could race their cartoon motorbike round the track safely after just two units and several of the boys had sworn off drinking and driving on the spot.

A part of her felt she should quit whilst ahead (and still undiscovered) but she knew the emotional impact of the computer evening would fade soon enough. She needed the last session to help them establish an alternative to swilling

pints in the pub before clambering into a car and heading home.

'The new senior's due early next month,' Sue added. 'You don't want to get off on the wrong foot with her.'

'Look, I know I'll probably never be able to run this course again,' said Alex. 'I might as well do it properly.'

Sue glanced at her friend and recognized the expression – Alex's stubborn face, she called it privately.

'Well, for God's sake be careful,' she said. 'They could sack you if you're caught.'

'Nah,' said Alex, rising to clear the empty plates. 'It's not that serious. Besides, they'd be even shorter handed if they got rid of me now.'

She sounded confident but inside she wondered if Sue might be right.

Friday morning meant a trip to the hostel for her appointment with Steve Wilson and Alex was up early, determined to get on with the report as soon as she could. The hostel was about a mile down the road from her house, just too far to walk on a busy work day but close enough for roaming residents to spot her car outside her home. The perfect combination and typical of her luck, she thought, as she manoeuvred her Citroën into a tiny space between the warden's huge camping van and the hostel's overflowing bins.

Sliding carefully out of the door, and trying not to touch the pile of rubbish spilling out over the paving stones, Alex made her way to the front door. There was no answer when she rang the bell and she walked around the side of the building to see if the back door was open. Occupied with trying to plan her schedule for the rest of the day, she almost tripped over Petey and Charlie who were kneeling on the path, hunched over something in the border.

'And what, exactly are you doing gentlemen?' she said.

The two young men jumped, Charlie falling backwards into the shrubs. Petey turned to squint up at her, his hand closing around something from the ground. Alex held out her hand silently and waited. Petey stared at her for a moment and then reluctantly passed over a battered disposable lighter. Waving them aside, she peered at the ground around the bushes, leaning forwards to poke about with one foot. There was a small pile of greasy paper with a few pieces of blackened cardboard nestling around the woody stem of one plant. The top of the lighter was uncomfortably warm she realized and hastily transferred it to her other hand. She took a deep breath, trying to contain her anger, before rounding on the pair.

'I repeat – just what the *bloody hell* do you think you're doing? And stand up when I'm talking to you!'

Petey and Charlie scrambled to their feet, brushing rather ineffectually at the twigs and earth clinging to their knees. Charlie stood with his head bowed, staring at the path, but Petey looked straight back at her defiantly.

'Look, we was just muckin' about,' he said. ''Ent much doing round here. Just a lark, passin' the time.'

'This is not "just passing the time",' Alex said angrily. 'This is dangerous, irresponsible and criminally stupid behaviour even by your standards.'

Charlie shuffled his feet nervously and even Petey looked a little abashed.

'If I ever catch you doing anything like this again I will report you. If I can make it stick as criminal damage I will breach you and send you both to prison. Do you understand?'

Petey's gaze finally faltered and he muttered something as he looked down at the ground.

'I beg your pardon?' said Alex.

'Okay,' he murmured.

Charlie nodded, never raising his eyes.

'Right. It looks as if this all belongs in the rubbish so you can clear it up and tidy the bins while you're at it,' said Alex. Petey opened his mouth to protest as she brushed past them, heading for the open back door.

'I'm sorry, did I not make myself clear?'

'You got my lighter,' said Petey, holding out his hand.

Alex glared at him, slipping the offending item into her back pocket.

'Tough. I've got an appointment now but I expect to see that whole area clear and swept up when I come out. And if there's a single mark on my car you'll both be very sorry.'

With that she swept into the kitchen of the hostel, her breakfast already sour in her stomach. By the time she had finished with Steve Wilson she also had the edge of a headache, warning flashes of light cutting across her vision and threatening a full-blown migraine. The hostel staff had handed over their copies of Steve's record on the promise she duplicate them and get them back by the evening and she couldn't afford to go home and sleep it off, so, driving very slowly and carefully, she made her way to the probation office.

For once she was grateful for the gloom in her tiny room and the cool air was welcome. Alison, her clerical assistant, had agreed to do the photocopying for her and Alex was able to relax for a few minutes, closing her eyes and breathing deeply in an effort to control the attack. Savouring the quiet, she felt the pain begin to subside a little but her peace was shattered by Alison bustling down the corridor and flinging open the door.

'Here,' she said, dropping the folder onto Alex's desk. 'Wasn't all that much in it anyway. Some of the stuff seems to be missing, especially his early years. He went to an Approved School out in Surrey but there's no details of why he was there or when he left. Spent some time in Borstal after that – just a few scrappy notes about that too.' She sniffed in disapproval. Alison was a bit of a trial sometimes but she did like to ensure all her records were up to date.

'Are you alright?' she asked, peering at Alex through the gloom. 'It's very dark in here. Hang on ...' Before Alex could stop her, Alison switched on the top light. The harsh neon seemed to beat on Alex's eyes causing her to curl up over the desk, groaning softly. Alison blinked at her anxiously. 'You look awful,' she said. 'Can I get you something? How about a nice cup of tea?'

'Just turn out the light,' said Alex. 'Thank you. Actually

I'd really appreciate some water,' she added as Alison opened the door, hurt by the abrupt rejection of her kindness.

'Okay,' said the admin assistant, slightly mollified. 'I'll be back in a minute.' She left, closing the door behind her, leaving Alex to sit up carefully, something she just managed without being sick. Good thing, she thought. Alison was likely to take her throwing up on the files personally.

'There's a meeting upstairs at four,' Alison informed her when she returned, glass in hand.

'Is it important?' Alex asked. She really wasn't feeling up to a full team meeting and was beginning to doubt she would make it through to four at all.

Alison shrugged, 'Don't ask me. They never tell us anything. Though if Gordon's called an extra meeting it's probably something we all need to know. Maybe it's about the new senior.'

Alex sat in her darkened room, sipping the water and musing. As she leaned back in her chair something dug into her hip. Fumbling in the pocket she pulled out Petey's confiscated lighter. Not a good thing for someone like him to be playing with she thought, turning the cracked plastic object in her hand. Flicking the wheel she confirmed it was still working but even that was too bright for comfort and she hurriedly turned it off and laid it on the desk next to Steve Wilson's file. Which needed to go back to the hostel before the meeting, she recalled.

There was a soft knock on the door and Sue poked her head round.

'Alex? Alison said you were feeling ill.' She slipped inside, gliding through the debris without even knocking anything over and laid a hand on her friend's forehead. 'You're running a bit of a temperature,' she said accusingly. 'You should have gone home and phoned in sick.'

Wordlessly, Alex gestured towards the pile of forms and files that teetered on the end of her desk.

Sue dropped into the chair opposite her friend and sighed.

'And there's Gordon's meeting,' Alex added, closing her eyes again.

'Oh bugger Gordon's stupid meeting,' said Sue crossly. 'What can be so important he's got to mess up everyone's weekend anyway? More management nonsense probably. I don't know why it can't wait until Monday morning.'

Despite her pounding head, Alex managed a grin. 'Listen to you,' she said softly. 'I remember when you first arrived, all eager and well-behaved. You've been hanging around with the subversives for too long.'

'That would be you then,' said Sue. 'And just for your information, I have never been well-behaved – at least, according to my mother. Look, seriously, you should go home. I can tell you all about it tonight. Oh, and maybe we should let people know so they don't all turn up this evening.'

Alex pulled a face at this. Friday evenings had become one of the high spots of her life, a chance to cook for the people she cared about. Friends arriving with bottles of wine or a cake for dessert, sometimes bringing a new record or book they had discovered. No-one knew exactly who would be there, what they would be eating and what the evening might bring, so much so that she and Sue referred to them as 'anarchist nights' in private. They were warm, happy times that often stretched into the small hours and she was loath to let one Friday pass unmarked. Then the flashes started up again behind her eyelids and she realized the futility of wishing for a speedy recovery.

Sue correctly interpreted her grimace of pain as the onslaught of a major migraine and grabbed the phone off Alex's desk.

'Gordon? Yes, I'm in Alex's office and she's not well at all. I'm going to take her home but I'll be back after lunch. No … no, she won't be well enough to get to the meeting but I'll make sure she knows what it's about. Right, thanks.' She replaced the receiver with a snort of disgust. 'As if,' she muttered. 'Now, come on, where's your case?'

Alex gestured to the side of her chair, too dizzy to resist as Sue helped her to her feet and guided her gently through the door. 'Keys?' Sue asked before letting the door lock behind them. Alex fumbled in her pocket and handed them over.

'Can we leave my car here?' she managed.

Sue nodded. 'I think so,' she said. 'I don't fancy driving your old monster anyway. We'll take mine so I can get back before my next appointment.'

Several young men in the reception area paused in their bickering, responding to Sue's glare by sitting up a little straighter as she led Alex out into the bright sunlight. 'Not long now,' she said soothingly, strapping her friend into the front seat. 'Just close your eyes and I'll have you home in no time.'

'I don't think I should,' Alex murmured. 'Don't know what you'll get up to without me watching.'

With Alex tucked up asleep at home, Sue used the rest of her lunch hour to ring around their friends and let them know the evening meal was off. Running through the list in her mind she realized there was one name missing – Margie, Alex's new friend who had just moved down from Bristol to work at Shepton Mallet prison. Alex was still a bit secretive about her relationship with Margie, understandable under the present climate of rising intolerance and ignorance, and Sue did not have any contact details for her. She paused for a moment but there was nothing she could do and already there was the sound of heavy boots on the stairs heralding the imminent arrival of her 2 o'clock appointment.

The house was quiet when she got back that evening, the absence of cooking smells indicating Alex was still asleep. Sue closed the door softly, leaving her bag full of files and paperwork on a chair in the front room and headed towards the small kitchen to make some tea. The sight of Margie sitting at the table brought her up with a start.

'Oh sorry – didn't mean to startle you,' said Margie. She had changed out of her prison officer's uniform, Sue noted. Always a good idea when going out in public, especially so close to a probation hostel. 'Alex gave us a key, couple o' weeks ago. She's still upstairs – wanted to get up but I told her to just lie a bit, see how she felt later.'

28

Sue experienced a stab of jealousy. Looking after Alex was her job, a way of showing how much she cared for her friend. 'Would you like some tea?' she asked, trying not to let her resentment show.

Margie looked at her and smiled. 'Would be lovely,' she said. 'Reckon we should take one upstairs?'

'I'll do it,' said Sue as she disappeared into the back of the house. The strength of her feelings had taken her by surprise and she paused before setting the kettle to boil, trying to make sense of the reaction. It wasn't as if she wanted Alex for herself – not in that sense anyway. It was more a feeling that things were going to change now.

Alex owned the house and Sue was a lodger, had been ever since she moved to Highpoint. She had always intended to look for her own place but the lack of time and money had led to her settling comfortably into life with Alex, who rapidly became a close and loyal friend. She liked the house which was convenient for the office and relatively comfortable despite their joint lack of decent furniture. She enjoyed the routines they had developed over the past few years, including the Friday meals.

She was going to miss the closeness she thought. This feeling mirrored her miserable early twenties when, one by one, her female friends had fallen for a seemingly endless succession of men, married them and drifted away from her. They had all vowed to keep in touch, of course. There had been phone calls at first, then holiday postcards, then baby pictures, often accompanied by an invitation to a christening. Finally, the friendships shrank to a Christmas card so that when she moved from university after graduation she hadn't bothered to let most of them know her new address. Here we go again, she thought, as she poured hot water into three beakers. It was a pity Margie was such a nice person. It was much easier if you could take a dislike to the person who was waltzing off with your friend.

Curfew at the hostel was 10pm, every day. Many of the residents chafed against this, especially at weekends, and Samuel resented the indiscriminate nature of this rule even though he was an early riser and despised those who tried to sneak back upstairs to crawl into bed again after breakfast. There was a big, wonderful world outside the hostel and Samuel was eager to sample as much of it as he could. He lay under a clean white sheet beside the open window, breathing deeply and focussing his considerable intellect on the obstacles facing his next assignation.

Although his room was supposed to house four occupants the hostel was half empty so Samuel had it to himself and he kept it spotless. The floor was swept every day, his meagre possessions were put away in the cupboard by his bed and he even cleaned the window once a week, much to the surprise of the official hostel cleaner who opened the door on his first morning and stopped short at this unprecedented sight. She was an older woman dressed in a faded housecoat that smelt of disinfectant and roll-up cigarettes and was of no interest to Samuel.

He fixed her with a bright blue stare and suggested he would take responsibility for the room's cleanliness for the foreseeable future. The woman mumbled her agreement and left quietly. Despite appearances, Hazel was no fool and close acquaintance with the hostel over the last ten years had given her a fine sense of danger. Samuel turned back to the windows, forgetting her before the door was closed, something Hazel would have found very reassuring had she known.

The sound of voices from the next room disturbed Samuel's thoughts and he scowled, considered going next door to shut them up and then dismissed the idea. The room would be dirty, it would smell and the inevitable fracas would probably bring the night staff running. Samuel preferred not to attract attention, though he made a mental note to have a little word with the occupants in the morning.

In the next room Steve lay sweating on his bed. The darkness was suddenly lit by a sputtering flame from the bed to his right, startlingly bright in contrast to the night.

'Don't waste 'um,' came Charlie's voice from the far corner.

The light flickered and dimmed and then Petey cursed, shaking his fingers as the match burned down to the end.

The still-burning match fell onto this chest and he jumped up, laughing and slapping at the vest he was wearing. The smell of sulphur mingled with the scent of singed wool as the hot match head landed on Petey's blanket.

'Dozy bugger,' said Steve calmly. 'Watch what you're doing. You'll set the fire alarm off if you're not careful.' He breathed in the rank air, enjoying the way it burned at the back of his throat.

Charlie got out of bed, coughing as he made his way to the window to clear the room.

''Ent no detectors in here,' he said as he fumbled with the latch. 'Got to push the button to set that old alarm off. They's only on the stairs an' the office.'

'Really?' said Steve. 'That's interesting. I'm not sure that's even allowed any more. No – leave it.'

Charlie stopped, the window half-open. 'Can't breathe in here,' he complained.

'I said leave it!' snapped Steve and reluctantly Charlie pulled the window closed again and shuffled over to his bed.

'Is my room too,' he said, rolling over so his back was towards his companions. For a few minutes he continued to wheeze and cough until finally sleep overcame him.

Steve smiled in the darkness, listening to the snores of his room-mates. Charlie was a bit of a wimp but Petey definitely had potential, he thought.

Chapter Three

The next morning Alex was feeling a lot better, so much better she needed to be persuaded to take it easy.

'It's a lovely day,' she protested, waving a piece of toast towards the garden. 'We could go for a drive, maybe have lunch out in a pub somewhere?'

Acting in unison, Sue and Margie quashed this enthusiasm and Alex was no match for their combined determination.

'We can sit in the shade in the garden if'n you like,' said Margie. 'You should have a rest after lunch an' all. Never seen you look so pale as last night.'

'I could do lunch,' Sue suggested. 'I'll pop into the market and see what's looking nice.' She rose from the table and glided up the open-plan staircase humming happily and rather tunelessly.

'Now look what you've done,' said Alex. 'Don't expect me to get better if Sue's cooking!'

Margie laughed, not at all upset by her friend's behaviour. 'Don't you worry,' she said. 'I'll go with her an' I'll do lunch, let her help me. Maybe she'll pick up a few tips along the way. But you got to promise to sit quiet and don't go rushing around or I'll let her loose in that kitchen, swear to God I will.'

Alex pulled a sulky face but even the slight exertion of getting dressed and eating breakfast had left her feeling a bit washed out and it was with a minimum of opposition she settled in the tiny back garden. Feet up on a stool and with her head in the shade from the house, she felt herself relax, watching a flock of sparrows as they swooped onto the bird table she had set up by the rear fence. There was much squabbling over the remains of an old sunflower, the seeds torn out and scattered as a small gang of starlings arrived and attempted to muscle their way into the smaller birds' territory.

Smiling at their antics, Alex felt her eyes begin to close and she shifted in her chair, enjoying the warmth of the morning sun. Her good mood was shattered by a loud banging on the back gate. Jerking upright she blinked in the brightness, then leapt to her feet as a large stone flew over the fence, just clipping the table. As the birds flew up with a great chattering and flurry of wings, Alex stormed up the back steps and flung her gate open.

Three young men stood outside, sniggering and pointing. They fell silent, frozen in shock as Alex yelled in fury.

'Charlie, Petey, Steve – what the bloody hell do you think you are doing? You nasty, vicious little vandals ...'

'I'm sorry, Miss,' stammered Charlie, almost in tears. 'Didn't know was your house, honest.'

'It doesn't matter whose house it is,' Alex stormed. 'That was an act of criminal damage. You almost killed those poor birds and if a child had been playing beside the fence you might well have killed them too.'

'We seen one of the screws from Bristol coming out the front,' said Petey. 'Thought was her house. Didn't know was yours. Must 'a got the wrong one,' he added, turning to his partners in crime.

'If anything that makes the whole thing worse,' said Alex. 'Get out of my sight, all of you. I'll be speaking to the hostel staff after the weekend so I suggest you behave yourselves in the meantime unless you want to find yourself back in Bristol nick on Tuesday.'

Slamming the gate angrily she turned away but not before catching Steve's voice.

'Pity it wasn't the screw's house. Bit of a diesel, by all accounts ...'

Alex went cold with fury and struggled with the temptation to wrench the gate open again and confront the speaker. 'Bit of a diesel', he'd said. Well, she thought glumly, that didn't take long. Now the fun really starts. She went over to her bird table, setting it straight again and replacing the feeders and water bowl. There was a faint rustling from the trees in the garden to her right, a sign the birds had not gone too far. Moving slowly so as not to alarm them too much, she finished tidying up and went back to her chair in the shade. Better put a bolt on that gate, she thought, as she relaxed again. She was fast asleep when Sue and Margie returned from the market.

Samuel had given his logistical problems considerable thought. He could replace a lot of his missing kit easily enough. He'd need to travel to Taunton for some of it – better not to be recognized in Highpoint and the market at Taunton was large, sprawling and anonymous. Here he could source some suitable non-descript clothes, the sort of things no-one would remember or be able to describe. Cotton gloves were easy to find too, as well as duct tape and a couple of bandages. He still had one of his torches, though another, just for the special evenings, would be advisable. Less chance of leaving any trace of his presence on it and no questions about where his had gone if it had to be abandoned in a hurry.

That just left one item, small but vital to the whole enterprise. Samuel had lost his precious straight-edged razor fleeing the scene of his last, thwarted outing. He didn't care about the rest of his kit but he was upset over losing that. It had come from Switzerland, one of the finest and sharpest blades he could find. It had been expensive too and would be very hard to replace. With the original razor now in the hands of the police at Highpoint, he couldn't go into a shop and buy another. Even a rural force like these bumbling hicks would have some sort of alert out, he thought.

There was always mail order but he couldn't have it turning up at the hostel. After some thought he set off down the track across the Levels to his new bolt-hole out on the marshes, an old Ordinance Survey map 'liberated' from the town library in his bag. First he'd make his new space secure and a bit more comfortable, then he'd use his weekend to plan exactly where he could get a new razor. The market in Taunton could wait another week. He was in no hurry now – the planning, the watching and the dreaming of his next adventure were enough to satisfy the cravings within for a while.

It was not until they sat down to lunch that Alex thought to ask about Gordon's meeting. Sue groaned and rolled her eyes, stuffing some cheese and ham mix from a baked potato into her mouth before replying.

'The worst possible news,' she said, putting her fork down rather reluctantly. 'Just as we get a new senior, the Home Office is coming for an inspection.'

'Oh, you're kidding,' said Alex.

'Four weeks' time,' said Sue. 'The new senior's due to start that month so I don't know how they feel about it.'

'God, I went through an inspection on placement,' said Alex. 'It was terrible. Not the actual visit – that wasn't too bad, though it was a bit nerve-wracking having a stranger sitting in the corner making notes on everything I did. It was the weeks before that were truly gruesome. The entire management team ran around like headless chickens yelling at everyone. We all had to work late every night and every single file was checked and re-done. And I was just a student. I dread to think what it'll be like now I'm an officer.' A thought struck her. 'They'll be looking at the day centre, won't they?'

Sue nodded.

'Oh, hells bells – that puts me right in the middle of the whole thing.'

Sue shrugged, turning her attention to the remains of her lunch. 'Gordon's not really the running about sort,' she said. 'I expect him to deal with it a bit more sensibly. And besides,' she added grinning wickedly, 'there's always Ricky. He's so incompetent I think we could wade knee-deep in uncompleted reports and still come out looking fabulous.'

Alex had to laugh at this. Ricky, the latest addition to the office, was one of her least-favourite people. Lazy, sloppy and snide, he had sloped through his first few months doing as little as possible and leaving everyone else to pick up the mess he created. He had improved slightly since Gordon took over his supervision but the change was minimal and he remained a liability to the team.

'Yeah,' said Alex. 'Let's throw them Ricky and we can just stand back and watch the show.'

'What's a probation inspection like?' asked Margie as she helped herself to more salad.

'They send a team from the Home Office,' said Alex. 'It'll be for a big area down here so we'll probably get just a day or two. They take the files away and check everything's up to date and you're doing everything by the rules. They sit in on sessions too so I'll have to have something really good planned for the day centre …'

'And something legal,' said Sue, searching through the salad bowl for the last bits of avocado. Alex gave a warning shake of her head but Margie had already picked up on Sue's comment.

'Thought the idea was to help 'em back onto the straight and narrow,' she said eyeing Alex. 'Don't tell me you's turnin' to the dark side then?'

'No,' Alex protested. 'Nothing like that. It's just – well, the alcohol education course has gone really well but it's all a bit theoretical and dry …'

'That's the point,' said Sue. 'It's *supposed* to be dry.'

Alex sighed, pushing her plate to one side and leaning over the table.

'They still think only something alcoholic is worth drinking,' she said. 'We can't hope to get them onto soft drinks – they'd be ribbed mercilessly by all their mates in the pub. Most of whom should be on the course too,' she added. 'Anyway, they won't touch the low-alc' stuff because they say it doesn't taste right. Actually they're pretty rude about it. So I want to finish off the course with a blind taste-testing, to show how much of their attitude is due to prejudice. But to do that ...' She tailed off thoughtfully.

'To do that you have to give them beer – in the day centre,' said Sue. 'And that is *so* not allowed.'

Alex glared at her, the epitome of stubbornness. 'Some of the alcohol-free beers are a decent drink and they look like the real thing. Not like an orange juice or something. If I can get even some of them to switch occasionally then that's a success.'

'No, it's not,' said Sue, rising to collect the plates from the table. 'You can't prove it works. If it can't be measured or counted or ticked off a list from headquarters it doesn't count any more. That's the way it is now. All you'll get is an official warning – if you're lucky.'

Margie looked at Alex and asked, 'Is it really that bad?'

Alex pulled a face. 'Actually it's worse,' she said. 'But that doesn't mean we have to give up.'

Across town Steve and his two new friends were drifting through the covered market in the old Corn Exchange. It was cool inside the old Georgian building and the dim light suited Steve perfectly. Hovering next to each stall in turn, he filled his pockets with whatever came to hand. It was not what he could acquire that interested him but more the act itself that Steve savoured. To Steve the whole thing was an elaborate game. At the end of the Cornhill in an enclosed side area was the Saturday auction. The small space was crowded with onlookers, all jostling and peering at the auctioneer, an elderly lady dressed in a baggy tweed suit and wearing a shapeless felt hat. This woman had ruled over the auction for thirty years, taking over the role from her father who, in turn, had run the sales from just after the First World War. Selling mainly local produce, the items on offer ranged from baskets and boxes of fruit and vegetables to pairs of rabbits still in their fur and occasional game birds, their heads lolling to one side as they lay in their finery on the worn wooden trestles. It was fascinating and slightly sad, very typical of the town.

'Now, I got a fine brace of big, brown pigeons here,' she boomed, her voice echoing around the stone walls as she flourished a pair of pheasants at the crowd.

'They don't look nothing like the pigeons we got in London,' said Steve.

Petey sniggered behind him. 'Them's pheasants, stupid. Only can't sell pheasants 'cos they's probably poached. So is called "brown pigeon" instead.'

Steve was intrigued by this law-breaking by a local institution and watched as the crowd began to offer bids for the birds.

'Ten bob,' called a man near the back.

Steve blinked in surprise.

'Ten 'n six,' came a counter offer.

'Yer joking!' he said, turning to Petey and Charlie. His interruption brought a furious response from the auctioneer.

'Silence,' she thundered in their direction. 'If'n you's not bidding you just keep quiet. This is a proper auction an' I'll not have it disturbed!'

Steve burst out laughing. 'Right,' he said. 'Two doubloons!'

'Who is that,' yelled the auctioneer. 'Stop that at once!'

'Three pieces of eight,' Petey called out.

'I bid my wife and my first-born child,' added Charlie as he wriggled through the crowd, heading for the wide doorway into the street. Petey and Steve followed just ahead of the enraged auctioneer who stood on the steps flourishing a walking stick in their direction.

'I know you,' she shouted. 'Don't you never be coming back here, you hear me? Bloody little hooligans,' she muttered turning back to her 'pigeons'.

Out in the sunlight, safely out of sight behind the Admiral's statue, the three lads took a moment to catch their breath.

'They give a good discount in there,' said Steve, dipping into his pockets and showing the other two a handful of his booty. Petey looked in admiration at the mix of small tools, crumpled handkerchiefs and a few root vegetables he displayed. In amongst the jumble were two disposable lighters.

'You got all that?' he said. 'How'd you manage it?'

Steve shrugged modestly. 'Got the knack, me,' he said.

Charlie frowned at him. 'What you want all that stuff for?' he asked.

'Don't matter,' said Steve. 'It's the getting away with it that matters, not what I got. Come on, I'm getting hungry. Let's go and see what them food stalls down the road've got to offer us, eh?'

'Give us one of yer lighters,' said Petey. Steve looked at him for a moment and then handed one over. Petey walked next to him as they wove through the happy crowd of shoppers and visitors, Charlie trailing several paces behind them. He'd been friends with Petey since their arrival at the infant school in Middlezoy and he'd always admired his nerve and slightly reckless approach to life but he was not happy with the way Steve influenced their actions. He was beginning to wish he'd gone over to Taunton for the day. Or got a jug of something strong and sat by the canal to drink it. Anything really in preference to following Steve around.

'Think I'll head back,' he said, stopping in the middle of the road, oblivious to the people around him.

Petey turned to stare at him but Steve walked on without looking back and after a moment Petey shrugged and hurried after him. Charlie stood in the crowd, jostled by impatient shoppers, and tried not to cry.

Margie was due at work on the Sunday afternoon so she headed back to her digs in Shepton Mallet just after breakfast.

'Reckon she should take it a bit easy today,' she said to Sue on her way out.

'I wish,' said Sue. 'Fat chance of that, I'm afraid. I should have waited until this evening to tell her about the damn inspection.' She glanced over her shoulder into the back room where Alex was seated at the dining table making a list of the files and notes she needed to bring up to date.

'I'll need to go into the office today,' she said without looking up from her work.

'Well I'm not going in today,' Sue retorted. 'It's Sunday, it's a beautiful day and we'll be slaving away for the next few weeks so I'm damn well going to enjoy myself before it all starts.' She leaned over and pulled the notebook away from Alex's hands. 'And you should do the same. Come on! Let's go out to the Quantocks. You know you always enjoy it up there.'

Alex reached for her book.

'We could drop in on Lauren,' Sue added, stepping back and still holding the notes firmly in her hand.

Alex hesitated. She was very fond of Lauren. 'After lunch,' she said finally. 'I won't enjoy it if I'm worrying and not knowing what I've got to do. If I plan it all out then at least I know the worst.'

Sue handed the book back without a word and went out into the garden where the birds were squabbling happily on the table, unconcerned by their recent near-death experience. Alex was something of a control freak, Sue thought, and the compromise was as good as she was going to get. Stretching out in an old reclining chair they had picked up at a second-hand sale, she closed her eyes and enjoyed the warmth of the sun.

Her enjoyment was cut short by a thump at the back gate, hard enough to make it shake in the frame. Recalling Alex's description of yesterday's incident with the rock and the birds, Sue sprang to her feet and ran to the back fence, anger overcoming caution. She opened the gate before thinking and stepped back as a dishevelled figure toppled forwards towards her. Instinctively she reached out and caught them before they hit the wall, grunting as she took the full weight.

'Bloody hell, Charlie? What are you …?' She caught a whiff of him and gagged, then swallowed and tried to take shallow breaths through her mouth.

'Alex!' she called. 'Alex – a little help needed here.' Struggling to keep her balance, Sue slid Charlie's semi-conscious body down the fence until he was seated on the grass. He'd been sick – very sick from the look of him and Sue reached behind, rubbing her hands against the rough wood of the fence to scrub her hands.

'What?' said Alex, her face twisted with annoyance as she trotted down the path and up the steps. 'Oh!' She blinked at the sorry figure propped up at her feet. 'Is that Charlie?'

She leaned over him but straightened up again hurriedly.

'He fell against the gate I think,' said Sue.

'Damn, damn, damn,' said Alex. 'I don't think it was just an accident he ended up here. My cover's blown now – he knows where I live and that means the whole bloody hostel will soon.' She sighed and shook her head. 'Nothing we can do about that. Do you think we should move him?'

Charlie slid over onto his side, his head knocking on the ground as he crumpled into a heap.

'He might choke if he stays like that,' said Sue. They glanced at one another, both reluctant to lay hands on him. 'We could call the hostel,' she suggested. 'He's supposed to be their problem.'

'I think you mean "under their care and supervision",' said Alex. 'Just how much help do you think they'll be? It's Sunday, the poor old relief warden's going to be rushing around trying to keep order, watch them all and cook the Sunday dinner too. Personally, if I were her I'd strangle him – and whoever called me out to get him.'

'I'll call an ambulance,' said Sue. 'You get him into the recovery position if you can.' Hurrying off down the steps, she left Alex staring down at Charlie. Gingerly, she knelt beside the young man, checking his pulse before trying to move him over onto his side. He was surprisingly heavy and she had to struggle to her feet and haul at his left arm at one stage but after a few minutes he was lying in the proper position, legs bent and one arm over his chest.

She had a fright when as she got him over on his side he made a sudden rasping sound. Just as she steeled herself to open his mouth to check his throat was clear he made the sound again and his head lolled over onto the ground. He was snoring, she thought. The little bastard had barged in on her Sunday, stinking and filthy and now he was sound asleep on her back step. More than anything else she wanted to kick him, but fortunately Sue returned before she could give in to the impulse.

'They're sending someone,' said Sue. 'What's wrong with him?'

Alex leaned over the recumbent form and sniffed, pulling a face as she straightened up. 'Natch, I think,' she said, using the local slang for farmhouse or 'natural' cider. In truth, there was not all that much that was 'natural' about some of it. Natch was fermented from windfall apples, complete with cores, skin, maggots and anything else nesting inside. It was rumoured to be flavoured by adding a raw onion to the barrel or occasionally throwing in a dead rat. A gallon container had almost as much alcohol as a bottle of whisky and if Charlie had drunk that much it was a good thing he'd thrown it up again. It might just have saved his life.

Once the ambulance had arrived and Charlie had been shovelled rather roughly inside, Alex telephoned the hostel to let them know what had happened. A very harassed sounding woman answered, thanked her for the information and put the phone down before Alex could even ask her name.

'I sense all is not well down the road,' she observed, returning to the table where Sue was clearing the notes away. 'What are you doing?'

'We're going out for lunch,' said Sue. 'Well, we are after I've had a shower. I'm not going anywhere until I've changed these clothes.'

Alex looked down at her own outfit and decided she would follow Sue's example. The rank smell of cider and vomit clung to her and she was suddenly desperate to wash it away.

Samuel was pleased with his new hideout. On his extensive exploration of the Levels he had found an old cottage, abandoned and almost derelict, down by the canal. Bushes had grown up around it, shielding it from the track that ran to the south, curving round the water meadows to link Weston-zoyland to the main road. The door had been locked and the grimy windows refused to budge but a rickety gate opening into a small passageway leading to the back door was loose in its frame, secured only by some baling wire twisted round the door jamb.

It was the work of a minute to untangle this and push open the creaking back door. The smell made him screw up his face in disgust. It was rank inside the tiny kitchen, the stink coming from an old, rusty chest freezer in the middle of the room. Samuel held his breath and risked a look inside. It was empty though the bottom was covered in a thick layer of brown sludge in which hundreds of dead flies were embedded.

Slamming the lid shut in disgust, Samuel decided it would be easier to get rid of it than to try and clean it out. The thought of touching that revolting mess made his skin crawl. Leaving the adjoining door ajar in case he had to leave in a hurry, he moved into the front room, the only other room on the ground floor. This was dusty, the cobwebs spanning the grimy ceiling a testament to the cottage's neglect. The only furniture was a battered armchair with a footstool, an upright chair shoved into one corner and an old trestle table with some rather ominous-looking stains. It was considerably more acceptable than the kitchen, however, and Samuel decided, looking around carefully, that it would do rather well.

He climbed the stairs in darkness, no light finding its way through the tiny, filthy window at the top of the stairs. A quick check around revealed a bedroom and two tiny box rooms, both covered in dust and draped with cobwebs. The bedroom looked as if it might have been used some time in the last year or so but whoever had slept there had not bothered much with proper bedding. The sagging mattress was draped in some old sacking and a few scraps of cloth and there was no pillow.

Samuel picked his way downstairs again, taking the stairs with great care. The last thing he needed was a bad fall, even possibly a broken ankle. The thought of lying in the gloom, helpless and unheeded, made him shudder. Despite the state of the cottage he was pleased with his find. It was well hidden, obviously long abandoned and a lot more substantial than any of his previous hides. Two useable rooms downstairs, once he'd dealt with the odious freezer, promised both shelter and privacy. It offered him a place to relax, plan and be himself. It had been a long time since he'd had such luxury. It would be worth the effort to get the place cleaned up, he thought.

In the kitchen he stood eyeing the freezer thoughtfully. It was very old and consequently likely to be equally heavy. He walked around it and almost tripped on the cable that snaked out of the back. That was odd, he realized. There were no electric lights in the place. Previous occupants had probably relied on candles – or gone to bed at dusk. The rusty stove was an antique wood burner. So what was an item of electrical equipment like the freezer doing in the middle of the room?

He went back to his rucksack and pulled out his torch. He'd been conserving the batteries, for he needed every penny of his meagre income to feed himself and replace his lost kit, but this could be important and merited using the fading light it produced. Scrabbling around the back wall he uncovered a floating socket. No switch, no light and hardly any insulation but when he rather gingerly inserted the freezer plug there was a faint humming from the unit and a red light came on near the handle.

Samuel unplugged it again and crawled backwards out of the gap, intrigued by this unexpected bonus. Someone had gone to the trouble of laying the cable, probably tapping the local mains to provide power for the freezer. He stepped outside, checking along the back wall until he spotted the cable snaking out and down through the long grass towards the canal where it disappeared into the waterproofed trunking.

He decided to check the garden for anything useful before dragging the freezer out, just in case he damaged something that he might need. A quick search revealed some broken boxes, possibly good for fuel if he lit the range, an old tyre and a pile of mud with various bits of wood, brick and glass embedded in it. Disappointed, he turned away and almost trod on a small pile of fishing gear hidden in the undergrowth. Disentangling his foot from a long-handled net propped up against a tree, he pulled a fishing rod free from a large stand of nettles, rubbing at the stings on the back of his hand as he stepped backwards. Samuel didn't have much experience of fishing but he knew the basics. He saw a chance to add to his meagre diet with some protein-rich fish and the stove, if he could get it to work, meant he could cook his catch.

Carrying the fishing gear in his arms, he retreated to the front room, placing his new possessions on the trestle before turning his attention back to the problem of the freezer. Unless he could deal with that the cottage was not going to be usable. Samuel gave it a trial shove, hefting it to check the weight and then turned his full intellect to the task.

Chapter Four

It was a predictably gloomy group of officers that gathered in the meeting room on Monday morning awaiting the arrival of Gordon, the acting senior. Most of them had gone through a Home Office inspection before and it was not an experience they were keen to repeat.

'I hope everyone's been using the new format for reports,' said Eddie Stroud. An officer for over ten years, he was alarmed to see the underlying ideology of his role begin to change as the emphasis slowly shifted from rehabilitation to punishment of offenders. Like most of those in the room, he was struggling to adjust to the new, more punitive practises. Eddie was a great believer in healthy exercise leading to healthy minds – and if that didn't work at least a few days on his outdoor adventure programme would tire the clients out, leaving them too exhausted to commit any further offences for a while.

Margaret Lorde, another experienced officer, sniffed in disapproval.

'I've been preparing reports for the court for fifteen years,' she said. 'This new template is really far too restrictive. There's no space to add any appraisal of the client's character or to discuss suitable alternative outcomes. They might as well give us a tick-box sheet.'

'Yes,' said Sue. 'One with several choices like "hang them", "beat them" or "lock them up for ten years".'

This drew a grin from Paul Malcolm, a young and idealistic officer in his fourth year. With his curly hair and freckles, Paul looked as young as some of his clients, but he handled the juveniles who made up most of his case load with skill and a fair measure of success. 'I'd be left with no-one,' he pointed out. 'By the time they were released they'd all be too old for my Intermediate Treatment programmes.'

Paul had the thankless task of trying to interest the youngest offenders in something other than their criminal activity of choice, preferably with a bit of education thrown in. His programme, a junior version of the day centre schedule overseen by Alex, had been surprisingly effective over the last few years with less than half the boys re-offending. Despite this he was under constant pressure to harden his stance towards the young lads on his list. The programme, which included trips to the local swimming pool and days out in the National Park had recently attracted some deeply unfavourable and ill-informed attention from the press with several articles accusing the Probation Service of "rewarding" young criminals for their bad behaviour.

Alex glanced over at Sue who was leaning her chin on one hand and gazing longingly out of the window. It was another beautiful day outside and already uncomfortably hot in the offices. After dealing with Charlie yesterday they had eventually set off for their walk on the Quantocks, though Sue's dream of lunch had failed to materialize. Arriving at 'The Albatross' in Nether Stowey just before two they had been informed it was too late to eat though the kitchen could probably rustle up a sandwich if they wanted to wait until the dining room was cleared.

'It says "Sunday Lunch" on the sign outside,' Sue said.

'Well, yes. But is finished now,' said the barman gesturing to the dining room. At least half the tables were still occupied by couples and families happily stuffing themselves with roast beef, Yorkshire puddings and a choice of vegetables. The serving counter from whence this bounty came was still laden with food and Sue rounded on the barman angrily.

'They've only just stopped serving – and it's not two yet!'

'They've finished,' he said. 'And is three minutes past. Now, you want that sandwich or not?'

Sue's response made it very clear what she thought of the offer along with a suggestion for the disposal of the proffered snack and they left, hungry and annoyed. Rummaging around in the glove compartment, Alex uncovered half a packet of Garibaldi biscuits and they munched their way through these as Sue guided her car up to the car park at the top of the hills. The walk was a delight, as ever, but hunger caught up with them part way around their usual route and they made their way home, Sue giving the pub a rude gesture as they drove back through the village.

Alex's musing was cut short by the arrival of Gordon, who was accompanied by Pauline, the senior administrator. Together they distributed a number of thick folders around the assembled company. Alex flipped through the top booklet, her heart sinking as she saw form after form requiring her personal details, professional qualifications and an itemized breakdown of everything she did at work. The final pages were headed 'Continuing Personal Development' and she blinked at them, uncomprehending for a moment. Surely they didn't expect her to do yet more training as well as run the day centre and manage a full case load?

It seemed they did. Gordon ran them through the top booklet briskly before turning to the final section.

'This is going to be a requirement soon,' he said, raising a hand to quell the groans of his officers. 'I know – we are all busy and we are all highly trained professionals and this can feel a little patronizing but things are changing and we need to demonstrate we are keeping up with current practice.

It doesn't have to be formal courses. If you read any of the probation or social work journals, for example, that goes in there ...'

'Only to look for another job,' muttered Eddie.

Gordon quelled him with a glare. 'We have a county officer whose only job seems to be locating and providing useful and informative articles for you. The least you could do is read one of them occasionally. Now, we've had a couple of days away for team-building and so on – those go in there. Alex, you went to visit the day centre in Yeovil last month – well that should go in too.'

'I watched *Prisoner of Cell Block H* on Friday,' said Paul. 'Does that count?'

The generally placid Gordon rounded on him, snapping in frustration.

'You may think this is funny but, believe me, it is not! Just in case it has slipped your mind we have a new senior starting in a month and she will be watching how we perform very closely. With all the changes in policy coming down from above, headquarters in Taunton are also determined to ensure we follow the new guidelines or they will be in here watching over you all as well. So I expect you all to concentrate on getting this right.'

'Sorry, Gordon,' muttered Paul, and he slipped down in his chair, hiding behind Sue. At that moment the door flew open and Ricky Peddlar, the latest addition to the team, hurried in making a great show of puffing with the exertion of climbing two flights of stairs.

'Sorry I'm a bit late,' he said, throwing his bag down and dropping into a chair at the end of the back row. 'Puncture.'

Gordon rounded on him. 'You have remarkably poor luck on Mondays, it seems,' he said. 'I can't recall you ever being on time for one of my meetings.'

Alex and Sue exchanged glances. It was unlike Gordon to criticize another officer in public and it showed how stressed he must be feeling.

Ricky's face coloured a bright red and he blinked in surprise. His hands clenched into fists as he controlled his temper but the look he gave Gordon was full of menace. Rumours concerning Ricky and the new senior were flying around the office and if he did know her from his training year then Gordon might soon come to regret his outburst.

After an uncomfortable pause Gordon continued with the meeting, laying out the timetable for bringing all the paperwork up to date, setting deadlines for getting typing to the admin pool and highlighting areas likely to be put under close scrutiny.

'A lot of the attention will fall on you Alex,' he said. 'We have one of the fastest-growing day centre provisions in the country and they are likely to be interested in how it tallies with the new policy document.'

Alex nodded, her face neutral. She knew how it tallied with the new policy guidelines – a lot of it didn't and she didn't much care. She saw the day centre as a way for her probationers to learn some new skills, access much-needed education in an unthreatening way and develop some interests that didn't involve a gallon of natch. She did not see it as any type of punishment.

'We will have a meeting later in the week to discuss this,' Gordon added. He gave her a hard look before turning his attention to Pauline, almost as if he knew what Alex was thinking.

After the meeting Sue cornered Alex on the stairs. 'You can't possibly go ahead with that Thursday,' she hissed. 'Gordon's going to be watching you and how are you going to write it up in the final report? Besides, you know the lads will talk. They always do. One of mine wanted to know how to get on the course because he fancied the idea of that stupid computer game!'

They paused as Ricky pushed past, his face still angry from the humiliation of the meeting.

'It was polite of you to wash up before coming in,' Sue called after him.

'What do you mean?' asked Ricky, turning on the stair to glare at her.

Well, look at your lovely clean hands,' said Sue sweetly.

Ricky glanced down at his hands, free of any taint of oil or grease, and his scowl deepened. 'Very funny,' he snapped and hurried away up to his room.

'Lying little gobshite,' said Sue. 'Just too lazy to get up in the morning. He's still wearing the same clothes he had on last week too. Did you get a whiff of him as he went past? He smells worse than some of the clients.'

The previous Thursday had been a court day for Alex, who was presenting her report on Steve Wilson. It was not one of her best efforts but she had done all she could to portray him in a favourable light. Given the fact he was facing a charge of actual bodily harm in addition to the attempted theft of his meal at the pub she was forced to move him up the tariff to keep him out of prison. Steve had not been impressed by her reasoning but agreed, somewhat sulkily, to her recommendations. They left the court with a two-year probation order and 60 days attendance at the day centre, a sentence that ensured Alex would be enjoying the pleasure of his company for some time to come.

'Don't see why I should stay down here,' he grumbled as they drove back to the hostel. 'Not as if there's anyfink for us. Waste of bloody time.'

'I hope the day centre will be useful,' said Alex smoothly. 'We have a lot of different groups and classes to help you in addition to links with the local college ...'

'Yeah, right,' said Steve, swinging his feet and kicking under the glove compartment.

'Do that again and you'll get out and walk,' said Alex sharply.

Steve sighed theatrically and stared out of the side window but he stopped kicking. Maybe there was some fun to be had, he thought. He had a place to sleep and was fed at the hostel. And the warden was useless – no problem fooling him. Charlie was a bit of a loser but he had high hopes for Petey, who was proving impressionable and easily led. Might not be so bad.

Steve left the hostel on Monday morning having persuaded Petey to part with some of his dole money for the bus fare.

'I think we should have a bit of a look around,' he said. 'Scout out some stuff and see what's on offer. Know wot I mean?'

Petey didn't but he was eager to see what his new friend had in mind. Life was so boring at the hostel, an endless round of grey days, tasteless food and limited money. It had been a lot more interesting since Steve arrived and the prospect of some excitement drove any caution out of his head. He even forgot his concern over Charlie, still languishing in the hospital across the other side of the river.

Taking the bus from outside the Town Hall, the two young men travelled deep into the countryside, Steve staring out of the window at the rich, flat water meadows with their pattern of ditches and canals to drain the ever-rising water into the river. In spite of the summer heat the rhynes were filled to a good depth, the water flowing sluggishly with twists and eddies as it wound its way between willows and reeds. The bus was old and smelled of dust, chips and diesel fumes. The suspension was wearing out and the vehicle rocked from side to side as it wheezed its way along the route from Highpoint to Street, wallowing around the narrow corners alarmingly.

For once, Petey was the experienced one, rolling comfortably with the bus and pointing out interesting features along the way. Steve was glad to get off when the bus finally stopped just outside Street. Breathing deeply to get the fumes out of his lungs he looked around at the wide, pale sky, a little disoriented by the silence that crept in as the sound of the bus faded in to the distance.

'I don't think I ever bin on no bus as old as that thing,' he said.

Petey shrugged. 'Gets you there an' is cheap enough,' he said. 'Specially for you.' He turned his back on Steve and was heading off down a faint path between two trees before Steve could think of an answer. Walking in single file, the pair made their way deeper into the Levels. Around them birds fell silent as they passed, only to begin their soft chatter once the human intruders were gone. A soft breeze stirred the reeds and made the willow trees sway and dip their branches in the dark waters.

Steve jumped nervously at the sounds from the river and stopped a couple of times as the path turned to slippery mud. Progress was slow as he picked his way along behind Petey, who was enjoying the experience of being in charge. Suddenly Steve gave a shout and jumped off the narrow path. His feet slipped on the waterlogged bank of the stream and he slid into the water, his hands grabbing frantically at the reeds as his legs disappeared up to his knees in mud.

Petey turned and began to laugh at the sight of Steve wallowing helplessly. Steve tried to take a step but his feet slipped and he landed in the water, glaring at Petey from the stream.

'Here, come on out,' he said, holding out his hand. 'How you manage to do that then?'

'Saw a snake,' Steve said as he hauled his sodden legs out of the water. 'Just down there it was. Big bastard, all stripy and stuff it was. Give us a right turn.

Petey stepped back from the bushes where he had been poking at the undergrowth.

'What sort of stripy?' he asked. 'Like a zigzag down they back was it?'

Steve stood on the bank shivering despite the warm sun. 'Yeah, big black zigzag. Can't stand snakes,' he added. 'One good thing about Stockwell – we don't get no snakes runnin' around the streets there.'

Petey gestured to him to walk on and they set off down the path again. 'Don't want to be hangin' around there,' he advised. 'Sounds like was an adder. Don't bother you most times but is still breeding season an' they can get a bit nasty if'n you get close to they nests.'

Steve picked up his speed on hearing this and was almost treading on Petey's heels by the time they emerged from the undergrowth surrounding the path and struck off across firmer ground.

'Adders are poison!' he panted as he hurried along. 'Poison snakes out here in the wild!' He glanced over his shoulder at the trees, relieved to have escaped without injury.

'Don't hardly no-one die from 'um,' said Petey calmly. 'Bit nasty if you get bit but 'taint likely to kill yer. Only get bit if'n you's daft enough to step on 'un or pick 'un up. Watch yer step mind. They's maybe out round here, it being a nice day an' all.'

Steve turned round, searching frantically for signs he was being followed by venomous reptiles. He had a vision of adder families crawling out of the woods and settling in small groups to gossip and play in the field, all the while keeping an eye on their tiny adder children ...

This fanciful idea was dispelled as Petey explained. 'They comes out into the open when is sunny. Just lie around, specially in the afternoon. Don't do no harm – 'less you tread on 'um of course.'

Steve stomped along behind Petey, hating the countryside in general and the Levels in particular. Flat, ugly, empty, boring place with nothing to see or to do – and to make his day even more miserable clouds of tiny insects gathered over the streams and canals. They were so small they couldn't be seen individually but they had one hell of a bite. By the time he and Petey had cleared the water meadows, Steve was scratching at his arms and face, all of which were covered in itchy red spots.

'What's that over there?' said Steve, stopping in the middle of the path and pointing into the middle of a patch of grassland. There was a humped shape with a few bricks sticking out at odd angles. Steve set off across the rough ground, all thoughts of adders and other dangers gone in an instant.

After a moment's hesitation Petey followed, though he moved with more care, avoiding the ruts and hollows in the field.

Steve walked around the mound, pulling at the long grass and climbing plants that obscured most of it.

'Bloody hell,' he said, snatching his hand away from a long stem of blackberry. 'This whole place is just horrible!' He aimed a kick at the base of the bush but succeeded only in entangling his foot in the thorns and had to be freed by Petey, who seemed as impervious to the sharp thorns as he was to the biting midges.

Moving with more caution he circled the structure again, this time using a stick to pull the vegetation aside. On one side was the remains of a wooden panel and a few good kicks disposed of this obstacle. Leaning into the black space, Steve tried to see what was inside but the only light was blocked by his body. Fumbling in his pockets he pulled out the remains of a box of matches, sodden and useless from his dip in the river. Cursing with frustration, he flung the soggy mess away into the bushes, groping around in the hope he had his lighter with him.

'Use mine?' asked Petey, holding out the lighter Steve had given him at the weekend. Steve took it with a grunt and wriggled back into the gap between the boards. In the flickering flame he saw a jumble of old, broken furniture and bits of wood strewn around a concrete-lined interior. He only had a few seconds before the lighter began to burn his thumb but the initial inspection suggested there was a closed-off doorway at the far end but no other windows.

Sliding out onto the ground he reported his findings to Petey, who sat down next to him, carefully removing a stand of nettles before leaning against the mud-covered wall. Looking around at their position, right in the middle of open ground with a clear view off to the south-west, he had an idea what they had found.

'Part of old defences from the war, I reckon,' he said. 'Probably had a few old buggers with a machine gun in there ready for when a load of tanks came rolling in. My grandad, he was in the Home Guard. Told us about it one time.'

Steve snorted in disgust. 'Fat chance they'd have 'ad,' he said. 'Waste of time anyway. Who's gonna bother with this?' He waved his arm, taking in the landscape that stretched as far as he could see. 'Now London, that was where the action was. Bombs every night, whole streets burnin' down – we still got a load of bomb sites round us. You know what? They sent half the kids from London down 'ere to be safe. You never got nothing. Cushty, you had it.'

Petey leapt to his feet, stung by Steve's implied criticism of Somerset's role in the war. 'We got bombed,' he said furiously. 'We got bombed in Weston an' Bath an' all round Bristol.'

Steve shrugged, unimpressed by this. 'Yeah, well they're all towns 'ent they. Not like round here.' He repeated the sweep of the hand.

'We did too!' said Petey furiously. 'My Gran told us – they set up these big fires, with petrol an' tar and straw so's the planes'd think was Bristol or some place they was after. My Grandad, he said we was used as bait. "Live bait", he said we was. Thousands of bombs was dropped, landed all over. There's still a load of 'um out here 'ent never been found too.'

Steve rose to his feet and went over to Petey, who was close to tears.

'Look, I didn't mean nothin.' He put his arm around the young man's shoulders. 'Come back an' tell us about these fires. And the bombs. You said there's bombs out here.' His eyes gleamed with excitement at the prospect. Fire was fun but the chance to blow something up was too good to miss.

Monday was a workshop day and Samuel was up early and waiting outside the door before the supervisor arrived.

'Sorry I'm a bit late,' the supervisor said, unlocking the old bike shed and beckoning Samuel inside. 'Meeting overran a few minutes.'

Samuel was tempted to look at his watch, checking just how long it had been, but instead he just nodded. That sort of implied criticism upset some people and he wanted the supervisor in a good mood. Still, he knew it was more than a few minutes and he resented being kept waiting. Inside the shed it was hot and smelt of sawdust, varnish and oil from the bikes stacked up at the back. Every workshop client had the option to choose a machine from the pile and repair it. When they had finished, the Probation Service put them in for the cycling proficiency test and once this was successfully passed they could keep the bike.

This was not something that attracted Samuel. He hated the idea of performing for the testers, being judged like a kid with their first bicycle. If he wanted a bike he'd get a job, earn the money and buy his own. He didn't need someone else's cast-offs, but he kept this opinion to himself. No point in deliberately antagonizing people, he thought. Anyway, he wanted a place on the raft race team very badly. He wasn't sure why he should care so much except it was something new, something potentially dangerous and something he knew he could do much better than anyone else from the sorry crowd that made up the workshop group. Samuel loved to win, almost as much as he loved his special evenings with young women.

'I had a chat with Alex,' said the supervisor as he unlocked the wall cabinets and pinned the doors open to reveal rows of woodworking tools. 'She said you might be helpful in designing our raft?'

Samuel hid a smile of satisfaction. Alex Hastings had remembered and she'd kept her word. She really was very different from most of the women he'd known in his life.

'I have a few ideas that might be useful,' he said, stepping up to a large drawing board at the back of the room. There was a faded diagram taped to the surface, its edges curling and starting to fray. 'Is this last year's raft?'

The supervisor nodded. 'Yes. It was our first time so we were just trying out things. Some of them worked – the rudder, for example. That was devised by one of our lads, Kevin Mallory. He was a revelation – couldn't read or write but he could do sums in his head and just seemed to see exactly what would work.' The supervisor pulled out a rolled-up drawing and smoothed it out on the board.

'We had a bit of a problem just as we rounded the cliff, half way from Minehead. There was a puncture in one of the barrels and the raft shipped a lot of water. Alex was knocked overboard and almost drowned. I think we need to look at the design and perhaps make it a bit more responsive.'

Samuel looked at the drawings and was amazed the raft had even floated, let alone made it from Watchet to Minehead by sea, a distance of some five miles. In his estimation the craft looked to have the handling characteristics of a drunken pig. He felt a twinge of admiration for the unknown Kevin Mallory who had designed a rudder capable of steering this monster.

'I think we might simplify it a bit,' he said, already running over the possibilities in his mind. 'Are there any rules covering the construction?'

'Not many,' said the supervisor. 'Must carry a crew of at least two people, no sharp edges or corners, at least four feet wide and no boat parts. For paddling only too – no oars and such …' He broke off as the first of the workshop group pushed their way in, shoving and jostling one another.

'Oih! That's enough now. Get to a bench and – you – John – yes you. No smoking in here. Not on the floor you little fool – outside with it!'

Samuel closed his ears to the mindless chatter around him, focussing on the problems posed by the raft. There was buoyancy to be balanced against number of crew – the more crew, the more paddlers but also the more weight. The craft needed to be streamlined but the rules said four feet wide. Stability – he needed to see what the currents were like on an average day and calculate likely stresses … He flipped a fresh sheet of paper over onto the board and taking a pencil from his pocket began to sketch.

Several hours later he was startled by the supervisor materializing next to him holding two mugs. 'Here you go. Got you a coffee – hope that's alright. You been right busy here,' he continued as he perused the drawing board.

Samuel stepped back, picking up the beaker. He sniffed, expecting the sour, metallic odour of steri' milk and instant coffee. Instead he smelt the dark, rich scent of ground beans.

Almost burning his mouth with eagerness he took a sip and gave a soft groan as the caffeine seemed to rush into his bloodstream. The supervisor glanced at him and smiled.

'Alex suggested you might like a drop of decent coffee for a change,' he said. 'You've certainly earned it. There's some right good ideas here.'

Samuel took a moment to savour the rich, buttery taste of his coffee before speaking. 'Decent milk,' he noted.

The supervisor nodded. 'She won't have steri' in the day centre,' he said. 'Bit of a nuisance, getting fresh each day but does taste better, I'll grant you. Now, let's look at these drawings of your'n.' He stood back and studied the sheet intently, leaning forwards to inspect a detail in places. 'Looks like you done some drawin' before. Very nice work, this is. Why didn't you say when you come here first, 'stead of lettin' us put you on all that basic stuff? Must'a been bored out of your mind.'

Samuel stood behind him, sipping his coffee in silence. In truth, he had been bored out of his mind but he was not about to reveal anything of his past. He lived in short bursts, every couple of years sectioned off from what had gone before. That made him hard to trace, almost impossible to follow. The minor offences on his record were wiped off regularly, classed as 'spent' and as long as he didn't want to work with children no-one was likely to go digging any deeper. He played the system to perfection.

'I did some technical drawing in school,' he said. 'I was always quite good at art too.'

The supervisor nodded. 'Maybe you should think about going back to it,' he said. 'There's a very good college over at Taunton with some excellent art classes. You have talent, you know.'

Samuel smiled, a tight little smile. The opinion, good or otherwise, of a nonentity such as this was of no interest to him at all and he certainly wasn't going to hang around Highpoint longer than was strictly necessary. It had very little to attract him and he intended to leave as soon as his probation order allowed. In the meantime he would amuse himself with the little people and the raft race promised to be very amusing.

'So how do you choose the crew?' he asked casually.

'Was volunteers last time, so Eddie says,' the supervisor replied. 'Will probably be the same this. Need to have lads as are keen, do a bit of training and so on. Had eight last year – we's aiming for the same again this time round.'

'What about the crew from last year?' asked Samuel. 'Their experience would be valuable if we are to have a chance of winning.'

The supervisor turned and stared at him for a moment. 'What you think?' he said laughing. 'We ain't entering to *win*. We entering for the fun of it – gives the lads a new experience, teaches 'um to work together and maybe gets 'um a bit more fit. Don't have no chance in hell of *winning* the thing!'

This brought Samuel up with a start. It hadn't occurred to him they weren't going all out for victory – the idea was completely alien to him.

'Oh,' was all he could manage. There was the sound of raised voices outside as the rest of the group trickled in from their break. A couple of the bigger lads stopped at a bench near the drawing board, eyeing Samuel and his coffee. He put down the mug and stretched his shoulders, meeting their hostile stares. After a few seconds the three young men turned away with some angry muttering – there was something intimidating about Samuel, something that warned off other predators.

The silent exchange had not gone unnoticed by the supervisor, who stepped up to the bench and had a quiet word with the culprits. Samuel turned his back on the room and within seconds was immersed in his drawings. He could not think of eight people from the workshop capable of rowing a raft five miles in open sea. Most of them could scarcely ride their bikes around the car park without getting hot and sweaty.

Still, he'd been told to design a craft for eight and that was what he would do. In his head he thought of the ideal raft – fast, light and elegant, a winning raft for two dedicated rowers. He would take the stern, paddling and steering. In the front, working in perfect sync, would be Alex Hastings. He focussed on his designs, calculating and refining the lines of the raft, his bright blue eyes fixed on the paper.

Chapter Five

Lauren was bored. Propped up on the sofa, a book in her hands, she gazed out of the windows at the Quantock Hills that shimmered invitingly in the hazy sunlight. Lauren, at under four feet tall, was not one for strenuous athletic endeavours but she longed to be outside enjoying a stroll with a friend. Or riding her specially adapted tandem with Dave, her boyfriend. Or just sitting in the sun. Anything but being stuck in this gloomy room on her own. Hell, she almost wished she could get back to work but the doctor had been adamant.

'You have suffered a minor cardiac incident,' he said. Before she could argue, he had continued. 'You should consider the emphasis to be on *cardiac incident* rather than on *minor*. This could have been very serious and I don't want you rushing back to work before I've been able to establish exactly what the cause was.'

Lauren knew what had caused her 'minor cardiac incident' (or 'not really a heart attack', as she thought of it). Assigned as admin support to Ricky Peddlar at the probation offices, she had been summoned to his office on the top floor four times in a quarter of an hour until she collapsed and fell on the way down. No-one who knew the facts had any doubt he had done it deliberately. In recent weeks Ricky had become increasingly arrogant and rude and some of his remarks to Lauren had bordered on abusive but he was always very careful not to say or do anything in front of witnesses. Lauren was popular and respected in the office and she had many friends ready to jump to her aid but her pride had stopped her complaining until it was too late.

Sitting by her hospital bed, Dave had talked to Alex and Sue as well as Lauren's brother, Jonny, and he had a fairly good idea of what had occurred. Lauren had recovered consciousness just in time to prevent him from confronting Ricky, though it had taken the combined force of all four of them to dissuade him. Lauren wasn't opposed to Dave having a 'quiet word' but he was due to leave for the police college at Hendon for three months detective training and Lauren wasn't going to allow him to jeopardize all he had worked for over the last few years. Dave had wanted to stay but the course was difficult to get on to and he might have to wait months for another chance.

Reluctantly he had left for London and Lauren was stuck at home, bored and sulky. A tap at the door made her sit up with a jerk. 'Come in.'

There was a pause and then Sue's face appeared round the frame.

'I haven't woken you, have I?' she asked.

Lauren smiled and shook her head. 'Saved me from another long and lonely day, you have. Here, sit down.'

Sue sank into an armchair and sighed happily as she slipped off her gold sandals and wriggled her toes, enjoying the freedom of being away from the public eye for a few minutes.

'Why d'you wear them things?' Lauren asked. 'I could never walk in 'um, never mind run around at work all day.'

'Yeah, well maybe I should get you a pair,' said Sue, 'seeing as you're not supposed to be running around all day. So, how are you?'

Lauren sighed. In truth, she was still feeling a bit shaky, especially when she ignored her mother's instructions and tried to get on with something when left alone in the house. Stupid little things too – it wasn't like she was painting the ceiling or anything like that, just a bit of pottering about in the house and garden, anything to make her feel less useless and to stop herself worrying about her job.

She really didn't ever want to see Ricky again and she certainly didn't want to continue as his assistant, but she enjoyed the job itself. She was proud of the work she did and liked almost everyone else she came into contact with during the day. Even the clients, many of whom she knew from school or through her extended family spread around the area. It gave her self-respect and it paid well enough, especially as she still lived at home with her mother and Jonny. She'd thought a lot about what had happened and decided that no-one, never mind a worthless little worm like Ricky Peddlar, was going to drive her out.

'All right I guess,' she said. 'Better than a few weeks ago anyway. How's it going at the office?'

Sue groaned softly. 'Inspection,' she said gloomily.

'Ahh.' Lauren had heard about the Home Office inspection team. For the first time since her accident she was rather glad not to be at work.

'Alex is a bit stressed,' Sue continued. 'They'll be looking at the day centre so she's got more work than the rest of us. She seems to be coping though. I think having Margie around makes all the difference.'

'She there all the time then?' asked Lauren, quick to pounce on some interesting gossip. 'Moving in? Thought she was out near the prison at Shepton.'

Sue flapped a hand at her friend. 'Yes, she's in the staff quarters there at the moment. I suppose she'll look for somewhere of her own after a few months …' Her voice trailed off. It hadn't occurred to her that Margie might move in with Alex. The thought brought a mix of emotions. She liked Margie, who was friendly, clever and fun. And she was very good for Alex who, wonderful as she was, tended to be far too serious about everything. Still, Alex had been her closest friend for the past few years and Sue wasn't sure the little house in town was going to be big enough for the three of them. Some time in the future she was going to need a place of her own. She pushed the thought away but the sense of dread stayed with her, a small cold ball in the pit of her stomach.

'Tell you what,' said Lauren, oblivious to Sue's concern. 'I got a couple of tickets for the play up at the college next week. Jonny said he'd come and got one for Kurt but he can't make it 'cos is working. Wanna come along? Should be a right laugh.'

Sue blinked at her in surprise. She hadn't considered Lauren much of a theatre-goer. Then a thought struck her. Maybe the college productions were really bad and she was being invited to go along and mock. The thought did not appeal to her and she was about to decline as politely as she could when Lauren continued.

'Loads of the students is going an' they's going to dress up. Sing along too. Saw it at the cinema last year and was a riot.'

'What on earth are they performing?' Sue asked.

'The *Rocky Horror Show*,' said Lauren with a wide grin. 'Never seen it live so I's really lookin' forward to it. Go on, say you'll come.'

Sue was tempted. Apart from the cinema and the carnival there wasn't a lot of entertainment in Highpoint and even amateurs could normally manage a decent performance of the *Rocky Horror Show*. She'd been to one performance where several of the performers couldn't carry a tune in a bucket but it hadn't mattered because a significant part of the audience sang their numbers for them. She had even dressed up once, swept along by the enthusiasm of her friends. Probably not a good thing to do in Highpoint under the circumstances, but a chance to see the show again was too good to pass up.

'I'm in,' she said. 'Oh – when is it? I forgot – we've got all these extra early evening sessions to get everything ready for the inspectors.'

'Thursday,' said Lauren. 'First night – thought we'd go along to give 'um some encouragement, though from all accounts is selling really well. Don't suppose Alex can be persuaded …?'

Sue shook her head. 'That's her last alcohol education session,' she said. 'It's already been postponed once so she'll be desperate to finish the course. Perhaps another time – do they do many shows?'

''Bout four or five a year,' said Lauren. 'Got a decent drama department there an' Saturday classes for kids an' all. I went for a bit when I was young. Thought I might learn dancing but …' She shrugged, glancing down at her heavy torso and short legs. 'Don't reckon I'm built for nothing elegant like that.'

Sue resisted the urge to go over and hug her. Lauren had a certain dignity about her and was a proud and independent person despite her lack of inches. Moments of self-pity were very few and usually fleeting, as this one proved to be.

'Still, I can do the "Timewarp" with the best of 'um, so I'll be dressing up. Jonny will too. Any excuse getting into his fishnets for him.'

Sue had a vivid and disturbing mental picture of herself arriving at the local college with Jonny in full drag on one side and Lauren done up as a Transylvanian on the other. What if a group of clients saw her? She dismissed the thought with a smile. It was a play at the local college. There would be students and parents and members of the staff there – it was just some fun. What was the worst that could happen?

Charlie Dodds finally returned to the hostel in a hospital car in time to be put out again around lunch time. Despite the medical certificate from the doctor who had attended him, Peter Marks, the hostel warden, refused him permission to stay in his room and rest. Reluctantly, he did allow the wretched young man to go upstairs and change his clothes, which still bore signs of the weekend's excesses, but he drew the line at allowing him to use the washing machine out back.

'I'm not having those revolting things in the hostel washer,' he said. 'Besides, is being used for bedding today. You'll have to sort it out yerself.'

Upstairs, Charlie opened the window to get the sour smell of the room out of his head as he stripped off, bundling the stained garments into an old carrier bag. He checked the change in his pockets and realized with a sinking heart he didn't have enough for laundry unless he gave up eating lunch for the rest of the week. Make that the next fortnight, he thought gloomily as he remembered it was almost two weeks to benefit day.

Slipping downstairs in his bare feet, Charlie crept towards the kitchen. It was deserted as there were no classes scheduled for that day and the cleaner was busy trying to bring order to the recreation room after the weekend. A glance around revealed nothing edible left on the side counters. All the breakfast stuff was put away in the fridge, which was securely fastened by a large padlock. Charlie looked over his shoulder nervously but there was no sign of the warden.

Moving with exaggerated caution he tiptoed over to the big larder, a cupboard built into the back wall of the hostel. To his surprise it was not locked and the door opened with a creak. He stopped, heart pounding as he waited for the wrath of the establishment to fall on him. After a moment he reached in and grabbed the first thing that came to hand, closed the door and ran as quietly as he could back up the stairs towards his room. Just as he turned onto the landing the office door opened and the warden stepped out.

''Ent you done yet boy?' he shouted. 'Come on, hurry up. I want you out in ten minutes!'

'Sorry, Mr Marks,' Charlie said. 'I was just in the bog. Feel a bit sick still.'

'Serve you right,' grunted the warden. 'Bloody silly thing to do – could'a killed yerself, drinking all that. Lucky you was found in time. Go on, hurry it up now.'

Safe behind a closed door, Charlie examined his haul – two mini packets of cereal, one composed almost entirely of bran, and a half-eaten pot of mixed fruit jam. He turned his attention to the other mini cereal, a box of sugared cornflakes. Ripping off the top, he upended the tiny cardboard package, pouring half the contents into his mouth and almost choking. Sputtering and spitting half-chewed cereal, he staggered to the sink in the corner of the room and drank from the tap, trying to swallow his impromptu breakfast without throwing up again.

It was a close thing and his heart was thudding in his chest when he sat down. The rest of the box went down a lot more slowly and the warden was calling for him to come along before he had finished. Stuffing the two boxes and the jar into his carrier bag of dirty clothes, Charlie rose to his feet and wearily set off down the stairs into the bright, hard light of a summer morning.

It was with a sense of relief mixed with impatience that Alex greeted Charlie when he arrived at the offices unannounced and unexpected. Whilst pleased to see he was out of hospital and relatively none the worst for his misadventure, she was overwhelmed with extra work and didn't have time to listen to Charlie's woes. He looked decidedly ragged, she thought, eyeing his pale face and dark-rimmed, red eyes. Alcohol poisoning would do that to you every time.

'I'm not going to ask how you're feeling,' she said briskly. 'I can imagine how you feel. I just hope you remember how bloody awful it was and next time make a better choice of weekend activity.'

Charlie dropped his aching head until his chin was resting on his chest and muttered something.

'What? Come on Charlie, I can't hear you. What did you say?' Alex had a twinge of guilt at her lack of sympathy but she'd tried reason and she'd tried being supportive and here was this young man, not much more than a boy, still determined to drink himself to death in one afternoon. Perhaps some 'tough love' was what he needed.

'Wasn't my idea,' said Charlie.

'Oh, really? So whose idea was it?' asked Alex. 'I thought you were on your own on Saturday.'

'No, I mean was not what I planned for the day,' Charlie said. 'Was in town, up Cornhill with Steve an' Petey but the old bat from the auction throwed us out an' they went off an' I didn't know what to do. Had a bit of money from my dole an' didn't want to be with them anyway 'cos ...' He stopped abruptly and his pale face flushed. 'Just 'cos,' he finished rather lamely.

Alex gave him her best hard stare. 'Just because ... just because of what, Charlie?'

Charlie didn't mind getting Steve into trouble but he still felt a strong sense of loyalty to Petey and he suspected anything he said to incriminate one would cause problems for both.

'Just – felt left out,' he said. 'Been friends for all my life but Petey went off 'n I didn't want to go back on my own.'

Alex waited but that was all she was going to get. She sighed and leaned back in her chair. Charlie was wearing clean clothes but the bag resting at his feet was emitting a pungent odour.

'What's in there?' she asked.

'Got to get them washed,' said Charlie. 'Warden won't let us use the hostel machine so thought maybe I'd go to the laundry or summat.'

Before she could stop him he lifted the bag and pulled out his vomit-stained shirt to show her. The two boxed of cereal popped out of the top, one scattering sugared flakes across her desk and the floor.

'Oh – sorry 'bout that. Is my breakfast,' he said, grabbing for the boxes and trying to stuff the spilt cereal into the open box again.

'Stop,' said Alex. 'Put that all down and we'll clear up the mess. You can't eat it now it's been in there with – that.'

She fished some tissues out of her desk drawer and began to wipe the sticky crumbs off the table and into her rubbish bin.

'Hang on, what do you mean, that's your breakfast?'

'Didn't get nothing at the hospital 'cos they said I was eating at the hostel,' said Charlie. 'Is already paid for so they don't give us it twice. But was too late when I got back.' He stopped as he realized the next question would be where the cereal came from and there was no good answer.

Alex stopped her cleaning and looked at him. 'You must be hungry if you were reduced to eating cereal out of the box,' she said. 'Wait here and I'll see what I can find.' She stopped at the door. 'Do you have sugar in your tea?' Charlie nodded. 'Okay. Finish putting all that debris in the bin – and dump those boxes too. I'll only be a moment.'

Up in the Day Room, Alex made a large beaker of strong tea and added two sugars. There was nothing going spare in the fridge and so she pulled out her own sandwiches from a container on the top shelf. Ham and tomato, no mustard – fairly neutral she thought. After a moment's hesitation she took her biscuits too, walking awkwardly back downstairs as the tea sloshed over the edge of the mug leaving a trail of tell-tale spots behind her.

Charlie fell on the food, eating as fast as he could cram it in to his mouth. Alex watched him, revulsion just shaded out by pity.

'Didn't they feed you at all in the hospital?' she asked. Charlie shook his head, still chewing the last of her sandwiches as he reached for the packet of biscuits.

'Had us stomach pumped,' he said when he finally stopped for breath. 'Didn't feel like nothing, kept chuckin' up water for a day. Then was time to go.'

Too much detail, thought Alex. *Way* too much. She nodded to the bag of soiled clothes. 'Can you manage those on your own?' Charlie took a large gulp of his tea and shrugged. 'Hold on, I'll see if I can get a sub for the washers,' she said.

Alison was reluctant to hand over the money. 'He was in hospital because he drank a whole gallon of natch,' she said, keeping a firm grasp on the key to the petty cash box. 'That's self-inflicted injury if ever I heard it. Don't see why we should have to pay for him to wash his clothes.'

'He's obviously not got much money,' Alex argued. 'He was starving hungry when he got here and I think he's probably not got enough to feed himself at lunch time if he has to pay for the laundry.'

'And whose fault is that?' sniffed Alison. 'I heard he spent everything on Saturday. It won't help him learn to budget if we just bail him out every time.'

Alex gritted her teeth in frustration. Alison was right of course, but she wasn't going to let a vulnerable young man like Charlie go hungry on a point of principle.

'What about his family?' Alison continued. 'He used to live with his Gran didn't he? He could go there and get fed.'

Alex's patience was exhausted. 'For God's sake Alison, just give me the money! His Gran lives out on the Levels. How the hell is he supposed to get out there without his bus fare?'

The office fell silent, every woman bent over their files, busily making notes whilst straining to hear every word.

'He should sign on at the college or something,' said Alison defiantly. 'He'd get a bus pass and he might even learn something useful.' Reluctantly she unlocked the tin and handed over several pound coins. 'You'll have to sign for it,' she said, holding out a petty cash slip. Alex took the money, signed and beat a hasty retreat before Pauline came to Alison's defence. She knew she was in the right but there were protocols to be observed and shouting at her assistant in front of the whole office was not considered acceptable behaviour.

She felt slightly ashamed of her outburst and so was more abrupt with Charlie that she would be normally.

'Here, get down to the washers and get that lot clean,' she said, thrusting the money into his hands. Charlie's thanks were cut short.

'You really need to start thinking things through you know. You can't keep on expecting other people to look after you. We'll look at finding you some kind of training programme in your next appointment. If there's anywhere left that will take you. In the meantime just try to stay out of trouble.'

Charlie gathered his belongings and shuffled to the door, muttering apologies and more thanks as he went. He looked utterly wretched and Alex relented. It was like kicking a puppy, she thought.

'Charlie? I do think it might be a good idea to find you a course at the college if we can. We need to get you settled into something and you'll probably get an allowance too. Think about what you like doing and we'll have a chat later in the week, okay?'

Charlie managed a smile before slipping out into the corridor, taking his noxious washing bag with him. Alex waited a moment and then cranked her tiny window open. It didn't do anything to clear the air but nevertheless it cheered her up a bit. She really should go and apologize to Alison she decided. There was no excuse for rudeness and actually she liked and respected the admin team. She didn't want to lose their good opinion – or their support during such an important inspection.

Glancing at her watch she saw it was almost coffee time. Charlie had eaten her lunch and she had a full schedule after mid-day. It seemed a good time to run out and get something and while she was in town she'd pick up some biscuits – or a cake for the office staff. Nothing said 'sorry' like a chocolate cake.

Tom Monarch drove his van carefully across the rutted roads that crossed the deserted area of the Levels, mindful of the age of the suspension. Brian sat beside him, clinging on to the dashboard and giving occasional squeaks as they lurched over a particularly rough patch.

'Why we goin' this way?' he asked. It was early for Brian, who was still adjusting to a life away from his family, a life that mainly comprised heavy drinking, neglect and physical abuse. Brian had ambitions for the first time: the dream of going to the agricultural college and becoming a goat man but he didn't like getting up before mid-day and rarely had a civil word to say before arriving at Ada's cottage.

Tom didn't seem to mind. He just carried on with his normal routine, offering tea to his barely roused lodger before bundling him into the van ready for a day's work. Today, however, they were engaged in something slightly different, a side-trip before they headed for Ada's.

'Got to check summat,' he said. 'Won't take long but could do with a hand if you's up to it.'

They rattled along for another mile before Tom pulled up under a thick stand of willows beside one of the medium-sized channels cut to drain the vast floodplain. Climbing out of the van, he went to the back and pulled out a large, round net with a long handle and a wicker basket. Intrigued in spite of himself, Brian followed Tom down to the edge of the slow-moving stream, kneeling down on the dry earth to peer into the water.

Under the trees, hidden in the shadows, was a large tubular net, one end open and the other, sunk a few yards down-stream, closed and filled with a rippling mass of trapped fish. Following Tom's instructions Brian helped him ease the net towards the surface, bringing the catch towards the bank in gentle stages.

'Right, easy now. I'll take 'um out an' you lift it a bit at a time on my say-so, okay?' Brian nodded, intent on the sight of the fish as they slid over one another, fighting to keep as far down in the water as possible. Tom reached in and flipped the fish one at a time into the smaller net, his 'keep net', which was wedged firmly into the bank between them. Once he had half a dozen he lifted it out of the water, dispatched the flopping, gasping creatures swiftly and laid them in the open basket.

One medium sized specimen, a fine, glossy bronze colour, jerked free, sliding through his fingers to escape into the water. Tom swore and wiped his hands on an old towel from the basket before reaching for the next fish. 'Bream,' he said. 'Right slippery they is. Tricky little buggers but good eating.'

Brian peered at the dead fish Tom held up. Its body was coated in a thick layer of slime. 'Hold 'um by the tails when you get one,' Tom said. 'Less likely to get away then.'

They continued to empty the net, Brian lifting and holding and Tom capturing and killing until there were only a few fish left. Tom reached in for a large specimen that was right at the bottom, immobile and partly hidden in the deep shade. Suddenly he jerked his hand away as the fish spun towards him, lightening fast. Brian almost dropped the net in shock at the movement and the flash of teeth.

'Woah,' said Tom, sitting down a little way back from the net. 'Watch yerself lad. Pike in there. Not a big'un, else he'd a' had the whole catch, but even a young'un 'ent to be messed with.'

Brian shifted his hands on the net, making sure they were clear of the water but he couldn't resist leaning over to peer at the pike. He'd never seen one close up – not alive anyway – and the sight of the broad, pointed face and scaled body sent a delicious frisson up his spine. 'How we gonna get 'um out then?' he asked.

Tom shook his head. 'We 'ent. I'll come get the net and turn it so's he swims off. Let the others go too. We got most of 'um and I 'ent thinking to lose a finger or two fighting no pike at my age, specially as Ada won't eat 'um an' can't sell 'um without likely attracting a look from the *beng* river wardens.'

'Why won't Ada eat pike?' Brian asked as he watched the fish slide out of the net.

'Says is a carrion eater. Pike, they eat most things, dead or alive. Ada reckons is unhealthy. Won't even have 'um in the house.'

Brian considered this for a moment, eying the fish as it floated, tantalizingly close to the bank. 'Oh,' he said.

'Don't be trying to make no sense of it,' warned Tom with a grin. 'Women think different from us. Just got to go with it sometimes. Now, give a hand to fold this all up.' Together they bundled the nets into the van and heaved the basket in after them. Tom swung the van round and cut across the narrow strip of land separating the stream from the road. With a bump and a slight grinding of the undercarriage they were back on a gravelled surface and speeding off towards Westonzoyland.

'Don't you worry 'bout someone finding the net when is out?' Brian asked.

Tom shook his head. 'Only put it in every couple of days or so,' he said. 'Don't get too greedy so folks don't notice the lack further downstream. 'Sides, not many live round here and a lot of them what do is doing similar. Lot of empty places scattered over here, overgrown some of 'um. Ada's old home is just over there.' He pointed through the windscreen as the van slowed slightly to round a bend.

Brian looked but there was nothing to see except thick hedge with the very top of a chimney poking up over the top. 'How come Ada's got two places then?' he asked. Brian was one stupid action away from returning to a homeless state. It was inconceivable that someone he knew might own two properties, let alone leave one to rot, empty and neglected.

'Got a bad history, that place,' said Tom as he turned the corner, leaving the remains of the cottage behind him. 'Was Ada's family home but then she an' Frank got her house down the road here when they was married. Frank come back out of prison an' got hisself killed in that old place. Don't blame Ada for not wanting to go back.'

Brian's eyes stretched wide with fascination. 'Was where Derek Johns was hid?' he asked. 'Heard about that. Found bits of Frank in some old freezer …'

'Don't you go saying nothin' to Ada,' warned Tom as they drew up outside Ada's cottage. 'Maybe he weren't the best husband, nor father come to that, but was a shock to her. Right nasty carry on, an' I'll not have her all stirred up about it, you hear?'

'Promise,' said Brian. 'Been right good to I, you 'n' Ada. Not going to do nothin' to upset her.'

Together they walked up the front path and let themselves in through the side gate. 'Don't say nothin' 'bout them fish neither,' Tom whispered as Ada opened the back door and smiled at them both. Mouse came bounding out to greet them with Mickey, now very grey around his muzzle, following more sedately. Brian stopped to fuss the dogs before going over to Pongo's enclosure. The goat had been busy over the last week and where once there had been thick under-growth and brambles there was only short, cropped grass and stems.

'Reckon Pongo's gonna need a new patch in a day or so,' he said cheerfully as he entered the dim kitchen. Tom glanced up at him and sighed.

'Well, that's up to you, Ada,' he said. 'Want any more land cleared?'

Ada was busy at the wood range, pouring water into a pot and setting the tea to stand. 'Don't know if I dare,' she said. 'We's pushed the garden out a fair bit already. Might get away with that but don't fancy some Water Board type turnin' up with a ruler and takin' it all back again. Think I should stop for a bit, see how it goes.'

Boundaries were somewhat hazy on the shifting land of the Levels and Ada's addition to her land, thanks to Pongo's superior clearing abilities, could be justified on the basis on a very old map from the Land Registry but beyond her garden the land belonged to someone else – maybe a long departed farmer, maybe the river authority, perhaps an absentee land-owner. Whoever the rightful owner might be, Ada had no desire to provoke them.

Tom stared thoughtfully at his tea, stirring it round and round until Ada reached out and snatched the spoon away.

'What's biting you then, Tom?' she asked.

'Well, see, Pongo's gettin' on now. Not much demand for an old stud-goat like him an' if we not needin' him for land clearing, could be hard feeding him, specially in winter. Might be time for him to go.'

'Go where?' Ada demanded. Despite her initial reserva-tions she had become fond of Pongo. She'd even got used to the smell.

'Normally they go for meat,' said Tom rather reluctantly, keeping his eyes fixed on his tea.

'You can't eat Pongo!' said Brian horrified.

'That's right horrible,' snapped Ada.

'Well, wouldn't be for humans,' said Tom. 'Bit old and tough, he'd be now. Probably be used for dog meat ...'

'You're not sending Pongo for dog meat!' Brian shouted. He pushed away from the table and left the room, slamming the outer door behind him.

'Is the way it is, in farming,' said Tom. 'Can't be sentimental about stock animals. Once they done their job is time to let 'um go an' get another. Lad's got to learn that if'n he wants to be a goat man. Or any type of stockman.'

'Maybe so,' said Ada, who cheerfully popped her non-laying chickens in the pot. 'Still, don't seem right. There's a bit more down close to the bank we 'ent got clear yet. Would be helpful, having a path down there.'

Tom nodded and sipped at his tea. 'I'll go have a word with the boy, get him to start moving the posts ready. Not a very big bit though. Won't keep 'um busy for long.'

Ada fixed him with a fierce look. 'When is done, then we'll talk,' she said. 'Till then he's still needed.'

'Right,' murmured Tom and he rose from the table, heading outside to talk to Brian. At least all the fuss about the goat had diverted his attention away from the abandoned house a mile down the road.

Chapter Six

Samuel noticed the tyre marks as soon as he rounded the bend. The gravel road left little sign of passing traffic but the land next to it was baked dry and hard in the heat of the summer. A layer of dust had settled over the grass, showing evidence of a vehicle joining the road a few hundred yards shy of his new base. A closer examination of the area revealed some flattened grass by the drainage channel and marks where a low bodied vehicle had hit the dried mud beside the road.

There was no indication of anyone in the area any more and after checking around carefully Samuel slid behind the high hedge and through the side gate to the small back garden. The run from Highpoint had taken longer than he'd expected and he was tired. There was the start of a nagging headache behind one of his eyes and his legs felt stiff and uncomfortable. He needed more food and better food too. Some good quality protein would set him right, if he could only get hold of some.

It was beneath him to shoplift, despite the fact he had several convictions for just that offence. Besides, it was just too easy to get caught, especially in a small community where everyone seemed to know everyone else. Samuel preferred cities, large anonymous communities where it was possible to drift away and disappear – or to make someone else disappear. In Samuel's distorted view of the world the crowds thronging the streets of Bristol, Liverpool and London were shoals of smaller fish, prey for him to take or exploit as he wished. There were few such opportunities in rural Somerset and Samuel was getting hungry.

With the freezer safely hidden in the wrecked shed by the canal he could turn his attention to the protein problem and the fishing gear seemed just what he needed. He was no expert but really, how hard could it be? He'd seen small boys and aged grandfathers who looked too frail to haul themselves out of the water catch a decent supper with no visible effort. Rummaging through the pile of salvage on the kitchen table he located the rod and then spent some time trying to untangle the line from the net and get it back on the reel.

He needed something for bait, he realized. And a hook of course. His only previous experience had been fishing for crabs in the harbour at home, an activity that involved tying an old chicken carcass to a ball of string, chucking it in the water and pulling it out a few minutes later. The local crabs grabbed on to the chicken and could be picked off, kept in a bucket and then thrown back to be caught over and over again.

He doubted the local fish would be so obliging and had a quick look around the kitchen in the faint hope there might be something he could use in the dresser or sagging cupboards. To his surprise he found a box of assorted fish hooks buried under the remains of a pillow in the corner of the room and some brand new line on a reel. The previous occupant had been a fisherman, he thought – or perhaps had the same idea as him. Either way, he had what he needed except for the bait.

Glancing at his watch he saw it was late afternoon. If he ran and took the roads rather than the longer but less obvious route across the marsh he should get back to the hostel in time for the evening meal. For once he was going to have dinner. With a bit of luck there would be something he could slip into a plastic bag and use for fishing.

After a moment's hesitation he took the fishing rod and net upstairs and hid it in the grimy bed. He'd not seen anyone all day but the tyre marks were a warning there were others roaming the area.

Petey followed Steve through the mid-week market and marvelled at his skill. Without seeming to move, Steve deftly collected all manner of small items, some useful and some just for show. Only one stall-holder noticed anything, a large man with a thick head of black hair and even thicker forearms. Spotting Steve as he drifted closer to a display of glossy apples he stepped forwards and held out his hand.

'Now then, what you doin'?' he asked.

Steve looked at him, radiating innocence and hurt feelings.

'Dunno what you mean,' he said. 'Just lookin'. My Dad's a greengrocer in Romford and I'm prob'ly going into the business so I'm just interested, right?'

'That so?' said the stall-holder. 'So you could tell us what's them apples then?'

'Look like Braeburns to me,' said Steve casually. 'Course, is hard to tell sometimes without tasting one.' He reached out his hand and the stall-holder made a swipe at him. Steve ran off laughing with Petey in his wake.

'What you do that for?' Petey asked when they stopped round the back of the Cornhill to catch their breath.

'Stopped him looking at us too closely,' said Steve. 'We don't want him turning out our pockets now do we? He thinks he's chased us off an' no harm done but actually ...' He reached into his jacket and pulled out two shiny apples, passing one over to Petey before taking a bite out of the other.

'How did you know them's Braeburns?' Petey said, juice dribbling from the corner of his mouth.

Steve grinned and turned his apple over to indicate a small plastic sticker on the back. 'Silly bugger forgot about that didn't he.' He tossed the half-eaten apple away into the street, earning him a sour look from a passing shopper, and wiped his hands on his shirt. 'Got any change on you?'

Petey finished off his apple and put the core in a bin by the steps before answering. 'A bit,' he admitted reluctantly.

'Good-oh,' said Steve cheerfully. 'Come on, off to the bus station. I wanna get another look at that old pill box.'

On the way out of town Steve kept up a running commentary on the shortcomings of the hostel, Highpoint and the Levels before turning his attention to the transport system.

'You ain't half got some crap buses,' he observed loudly as they jolted along. 'How old is this thing? Back home we'd call it a charabanc an' it'd be in a museum.' He leaned back against the side of the bus and stretched out on the seat, his arms behind his head, and the driver, who had been watching him in the mirror, slammed on the brakes, skidding to a halt in the centre of the narrow lane.

'You there!' he called down the vehicle. 'Yes, you – take them feet of'n my seat or you'll be walkin' home.'

Steve sat up slightly and looked at him over the back of the seats. 'You mean me?' he asked.

'Course I mean you. Who else is there?' He glared around the bus, empty but for an old lady with a pile of shopping in carrier bags on the seat next to her.

'Could've meant her,' said Steve nodding towards the woman. 'She's got all them bags an' stuff. Bet they've been dragged around in the dirt a bit so why pick on me?' He spat on the floor and sat back, feet up on the seat again.

'That's it,' said the driver, flinging the door open and stamping his way down the aisle. Grabbing Steve by his collar, he frog-marched him swiftly up from his seat and out onto the road. He turned to look at Petey who rose without a word and followed his friend.

'Wot about our bus fare then?' Steve shouted as the driver closed the door and drove away. The driver responded with a universally recognized hand signal as he turned the corner, leaving the young men standing by the side of the lane in a cloud of dust.

'Why does you *do* that?' Petey demanded. It was hot and the sun was almost directly overhead, beating down on them with relentless intensity.

'Do what?' Steve asked, peering hopefully around him as if expecting another bus to materialize at their convenience.

'Why'd you wind people up like that. Seems you trying to make 'um angry. Was the bloke in the market an' now that bus driver ... Shouldn't 'a picked on that lady neither. Is Charlie's Grandma. He 'ent gonna like it an' you don't want to be upsetting her neither.'

Steve sniggered and spat in dust by the road. 'That old biddy?' he said scornfully. 'What's she supposed to be then? Some sort of witch or something? Looks just like a little old lady to me and I ain't scared of *them*.'

'Well you should be,' mumbled Petey. ''Specially if she goes an' talks to Ada Mallory. An' maybe *she's* a witch. Charlie got this burn on his hand – real bad it was an' Ada put this stuff on from some plant she had an' it just went away.'

Steve ignored him, busy looking around at the flat, open land that stretched away beyond the hedgerows. It looked, to his city eyes, almost featureless. 'Where's that old pill box then?' he demanded.

Petey turned to the left and pointed over a field, then down to the right along the side of a small channel. ''Bout a mile over that way,' he said.

'Bit of a hike,' complained Steve. 'Well, lead on. Keep an eye on the time so's we can get the bus back. I ain't missing my tea.'

'Can't see old Simons lettin' us back on the bus,' said Petey sulkily. 'Have to walk back to town.'

'Well, we'll wait and get the next one,' said Steve with exaggerated patience.

Petey looked at him and gave a short, barking laugh. ''Ent no *next one*,' he said. 'Is only old Simons an' his bus. When he goes there'll be no bus 'cept for the free one out to the new supermarket.'

Steve grunted and turned away, starting off towards a gap in the hedge. 'I knew it was backward down here,' he said as he went. 'Didn't think you yokels were that behind the times. God, what a pit ...'

Petey stood by the road, hurt and angered by his new friend's words. For a moment he considered turning round and leaving Steve to his own devices. Then he remembered they shared a room at the hostel and he'd already alienated his oldest friend Charlie. Caught in the trap of the lonely, Petey followed Steve out across the Levels, hauling his wretchedness behind him.

Half a mile to the east of the two lads, Lily Dodds stepped off the bus and headed up the lane towards Ada's house. The bus service was a godsend on the way into town, for despite her age Lily was still fit and healthy, but she was finding the walk back from her nearest stop harder with the weight of her shopping. Ada's house was closer to the bus route and she could count on a bit of a sit-down and a cup of tea. Recently, Tom Monarch had offered a drive back to her home when he was there, which was most days.

Well, good for Ada, she thought. Some people didn't approve of her friendship with Tom. They thought she was too old and it was undignified, some of them considered Tom a dangerous man, a *Rom* with a criminal past, and some of them were, in Lily's opinion, just plain jealous. She had to admit to the occasional twinge of jealousy herself. Watching them together in the garden or sitting companionably in the kitchen she experienced a yearning for that sort of friendship. It didn't matter to her that Tom was from the Gypsy community. He was a good man and it was obvious he adored Ada.

The two women took their tea into the little side garden, away from the smell of Pongo. Lily sat in the shade, recovering from the walk, and gazed out over the open land.

'Nice bit o' extra land you got,' she said thoughtfully. 'Must be a godsend, what with prices bein' what they is fer veggies and such.'

Ada glanced at her but didn't rise to the suggestion. 'Been lying fallow many years now,' she agreed. 'Do it good to be used again.'

Lily smiled and sipped her tea. 'Got a bit of my own,' she said. 'Fancy trying my hand at a few veggies but is too much to be digging and young Charlie, he's away at that hostel now. Not that he was much of a one for digging anyway. Too busy doing them drawings of his or running after the big boys, gettin' into trouble.'

'Never knew he liked drawing,' said Ada. 'He any good?'

Lily nodded, setting her cup down on the ground to rummage in her bag. She pulled out a folded sheet of paper and passed it over. Ada opened it to find a picture of Lily standing at her kitchen table. Rendered in pencil it still had a brightness, a sense of light that flooded into the room illuminating the figure. Lily was drawn with tremendous care, her features clearly recognizable and set in a gentle, distant smile. The whole picture seemed to radiate love and Ada could see why Lily chose to carry it with her.

'Not bad is he,' said Lily as she folded the drawing again and replaced it in her bag.

'Not bad at all,' agreed Ada. 'Pity he never did nothing with that at school.'

Lily sighed, staring out into the distance. 'Never did nothing at all at school,' she said sadly. 'Not that surprising, looking at his worthless upbringin', mind. Lad never had much of a chance.'

Ada's reply was cut short by an exclamation from Lily.

'Where's that to then?' she asked, rising from her chair and pointing to the west. A faint plume of smoke was rising from the emptiness, grey at first but rapidly turning darker until it was clearly visible against the bright blue sky.

'Don't like the look of that, what with the whole place being so dry an' all,' said Ada. 'Shouldn't bother us – not much wind today and is blowing over that way but can cause a right lot of damage, left to itself. Where's Tom when is needed, eh? Could pop over there 'n' see what's doing in that van of his.' She moved to the fence at the edge of her garden and strained her eyes, watching anxiously as the smoke thickened into a black column in the distance. After a moment Lily rose and joined her.

'Can't do nothing,' she said. 'Likely someone with a phone's already called it in and, like you says, isn't coming our way.' She looked around Ada's garden again before returning to the subject of her garden.

'My garden – I was wondering if you would consider lending your goat. Seems he's just what I is needing, it being all overgrown. Get it cleared and would be much easier setting out and stuff. What d'you say, Ada? Maybe Tom could have a look next time he's over.'

Ada was suddenly struck by a wonderful idea. Pongo needed feeding, a lot more than she could provide every week. People on the Levels were constantly struggling against the encroaching plants, fighting the sheer power of nature that surrounded them. Why not put the two together and hire out her goat to the small holders and cottage gardeners in the area?

Pongo was the perfect land-clearing instrument – quick, efficient and quiet. She'd not come across anything he wouldn't eat, though Tom advised against any member of the onion family. Unfortunate side-effects, he said with a wicked grin.

She nodded her agreement. 'Don't see why not,' she said. 'Need to talk to Tom mind, make sure he's safe an' can't get out. Don't want him wandering round lost on them roads.'

In the distance there was a faint popping sound and the smoke billowed up in a cloud as if the fire had caught something explosive. The two women watched anxiously until it began to die down again.

'Now what the holy hell was that then?' mused Ada.

Steve was enjoying his experiment. Faced with a mile of tramping over parched meadows and round midge-infested streams of stagnant water, he'd decided to leave exploring the bunker for another day. Stopping in a small clearing a few hundred yards from the road he flung himself down on the grass that was burned a pale gold by the summer heat.

'I'm beat,' he said, squirming into the shade offered by a stunted tree. 'I'm not going no further. 'Specially if we gotta walk back.' He felt in his pockets and pulled out some of the items he'd stolen from the market, laying them out in front of him.

'What's all that for?' asked Petey as he sat himself down next to the tree. It was hot and he was thirsty but nowhere near as tired as Steve seemed to be. Had he thought about it he would have reached the conclusion that, despite his posturing and big talk, Steve was actually a bit soft.

'Shuddup,' Steve growled as he arranged the items on the ground, muttering as he did so. 'Yeah, think that's alright for a try out. So.' He looked up at Petey. 'You really don't have a clue does yer?'

Petey looked at the items set out carefully on the grass and he had a good idea what Steve was up to but it seemed better just to shake his head. If it all went wrong he could claim he was just an innocent bystander and who could contradict him?

Steve took a knife from his pocket, a red-handled multi-tool with every type of accessory anyone could possibly want or need, including a pair of scissors. He was very proud of his knife and had special permission to keep it in the hostel after a spirited argument with the staff. It was not really a knife, he'd insisted, it was his tool kit, all bundled into one handy package. To take it away and lock it in the safe would be to deprive him of his scissors, nail file and a pair of tweezers. Bennie Sands, the deputy warden, had her doubts about Steve's level of personal grooming but Peter Marks overruled her reservations, arguing that anything that helped to develop a sense of personal hygiene and pride was to be encouraged. As a result Steve took great satisfaction in producing his knife at the slightest excuse, opening the many blades and strange attachments as he pretended to search for something.

Now he used the large blade to cut handfuls of the long, dry grass and arranged it around the trunk of the tree. Then he stripped some bark from the thicker lower branches and cut it into pieces, placing these on top of the grass. From his pile he took a packet of tissues, courtesy of the Highpoint Market and laid them between the bundles of foliage. Finally, he gave the whole thing a good squirt of lighter fuel.

'What you doin'?' Petey demanded. 'You can't burn a tree. Not when is alive anyway. They's full of water and stuff ...' He hesitated, his limited botanical knowledge exhausted. 'So, 'ent like wood is. Why d'you want to burn it anyway?'

Steve stepped back to admire his handiwork before turning to look at Petey. His eyes were gleaming with excitement and there was a disturbing look on his face. He appeared much more dangerous than the young man who had run away from the adder last weekend. Petey shifted uncomfortably on the ground. He was beginning to wish he was back in town, talking to Charlie or hanging around the river throwing stones. Somewhere away from this unfamiliar and frightening person.

'I always wanted to try,' said Steve. 'Ain't much chance in London but you got more trees than you know what to do with, eh? Let's give it a go. Betcha I can.'

Scooping up the remains of his stolen goods he motioned to Petey to move further away from the tree. Then he struck one of the matches from his pile and threw it at the grass. The flame flickered and went out with just a tiny trickle of smoke.

'Told ya,' muttered Petey.

Steve glared at him and went over to his fire, poking at it with a stick he found lying beside the singed grass. 'That was just the wind,' he said. 'You watch.' This time he struck two matches simultaneously, holding them to the grass until it fizzed into life. He stepped back to admire his handiwork, chuckling as the bark began to smoulder and then burst into flames. The fire licked greedily at the tree, trying to gain a foothold on the dry trunk but it wasn't hot enough and after several minutes it began to die back, spreading instead to the surrounding grass. Within seconds a cloud of thick, grey smoke billowed around them and Petey began to stamp at the fire instinctively.

'Get some water,' Steve shouted, his voice roughened by the smoke. 'Put it round, couple of feet away. Keep the fire next to the tree, okay?'

Wordlessly, Petey hurried to the narrow canal and scooped some of the brown water up in his hands. By the time he'd stood and turned towards the fire it had run through his fingers. Steve laughed at him, mocking his efforts.

Don't be so bloody stupid,' he said. 'Use yer shoes or somethin'.'

Torn between fear of the fire that threatened to spread throughout the clearing and fury at Steve's behaviour, Petey hesitated. Then fear won and he stripped off his shoes, dipping them in the stream and hopping over to the edge of the burning area. A couple of trips was all it took to damp down the surrounding grass and drive the fire back towards the tree. Thick black smoke plumed into the air as the burning grass was extinguished and Petey backed off, his feet stinging from small cuts and scrapes inflicted by the rough ground.

'Better put 'em on again,' said Steve, his eyes fixed on the tussle between the fire and the tree. ''Cos any minute now you're gonna have to RUN!'

He threw the can of lighter fuel on the burning grass and set off across the field, whooping and laughing as he went. Petey grabbed the shoe he'd not managed to get back on and hobbled after him as fast as he could. Behind him there was an explosion and suddenly the back of his head was stinging and burning. He screamed, slapping at his neck as he limped after Steve who was well out of range and had stopped to admire the blaze.

'You're not hurt,' said Steve as Petey reached him. 'Just a bit singed. Oh – I think a bit of the can got you on your ear too.'

Petey felt round his face and his fingers came away red and sticky.

'I'm bleeding!'

'Don't be so soft. It's just a little cut. Should have run faster.' Steve turned away again, his eyes fixed on the tree that was now fully alight. 'Told you it'd burn,' said Steve with satisfaction. 'Come on, let's be off before some nosey bastard decides to come round and see what's going on.'

Petey stood rooted to the spot trying to staunch the blood running down his neck. 'I'm hurt,' he wailed.

Steve rounded on him, his fists clenched. 'No you're not. Just a cut – always bleeds a lot, a scalp wound. Now shut up and come on. And don't think of talking about this to anyone else – or the next fire'll be for you.'

Petey stared at him in horror, seeing a stranger glaring back at him. This was a different person from the slightly mad but all-good-fun Steve he thought he knew. This was a fierce, angry young man and Petey had no doubt he meant what he said. He limped off over the meadows towards the road, his fingers probing the gash in his scalp. This was turning into the worst day of his life.

As Thursday evening approached, Alex began to get increasingly nervous over her final session for the alcohol education course. She knew it was exactly what the group needed. She knew it could be the most convincing evening of the whole thing. She also knew she would be in big, big trouble if headquarters happened to find out about it. The low-alc beers were all hidden away in her filing cabinet, safely locked up just in case Alison decided to tidy her files or stumbled on the bottles searching for something. Plastic glasses were tucked up next to them and she had prepared score sheets ready for the blind tasting. In a fit of panic she had also spent several hours on Tuesday evening planning and writing out an alternative session, one much more acceptable to the powers above but considerably less inspired – or effective.

On Thursday afternoon she took out the two folders,

opening them at her desk and reading through the plans. The alternative was fine – a summing up of the whole course, some words of encouragement, an exchange of stories to reinforce just how much trouble each of them had experienced in the past. Good, solid social work stuff but nothing to really inspire or challenge them. She closed the files with a sigh and put them back in the drawer. She still had the afternoon to decide, she thought, as she set off for the workshop where a new crop of bicycles were waiting to be repaired and distributed.

Ricky stood at his office window and watched Alex as she crossed the yard to disappear into the shed in the corner. A strange woman sat at his desk. Dressed predominantly in pink with a large number of lacy frills at the neck and elbows, she nevertheless radiated a sense of authority. Her eyes were a pale grey and her hair was teased into tight black curls. Her long pink fingernails tapped impatiently on the desk top and Ricky turned towards her with a start.

'I expected to see you fulfilling your potential a little more,' said the woman. Her voice was light and she spoke with a slight sing-song intonation, ending her sentence with a tiny smile. It was intended to be friendly but succeeded in appearing rather sinister.

'It's not my fault,' said Ricky. 'It's a little clique in this office. Everyone looks out for everyone else and no-one gives me any credit for all the work I do. They give me all the shit jobs and I can't even go out to do a report without someone looking over my shoulder.' He sounded like a petulant child and a brief flicker of distaste crossed the woman's face.

'I'm sure things will improve now I'm taking over,' she said. 'You will be able to show what you can do and maybe we can get you on a fast track to senior.'

Ricky gave a pleased smile at this. Senior had a nice ring to it, though he had his eyes on becoming at least an Assistant Chief Probation Officer if he could. Maybe Chief one day. In Ricky's mind there was no limit to his ambition – which made him very useful to Rosalind Marchent as she prepared to take up her post at Highpoint.

'Now,' she said, leaning back in Ricky's chair. 'Tell me about the day centre. You expressed some concerns last time we spoke.'

This was the opening Ricky had been waiting for. Pulling up the hard 'client' chair, he leaned over the desk and all the resentment, jealousy and bile he had stored up against Alex came pouring out.

Gordon glanced at his watch and noted the new senior was late for their meeting. He called down to the front desk and discovered to his surprise she was already in the building and had been for almost an hour. Disturbed by this news he decided to look for her. Apart from concerns about her getting lost in the old, rambling building, it was most impolite for her not to let him know she was on the premises. It might only be for a few more days but he was still the senior officer at Highpoint and it was simple courtesy to let him know if she wanted to look around.

He opened his office door, stepped into the corridor and spotted her heading towards him, a billowing cloud of pink and silver topped by hair of a startling shade.

'Ah, there you are,' she said, holding out her hand.

Gordon accepted the proffered handshake and held the door open politely. Rosalind stood in the centre of the room, appraising the furniture and view from the window. Gesturing towards a spare chair, Gordon slid hastily behind the desk.

'This isn't the senior's room,' he said, correctly interpreting her examination of the office. 'I didn't bother to move up to Garry's old office – I knew it was only temporary. Would you like to see the senior's room?'

'Oh, I've seen that,' said Rosalind with a flick of her fingers. 'Debbie, my assistant, is measuring it up now. I will need someone to clear it out of course. It's still full of the previous occupant's clutter.'

Gordon took a deep breath and controlled the anger he felt at this woman's presumption. 'Of course,' he said. 'I'll have a word with the caretakers and see what we can do.'

Rosalind nodded vaguely, not really concentrating on him.

'I will need all the personnel files on my desk for the week-end,' she said. 'Court rotas, client lists – everything pertaining to the allocation of resources.'

'I'll have a word with Pauline, our admin chief,' said Gordon evenly. 'Have you met the office staff yet?'

'Debbie will deal with all that,' said Rosalind. 'I wanted to get an idea of the feel of the office, especially with the inspection pending. I assume you have measures in place for that?'

What measures? Gordon wondered. Were they supposed to put on a welcome banquet? Or perhaps have a secure room to lock up any meddlesome inspector until they signed a glowing report?

'Of course,' he said. 'Everyone has been fully briefed and the bulk of the paperwork is up to date.'

'See it is,' said Rosalind. 'I don't expect anything less than a good report for *my* office. Now if you'll excuse me I want to have a look around. You have a very large building here and I'm curious to see what you're doing with it all.'

'Can I get someone to show you round?' Gordon said, rising to his feet.

'Oh no, I want to look around freely, not be guided away from anything that might not be up to standard,' said Rosalind, and she flitted through the door leaving Gordon fuming but helpless.

When seven o'clock arrived Alex was still staring at the two folders. Finally, she reached out and lifted one from the desk and headed down the narrow corridor to the day centre where the alcohol education group waited.

Upstairs in Ricky's room, Rosalind waited, seated behind the desk, her sharp fingers steepled under her chin. The lights were turned off apart from a lamp on the desk and in the shadows her face took on a cruel look.

'They've arrived,' said Ricky from the window.

'Let's wait a little while,' said Rosalind. 'I think I should wait until they finish and then go to investigate once everyone's left don't you?'

Chapter Seven

Sue was waiting to pounce when Alex got home.

'How did it go?' she demanded. 'Which session did you use?'

Alex smiled wearily, struggling to get in through the front door as she was laden with a backpack and two heavy shopping bags.

'Give me a moment,' she said, dropping the bags on the floor and flexing her hands. 'Ooff! That's better. Give me a hand with this will you?'

Sue obligingly helped lift the backpack off her friend's shoulders. 'Now, tell me!' she demanded, resting the bag on a chair.

A slow grin spread over Alex's face. 'It was terrific,' she said. 'I wasn't sure, even when it was time to start, but we did all the social working stuff – you know, what I've learnt, what I feel, what I'm going to do. All that, and it was dragging a bit so I decided to do the blind tasting as we went along. They all filled in the forms and seemed to be having a good time. Just as well the office was empty – they acted a bit drunk towards the end and I had to spill the beans before we'd finished all the samples. Anyway, I've got the forms here and most of them can't tell the really low alcohol beer from the ordinary stuff. There's one in particular.' She stopped and flipped through the sheaf of papers in her hand. 'Yes, a new one from Australia. About half of them thought it was one of the "extra strength" beers.'

Sue stood in the middle of the room shaking her head, torn between concern and admiration. 'That was one hell of a risk,' she said. 'What if someone had been working upstairs? Especially if they were getting rowdy – no-one would believe they'd only been drinking the low alc stuff.'

'Yeah, but no-one did come down,' said Alex smugly. 'The office was empty. And it was really interesting, the way they got themselves drunk on expectations and fresh air. Once I'd done the big reveal bit they all got rather quiet and chastened, like they were embarrassed. That was a great moment because they actually felt how dumb their behaviour was. They maybe realized for the first time they are responsible for their actions instead of blaming it on too much natch.'

'All right!' said Sue. 'You did a good job, you got away with it. Can we please agree you don't do anything that stupid again?' She turned abruptly and left Alex standing in the front room, her mouth open in surprise. After a moment she followed Sue through into the kitchen and unpacked the shopping in silence.

'How was the play?' asked Alex finally. 'You're home a bit earlier than I expected.'

Sue was still sulking but the story was too good and she relented, turning to her friend and grinning broadly.

'You will never believe what happened!' she said. 'It was packed and at least half of the kids were dressed up. Everyone was happy, all bouncing in their seats and I have to say the drama department have done a really good job. The castle looked fabulous and the lighting was great. So, we're rolling along, everyone having a great time and then Frankenfurter comes on – in that amazing costume. You know, the basque and fishnets with high heels right? Well, suddenly the principal leaps to his feet, hurries onto the stage and starts shouting. The chorus kept going for a bit but then it all ground to a halt. I thought someone would lead him off the stage because he was ranting like a total looney.'

'What was he saying?' demanded Alex.

'It was something about stopping the show. He said it was cancelled and we all had to go home because the council would withdraw the college grant under Section 28!'

'What?' Alex was horrified, yet the whole incident was farcical and a part of her wanted to laugh out loud. 'He actually said that?'

Sue was laughing now. 'Apparently, the *Rocky Horror Show* depicts homosexuality in a positive light and so it is now banned in Highpoint College!'

The morning after their adventure on the Levels, Steve was up early, sneaking his smoke-tainted clothes down to the washing machine in the basement and relying on a hot wash to remove all evidence of the previous day's activities. Petey, meanwhile, found it hard to get out of bed. Every time he sat up his head throbbed and there was a burning pain behind his ear where the shrapnel from the lighter fluid can had gashed his scalp. After the third attempt he flopped back on his pillow, groaning softly and cursing Steve for his mad antics.

His mood was not improved by Bennie, the assistant warden, who banged on the door and demanded he get up and come downstairs immediately. Petey was not one for improving himself and so none of the classes offered by the hostel interested him in the slightest. As he was not on the day's cleaning rota he was obliged to leave the building with or without breakfast by nine, ostensibly to look for work.

Nursing his sick head and equally sick stomach, Petey crawled out of the bed and rummaged through the pile of clothes thrown down in front of his chest of drawers. Most of them were in need of a wash and the rest were in need of replacing but he found a pair of underpants he thought he'd only worn once or twice already and was hunting for a top that didn't announce to the world the last few days' menus when Charlie Dodds stuck his head around the door.

'You'm gonna be late for the dole office if'n you don't hurry up,' he said. He wrinkled his nose in disgust and added, 'Smells like a bonfire in here. What you b'n up to then?' Petey ignored him and carried on his futile search for something to wear. Charlie watched him for a moment, then slipped down the corridor into his new two-bed room, evidence of his progress over the past few weeks. The incident over the gallon of natch had been the wake-up call he needed and since then his behaviour had been impeccable.

He shared the room with a quiet, earnest young man called Mick, who had decided to take advantage of every class and work experience offered and his influence on young Charlie was both striking and positive. Charlie opened his cupboard and took a clean T-shirt from the pile folded neatly inside. He hesitated over the jeans but there was a limit to friendship and Petey was the worst slob in the hostel. Finally, he grabbed a clean pair of socks and hurried back to the room he had recently shared with Petey and Steve.

'Here,' he said, thrusting the clothes in Petey's direction. 'Want 'em back mind. Reckon you should do a bit of laundry this evening an' all.' He skipped down the stairs, reported to the warden, who was sitting at his desk writing up the day book and set off into town to sign on. He almost trotted down the back path that ran beside the river into Highpoint, eager to get the formality of signing on over with so he could return to the hostel.

It was an art class this morning and many of the residents attended, mainly as it was seen as a soft option and it was better than tramping round the increasingly bleak roads of the area. Charlie, however, found he quite enjoyed it. He was exploring a hitherto neglected talent for drawing and the praise of the class leader, a highly eccentric and exceedingly formidable woman called Molly Brown, was both new and rather addictive. Absorbed by his own thoughts, Charlie failed to attend to his surroundings and a shove from behind almost forced him onto the sloping bank of the river.

'Eh! Watch what you'm bloody doin',' he said as he turned to face his assailant, fists clenched by his side.

'Or you'll do what?' asked Samuel Burton, towering over him. 'Get out of my way.'

Charlie swallowed nervously and moved to one side. In common with most sensible people, he was afraid of Samuel. However, despite his fear he was not willing to capitulate completely.

'Could've just said,' he retorted, resisting the temptation to step back again as he spoke.

Samuel was already past him and about to break into his perfect, seemingly effortless stride but he hesitated, looking back at Charlie's scrawny figure. There was a moment of silence as Charlie prepared to be thrown into the muddy river, then Samuel gave a tiny smile, just a twitch on one side of his face, before turning away again.

Charlie watched Samuel disappear down the path and under the bridge leading into the town gardens. Despite the trembling in his still-clenched hands, he felt a twinge of pride at standing up to the other man. The town clock began to chime the half-hour and he followed Samuel along the river bank, anxious not to arrive late.

Half an hour later he was back in the gardens but in a far less positive mood. Times were tough and the government was not happy about the unemployment figures, especially those relating to juveniles. A whole slew of new regulations were being unrolled and, once more, young people like Charlie and his peers at the hostel were expected to do more for their money than turn up every two weeks, answer a few questions and sign for their giro. Charlie had gone through a bit of a bad patch, which was why he was in the hostel in the first place. He'd already tried several 'training' schemes and been enrolled at the local community college with a measure of success that began at very little and sank to none at all. This meant there were very few places left willing to offer him another chance, especially as most of them were now paid by results – and that meant only good results. Charlie was a bad bet and no-one wanted him.

'Oh bugger,' he said, staring out over the rose beds. He hadn't the heart to go back to the hostel, even for Molly Brown's art class. For the first time, he had found something he was good at. He'd started to think about his life and how he might, just might, do better with it, and now he was about to be sanctioned and left without any income or support. He didn't even know if he'd be allowed to stay at the hostel without his benefit money and if they threw him out then he was in breach of his probation order. And that meant he would be back in court and possibly on his way to a Young Offenders Institution. Charlie had spent a week in one of those whilst remanded in custody and he had no desire to go back.

A shadow fell across his hunched body and Charlie looked up, squinting in the bright sunlight. Samuel Burton was looming over him, staring with his hard, cold eyes.

'Tough luck,' said Samuel. Charlie blinked at him, surprised by even this miniscule display of empathy.

'Thanks,' he managed to reply. For a moment they remained frozen looking at one another, Charlie gazing up like a small animal mesmerized by a snake. Then Samuel turned away, striding down the footpath to the underpass.

'Go and see Alex,' he called over his shoulder before disappearing round the corner. It was actually very good advice. If anyone could unpick the mess he was in then it was Alex and she would know what the hostel could or could not do to him. Charlie hauled himself off the seat and set off towards the probation office, shivering despite the warmth from the sun.

Samuel wasn't sure why he had stopped for Charlie Dodds. It was certainly out of character and generally he felt nothing but contempt for those residing in the hostel. Charlie was weak, physically and emotionally, and that meant he was only of concern if he got in the way. Despite this, Samuel had noted the improvement in Charlie over the last few weeks.

He washed every day – not as often as Samuel, who showered three times and changed his clothes at least twice a day, but still better than most of them. Charlie had also started to behave in a more adult manner, both in the way he treated others and in how he looked at himself. There was a spark of pride in him and Samuel respected that. Deep down inside, a tiny piece of decency saw Charlie's dilemma as unjust.

Samuel gave himself a mental shake, dismissing such foolish ideas as he swung round the corner and on to the canal path. There was a lot to do, getting his new base ready, and he had no time for distractions or the concerns of others. The tightness in his legs and shortness of breath reminded him of the need to find a new food source and as he ran he felt his jaw tighten in anger at the indignities piled upon him by the minnows in his surroundings.

The blank-eyed, chubby girl at the benefit office who sweated came to mind. Her fingers had left a damp smear on the form as she pushed it over the counter for him to sign. She had rolled her eyes with impatience when he politely asked for a pen, slapping an old biro down whilst looking up at the clock on the far wall. He had picked it up, trying not to touch the top which was scarred by teeth marks. He wondered how anyone could put that filthy thing in their mouth.

His distaste must have shown on his face, as the girl snatched the form and pen back and told him to bring his own next time. For an instant he toyed with the idea of choosing her to be his next special friend but the thought of touching that pale, damp, slippery flesh made him feel sick. He'd have to wear protective clothing before he'd go near her.

Samuel slowed as he approached the banks of Kings Sedgemoor, turning left onto the track to Ada Mallory's cottage. Keeping to the far side of the road, he walked briskly past and picked up his pace again a few hundred yards further on. She had dogs who were attuned to the sound of running feet and Ada was a nosy bitch. He didn't care about disturbing her but the less attention he attracted the better as he began his preparations in earnest.

There were fresh marks in the dust near his cottage and Samuel crossed the road, slipping into the cover of the willows shading the river bank. Twice in a week was a lot of traffic to be stopping in this empty spot and he wanted to see what was attracting these unwanted visitors. At first he saw nothing unusual but then the sun dipped behind a cloud and he caught a glimpse of movement in the shallows. Samuel crouched down, edging forward until he was right by the water.

Only then did he spot Tom's net pegged out in the shadows, now half-filled with fat, fresh fish. Samuel glanced around instinctively but there was no-one in sight. The air was still and any vehicle could be heard coming a long way off. After the briefest of hesitations Samuel stripped off his shirt, tying the neck and sleeves closed before dipping it in the river where it ballooned out into an improvised net. Kneeling on the sleeves to hold it steady in the current, he leaned over and grabbed the nearest fish, only to have it slide though his fingers.

'Damn it,' he muttered, shifting his position. The shirt broke free and drifted just out of reach, rippling in the gently moving water. Reaching for it, Samuel almost ended up in the canal but he managed to grab a willow branch and hauled himself and the shirt back to the bank. The thin branch slid across his palm, slicing it open and sending a jolt of pain through his hand. He rocked back on his heels, teeth gritted against the burning from the cut, then he took a deep breath and focussed his considerable intelligence on the problem.

The obvious solution was to go on to the cottage, get some twine or the old keep-net from the fishing box and come back, but Samuel was loath to make two trips, possibly attracting attention to himself and to the net in the water. The owner might return at any moment and the thought of the fish, so tantalizingly close, had reawakened his appetite. After a moment's thought he raked around under the trees, pulling a couple of old bricks out from the roots. Remains of an old wall, he thought, as he piled them on top of the edge of his shirt. This time it settled in place, billowing slightly in the water. The water was clear again, the silt settling on the bottom, and Samuel rinsed his injured hand before turning his attention to catching his dinner.

After a couple of failures he was able to flip several of the small, slime-covered fish into his shirt. Their mucus coating made him curl his lips with distaste but he knew it was a protective device and a good one too, so he overcame his disgust and reached into the net once more. His hand was still bleeding, a thin trickle of blood oozing out into the water, and the strike, when it came, almost sent him into the water again. As the young pike shot out from under the bank, Samuel reacted by flinging himself to one side, jerking his hands up as the wicked jaws with their interlocking teeth snapped at his fingers.

Not much frightened Samuel but he was shaking as he pulled his shirt from the water and hurried back up the bank. Despite his meagre haul he was not at all tempted by the remaining fish, now squirming frantically in the net as the pike floated next to them, its tail flicking lazily as it held its position in the stream. Note to self, he thought grimly, as he tramped the last few hundred yards to the abandoned cottage. Don't try wading through the canals on this God-forsaken marsh. Still, the prospect of a decent meal, his first for a month, soon restored his confidence. Not many people could say they had escaped from a pike attack. It was a shame he couldn't tell anyone, though if he was being honest there was no-one he needed or wanted to impress that much.

Charlie had to wait to see Alex and he sat in the corner of the main entrance, slouching against the wall with his legs stretched out in front of him, a picture of misery. Not so much a client as a tripping hazard, thought Alex, when she finally reached the end of her appointments and went through to collect him.

'Where's Lauren to, then?' Charlie asked. 'Don't like that'n.' He threw a scowl over his shoulder at Alison who was seated at the reception desk and pointedly ignoring him.

'You don't have to like her,' said Alex. 'You have to do as she says and behave yourself. Lauren's off sick,' she added. She wanted to say a lot more but Charlie was a client and she took her professional role very seriously.

'Heard that Ricky pushed her down stairs,' said Charlie, settling into the chair in front of her. Alex was startled by this. There were bound to be rumours about Lauren's accident but she hadn't expected anything so serious.

'Nonsense,' she said briskly. 'Lauren tripped and fell. Ricky – Mr Peddlar to you – was in his office when it happened. I don't want to hear you've been spreading rumours about what happened, understand?'

Charlie ducked his head and stared at his hands.

'Sorry,' he mumbled. 'Never meant nothin', honest. Was just what I heard.'

Alex softened her voice. 'That's okay. Just don't be gossiping about things you know nothing about. Now, what is so urgent you need an extra appointment this week?'

Alex peered at her watch as Charlie left the office and gave a soft groan. She had just ten minutes before her next meeting, this time with the new senior and her assistant. Being confined to the day centre for much of her work, Alex had not yet met the new team though she had been hearing rumours for a few days. It was the woman's first official day in post and they were all summoned to the Day Room for 1pm. Fumbling in her pockets Alex unearthed a handful of coins, just enough for a sandwich at the local supermarket, and if she ran she could probably make it there and back in time. In fact she was two minutes late.

'So glad you could join us,' said the woman standing in the centre of the room when Alex, hot and out of breath, opened the door. They stared at one another for a moment before Alex managed a mumbled apology and slid round the room, heading for the empty space next to Sue.

'There's a place here,' said the woman, pointing to a chair in front of her. It was next to Ricky Peddlar and Alex perched herself on it trying to keep as far away from him as possible. Ricky turned to look at her for an instant, his eyes cold and blank beneath the washed-out eyelashes. It was like being sized up by a fish, Alex thought. Ignoring his tight-mouthed smile she turned her attention to Rosalind Marchent, who was holding up a hand for attention though none of the staff was moving, let alone talking.

She looked like a meringue, thought Alex. A pale, pink meringue done up in a swathe of fluffy violet material and topped by the most unlikely black hair she had ever seen outside of a child's cartoon. A bright red rosebud mouth sat under puffy cheeks but the eyes that slid around the room were hard, sharp and a dark, stormy grey.

Rosalind had run through the standard platitudes of welcome, team work and anticipation of a fruitful relationship and was moving on to the new management structure she was putting in place. This was important to them all and Alex, along with the rest of the officers, gave it her full attention.

'This is Debbie,' said Rosalind, gesturing to a small figure seated beside a whiteboard in the corner. 'She is my personal assistant and will be overseeing a number of routine aspects in the office. You may consider what she says as having come from me.'

Debbie rose from her chair and stepped forward, a miniature Rosalind – not quite as plump, not quite as pale and dressed in a green suit that matched her eyes. The overall effect was of one of Santa's elves, thought Alex. She was starting to have a very bad feeling about this new regime. From the look on most of the faces around her she was not alone in her opinions. The exception was Ricky Peddlar, of course. He was smiling at his new boss, nodding enthusiastically at every other sentence.

The rest of the meeting followed a predictable pattern with hints at new regulations to come, some half-hearted praise for Gordon's efforts in maintaining the service without the guiding hand of a senior officer and a request they all arrange a private appointment in her office before the end of the week.

With one final and totally false smile Rosalind swept from the room leaving Debbie in charge.

Like naughty schoolchildren they were shuffled into a line to book their meeting with Rosalind before they could leave and get back to work and Alex was grinding her teeth in frustration by the time it was her turn.

'Ah yes, Rosalind wants a full hour with you,' said Debbie flipping through the pages of the master diary. 'I think Friday at three would do.'

'I have a session in the day centre then,' said Alex. 'Actually I've got sessions most days. Perhaps I can get my diary and we can ...'

'No, you will be meeting Rosalind at three on Friday,' said Debbie. 'You'll just have to make alternative arrangements for your group.' She turned her back and walked out of the room leaving Alex open-mouthed and fuming.

'Who the *fuck* does she think she is?' asked Sue, walking over to her friend. 'I hope this isn't how things are going to be from now on. I'm not being bossed around by someone who looks like Little Jimmy Krankie!'

Despite her fury at Debbie's presumption, Alex laughed aloud and the remaining officers joined in around them. Unnoticed, Ricky slipped out of the door and headed upstairs.

Petey made his appointment at the dole office though he received a stern warning for being late. He'd not been on the register as long as Charlie and actually as he'd done absolutely nothing in the past he was still considered suitable material for the various youth training schemes around the area. After his meeting with a youth advisor he went into the park and sat on the same bench Charlie had occupied a few hours earlier, casting an unenthusiastic eye over a handful of brochures, all of which promised him an excellent learning environment, good prospects and £30 a week plus travel.

Petey had never been one for learning anything. In fact it was his total lack of attention that had saved him from being drawn deeper into the local criminal world. Assorted burglars, pick-pockets and drug dealers had tried to attract him to their side but Petey was too lazy to take any of it seriously. Consequently, he was a small-town shoplifter with a couple of convictions for affray and ABH, mainly after drinking too much and getting into a fight he could not hope to win.

The idea of having 'prospects' was so alien to Petey he wasn't even sure what it meant. In rural Somerset there was little work apart from seasonal farm labour and the dreaded chicken factory and he was not about to take up either. And he certainly wasn't going to get up early every morning for £30 a week. He got almost as much from the dole after the hostel took his board and lodging. Mug's game, he thought, screwing up the brightly coloured pamphlets and throwing them into the nearest bushes.

'Oi – you!' came a shout from across the park. 'Pick that up now!'

Petey looked across the rose gardens and saw the keeper heading his way. The man was old and slow and Petey stood, stretched and trotted off down the path, stopping to make a rude sign before disappearing under the road bridge.

'Bloody little hooligans,' muttered the park keeper as he retrieved the abandoned papers. 'No respect for public property.' He'd seen Petey around before and noticed the boy always threw his fag ends away into the flower beds. He'd have him next time, he vowed. Lads like that needed teaching a lesson and littering was an offence.

On the other side of the bridge Petey stopped and peered back through the tunnel. The parky was too busy muttering and picking up things to follow, which was just as well as his head was swimming. Petey felt along the back of his ear, his fingers touching the sticky wound, and gingerly he probed the large bump at the base of his skull. He suddenly felt very sick and stumbled over to the edge of the River Parrett, reaching the railings just as he threw up.

'Disgusting!' snapped a woman's voice and he tried to turn his head to swear at a mother as she hurried past, one child in a pushchair and a second held firmly by the hand. The scenery dipped and swayed before his eyes and he was sick again, this time over the path. Wiping his mouth with the back of his hand, Petey stumbled towards the hostel, his head pounding and his eyes watering.

What he wanted was to lie down somewhere cool and dark but all he was allowed was Molly Brown's art class. The thought of the hot little room filled with sweaty bodies was more than he could stand. Dragging his reluctant body along, Petey sought the dubious comfort of the old lock gate where he stripped off Charlie's T-shirt, now spotted with vomit, curled up in the shade and closed his eyes. The sun moved around slowly, shrinking the patch of shelter until it shone full onto a bare arm. The heat did not wake him but he rolled over, his head still in the cool grass and his back to the sunlight. By the time he woke he was bright red and the skin was threatening to blister.

'What the hell do you mean, coming in here in this state!' demanded Peter Marks when Petey staggered through the door to the hostel. The young man leaned on the wall swaying slightly as he tried to focus on the passageway leading to the stairs. He was still bare-chested, the shirt forgotten and abandoned on the canal bank and his clothes smelt even worse than they had when he left in the morning.

'Get out at once and don't come back until you are sober,' shouted the warden.

'I 'ent,' Petey muttered. All he wanted was to get upstairs and to fall into his bed. His head was ringing and his back felt as if it was peeling off with the heat of the sunburn. 'Just need to lie down a bit, is all.' He lurched forward, tripped and fell flat on the tiled floor in a dead faint. The noise brought most of the art class into the hallway, closely followed by Bennie. She took one look at Petey and immediately called two of the residents over.

'Help me lift him,' she said, gently turning the boy over until they had him in the recovery position. 'Have you called a doctor?' she added over her shoulder.

'I told him to get out,' said the warden. 'I won't have residents coming back in that state.'

Bennie stared at him for a moment. 'I think he's got sunstroke,' she said softly. 'He fainted. Now he really needs a doctor.'

The pair locked eyes for an instant whilst the two young men fidgeted, waiting to see what they should do.

'Go back to class now,' Bernie said. 'All of you. And thanks for your help. Oh, Mick – .' She addressed Charlie's roommate. 'Could you go to the medical room and fetch a couple of rugs for me? Thank you. Go on,' she said firmly to the gawping crowd still hovering in the hallway. 'Back inside.'

Peter Marks turned round and stormed into the office, slamming the door behind him. When Mick returned they folded the rugs to make supports for Petey's neck and arms, settling him as comfortably as they could before Bennie dismissed him and rose to her feet, hesitating for a moment outside the office door. Giving Petey's prone body one more glance she opened the door without knocking. The boy really did need a doctor and she was fairly sure Peter Marks had not bothered to make the call.

'Don't you ever contradict me in front of the residents again,' he snapped as she stepped inside. 'I have a good mind to report you.'

Bennie ignored him, reached over the desk and pulled the phone towards her. The warden slapped her hand away, pulled it back and pointed to the open door. 'Out, now!'

Bennie's patience finally failed her and she snatched the phone away, dropping it on the spare desk with a loud bang. 'He needs a doctor,' she shouted. 'Do you want to be responsible if he dies in the hallway? Because there are enough witnesses to your tantrum to make sure the blame falls where it belongs!'

Peter Marks was speechless for a moment and Bennie dialled the emergency number for the local surgery, gave the receptionist a rapid account of events and slammed the receiver down, pushing the phone back over the desk before stepping back into the hall. She hoped he'd let it go but it was not to be.

'Right,' said the warden from the doorway. 'I've had enough of you and your attitude. You're fired! As of now, I don't want you in my hostel so get out.'

Bennie knelt next to Petey, checking he was breathing and feeling his forehead. Without looking at the warden she said, 'You can't do that. And it is not your hostel, thank God. If you want to make a complaint you can contact headquarters in Taunton. It can go in with mine against you.' This time the door slammed so hard the wall shook but Bennie stayed next to Petey, talking to him softly until the doctor arrived.

Alex and Sue were the amongst the last staff members to have their meetings with the new senior and by the time Friday came around they were already acquainted with the new management's agenda. Most people were being moved, allocated new duties and expanded case loads in advance of the dreaded inspection. The exceptions seemed to be Pauline, who was insulted to be offered three months on trial as senior admin, a post she had fulfilled with astonishing skill and diplomacy for over ten years, and Ricky, who just shrugged and smiled knowingly when anyone asked what he was going to be doing.

'What's the point of moving us all just before an inspection?' Sue had asked on the Thursday evening. 'Surely they want us to show we know our jobs. I thought we needed to be at our best for the Home Office. Now everyone's running round frantically trying to swap files and work out what the hell they're supposed to be doing.'

Alex had given the process some thought and had her own suspicions.

'If they come in and we're all starting new jobs they can't really pick us up on any shortcomings. Well, they might pick on us but the management can't be blamed because the system's not had a chance to settle. So anything wrong is down to individual officers and not the new senior. They're covering their backs on this one.'

'But Gordon's done a great job keeping us all going!' Sue had protested. 'In fact it's been running better than it did when we had bloody mad Garry in charge.'

'Yes, well that might be a problem too,' said Alex. 'Forgive me for being cynical but I don't think Rosalind wants Gordon getting any credit for anything. She knows we like him and that he has the respect of the whole team ...'

'Except for Ricky,' Sue said.

'Well, yes, except for Ricky, the little weasel. So, if there's anything good she'll claim credit and if there are any problems that will be on Gordon's head.'

When Sue came out of her meeting she was looking pale, her face rigid with anger.

'I'll tell you later,' she hissed to Alex who was waiting in the corridor. 'Just – watch yourself. She's spiteful as hell but very clever. Oh, and be prepared for the room!'

Alex blinked at her friend in surprise but before she could ask any questions the door opened and Debbie beckoned her inside. As she stepped over the threshold Alex understood Sue's final remark. The whole room was a festival of pink and purple. Pink candy-striped blinds hung from the tall, elegant windows, the carpet was a swirl of purples and mauves and the desk was covered in pink plastic dolls. A feather boa was draped over the computer monitor and strings of pink and purple feathers hung from the ceiling. It would have been shocking if it hadn't been so ludicrous.

Debbie waved her towards a hard chair in front of the desk, the only object in the room not graced by a purple cushion, and Alex sat without a word, folding her hands and waiting. Rosalind was seated on what looked like a pink plush throne, her eyes sharp and eager as she searched Alex's face for any reaction to her surroundings. Alex took a moment to let her eyes focus on the small areas of visible wood panelling. She was a little surprised not to see a portrait of a Barbie doll hanging behind the desk.

'So,' drawled Rosalind, reaching for a grey folder on her desk. A remarkably tidy desk Alex noted. 'Cassandra Hastings Norman – Alex as you prefer to be called, not surprisingly.' She flipped open the cover of Alex's file seemingly at random, made a show of reading a few lines and then turned to another page. Alex sat in silence holding her hands loosely in front of her, waiting out her new boss. She knew exactly what Rosalind was doing and had no intention of giving an inch to this woman whom she already disliked heartily. It was Debbie who finally broke the stand-off, shifting awkwardly in the corner and giving a little cough. Rosalind closed the file with an angry slap, throwing a frown at her assistant before giving Alex a smile that oozed insincerity.

'You have certainly made your mark here at Highpoint,' she said. 'Quite an eventful time for your first appointment.'

Alex waited, sure something nasty was on its way.

'Let me see, a bit of a rocky start with that unpleasant business on the Levels,' Rosalind continued smoothly. She didn't bother to open the file again, which suggested she had already read it several times. Not a level of scrutiny Alex found reassuring under the circumstances.

'After that you ran foul of some smugglers at night, is that right?' Rosalind paused but moved on before Alex could reply. 'And then you took it on yourself to assist the police with some sort of psychological mumbo-jumbo. I'm not sure that should be encouraged in the modern world, do you?'

Alex refused to react, concentrating on stopping her hands from curling into tight balls. If Rosalind was disappointed she did not let it show, turning her attention to a large multi-coloured chart on the desk and running her finger along one of the rows.

'You have made a reasonable start with the day centre,' she continued. 'Though there are a few ... *issues* ... with some of the groups.'

Alex felt the last flicker of hope die inside. She knew what was coming.

110

'Your latest session with the alcohol education group, for example.' Rosalind lifted her cold, grey eyes from the chart and stared at her, letting the silence grow to an uncomfortable length before giving her hateful smile.

'Well? Tell me about it please.'

Damn, the woman was good, Alex thought.

'It was designed to demonstrate there are alternatives to the unhealthy drinking habits our group have developed,' she began.

Rosalind cut her off with an impatient gesture. 'I am sure it was undertaken with the best of intentions. However, I am more concerned with the practicalities. I understand alcohol was involved in this final session. And it was not the first time either. Your group spent one evening drinking and playing a computer game – correct?'

It was both an exact description of events and a brutally unfair interpretation of her course and Alex realized she would be lucky to get out of the room with a job. Forced into defending her work, she tried to explain what she had been doing and exactly what she had achieved. Rosalind listened for a minute, her head to one side and a slightly puzzled look on her face, before cutting in.

'So you did supply alcohol to clients on these premises?' she said. When Alex hesitated she added, 'A simple "yes" or "no" is sufficient.'

How the hell did she know about the last couple of sessions, Alex wondered. Obviously someone had been spying on her and it didn't take much of a detective to work out who it was.

Rosalind's summing up was swift and ruthless. 'I feel you have been allowed too much freedom, partly due to the regrettable lack of proper supervision,' she said. 'I am tempted to set up a trial regime to help you develop a more professional vision but we are very short of officers and I need to be sure the important aspects of our work – court reports, the day centre and so on – are of the highest standard for the forthcoming inspection.

'There is a new emphasis on a more holistic approach to supervising offenders and so I am placing you in the hostel for the next few months. You will be able to continue your more *pastoral* approach on a daily basis whilst the rest of the team focus on the compliance and legal aspects. We can review this later but in the meantime you will ensure the day centre records are up to date and all planned sessions are available for Debbie to collect and inspect in a fortnight's time.'

Alex went cold in fury. All her hard work in the day centre was to be wasted. All the trust she had built up between the system and the clients was dismissed without any consideration. And the hostel? Somerset didn't put trained officers in probation hostels, they used people like Peter Marks. Not that she necessarily approved of his appointment. In her opinion he was lazy, incompetent and a bully but still, this was more than a demotion. This was only one step above dismissal.

'You will hand over the day centre to Ricky Peddlar,' Rosalind continued, happily destroying any illusions Alex might still be harbouring over her impartiality. 'I want you in post at the hostel as soon as possible. I understand there are some problems with the current warden and he will be moving to Taunton to undergo a period of further training.' There was a glint of satisfaction in Rosalind's eyes as she rose and offered Alex a limp and slightly damp handshake.

Whisked out of the room by the odious Debbie, Alex stood for a moment, the noise of her heart pounding in her ears. Still stunned by events she walked down the corridor in a daze, turned the corner and bumped into Gordon who was heading to his interview.

'Alex – are you alright?' he asked. He reached out and touched her shoulder, radiating concern. Alex blinked away tears of anger, shaking her head as she struggled to find her voice. She respected Gordon immensely and hated the thought of telling him of her new post. It was an insult to her but also to Gordon and the trust he had placed in her work.

'I think there's a hidden agenda going on,' she managed. 'Be careful, Gordon. She's – well, be prepared for the room.'

Gordon gave a puzzled look but a glance at his watch sent him hurrying off to his own appointment.

As Alex shuffled down the stairs she mused on the surprising fact that she and Rosalind at least agreed about Peter Marks.

Chapter Eight

Much to Ada's surprise Tom had reservations about her scheme to put Pongo to work in Lily's garden.

'Don't see him being happy, sent somewhere else all on his own,' he said. 'Social creatures is goats an' he's got used to us bein' around. Need to look see what'n he'll be eatin' and all.'

'Thought goats ate anything,' said Ada, drying her hands on the apron tied around her waist.

'That's problem, see,' said Tom. 'Eat anything they come across, even plants all bitter like, supposed to put any sensible animal off. But not a goat. If is poison they'll still keep chompin' away 'til they falls down dead.'

'Really?' said Ada, going to the kitchen window. 'Never knew that. Probably just as well, when he first got here. Could have cheerfully poisoned him, first few weeks when he got into my veggies. And ate the washing too, line an' all. Good job weren't one of them plastic ones.'

'Hemp ain't no good for 'um,' said Tom. 'An bulbs neither. Lily got daffies in her garden?'

'He 'ent for clearing the garden,' said Ada. 'Is for round about, old pasture and such. Just like here.'

Tom nodded and took a swig of tea from the mug Ada placed in front of him. 'Well, I'll go over, have a look round. Don't want to be sending him on his own, mind.'

'Well I ain't going too,' said Ada sharply. 'Mebbe could be a job for young Brian? He could sit next to 'um, reading them books for his exams.'

Tom laughed and shook his head. 'No, not what I mean. Old stud goat often has a young 'un, like a companion. Can't be another buck mind so a wether's best. Keeps both of 'em happy 'cos the wether gets right friendly – and wethers don't smell like old Pongo neither.'

Ada thought about this for a moment. Despite her initial reluctance she had become very fond of Pongo.

'I reckon Pongo could earn his keep,' she said finally. 'Long as he 'ent around anything bad for 'um then let's see about getting him this companion you's talking about. Done wonders for my patch out the back and I'd like to do Lily a favour. Been a hard life for her, having that young lad to look after, though I hear he's doing better now in the hostel. Would be something, him getting settled into a job maybe.' She turned to look at Tom. 'So tell me, where's this wether goat comin' from? I know you, Tom Monarch. You got something planned here.'

Tom chuckled and took another drink from his mug. 'Well, maybe I have. Got too many billies this year from his breeding, my friend has. Could do with having one taken off his hands. Could send 'um for meat but takes a while to get 'um fattened up and they's eating him out of pasture at the moment. Would be good for Brian too, bit of practice with the two.' He gave a sly glance over the top of his beaker. Ada was silhouetted against the window, arms folded as she looked at him. Then she burst out laughing.

'You's a cunning one, Tom. Had this in mind from the start I reckon.'

It was a cheerless Friday evening at Alex's house following the meetings with Rosalind. Sue was home when Alex arrived but there were no lights on and she stumbled through the front room, almost tripping over her friend who was hunched over the table in the dark.

'Bloody hell! Why are there no lights on?' snapped Alex as she fumbled for the light switch. 'I nearly broke my leg. Was the interview that bad?' She stamped off into the kitchen without waiting for an answer. 'Margie's due home soon. You could at least have put the kettle on.'

There was a loud bang as Sue stood up, pushing the chair over behind her. 'Oh, Margie, Margie, Margie – that's all you care about now isn't it!' She stormed up the stairs, slamming the door to her room just as the object of her complaint came in through the front.

'Hello,' said Margie, hurrying across the space and giving Alex a hug. 'Didn't half miss you this week.' She paused and pulled away a fraction. 'No Sue, then? An' you look upset. Sit down and I'll make some tea 'n you can tell all.'

'Sue's upstairs,' muttered Alex, but she allowed herself to be shepherded to an armchair. 'She's a bit mad about something. We've both had pretty dreadful interviews I guess.' She sank into the comfort of the cushions and sighed heavily. 'I didn't get a chance to ask her – she just flew off in a rage when I turned the light on.'

Margie peered round the kitchen door and frowned. 'Don't sound like Sue,' she said. 'Must 'a been a really rough meeting to set her off like that. Unless you missed out a bit?'

Alex took a mug of tea and sipped at it, relaxing a little as the hot drink settled her jangled nerves. 'Well, I did ask why she was sitting in the dark,' she admitted reluctantly. Margie raised her eyebrows but didn't speak. 'Okay, I think I might have snapped at her a little but whatever that bitch Rosalind said to her, it's nothing to what she's done to me!' and to their mutual surprise Alex burst into tears.

In an instant Margie was on her knees, removing the hot cup from Alex's shaking hands and cradling her in.

'Now then, that's it – you let it all out. Been a nasty week for you waiting for this, but now is over and whatever is happening we can deal with it.'

There was a shuffling on the stairs and Margie looked over Alex's shoulder at Sue who was peering over the banisters. Her face, too, was streaked with tears.

'Come on,' said Margie, beckoning Sue down. 'You two's been friends since you came here. Don't you let some new arrival damage that.'

Sue came down and sat in the armchair on the opposite side of the fireplace. After a moment she reached out and took Alex's hand and they sat in a quiet little group for a few moments, drawing comfort from one another.

'Well, my meeting was awful but yours must have been absolutely terrible,' said Sue. 'I don't think I've ever seen you cry before.'

Alex had reached the red-nosed, snuffly stage of a good cry and started hunting in her pockets for a tissue.

'We've always got plenty of the damn things ready for clients,' she said. 'How come I can never find one at home?'

Sue fished a small packet out of her pocket, took one and handed the rest over to her friend. 'Because we keep them at work,' she said. 'And you never cry anyway.'

'You're both making up for it now,' said Margie, returning from the kitchen with tea for Sue. 'Get this down you first. I'm popping out for something stronger. You both going to be okay?'

Alex and Sue nodded and Margie picked up her keys and hurried out in search of the nearest off-licence.

'I'm sorry,' said Alex softly. 'I was really thoughtless. I was so upset about losing the day centre …'

'You lost the day centre?' said Sue. 'Oh God, no wonder you were upset. What's going to happen to it now? And where are you going to be working? Oh no – she's not sacked you has she? Get on to NAPO. They'll know what to do. She can't sack you without using the proper procedure …'

'She's not sacked me,' said Alex. 'Though it feels as if she has. She's sending me to the hostel.'

There was a moment's silence as Sue gaped at her friend. 'The hostel?' she said finally. 'The *hostel?* Somerset doesn't have officers in the hostels, they have half-wits like Peter Marks!'

Alex managed a rather shaky grin at this. 'Well, it seems he has finally gone too far and they're sending him off for some training or something. I'm to step in and continue with what she calls my "pastoral approach". Don't know how long for – she didn't say.'

'Oh my God,' said Sue. 'I thought my interview was bad.'

Alex realized she had been so wrapped up in her own misery she had forgotten other people were also affected by Rosalind's reorganization.

'I'm sorry,' she said. 'I'm being really selfish. What happened with you?'

Sue pulled a face, then brightened up as the front door opened and Margie appeared with a carrier bag that clinked merrily as she put it on the table. 'Drink first,' said Sue. 'There's nothing like a glass of wine to make even the worst news seem tolerable.'

Margie had gauged the atmosphere in Alex's house just right and purchased accordingly, bringing three bottles of wine.

'Could be one each,' she said, wielding a corkscrew. 'Though wouldn't recommend it.' Alex took her advice and poured a half-glass, adding water to the deep red liquid. 'A toast,' she said. 'Mud in their eyes!'

'Mud in their eyes!' the three chorused before drinking.

'And perdition to all their families, relatives and pets,' added Sue, taking another swig.

'Bit harsh,' Margie objected. 'Don't see why the pets should suffer. Relatives, though, they should take some responsibility for not straightening 'em out over the years.'

'Oh, all right – pets are exempt,' said Sue, refilling her glass. 'So, what's the absolute worst duty you can think of?'

Alex took a sip from her glass and frowned. 'Court duty,' she said finally.

'Go on,' said Sue grimly.

'Family court?' Alex suggested.

'Nope.'

'Can't think of much worse than that,' Alex mumbled. Family court was never popular but it was one day a week and Sue would be keeping control of some of her case load, at least. 'Go on then.'

'How about pre-release officer,' said Sue. 'All of them over this part of the county. That's five different prisons with clients I've probably never seen before and who I'll not see once they're out. God knows how many days travelling from one end of the county to the other and a few days for reports and all the rest of the crap they're going to throw at us.'

'But that's ridiculous!' said Alex in horror. 'There's all the follow-up work and what about the travelling? No-one can do that for long.'

'Well, it's been made very clear to me I don't have any choice,' said Sue grimly. 'Do you get the impression she doesn't like us very much?'

'What about other officers getting experience in that role?' Alex asked. 'It doesn't make sense, lumping all that on one person. My move into the hostel's an insult but at least it's possible to do. That's not.'

Sue shrugged and rose to her feet. 'Yeah, I know. I'm wondering if I can make a case for constructive dismissal but I'll need to run it past NAPO first. And the union doesn't seem to be very well organized down here. Anyway, if we're going to carry on drinking like this I think we should eat something don't you?'

At that moment there was a knock on the door. Alex and Margie exchanged puzzled glances before Alex slid off her chair and went back into the front room. Margie hurried after Sue hoping to thwart any attempt she might make to rustle up dinner. The evening was grim enough, she thought, without being confronted by Sue's well-meaning cooking.

Alex opened the front door and blinked in surprise to see Lauren and Jonny standing there clutching a bottle of wine.

'Didn't want to miss another Friday,' said Lauren cheerfully. 'What's for dinner then? Been looking forward to this all week.' She slid round Alex and hurried through to the kitchen.

Jonny held out the bottle and Alex stepped back to let him in. 'No Kurt?' she asked as she closed the door.

Jonny shook his head and smiled ruefully. 'Says he's busy tonight. Been busy a lot recently. Don't expect we'll see much of him again to be honest.'

Alex reached out and touched his shoulder. She was very fond of Jonny.

'Sorry,' she said. 'He was fun. Still, I'm glad you're both here. We could all do with cheering up a bit and Lauren looks so much better.'

The object of their appraisal re-emerged from the kitchen, full glass in hand, and hopped up onto a chair at the table.

'Is okay,' she said. 'Margie's got the cooking in hand. So tell us about this new senior then. Sounds a bit of a shocker so far, what I hear. Pauline rang earlier, right upset about Gordon.'

'What about Gordon?' Alex demanded, sitting at the table opposite Lauren.

'You doesn't know? Kicked out of Highpoint, he been. Sent all the way to Yeovil office. Seeing as he's living in Weston now, is over an hour on the motorway each way.'

'Closer to hour and a half,' said Jonny. ''Specially in summer when is full of grockles. Can't get nowhere for dam' tourists now.'

Lauren nodded her agreement. 'Seems wrong that and he won't get no mileage neither 'cos is travel to work so it don't count.'

'Why is he going there?' Alex asked. 'Gordon's our most senior officer. We'd never have got through the last few months without him. Hell, without Gordon's support half of us would have left when Garry was here as senior. Why send him away now?'

Even as she spoke she saw the warped reasoning behind Rosalind's actions. In one afternoon she had purged the office of those most likely to resist her new regime. Sue would be too busy and had no fixed client list any more. The team had lost their trusted leader in Gordon and as for her – she wouldn't even be in the office any more. She looked at Lauren and sighed. 'I would give serious thought to finding another job,' she said. 'Ricky's got the day centre now. And I'm out in the hostel in a week's time. I don't think any of us are going to enjoy the next few months very much. I wonder if they'll give me a reference.'

Lauren put her glass down and leaned across the table. 'Been thinking about that,' she said. 'Even before all this started. Reckon I do a good job and I get on okay with the clients. Better than I do with some of the staff, to be honest. So I was wondering about training to do social work, like you done. Couldn't be no probation officer but could do maybe support work. Or in the hostel.' She raised an eyebrow at Alex. 'What you think then?'

Steve was mightily disgusted with his companions. First Charlie had run off and decided he was going to be a good boy and now Petey, who had been shaping up to be the perfect side-kick, got himself a bit knocked about and ended up on the sick. He'd gone up to the room they shared with another young man, a newcomer in for breaking and entering, but Bennie had caught him sitting on Petey's bed and sent him out of the hostel until dinner time. Steve walked down the road, hands in his pockets and dragging his feet in the dust. He was bored, hot and hungry.

Wandering through the town he noted the way several of the stall-holders watched him and realized they had finally wised up to his 'five finger discount'. He moved away from their hard stares, feigning indifference and adding a swagger to his walk whilst cursing them all in his head. He'd been hoping to get something to eat on his way through town but that was looking unlikely now.

He wasn't paying much attention to where he was going and suddenly looked up to see the probation offices looming over him. The gates to the courtyard were wide open and the sound of loud conversation echoed in the enclosed space. A radio was playing in the background and as he hesitated a burst of laughter aroused his curiosity. Peering round the brick wall he watched as a group of youths tried out several bicycles, pushing and riding them around the car park with mixed success.

'Mine's okay,' said one lad, his face a broad grin as he hopped onto a rather battered racing model. Despite the faded paint and rust spots on the chrome the bike was obviously in good shape and the rider circled the courtyard proudly, cutting in between the parked cars and narrowly avoiding his companions. A second young man climbed onto a BMX bike, pushed off gingerly and wobbled a few yards before the bike tipped over and he fell off.

'Got to turn the pedals, yer idjit!' jeered one of the crowd.

'Come on, give us a go,' said another, reaching for the bike.

''Tis mine!' said the fallen rider, scrambling to his feet and pulling at the handlebars. 'Was what we was promised. You go fix yer own.'

In seconds the mood in the yard changed from celebration to confrontation as the lucky bike owners tried to wheel their machines away from grabbing hands.

'Don't be tight,' shouted one boy at the BMX owner. 'You 'ent even ridin' yet. Let us try.'

Things were about to turn very nasty when Alex's voice rolled across the courtyard. 'Stop that at once or no-one gets a bike. Tim, take that machine back inside. Davie – let go now or you're off the project. The rest of you, get back inside.'

As the group slunk back into the workshop Steve ventured inside the gates, looking around to see where Alex was.

'And what do you want?'

He jumped, still unable to locate the source of the question.

'Over here,' she said and he finally saw the top of her head poking out from a basement window. 'Are you looking for someone in particular or just seeking some form of entertainment?' she asked as he walked towards her.

'Wot's that then?' Steve asked, jerking his head towards the workshop door.

'That is the beginners workshop project,' said Alex, a slight weariness entering her voice. 'As you would know if you had listened to a word I have said for the last few months. Everyone can select a bike from the unclaimed stock kindly donated by the police. They can work on their bike during sessions, repairing and restoring it. Once it is safe and roadworthy everyone takes the cycling proficiency test and if – and only if – you pass then the bike becomes yours to keep.'

'For nuffink?' said Steve. 'Just free? Sounds alright that. I could fancy a free bike. Sign me up then.' He gave his best jovial grin which was met by Alex's best hard stare.

'If you are serious then I would be delighted to get you doing something constructive. Come and see me ...' She glanced at her watch. 'Come in about an hour. I'll arrange to introduce you to the workshop manager and we can discuss your enrolment.' She closed the window with a bang.

'Strewth,' muttered Steve. 'What a fuss about a stupid workshop. It was more of a fuss than joining the army. Steve would know about that. He'd joined the army last year, skipped out after two weeks and sold his kit to fund a nice holiday for him and his then girlfriend. She'd disappeared when they had been chased down a hill in Cornwall by a couple of Redcaps, failing to see the humour of their situation. Steve had abandoned her in the B&B where they were staying, without paying the bill. He very much doubted he'd ever see her again.

'Not if I see her first anyway,' he added to himself as he ambled out of the yard. Maybe he could pick up a sandwich or something from the local supermarket. They only had one security bloke and he was too busy watching the booze aisle to notice a couple of missing snacks.

Alex watched him leave, staring through the grimy window until she was sure he was gone. It was a pleasant surprise, Steve showing interest in the bike project. Since his sentencing he'd stubbornly refused to involve himself in anything apart from the compulsory sessions on 'Challenging Offending Behaviour' and even then he sat off to one side, watching and occasionally smirking but certainly not contributing. She wasn't entirely convinced he understood exactly what the workshop involved, however. A lot of the lads had signed up in the early days, all eager to get their hands on a free bike. When they saw the amount of work involved, and especially when they realized the final cycling test was not a foregone conclusion, a lot of them drifted away.

Those left tended to become absorbed in the underlying skills needed to restore the bikes, some of them staying on and working on multiple machines. One had even got an apprenticeship at the local motorbike shop, in an age when real apprenticeships were as rare as tap-dancing fish. Somehow she doubted Steve would become absorbed in the delights of mechanical engineering but she rather liked the idea of luring him into the workshop and then leaving him for Ricky to deal with.

Samuel found his energy levels boosted almost immediately following his stolen dinner. The little fish had soon lost their revolting mucus coating once rinsed in cold water and he had fried them on the old wood-fired range, consuming them whole, removing the tails and guts but crunching through the rest with gusto. A few of those a week and he would be fighting fit again, he thought, staring out of the back window over the canal.

He returned to the pile of discarded fishing tackle, turning it over and sorting it into useable and junk. He had enough decent items to fish for himself but only using a rod and that took time. Samuel could not bring himself to sit on the river bank, idling the day away waiting for a bite. He was also aware of the danger from the river wardens who patrolled the Levels and imposed hefty fines for those fishing without a licence. Samuel had no desire to return to the magistrates court for something so stupid, especially as it would pinpoint his new hideaway, but he had no intention of buying a licence.

He considered setting the keep-net in the canal behind the cottage. That way he could return a few days later and collect the haul. The downside to that was the risk someone might find it and steal his fish and the idea of this made him tense and anxious. He knew he could not rest in the hostel whilst worrying about his net. The fact he was happy to rob another man of their catch did not concern him at all.

The sound of a car approaching made him turn towards the front of the building. There were always a few vehicles each day bumping along the dusty track. Often they were farmers or labourers taking a shortcut to or from work. Occasionally he spotted the car of a frustrated tourist, lost on the blank emptiness of the marsh. These could be identified easily by the maps flapping on the dashboard and accompanying shouting emanating from the car windows and he would watch from behind the curtains, enjoying their frustration.

This vehicle was neither, however. He watched as an old van slowed and pulled up a few hundred yards short of the front gate. As he peered through the grimy glass a thin and scruffy young man slid out of the passenger side and walked back towards the net hidden under the trees. A tall, stocky man got out of the driver's side and stood by the van, watching as his companion clambered under the branches and examined the net. Cursing softly, Samuel realized he had the misfortune to be on site at the same time as the rightful owners of the fish. Though they were actually poaching anyway, he thought. If he could keep out of sight until they left there were not likely to be any consequences. In fact it was probably a good thing. If the pair decided to relocate the net he would be able to see where they went and if they stayed on the same stretch of the canal then his next meal was secured.

The young man peered through the branches and waved to the driver, shouting something and calling him over. The driver reached into his van and took out a net on a pole. As Samuel watched impatiently the two of them disappeared behind the foliage. Finally they re-emerged, hauling the keep-net between them. Inside the net the catch writhed and struggled, flashes of silver and brown visible through the mesh as the fish gasped, drowning in the air.

When they reached the van the man pulled out an ancient blue cool-box and together they emptied the fish into it, clambered into the vehicle and set off down the road, bumping and sliding on the dusty surface. Samuel's mouth watered at the thought of all that lovely food now lost to him. Patience, he thought. At least they hadn't moved the trap so they probably had no idea anyone had found the net. Next time he would take a couple more, he thought. They'd not miss them.

Brian clung to his seat as the van jolted away from the canal bank. The springs on Tom's van were a long way past the recommended replacement date and the seat had lost most of its padding over the years.

'Not so many this time,' he said, the words coming out in jerks. 'Could be that pike we got last time scared 'um off?'

'Mebbe,' said Tom. 'Not like they talk to each other though. No signs up saying "Beware Pike". Think someone's been at the net. Was not in the same place exactly an' I puts this bit of a twig round the ropes when pegging out. You move that when you got there?'

Brian thought for a moment. 'Not sure,' he said. 'Didn't see nothing like that but then didn't know to look for it.'

Tom chuckled to himself. 'Ada'll be glad to hear that,' he said. 'If'n you was wise to the ways of poaching you'd 'a known about it. Ever been out lamping?' he added.

Brian shook his head. 'My dad done a lot of that but that's what landed him in Bristol nick. Mum wouldn't let us near his old shotgun whilst he was gone so I never got no chance. Always fancied it mind.'

'Well now', said Tom. 'Trick with lamping is choosing yer time. Is only poaching if is dark, see. Otherwise they can only do yer for trespass, long as they don't catch you with a deer or summat daft like that. Ada won't admit it but that dog a' hers, Mickey – right good dog fer rabbits an' such. I seen her bag a coney across the fields and Mickey's gone and got it straight off. She 'ent never even set foot on the field. What they gonna do her for then? Discharging a firearm maybe – if they can prove it.' He shook his head in admiration. 'Clever girl is our Ada.'

Brian mulled this over for a moment before returning to the problem of the fish.

'What you gonna do 'bout the trap then?' he asked. 'If someone's stealing from 'um, why not move it?'

'Firstly is in the best place on that bit of river,' said Tom. 'I move it now an' some other bugger'll come along an' put his net there an' I've lost my spot. Second, I'll be keeping an eye on it, next few weeks. Nothing like getting caught red-handed on the wrong end of a shotgun for a deterrent.'

Brian turned to look at Tom. 'You wouldn't *shoot* no-one would you?'

Tom looked at him in surprise. 'Course not. Just scare 'um a bit. 'Ent many would come back a second time after that. Now,' he added as they rejoined the metalled road and turned down towards Ada's house. 'You don't say nothing about this an' I'll see about taking you lamping one evening okay?'

Brian gave a broad grin, revealing his broken front teeth. 'Deal,' he said happily.

Ricky was delighted with his new post and so eager to move into the day centre he took to pestering Alex every time he saw her for course notes, client lists and contact details for the staff she used. He was especially keen to take over the budget and Pauline, in her role as senior administrator, had turfed him out of the office several times when he was caught rummaging through the main files looking for relevant paperwork.

'Unless I'm told otherwise this is still the responsibility of another officer,' she told him when he protested. 'When you take up the post it will all pass over to you and you can check the accounts and inventory if you wish. Until then you might consider getting some of your own files ready to transfer.'

Ricky left with a scowl on his thin, pale face. He loathed paperwork – most of the officers did. Unlike them, however, he rarely did even the bare minimum, relying on his own clerical assistant to fill in the forms using a few sentences dictated onto a portable tape machine.

'I feel sorry for whoever gets his cases next week,' said Alison, drawing a warning frown from Pauline. Whatever her personal opinion, Pauline was always professional in her dealings with everyone in the office and she demanded no less from her staff. 'Does anyone know if Lauren's coming back?' someone asked. There was a pause in the room as the women stopped work for a moment and looked at one another.

'I heard nothing,' said one.

'Nope. Think she's doin' all right but don't know if she *can* come back,' said another.

'Probably won't want to, with him still here,' muttered Alison, who then ducked her head hastily and made a show of setting her typewriter for a court report. Pauline gave the room one of her long, hard stares and work resumed, the sound of keys clicking industriously to counterpoint the shrill sound of the office phone.

'Ah, excellent. I was hoping to catch you,' said Rosalind when Pauline answered. 'Could you come up to my room please?' Replacing the receiver, Pauline left the main office, reluctant to venture upstairs and leave the women unsupervised when there was so much to cram into a single week. People just did not realize how much effort was needed to transfer a single officer from one role to another, let alone shifting everyone round at the same time. There would have

128

to be overtime payments, she decided on the long climb to the top floor. She wasn't having her staff exploited on the whim of the senior.

The room was almost as shocking the second time round but Pauline managed to keep a neutral expression as she entered what she had labelled mentally 'a tart's boudoir'. Rosalind waved her towards the hard chair and returned her attention to a letter on the desk in front of her. Pauline waited, trying not to fidget as the minutes ticked by. Finally, Rosalind looked up and gave a tiny smile. Pauline thought she detected a glint of disappointment in those cold eyes and felt a flicker of satisfaction at her small victory.

'I understand you have one member of your staff off on long-term sick, is that right?' said Rosalind. It was not a question but Pauline nodded anyway.

'Yes, Lauren. One of my most experienced clerical women. She was mentoring the new arrivals – Mr Peddlar this year.' She could not bring herself to refer to him as 'Ricky'. Pauline was firmly of the opinion that Ricky Peddlar had deliberately pushed Lauren to the limit of her physical ability until her frail, small frame had given way. Ricky, in Pauline's eyes, was the worst sort of bully – one who mocked anyone different and picked on those smaller and weaker than himself. Lauren might be two feet shorter than him but she was his superior in every other way and Pauline had longed to hear that Gordon had been confirmed as senior, with the power to deal with him as he deserved.

'Yes,' said Rosalind setting the letter aside. 'We have had a report from her doctor concerning her progress and a request for a medical examination prior to her returning to work.' She gazed out of the window for a few seconds, her fingers drumming on the desk top. Pauline watched the pink-tinted nails, fascinated by the complex patterns they made.

'However,' Rosalind continued, turning back to the letter. 'We are undergoing an inspection soon and there are already serious staffing issues. Sadly this person was unable to cope with a normal workload or the basic requirements of the job.

I do not feel we can offer her a safe working environment at the moment. Don't you agree?'

Pauline felt her pulse race as a wave of anger boiled up inside. She struggled to keep her voice calm as she sought a reply that would not get her dismissed too.

'Lauren has been a highly valued member of my staff for five years,' she said. 'She had been sick for fewer days than almost anyone else until her fall and I suspect any of us could have suffered a similar accident if we had been forced to run up and down three flights of steep stairs for twenty minutes!'

There was silence for a moment and Rosalind resumed drumming her fingers on the desk. As Pauline watched, her face gave a tiny spasm, the rosebud mouth pulling into a pout before setting into a thin, humourless line.

'I certainly hope you don't voice that opinion in public,' said Rosalind. 'It is the sort of unfounded, ill-informed allegation that can lead to serious adverse consequences for the service.'

Fighting the desire to leap to her feet and shout in response, Pauline sat in silence. Only her rigid posture and lifted chin gave any indication of her anger but anyone who knew her even a little better than Rosalind did would have been warned. The two women stared at one another over the desk, neither willing to give in. The impasse was broken by a tap on the door and Debbie slid into the room, hesitating before closing the door behind her.

'I'm sorry to interrupt,' she said. 'Only, the quality team from headquarters is here to discuss the inspection.'

Rosalind nodded and rose from her chair. 'Of course,' she said. 'Perhaps you will give this some thought and we can resume our conversation later in the week. In confidence, of course.'

'Of course,' said Pauline and she left the room, going slowly and carefully down the stairs. She was so angry, her head was buzzing and she experienced a moment's worry over falling the three flights to the entrance hall. 'In confidence,' she muttered as she picked her way downstairs. 'How *dare* she.'

Chapter Nine

It took quite an effort but Alex managed to get Steve enrolled on the workshop programme before she left the day centre for her new post. He seemed eager enough and scarcely bothered to read the agreement form before signing and hurrying over to the pile of bikes at the back of the shop. As Alex left, a grin on her face and the precious signed form clutched firmly in her hand, she heard the supervisor's voice calling Steve back.

'You don't touch nothing 'til I tell you, right? First you need to do your safety day and we got to fit you with boots and an overall. Then you got the practice sessions with the tools before you's allowed to move on to the machines. Be a while before you get a bike so you just knuckle down and you just might learn something.'

Alex was out of range before Steve replied but she was pretty sure it was less than complimentary. Good luck with *that* one Ricky Peddlar, she thought. In her room she continued packing up the books and reference articles amassed over her three years in Highpoint. Some boxes were still unopened from her last enforced move but a lot had been rifled through to find a particular item, the rest of the contents scattered nearby or lodged precariously in a pile on the floor.

'I'm a messy cow,' she said aloud.

'You are indeed,' said Sue from the doorway. 'But you're *our* messy cow and this office is really going to miss you.'

'I agree,' said Alison, following Sue into the office. She was carrying a stack of brown cartons, the sort that folded flat but could be easily assembled, complete with lid.

'Pauline thought these might help. You can do a rough sort out and I'll pack and label for you.'

Alex felt tears burn in her eyes. 'This is so good of you,' she said. 'I thought I'd be here until midnight. I guess I've been putting it off.'

'You'll be back,' said Alison briskly as she began to assemble the first box. 'You're one of the best officers we've had. Headquarters will soon realize what's going on when things start to go downhill.'

Alex and Sue exchanged looks. Alison had never been the most sympathetic member of the clerical staff and in the past she and Alex had argued over any number of things yet here she was, working through her lunch break and offering support both practical and emotional. Alex sneaked a glance at her assistant and recalled Alison's kindness when she had been so ill in her second year.

'Thank you,' she said gruffly before turning her attention to the piles of debris surrounding them. It was a good thing the room was so small, she thought. Experience with a number of bed-sits had shown her that clutter expanded to fill the space available, especially her clutter, yet here she was once more ... When will I learn from history? she thought.

After an hour the room was looking slightly better and there was a pile of cartons, each labelled neatly, outside the door. Alex looked around at what remained. The bookshelves were empty, the desk drawers contained a few paper clips and a discarded biro and the files for transfer were set out on the desk. Furniture for what was basically a half-converted storeroom was minimal – shelves, desk, two chairs and a filing cabinet. So what, exactly, was the wave of debris still filling the tiny space?

'Have you noticed that when you pack up there's always a point where you've got everything in boxes and you're still up to your knees in stuff you know you've never seen in your life?' said Sue cheerfully.

'Umm,' said Alex, surveying the room in dismay. 'I can't leave it like this, even for Ricky.'

'Oh, he's not using this room,' said Alison as she lifted the final box and placed it outside in the narrow corridor. 'He's keeping his office upstairs.'

'The sneaky, snivelling, jammy little bastard!' said Sue.

'Sue!' said Alex.

'Well, he is. He weasels his way into your day centre, sets himself up to take credit for everything you've done and still keeps his nice office – which was yours before you were forced to move into this black hole by Garry. It's just not fair!'

'No,' said Alex sadly. 'It's not fair but then life rarely is. At least I'll be away from the dynamic duo and the worst of the office politics out at the hostel. You've got to deal with all that, the staff in the prisons, half of whom think hanging is too good for shoplifters and all the probation officers you're passing your released prisoners over to when they get out. I couldn't do it. I certainly couldn't do the driving either.'

'Not in your car,' Sue retorted. She cleared a space on the desk and began to sort through a pile of papers from the floor. 'Do you need all these old newspaper cuttings?'

'What about my car?' asked Alex. She was inordinately attached to her aging Citroën even if she did hold her breath and cross her fingers every time she tried to start it.

'Look, there's old and eccentric and there's just plain old,' said Sue, heaving more paper onto the desk. 'You can't carry on without decent transport.'

'I can't afford a new car,' said Alex. 'You know that. And anyway, there's nothing wrong with my car – well, nothing wrong for now anyway.'

'Get a county loan,' said Sue. 'Go on – it's the cheapest way and you don't know how long they'll be available. Grab one now while you can.'

Alex glared at her over the waste paper bin.

'What, before they sack me you mean?'

'No, of course not! Just, everything's changing and county's looking to make savings everywhere. I can't see the cheap loan scheme lasting much longer. Still, suit yourself. I won't be able to drive you if you need a lift though. I'm flying all over the place from next week.'

'Sorry,' said Alex. 'I'm finding this all a bit hard. You're right – about the car I mean. I'll look into it as soon as I'm settled in the hostel.'

The sound of footsteps accompanied by women's voices brought the friends to the doorway. Coming down the corridor was the entire office staff.

'Keys,' said Alison holding out her hand. '*Car* keys, Alex, not house keys.' Each woman lifted a box and set off towards the front door and within five minutes the car was packed.

'Thank you,' Alex called as Pauline whisked them all back to work. Pauline stopped and gave a wave, adding, 'See you before you go,' before disappearing through the door.

Alex had a lump in her throat as she stepped back into her office. Small kindnesses, she thought, surveying the wreckage around her, get you every time.

'Right,' said Sue. 'I'm off too. Got to get my files in to be typed before I go tonight. See you later.'

There was a rustling behind Alex and Bill, the evening janitor, appeared in the doorway.

'Bill? You're early aren't you? I thought you didn't start until about half four.' Alex glanced at her watch, suddenly concerned she had lost an afternoon somewhere. Bill gave a big, easy smile and stepped into the room hauling a broom and several large black sacks behind him.

'Couldn't let you go without sayin' goodbye,' he said. 'Then thought I might as well lend a hand if'n you need it.' He looked around at the mess. 'Looks like you could do with it.'

He set to, sweeping and shovelling around Alex, who always seemed to be in the way. After a few minutes he stopped work and leaned on the broom.

'Why don't you go see them lads out in the day centre?' he said. 'I'll finish up here for yer. Go on.'

'There's no-one in this afternoon,' said Alex. 'All the sessions are finished so there's nothing on until ...'

'Didn't say was a group waiting for you,' said Bert gruffly. 'Some lads with a plant or summat is waiting out there.'

Alex hurried down the corridor, concerned for her pool table. She knew most of the clients found it utterly irresistible and she did not want her last afternoon to be one where Rosalind or Debbie found her lads betting on probation premises. It was suspiciously quiet as she approached the door into what had been her domain for the last year. The pool table was shockingly loud, especially when some of the more flamboyant players were involved so they were not messing about with that. What on earth were they up to, she wondered.

They were standing in a loose semi-circle, a dozen young men and Cider Rosie in the centre of the line clutching a potted geranium and a purple box of chocolates. There was some shuffling and nudging in the group as she appeared before Rosie was pushed forwards.

'We wanted you to have this,' she said in her deep, gravelly voice. 'You done a lot for us and you always b'lieved in us an' all. So – well, thanks.'

Alex took the gifts in a daze, almost dropping the plant as she juggled it and the chocolates. Her eyes filled with tears and suddenly her voice failed completely. Standing in the middle of the room, tears spilling on to her face, she felt the depth of her loss and the bitterness of her betrayal.

'Could maybe have a last game afore we go?' said Charlie from the back of the group. It was only two thirty and the table was only ever used as a reward after a particularly successful or challenging session. Alex walked over to the corner and set the plant and box down gently.

'Well gentleman – and lady, I think I should show you just how well *you* have taught *me* these past few months. Who's first?'

Tom arrived at Ada's early on Sunday morning and opened the back door to his van to reveal Pongo's new companion goat. The young wether was only about half Pongo's size and he was lacking the fearsome-looking horns that curled round the stud goat's head but he had the same strange slit eyes and long ears falling down past his face.

'Come on now,' said Tom, tugging at the rope halter and leading him across the grass towards Ada's gate. Ada stood at the door to the kitchen as Pongo poked his head over the fence and sniffed, rolling his head to one side at the new arrival. Tom walked the new goat over to Pongo's pen and let them sniff one another, smiling as they rubbed noses.

'Gonna be alright,' he said happily. 'They like each other.' He led the little wether to a stake set close to Pongo's pen and tied him up before beckoning Ada over. 'Come an' say hello,' he called.

Ada hurried down the path, gathering a handful of long grass that she offered to the newcomer. He sniffed at her before taking the grass delicately, nibbling at the lush plants with every sign of enjoyment. Behind her Pongo snorted and pushed his head over the fence. Ada laughed and pulled up another handful.

'Here you go then,' she said. 'Right gentle 'ent he?' she said, watching the new goat. 'And lovely soft coat too.' The wether shivered with pleasure and leaned against her hand, giving a gentle squeal of pleasure.

'So what's this one called?' she asked. There was a slight pause and Tom cleared his throat.

'Quentin,' he said finally.

'Quentin? *Quentin?* What sort of a name is that?' demanded Ada.

'Well see, he names 'um through the alphabet,' said Tom. 'Pongo – he was an "M" an' rightly called Marmaduke.' Ada snorted in disgust and he hurried on. 'So he's got to "Q". Called the girls Quince and Queenie but was coming up a bit short for the boys. Most of 'em going for meat anyway and his wife says they should just call 'em "Curry", "Mince" and "Chops", to stop the kids getting too fond of 'em but this one needed a proper name. Was his daughter called him Quentin for a writer she likes. Seen it on the book cover ...'

'Don't care if is named for foreign royalty,' said Ada. 'I 'ent standing at the gate and calling "Quentin", so you just think of something else.' She swept back into the kitchen to check on the progress of lunch, leaving Tom grinning foolishly at her retreating form.

'She's alright,' he murmured as he stroked the goat's soft ears. 'Bark's wors'n her bite. Though the bark can be fearsome. You wait here and I'll be back soon an' put you 'n Pongo together for a bit.'

The kitchen was cool after the heat of the summer sun and Tom sat away from the wood-fired range in the corner. Ada put the finishing touches to a salad composed of home-grown vegetables and a fair amount of wild gleanings, plonking it on the table in front of him next to a crusty, lumpy loaf of bread.

'Just got a bit of cold chicken to go with,' she said, reaching into a camping cooler. 'Got to eat it up afore it goes off in this heat.'

Tom sliced the bread which was still slightly warm and sniffed the rich, yeasty smell.

'Perfect for this weather,' he said. 'You given any thought to getting a fridge? Could afford one now you know.'

Ada had been astonished to receive a cheque as compensation for her husband, who had been murdered on the Levels several years ago whilst staying in her old cottage. She had opened a post office account with the money but so far had resisted any suggestion to actually spend any of it.

'Don't know about that,' she said. 'Don't seem right somehow. Blood money ...' She stared into the distance for a moment.

'Would be nice though,' said Tom, concentrating on his plate. 'Specially in summer. Not having to worry 'bout stuff spoiling.'

Ada sat down opposite him and began to dissect a chicken thigh.

'Quinn,' she said and popped the forkful of meat in her mouth.

'What's that?' asked Tom, startled and slightly alarmed.

'Quinn,' repeated Ada. 'That's what we call the new goat. Still a "Q" but less of a shamer.' She nodded in a pleased manner and turned her attention back to her lunch.

'If'n you say so, Ada,' said Tom. 'Quinn it is then. I'll get him settled in with Pongo for a few days afore we try taking 'em out. Might be an idea to have young Brian pop by and sit with 'em for a few hours, first off. He got his bike now, I see.'

'Had a word with Alex Hastings 'bout that, last week. She's moving over to that hostel place this week an' a young fella's taking over her centre. Crying shame that, seeing all the good she done for the lads round here. Still, she had a talk to Brian and he got a bike, provisional like. Should have done the rest of his hours in the workshop first and took some test too, but I got the feeling she didn't think Brian'd get a fair crack at it with this other fella.'

'Good of her,' said Tom. 'Not many would take a chance on young Brian.'

'You did,' said Ada.

'So did you,' Tom replied, setting his fork down on the edge of the plate. He reached out tentatively and touched her hand. For a moment he thought she was going to pull away but then her face relaxed into a smile and he felt her fingers curl around his. They sat for a moment in companionable silence and Tom felt his heartbeat quicken. Perhaps this was the moment, he thought. Just as he took a deep breath there was a loud crash as the side gate flew open followed by the metallic screech of a bike sliding down the cottage wall.

'Girt magic!' came the voice of their protégé as he spotted Quinn standing patiently next to Pongo's enclosure.

'In here, Brian,' called Ada, rising from the table. A wave comprising equal amounts of disappointment and relief swept over Tom. Damn the boy! Despite his annoyance he managed a civil nod when Brian burst through the door, full of enthusiasm and questions. Together the three of them sat round the table, eating lunch and talking until Tom's disappointment faded away and he could lean back in his chair, watching those he now considered family.

Alex's arrival at the hostel was greeted with relief by Bennie, apprehension by many of the residents and a deep, quiet satisfaction by Samuel. It was a sign, he thought. Not only would there be some changes in the hostel routine and rules but he had Alex where he could see her, watch her, even get up close to her on a daily basis. The morning she began work he was downstairs in the breakfast room, plain toast and a glass of water on the table before him, waiting for her arrival. He chose a place away from the others but one that offered a clear view of the front hallway and the door leading into the office. As he waited he nibbled at the toast, taking as long as possible over the frugal meal. As he watched his eyes shone a bright, hard blue.

Alex really didn't know what to expect of the hostel. There had been little notice of the move and no time to visit and get to know what the role entailed. That first Monday morning she walked in blind carrying her battered old satchel, a packed lunch and all the optimism she could muster. The dining room fell quiet as the residents heard the front door open and several of them leaned over in their chairs to catch a glimpse of the new warden. Alex was familiar to some of them but many of the residents had other probation officers and knew of her only by reputation.

Bennie was sitting at the desk when Alex pushed open the office door and she jumped to her feet, stepping round to greet her new boss.

'God, you have no idea how happy I am to see you,' she said. 'Here, sit down – that's your desk now. Can I get you some tea?'

Alex nodded and managed a smile as she slid behind the desk. After a year in her cramped little basement room the office seemed almost luxurious – two desks with comfortable chairs, a rug on the floor, plenty of shelf space and, best of all, windows on two sides that opened to let in the warm summer air. Bennie returned carrying a beaker that she set down on the desk.

'I'm sorry,' she said. 'The kettle's broken in the kitchen. I meant to replace it yesterday but I completely forgot so we're making do with tea from the urn this morning. I'll go into town and get a new one this afternoon if you like.'

It was a novelty for Alex to be in charge of anything and she hesitated for a moment.

'Yes, of course,' she said and took a large mouthful of tea. 'Oh my God!' she said spitting half of it back into the mug. 'Sorry – I just wasn't expecting ...' She peered at the grey liquid in her cup, swallowing to clear the taste from her mouth. 'This came from ...?'

Bennie looked sheepish. 'The urn in the dining room,' she said.

'So this is what we give our residents to drink?'

Bennie nodded. 'It's the steri' milk I think. But anything else goes off and costs more anyway.'

'There's sugar in this – what about anyone who doesn't take sugar?' asked Alex, pushing the offending drink as far across the desk as she could.

'I think they all do,' said Bennie.

'Well, they certainly do at the moment,' said Alex. 'Right, as soon as the dining room is cleared we're moving the urn out into the kitchen. Where is the petty cash?'

Bennie pointed to the metal cabinet beside Alex's desk. Alex pulled at the top drawer but it was locked.

'Er, sorry – keys are in the desk,' said Bennie.

'How secure is that, if the keys are in an unlocked drawer?'

demanded Alex pulling them out and hunting through to find the right one for the cabinet.

The petty cash tin was almost empty apart from a sheaf of slips covering minor expenses.

'Okay – how do I get more?' Alex asked. Bennie pulled a cheque book out of the second drawer and handed it over.

'I can't sign for it so it's been running down since Peter left,' she explained.

Alex paused, considering her options. What were the chances anyone at headquarters – or even the Highpoint office – had thought to arrange a transfer of the budget? She lifted up the phone and dialled the probation office and breathed silent thanks when Pauline answered. The ever-efficient senior administrator grasped the problem immediately and promised to contact the bank in town to make arrangements for Alex to go in and sign for the account.

'I'll call you back as soon as I've set it up,' she said. 'Do you need a float from us for today?'

Alex was tempted but she didn't want to go through the main office unless it was absolutely necessary. Despite the fact she'd arrived without any proper transfer from head-quarters it would still be seen as poor organization on her part. Alex was not happy about being dumped in the hostel but she was determined to do a decent job there.

'I'll manage, thanks,' she said, replacing the phone. Hunting through her pockets she managed to dig out the princely sum of three pounds which she added to the tin, carefully noting the loan in the petty cash book.

'Change of plan,' she said. 'Who have we got in the kitchen today?'

'Only Hazel, the cleaner,' said Bennie. 'She makes lunch on the days there are classes or if we've got any lads in doing work for us. I don't think there's anyone in today though.'

Alex rose from the desk and marched towards the office door.

'Time to call for volunteers, then' she said.

Samuel had been tempted, very tempted, by the chance to work next to Alex but he had long resolved never to volunteer for anything and, besides, looking at the other scruffy little toe rags who offered to help out in the morning in exchange for a meal at lunch time, he didn't think he wanted to be considered in the same group as them. Once the meal was over he quietly cleared his plate and glass, collected his small back pack and signed out of the hostel, setting off on his familiar run down by the canal and across the Levels.

As he strode over the dried edges of the marshlands he pondered on his feelings for Alex. It was not that he found her attractive. She was too old for a start. Just outside his preferred age range and a bit too – not masculine exactly but she didn't make any effort to appear attractive. Her hair was short and already showing some grey streaks at the sides, her fingernails were clipped and free of varnish and her dress sense bordered on the abominable.

Yet she fascinated him. She was clever, certainly. Astute, principled and very strong-willed, she was the opposite to most of the women he had known in his life. He wanted to talk to her, to probe that keen mind and share ideas with her. He wanted her to be a partner in his life, to see him not as a criminal or a danger but as someone just as principled as she. They both despised fools, he thought. They just had different ways of dealing with them.

Steve also declined the chance to stay inside and get a free lunch. He was quite capable of getting his own free lunch and without being under the eye of his probation officer, so he scurried through the front door and set off into town to see what might be available. A lot of the smaller shops were closed up he noticed. A few larger stores were trading but they tended to have decent security. Steve preferred easier pickings, especially as he was now on his final chance with the magistrates. Getting nicked for shoplifting so soon after starting his probation order was a quick road to the Young Offenders unit.

His face was familiar to the few stall-holders set up in the little market and he hurried past, hands in his pockets, wearing a fine air of indifference. Time to branch out a bit, he thought. He had a new lighter in his pocket but needed more fluid as well as something to eat. He wouldn't mind some ciggies either but all the tobacco and stuff was kept behind a counter nowadays. It was next to impossible, luring a shopkeeper off the till on your own. Once more he was missing his little stooges, especially Petey who was back in the hostel and not much the worse for his sunstroke.

Charlie has always been a bit of a soft lad, though he would have been useful as a diversion, or even a patsy if things went wrong, but Charlie was a new man. Full of big ideas and eager to change his life around, Charlie had even begun to influence Petey, who been the first to volunteer for a day in the hostel kitchens. Steve snorted in derision as he walked out of the town centre and headed towards the Burnham road.

Off to one side was the local college, a sprawling collection of buildings with a ring of portable classrooms round the perimeter. A steady stream of students flowed through the main gate and Steve decided to try his luck, slipping in through the wide-open doors and mixing with the flow of young people that milled around in a seemingly aimless fashion. The trick, he knew, was to look as if you belonged. Everyone else knew where they were going with a lot of them heading to exams from the sound of the anxious chatter around him. That meant the corridors would empty soon, leaving a lone figure looking very out of place and Steve had no idea of the layout.

On a whim he turned to the right, attracted by the sounds of a canteen and his instinct proved correct when he passed the entrance to a good-sized dining hall. Fishing in his pocket he dug out a few coins, enough for a cup of tea served in a heavy white beaker. Taking his drink Steve positioned himself near the main door at a table that offered a clear view of the room. Students were so careless, he thought. They dumped their bags all over the place, spilling items on the floor or scattering their possessions across tables. Most of the stuff was junk – books and folders with pencil cases jumbled in but a few had a Walkman sticking out of the side pockets of their bags. He could even see a couple of purses clearly visible and unattended.

There were a decent number of people milling around, enough to cover his movements, and Steve picked out his target. A couple of girls sat at a table deep in discussions over something boring – they were poring over a textbook so Steve assumed they were doing some last minute revision. Their bags were thrown down on an adjoining table, open to display two purses, a Walkman and a rather nice looking pen with what looked like a gold clip. Steve rose from his post and strolled over towards the toilets, brushing past the table and lifting a purse and the tape player without breaking stride. At the last minute he turned and headed for the main door, annoyed at missing the pen and one of the purses. He was beginning to lose his touch.

Lost in thought he didn't notice the figure stepping into his path until they collided heavily. Steve instinctively put his head down to hide his face and stepped to one side but a hand grasped his wrist and held him fast.

'Put it back,' hissed Charlie in his ear.

Steve looked up, blinking in astonishment.

'Wot you doin' here?' he demanded, too surprised to deny his actions.

'Joined a course last week,' said Charlie softly. 'Not that is any business of your'n. Now, you go over there an' you smile and tell 'em you found these on the floor.'

'Or what?' Steve sneered.

'Or I'll call the staff an' they'll call the police an' you'll be back in the nick where you belongs. Now – you goin' over there?'

Steve gritted his teeth and tried to pull away but Charlie had too firm a hold. Defeated and burning with humiliation he shrugged his shoulders.

'Can't while you got hold of me, can I?'

Charlie loosened his grip and stepped back, positioning himself between Steve and the exit. He watched as Steve sauntered across the room, handed the items over and accepted the effusive thanks of the two young women. Steve kept a pleased smile on his face until he turned away from them and headed back towards the door. As he passed Charlie on the way out he stuck out an arm, catching the young man in the ribs and knocking him backwards.

'You'd better stay away from me, you little grass,' he muttered as he headed for the exit. Angry and frustrated, Steve set off down the road, his head humming with fury. Someone was going to pay for Charlie's actions and he didn't much care who or what it was.

Chapter Ten

For the first time in his life Brian walked into an exam room and actually cared about the outcome. In fairness, it was almost the first time he'd walked into an exam room, for his attendance at both primary and secondary school had been sporadic to put it politely. Tom got him up early on the Monday morning, made him some breakfast, persuaded him to actually eat it and shoved him into the front of his old green van for the journey off the Levels and out to the agricultural college near Cannington. On arrival, Tom accompanied him to the main office where he signed in and registered for the entrance test, then pressed two biros, a pencil and a small packet of boiled sweets into his hands.

'Go on, lad,' he said before Brian began the long trek down the cloistered walkway to the main hall. 'Just keep calm an' you'll do fine. You know this all now – just got to show 'em you does.'

Brian trailed after the chirpy little office girl looking like a man off to his own hanging. Tom stood in the doorway watching until he disappeared round the corner, then gave a great sigh.

'Grandson is he?' asked the woman at the reception desk. 'Don't worry, we'll take care of him.' She smiled and Tom, who had been ready to correct her, just smiled back and nodded.

'Pop back about three,' she said. 'We give them lunch after the written papers and then they have a chance to look around and meet the tutors. And some of the livestock of course.'

Tom nodded again, angry with himself for not checking how long the process would be. He might have abandoned Brian with no lunch and no money to buy something. Some Grandad I am, he thought. Need to do a lot better if I'm going to be any help. He climbed behind the wheel of his van, pausing to admire the green Land Rovers lined up in the yard. He'd always fancied one of those but never had the money to get one. Now he'd struggle to run it, what with fuel going up in price every week and most other costs through the roof.

On his way back he cut through town to pick up some sausages. Ada did wonders in the kitchen and could go out into the fields, returning after a couple of hours with the most unlikely ingredients for an appetizing meal, but just occasionally Tom hankered for something shop-bought. Sausages were a rare treat – one of the things Ada couldn't source through her gleaning – and he thought how much Brian would enjoy them after his day at the college.

Driving towards Burnham, Tom wound down the window and felt the warm summer air flow through the vehicle. Turning off onto a smaller road he began the twisting journey out to Ada's cottage but spotting a side road decided to pay a visit to his net. There had been no evidence of tampering the last couple of times he'd been out but the catch was definitely down on earlier in the year.

Humming softly to himself, he was almost driving automatically when he caught a whiff of something unexpected. Slamming on the brakes, Tom turned off the engine and leaned out of the open window, sniffing the breeze. For a moment he thought he was mistaken but then he caught it again, stronger this time. Somewhere close by something was burning.

By the time Steve reached the first narrow paths that wound across the Levels away from the main road he was hot, tired and still furious. Having spent the last of his change on a beaker of tea at the college he had nothing left for the bus fare, even if the bastard of a driver had been willing to stop for him. Despite his optimistic waving, the battered leviathan that was Simons' bus swept past him and rolled round the next bend leaving him coughing in a cloud of fine dust. No chance of a lift then, he thought as he brushed at his clothes. Miserable old bugger.

Steve took a shortcut across the fields, ignoring the red warning signs scattered around the flat, uneven landscape. Some warned of soft ground now baked hard in the emerging heat wave, some simply demanded he keep off. All were treated with contempt until he jumped a narrow stream, tripped and landed in a thick clump of blackberries. Cursing and wriggling about as he tried to get to his feet, he felt something move across one hand and saw the shape of a snake sliding smoothly over his arm.

Steve gave a yell, jerked his hand away and tried to get up, limbs flailing in panic. In front of him the reptile turned its body to face him, its mouth slightly open and its tongue flicking rapidly back and forth. Suddenly it struck at him and Steve slid backwards into the water of the stream, escaping the snake by a fraction of an inch. As he slid over in the mud he felt a second strike on his leg and then the horrible thing was gone. Shaking with fear Steve crouched in the ditch fighting a terrible urge to wet himself.

Finally, he summoned the courage to edge further downstream where he was able to clamber onto the dry grass in safety. He was wet, muddy and extremely frightened, his loathing for this alien landscape roiling in his stomach. Keeping a wary eye on the immediate vicinity, Steve tugged at his sodden jeans, probing the area where the snake had made contact. After a few frantic minutes he realized the skin was unbroken and he relaxed slightly. Despite Petey's assurances, he was deadly afraid of adders and had a vision of his body stretched out on the bank of the stream, frozen in agony as the snakes slid over him. Slowly his fear subsided to be replaced by anger – at the Levels, the regime that kept him in this place and the reptiles that seemed to think they could taunt and menace him.

After a couple of tries the lighter flared and sputtered but then burned with a steady flame. Steve grunted in satisfaction, turned it off and shoved it back in his pocket before turning his attention to the grass and leaves scattered along the bank. Working carefully to avoid disturbing any more snakes he gathered a pile of dried vegetation, arranging it carefully upwind of the brambles. Grass dried to straw at the bottom, papery leaves next and then some small twigs across the top to build the heat – that was the way to get it going properly. He edged some grass and leaves as close to the bushes as he dared, hoping to lead the fire to the nest and any more of the hated snakes.

Finally, it was ready and Steve flicked the lighter on again, touching the flame to three sides of his kindling. For a moment there was only a disappointing trickle of smoke and his heart sank. It was much more difficult without an accelerant and the lighter did not generate enough heat to get the fire going properly. Then he saw a faint glow off to one side and the smoke thickened around it. Steve leaned over, blowing gently on the tiny flames and almost lost his eyebrows as the fire took hold and exploded upwards with a faint whooshing sound. Steve jerked his body backwards and retreated a few feet, then crouched down fascinated as the fire grew, creeping towards the brambles. That was what they deserved, he thought with satisfaction. Filthy, evil things.

He was jerked out of his happy thoughts by a shout in the distance and looking up saw a man running across the meadow towards him. Time to go then. Clutching his precious lighter he hared off in the opposite direction, pausing at the edge of the stream to get one last look at his fire. As expected, the man had stopped by the bushes and was trying to extinguish the flames. Maybe he'd get bitten, thought Steve. Serve him right, interfering old sod. He hopped over the stream and headed back towards the road. It was nearly lunch time and he was hungry. Time to see if he could pick up something in town.

Tom saw the smoke rising a few fields off and leaped from his van, heading towards the fire as fast as he could. Getting too old for all this, he thought, as he stumbled over the rough ground. Couldn't leave it though, not in this weather. It had been a glorious start to the summer without a drop of rain and the Levels were bone dry. A fire could spread in minutes if not caught and there was always the danger to animals and the isolated properties dotted across the land, not to mention the fields of wheat and barley tucked in between the water meadows. A fire sweeping through those could ruin a farmer, especially with times so hard and prices as low as they were.

As he ran he saw a figure rise from the far side of the fire and hurry away, stopping to glance back before disappearing over the stream. He waved and tried to call for them to stop but the smoke got into his throat and all he could produce was a series of coughs. Some grockle with a cigarette end maybe, he thought. Typical stupid behaviour. Couldn't blame them for running off though. A fire on open ground was a frightening thing and the penalties for causing one were hefty.

Tom turned his full attention to the fire, stamping around the centre and trying to prevent its spread. Once it was contained in a stand of brambles he scooped water from the stream to soak the bushes using his hands. When this made little impact he cursed softly and removed one boot, filling it and throwing water as fast as he could on the hot centre of the blaze. There was a lot of hissing as the water doused the flames and the wet stems began to smoulder rather than burn. A pillar of thick smoke rose into the clear blue sky, drifting with the light breeze and causing Tom's eyes to water as he stuck to his task, baling out the little stream until the fire was doused completely. Only then did he straighten up, groaning loudly as his back and hips protested at the exercise. Definitely getting too old for this, Tom thought, as he struggled to pull his sodden boot back on.

Curious as to what might have started the fire, he pulled a half-burnt branch from the bramble bush and poked through the wreckage. There was no sign of a bottle – often the cause of wild fires in the summer – and neither could he spot any evidence of a carelessly discarded cigarette though it was possible the butt had burned up in the flames. Interestingly, there seemed to be signs it had started a bit away from the brambles and he moved round the charred mess to get a better look. It was then he spotted the remains of a snake, twisted and blackened, almost buried in the roots of the bush.

Gently, Tom rolled the little body out into the open, uncovering two other much smaller snakes curled up under the adult. They were both dead, the young sheltered by a parent in an effort to save them from the heat that had engulfed their nest. Tom was no fan of adders but from the size of the adult he suspected these had been harmless grass snakes – and even adders deserved better than to be burned alive.

He looked again at the charred grass leading to the bush and twisted his mouth to one side thoughtfully. It was inconceivable someone would set a fire deliberately, especially in this weather. But he had seen a figure run from the scene and it certainly looked as if the fire had been coaxed towards the bushes where the grass snakes were nesting. It was not a pleasant thought and he walked slowly back to his van hoping it was all just coincidence.

He became aware of a deep throbbing pain along one arm and when he touched it he yelped at the sudden surge through to his hand. Fingering the area he realized he must have caught it in the fire. Now he would have to tell Ada, he thought. Still, she would be able to treat the burn better than any doctor. Magic herb garden had Ada. Moving carefully to avoid bumping the raw patch along his arm, Tom put the van into gear and drove back onto the road. He hoped she'd be able to patch him up quickly. Brian would need to be collected from the college at three and there was no way Ada could drive him.

Samuel returned to the hostel that evening feeling a strong sense of personal satisfaction. The net in the river had been full and he had liberated half a dozen small fish for his lunch using the long handled net from the cottage to transport them along the road to his cottage. Well fed and relaxed, he had turned his attention to the upstairs room, which was still filthy. He didn't think he would ever want to use it for sleeping but the thought of all that dirt above him was sickening.

Last week he had found a large plastic barrel lodged near the canal bank by the big sluice gate and after scrubbing and rinsing it several times had set it up under the downspout beside the back door to act as a water butt. A somewhat optimistic waste of a day, he thought as he peered into the empty barrel. Not a drop of rain had fallen for almost a month. Rummaging through the sagging cupboard by the sink he located a bucket and used it to carry water from the canal to the stove, where an old tin bath sat, balanced precariously on the narrow top. Samuel didn't mind the cold but hot water cleaned much more efficiently.

Several hours later the top room was cleared of debris and the worst of the dirt washed away, poured out a distance from the cottage onto the river bank. It was still far too dirty to use but Samuel was tired and the ingrained dirt would have to wait for another day. He stood on the back step, examining his arms, which were grey and streaked with soot and cobwebs. His fingers were wrinkled from immersion in water for so long and the nails were black around the edges. Disgusted by his own appearance, Samuel bent over the canal, washing the worst of the dirt away before having a final wash in the kitchen, using the last of the hot water.

He checked his reflection in the shard of mirror lodged over the sink and gave his face one last rinse before tidying up and preparing to leave. His clothes were wet but they would dry quickly enough on the journey home. As he jogged along the tow path to the hostel he decided to fetch some soap with him next time. There was a bar in the middle bathroom that was hardly used and could be easily appropriated.

His progress across the hall to the stairs was checked by the sounds of happy voices chattering in the dining room. Curious to see what might have brightened their drab little lives he looked in and was astonished to see several small groups of residents sitting at the tables drinking tea with every evidence of enjoyment. Even more surprising, Alex Hastings was seated at the end of one table, near the urn, talking to Charlie and laughing at something he said.

She glanced up and for a moment their eyes met, then she gave him a nod of acknowledgement before turning her attention back to the conversation. Samuel stepped into the room and made his way over to the tea table. The urn was gleaming, he noticed. All the old crud and greasy splashes had been washed away and even the tap looked clean. Picking up a beaker he turned it over and peered inside, catching the faintest whiff of bleach as he did. The whole area had been cleaned, scrubbed, disinfected – if the place served something decent he might actually consider using it now.

Alex rose from the table and stepped over to the urn.

'Would you like a tea or coffee, Samuel?' she asked.

Samuel blinked at her. The hostel did not serve coffee, though on the evidence of the past few months they didn't really serve tea either.

'Coffee?' he said.

Alex took the cup from his hands, reached round the back of the table beside the urn and lifted the lid to a large drum of instant coffee. Taking a spoon from a glass container – clean, he noted – she put a measure into the beaker and held it under the tap. Boiling hot water poured out and the heady aroma of his drink filled the space between them.

'Here you go,' she said. 'Milk in the jug – there's more in the fridge if you need it – and sugar on the tables.'

Samuel moved away from the rest of the group, taking a seat across from the door. He took a cautious sip of his drink. Not bad, he thought. Not as good as the coffee she had sent across to the workshop but many times better than the swill usually dished up in the hostel. The front door opened and Pauline walked into the room clutching a large brown envelope.

'I thought you'd need this tomorrow morning,' she said to Alex. 'That's a letter for the bank and the cash-and-carry account details. I'm working on the other details but this should keep you going for a bit.' She looked around the dining room, her eyes sliding over Samuel and then turning back. He met her gaze for a moment before dropping his head and sipping at the coffee. Pauline watched him for a few moments before returning her attention to Alex.

'You could have given them to Sue,' said Alex. 'You didn't have to come round – but thank you.'

'Sue's been out all day,' said Pauline. 'I wanted to make sure everything was alright with you.'

Alex smiled and took the envelope. 'I forgot,' she said. 'Sue's started her new job today. Would you like a tea or something?'

Pauline hesitated and Petey, who was standing at the end of the table, said, 'Is proper tea. Can make it yerself an' have decent milk too.'

Pauline raised her eyebrows at Alex, turning to look at the tea table.

'Do you think that's wise?' she asked.

'Wait and see,' said Alex. 'Now gentlemen,' she continued, raising her voice above the hubbub of conversation. 'It will soon be dinner time. Can you all clear your cups and wipe up any spills please. Who is on table duty today?'

A couple of young men raised their hands. 'An' Charlie too,' said one. 'He 'ent here though.'

'He may have been delayed at the college,' said Alex. 'I'll

have a word with him when he gets in. Now, everyone out please.' She gathered up the envelope and headed to the office to sign a receipt for the documents.

As they returned their beakers to the table most of the residents took the opportunity to grab a fistful of tea bags from the tray, sloping off to their rooms to hide the bounty against the return of the dreaded urn tea. Samuel moved smoothly over to the table and laid a hand on the shoulder of one lad who was lifting the coffee drum.

'Don't,' he said softly.

The young man dropped it and stepped away, a look of alarm on his face. The rest of the residents scattered, leaving Samuel alone apart from the two table-setters who were working at the other end of the room and trying to ignore him.

'I hope this will all still be here later,' said Samuel to no-one in particular. He left the room to the sound of cutlery being placed rather forcefully on the tables.

In the office Pauline was shaking her head over Alex's tea table.

'They'll just steal it all,' she said. 'There's not much of the budget left for this year – who knows what it's gone on but the food budget is already overstretched. You can't afford to let it disappear in boxes of tea bags.'

'Wait and see,' said Alex again. 'Once they realize it will always be there they'll stop hiding stuff away in their rooms. And if I'm wrong then I'll pay for whatever they take.'

Pauline left the hostel still unconvinced but she knew Alex too well to argue. Stubborn, idealistic and sometimes downright bloody minded she might be, but Alex still seemed to get the best out of her charges. As she drove home she remembered Samuel, the way he had sat staring at Alex like a cat watching a bird on the lawn. A shiver ran up her spine and she made a mental note to warn Alex of his interest. Samuel was not someone you wanted to notice you.

Ada had carried on something terrible when Tom walked through the gate, his jacket charred and reeking of smoke.

'What you want to take risks like that for?' she chided as she peeled the sleeve off his arm and examined the burn beneath.

'Is getting tinder dry out there,' he said calmly. 'Don't know how far it could spread. Best way is to catch it early an' put it out. Was never that dangerous … ooh,' he finished, as she succeeded in freeing his arm from the jacket.

'That's for the bin,' she said, throwing the garment out of the kitchen door. 'Now, hold still whilst I get a good look.'

Tom bit his lower lip and let her bathe the burn with cold water. Then Ada reached over to her kitchen windowsill and snapped the fleshy leaves from a spiky plant growing there. Slicing them open with her fingernail she applied the sap to the injury, plastering the leaves over the worst affected places.

'Now wait whilst I get a bandage for that,' she said.

Already the arm felt better, a cooling numbness spreading through the pain and Tom closed his eyes and gave a sign of relief.

'Thank you,' he said softly. 'Don't know what I'd do without you.'

'Just don't be doing no more stupid heroics,' said Ada as she wrapped the arm firmly, keeping the leaves in place.

'Would 'a burned you as a witch, couple of hundred years ago,' said Tom, flexing his hand cautiously.

Ada gave a snort of disgust. 'Is only Aloe,' she said. 'Mexican plant and used in loads of kitchens fer burns. Takes all the sting out and helps it heal a treat. So long as you don't get it wet or fiddle with that,' she added, slapping his hand away from the bandage. 'Now be off and get young Brian. I've got to think of summat nice for his tea.'

'I forgot,' said Tom. 'All this excitement – hang on.' He hurried out to his van and returned with the sausages.

'Well, just this once I reckon he'll enjoy 'em,' said Ada. 'How d'you think he's done then?'

'Can't tell,' said Tom thoughtfully. 'Some days he's brilliant – seems to know everything I ask and others he's just plain dumb. Hoping he's had a good day today.'

Charlie arrived back at the hostel just in time for the evening meal. Alex had managed to find him a place on an experimental programme, labelled 'The Initial Training Initiative', which was designed to support young people who had already failed or been excluded from at least three other schemes. Run by a determined and seemingly unflappable woman called Mary, it had been remarkable successful in placing these misfits in more traditional places after their twelve weeks at the college.

'It's a bit like the YTS version of the "short, sharp shock",' she had said when Alex met her one evening. 'I get them in here in a small group – we never take more than ten at a time. They all try everything the college has to offer. Boys do cookery and girls do bricklaying. They can try motor mechanics, art, sewing – whatever they are curious about. There's a crash course in interview techniques and they all have an assessment with the educational psychologist as well as trying out the aptitude machines.' She waved her arm at a range of black and green boxes sited around the large portable classroom.

Alex walked over to examine one. It looked like a basic version of a fairground game with handles at one end and a maze to run a ball around.

'Yeah, that one's quite popular,' said Mary. 'I have to stop them playing on it until they've been assessed, otherwise they all get really high scores. Look,' she unlocked a box at the side and took out the ball. 'You begin here and navigate around the holes until you get to the end. It's timed and gives a measure of manual skill against speed as well as testing fine reflexes. Here,' she said, deftly fielding the ball and putting it in the starting position. 'Have a go.'

Alex began nervously and became increasingly flustered as time and again the ball refused to follow the maze, veering off into dead ends and disappearing down holes. After several tries her hands were sliding on the handles and she admitted defeat. Mary locked the ball away and gestured to a table where they sat facing one another.

'Don't think me rude,' said Mary. 'I was just wondering, have you ever been tested for dyspraxia?'

'No,' said Alex, adding 'Well, not really.' She had in fact begun an assessment with a friend at university, part of a research study for their dissertation. Alex had left part-way through, too demoralized by her performance to continue.

'All the psych students ran their experiments on each other,' she said, trying to explain away her reluctance to pursue the subject. 'I've probably done most of these or something like them over the years.'

'They didn't mention you were a psychologist,' said Mary. 'That must be useful in your line of work.'

'I'm not,' said Alex. 'I left uni before finishing my degree and when I went back a few years later I changed to philosophy.'

'Ah,' said Mary. It was obvious Alex did not want to talk about it so she changed the subject. 'This young man of yours, is there anything we should know about him? Apart from his inability to finish anything he's started, of course.'

'I think he is ready now,' said Alex. 'He's had a bit of a wake-up call recently and he's doing much better at the hostel. He's got no record for anything violent so I don't imagine he'll be any different from the rest of the group. I'm at the hostel from next Monday week and I'll keep an eye on him there and if you have any problems you can just call me.'

'I will need to meet him before we can offer him a place,' said Mary. 'Can someone bring him along, say on Wednesday? We start next week and I do have a couple of spaces left.'

Charlie had proved to be ridiculously grateful for the chance and despite his natural reticence made a good impression on Mary.

'Obviously we will need to keep a close eye on him,' she said, when phoning Alex with the good news. 'I had a bit of a tussle getting my management to accept a lad from the hostel, but I don't see why he shouldn't have the same opportunities as everyone else.'

Not just my lot then, thought Alex. The term 'management' seems to be taking on a whole range of new meanings nowadays, none of them particularly complimentary. She found the idea strangely comforting.

Alex stayed late at the hostel on Monday evening, waiting to speak to all the residents before she finally clambered into her car and drove home. The light was on in the front room and she pushed the door open expecting to find Sue collapsed in one of the armchairs. Instead she was greeted by the tantalizing smell of food cooking. Cooking, not burning, so it wasn't Sue in the kitchen. Her heart seemed to skip a beat and she dropped her briefcase and hurried out to the kitchen where Margie was sampling the contents of a large pan.

'Thought you'd like something cooked for you, this bein' your first day,' said Margie. She dropped the spoon hastily as Alex wrapped her in a hug.

'Give over now,' she said, but her smile softened the words. 'Is not much anyway. Getting to the end of the month so spaghetti's about all we can run to.'

'Spaghetti sounds perfect,' said Alex. She picked up the spoon but Margie grabbed it and threw it in the sink.

'You just wait,' she said. 'Is not ready yet. Be another twenty minutes or so. Can't rush a good sauce, you know. Now, fancy some salad with that?'

'Sounds perfect,' said Alex. 'It's a lovely evening. I could set up the picnic table and we could eat out the back.'

Margie grinned, nodding as she turned her attention back to the stove. In the tiny garden, Alex stood in the evening sun, stretching her arms above her head and allowing the warmth to sooth the ache in her shoulders and neck. The birds stopped their squabbling at the bird table for an instant, watching to see if she was coming any closer but decided she was neither a threat nor the source of more food and resumed their meal. Alex smiled, more relaxed than she had thought she would be after such a long and anxious day. The hostel was a challenge but she was in charge and the staff were inclined to listen to her and at least give her a chance. It was like having a fresh start after all the setbacks and obstacles of the past year. Maybe it wouldn't be so bad after all.

Chapter Eleven

Tuesday was now workshop day for Samuel and he woke to find he was reluctant to go. Recent Tuesdays had seen him leap out of bed, eager for a day that challenged him mentally as the design for the raft began to take shape. The supervisor treated him with respect, talking to him as an equal and offering encouragement and a measure of acceptance with which Samuel was unfamiliar. He found it easy to ignore the plebs making up the bulk of the group and they left him alone, wary of his physique and the elevated position he occupied within the hierarchy.

But now Tuesdays were different somehow. He lay under the cover and stared at the ceiling, trying to recapture that elusive spark of interest in the raft and the upcoming race. But in truth he didn't give a damn. The work had been interesting but not all-consuming and Samuel's interests lay elsewhere. The attraction of the workshop was its proximity to the probation offices, and particularly the proximity to Alex Hastings. Now she was no longer running the day centre and its various activities, Samuel had no motive to attend.

The fact she was now based in the hostel made his enforced absence even worse.

He was tempted to go into the dining room again and wait for her arrival over some toast but he remembered Pauline staring at him last week. He had not bothered with hostel meals up to now and it was never a good idea to suddenly change routines. That would attract more attention, maybe questions, and Samuel functioned best in the shadows where he was hidden, underestimated and dismissed.

Not a good idea to claim he was sick either, though he remembered the last time he'd been ill. Alex had come to his room and brought something to eat and a cup of tea – decent, staff tea – much to the disapproval of the warden. The memory washed over him as a warm glow and he allowed himself a moment to bask in it before rising and starting on his normal morning activities.

The only other person about early, apart from the night warden, was Charlie, who emerged from the middle bathroom towelling his hair. Samuel glared at him, pushing past to inspect what he considered his personal space. The sink was clean and the shower had been rinsed out though the floor was damp and the steam had not yet cleared. Samuel reached under the sink for the sponge and disinfectant he kept there, wiping down all the fixtures before stepping into the shower. Standing under the hot water he wondered whether to warn Charlie off. There were three bathrooms for the residents to use and not much demand, especially early in the morning.

After a moment's thought he decided against it. Charlie had smartened up his act recently and was moderately clean, unlike most of the dirty little pigs on the first floor, and he didn't want word of his actions to get back to Alex. He suspected she would disapprove. He turned the water from hot to cold, standing without flinching under the icy stream for a count of thirty before shutting off the water and stepping out into the room. It amused him to leave the tap on cold for the next user. Serve them right for not checking – and for using his bathroom.

Samuel signed out in the office before Alex arrived and set off down the road. Usually he took the path by the river but today he jogged round the longer route that took him past the houses bordering the main road. After a few minutes he tired of breathing in the fumes from commuters' cars and turned right into a street that followed the river. Past a small industrial estate was a bridge over the canal that led away from the river and towards Taunton. Beyond that was an abandoned building labelled 'Kingdom Hall' and after some waste ground the houses resumed.

Smaller houses than those on the main road, he noted; terraced and packed tightly almost up to the edge of the pavement. Most had just a single window on each floor, though some had dormer windows poking up from the roofs. He trotted along the quiet street and was approaching a turn to the right that cut through a gap between two houses when he spotted a familiar vehicle. Slowing to a walk he fought the impulse to stop and examine it, but even though he was past it in a few seconds there was no mistaking Alex's distinctive old Citroën.

His heart pounded in his chest and he had a sudden shortness of breath. Alex lived on this street. All this time, she had been so close and he'd had no idea. Crossing the main road, Samuel vaulted the railings round Admiral's Park with ease and trotted back through the tunnel to emerge behind the row of houses. This was the path he took every time he went into town. He had gone past her house every week, oblivious to her presence. But, he wondered, studying the fences enclosing the back gardens, which one was hers?

Steve sat next to Petey, leaning against his shoulder and whispering in his ear. Petey looked up from his cereal occasionally, scanning the room as if seeking an ally, but he did not move away. Despite the lack of response Steve became more animated, tapping on the table and wriggling in his chair.

'Alright,' said Petey finally. 'Just let I eat won't yer?' He dug the spoon in his bowl and scraped up the last of the cereal, pushing the bowl away with a sigh. 'Should try some,' he said. 'Is much better now with that proper milk.'

Steve sipped at his tea. He was too excited to eat, his stomach fluttering as he thought of his plan.

'Come on, hurry up, wontcha? Got a whole day without nuffink else we gotta do.'

'Thought I might stay in an' help,' said Petey. 'Was alright last week. Got a decent lunch an' all.'

Steve slammed his cup down so hard the remaining tea slopped on to the table. 'What's wrong with you?' he demanded. 'Sucking up to the new warden, just 'cos she's yer probation officer. Pathetic, you lot. You wanna watch out,' he said softly, leaning over Petey again. 'I make a good friend but you really want to keep me on your side, understand?'

Petey watched as Steve marched out of the room, his own stomach now clenching nervously. Despite his attempts at bravado he was a nervous young man and he found living in the hostel frightening. Sometimes it was like swimming in a shark pool, he thought. You never knew when someone was about to turn on you. He wished he had never taken up with Steve and although he mocked Charlie to his face he was secretly envious of his old friend's progress – and particularly of his double room, away from the pressure of sharing with three others.

'Petey?' said the relief warden. 'Come on, put your dirty crocks over by the door and get your things. We need the room for classes.'

Petey glanced around and realized he was the last one left. Rising reluctantly he gathered the remains of his meal, carried the dishes to the serving hatch and handed them in to the lads in the kitchen.

'Need any help today then?' he asked hopefully.

'Not today,' said the relief warden cheerfully. 'Already got our volunteers and the groups will be helping out too. Go on now, off you go.'

Petey slouched out of the room, pausing to glare at the warden's retreating back. A long, lonely day stretched ahead of him until he spotted Steve through the side window. He was rummaging through the bins, pausing occasionally to look over his shoulder at the drive. Petey hesitated for a moment but past ties and old habits were too strong and he slid out of the door and round the corner of the building.

'Wot you bloody want?' Steve snarled.

'Thought you might want a lookout,' said Petey, taking up position between Steve and the driveway. Steve slowed his search and looked at him, eyes narrowed.

'Yeah? Thought you was too busy trying to weasel up with the new warden,' he said.

'Not me,' said Petey. 'Don't mind if'n there's something in it but not just if is sitting in classes and doin' all they dirty work.'

'Well, I got plans for today so you better be sure whose side you're on,' said Steve. 'Got any dosh left?'

Petey felt in his pockets and came out with a handful of small change.

'Ain't much but it'll do,' said Steve grabbing the money. Petey's protest was cut short by the arrival of Alex's Citroën, which bumped across the pavement and swerved round the corner before stopping just shy of the bins. The boys fled before she could get out of the car to catch them, running towards the back of the hostel and jumping the low wall to land on the hard earth path that fronted the river.

'Just in time,' puffed Steve. 'Though you was supposed to be a look-out.'

Petey rubbed his palms together to take away the sting where he had grabbed the bricks of the wall. 'Forgot how fast she drives,' he said.

'You think she was tryin' to hit us?' asked Steve, quite seriously.

Petey was taken aback by this. 'Course not,' he said. ''Ent nothin' like that in her. Just 'ent so much of a driver. In the office, she was allus hitting them bins. Saw her drag 'um right round the car park once. Don't think she was after us. Not on purpose, any road.'

Steve grunted and reached in his pocket to pull out their combined wealth. 'Come on then,' he said, counting out the meagre coins. 'Need you to go in an' get some lighter fluid in that shop on the corner. I was in a couple 'a days ago and the nosy cow asked all kinds of questions. Don't want her remembering me.'

'What about her remembering me?' said Petey.

'You ain't bin in recently so there's no reason for her to bother 'bout you,' said Steve. 'And you're local, so they ain't so likely to pick on you. I thought you said you was on my side?'

Petey wasn't sure he'd said he was on any side at all but it was too late to take issue with Steve now. He held out his hand in silence and Steve counted out the exact money, putting the rest back in his own pocket. Petey had to play along now or he would be penniless until dole day. Shuffling off down the tow path into town he wondered how the hell he'd ever got into this mess.

Alex arrived at the hostel late after stopping off at the bank in town to collect more funds for the still depleted petty cash tin and her near-miss in the car park did not make for a happy start to the day. Locking her car carefully she stopped for a moment, staring after the retreating figures before replacing the lids to the bins and making her way inside.

'Any idea what Steve and Petey were after in the bins?' she asked Bennie.

'Who knows with them two,' said Bennie. 'Might need to think again, over the tea,' she added. 'Tea bags is all gone again an' sugar jar's missing an' all now. Should do a search of the rooms now they's all out, see who's taking it all.'

'No,' said Alex. 'We should wait, at least until the end of this week. And I don't think we should be doing room searches without them being here. This is a hostel not a prison.'

Bennie sighed and shook her head. 'Never know what they hiding up there,' she said. 'Could have glue or drugs or anything.'

'If we have evidence of illegal activity then we can do a search,' said Alex. 'Even so, I would prefer they were here – that way no-one can claim we planted anything. But I'm not stirring everyone up over a few tea bags!'

Bennie lapsed into silence, shuffling papers around on her desk whilst keeping her head bent. Alex waited a minute and then picked up the day book and leafed through, reading the most recent entries. After going back a few pages she stopped, marked a place with a strip of paper and carried on reading.

'Bennie,' she said, after going back over the previous month.

Bennie glanced up briefly. 'Yeah?'

'Can you help me out here,' said Alex, flipping between pages. 'We've had four call-outs by the fire brigade since – well, I think since Peter Marks moved on to Taunton.'

Bennie put the file she was holding aside and leaned back in her chair.

'So?'

'These calls are expensive,' said Alex. 'They charge us for every false alarm. And it means someone in the hostel is getting away with setting the alarm off, which should be something they get breached for.'

'Is at the weekends,' said Bennie. 'Don't try that with our usual staff 'cos they know they can't get away with it. Weekends they're struggling to get cover from Taunton so we don't know who they is half the time. Some is okay but had a couple of students in and they was no good at all. Didn't know the first thing about probation work and was useless at keeping order too.'

Alex nodded, examining the pages closely. 'These entries seem to be written in different handwriting,' she said carefully. 'How many staff do we have on at night?'

'Is my writing,' said Bennie tersely. 'Only found out about them calls when the bill came in. I had a word, told 'um in no uncertain terms they had to put everything as happened in the book for their shift. Reckon they thought we'd not notice if it weren't logged. Dumb bunnies.'

'So we actually use untrained staff for the weekends – unsupervised?' said Alex. 'That can't carry on. We're not full at the moment but the clients are coming in higher up the tariff and some of them can be dangerous. They're here because they need proper supervision not just a roof over their heads to keep them out of prison for nicking a couple of bottles from the supermarket!'

'I couldn't agree more,' said Bennie coolly. 'So where are we supposed to find these trained people who are willing to do 24-hour shifts at the weekend? And if we can find them, how are we supposed to pay for them, even though headquarters insist eight hours count as "sleeping shift" so it's a cheaper option? I don't think anyone should work alone but that's what we've got and some of the little toe rags are only too happy to act up. We've already lost a couple of good people because of it and I'm never sure who, if anyone, is going to walk through that door some evenings.'

It was Lauren who walked through the door at that moment, looking fit, rested and extremely determined. Alex jumped to her feet, banging her knee on the desk as she tried to skirt around it.

'Lauren, what are you doing here?' she asked, searching the space for a spare chair.

'Nice to see you too,' said Lauren. 'I come to talk about getting some experience here. Sounds like I 'as arrived at the right time too.'

Alex looked over at Bennie's face and tried not to laugh. Lauren might be small but she was extremely smart, tough and took no prisoners. She had managed six years at the probation office in Highpoint, a lot of it dealing with the clients in reception. The hostel was a step further, granted, but apart from Pauline she could think of no-one from the office more able to cope with a hostel shift.

'Let's have a look around,' she said. 'Bennie, can you hold the fort here for a bit?'

Bennie nodded, her eyes still fixed on Lauren's diminutive figure.

'What's her problem?' asked Lauren as they headed down the hall and into the dining room.

'It's always a bit awkward when you get a new boss,' said Alex. 'Between us two, I'm very awkward about being someone's boss.'

'Don't get too used to that idea,' said Lauren. 'Way I see it they put you here to do what headquarters wants. Part of a new type of service, all joined up and everyone pushing together on account of the national policy. Hostel could become more of a holding cell, like the bail hostel. You keep 'em off the streets and watch 'em but when they get to be a problem is your fault and they get pushed off to prison anyway.'

'Where did you get that cheerful little summary?' asked Alex.

Lauren hopped up onto one of the chairs and swung her feet back and forth. 'Pauline comes over on the way home most nights,' she said, looking around the room critically. 'Bit Spartan 'ent it? What about some pictures or something. Looks like a works canteen in here.'

She was right, Alex realized. Strange she'd not noticed it before. Now, looking round, she became aware of how shabby the place was. It could do with repainting – or at least a decent spring clean. Sugar soap on the walls, windows polished inside and out and new paint on the front door, then some bright pictures and maybe coloured woodwork would smarten the whole place up. Mentally she began to work out how much that might cost and was brought back to the moment by Lauren poking her on the shoulder.

'So, what about it, then?' she demanded. 'I fancy moving on a bit, going back to college an' getting qualified. Would be a lot easier gettin' on the course if I got a placement.' She tilted her head to one side and raised her eyebrows. 'Said you was needing people an' you know I can handle 'um. Bin doing it for the last six years and besides, I grew up with half of 'um.'

Alex had tremendous respect for Lauren and would never do anything to hurt her feelings, but she had serious misgivings about taking her on to work in the hostel, especially after the recent fall had revealed her physical frailties.

'I'll need to think about it,' she said finally. 'You'll have to get your doctor's approval too – no, don't look like that! You have been very ill and I can't just fling you into an atmosphere as stressful as this without his agreement. Apart from anything else, headquarters would overrule me and then you'd never get a job here.'

Lauren scowled, but she knew her friend was right. She had a strong suspicion Rosalind was going to push for some sort of ill-health severance for her and she needed to move first before that went on her record.

Alright,' she said reluctantly. 'Let me have a word and I'll get a letter or summat. Now, how about you show me round proper?'

It was fortunate for Steve that Samuel had left the river bank and headed off to his session in the probation workshop before he and Petey arrived at the back of the row of houses. Steve had made a note of the gate and he knew exactly where Alex lived. He also remembered there had been no lock on it and she hadn't pulled a bolt back to open it following the incident with the bird table. He was hoping that, like most people, she had forgotten about securing the back way into her home.

A quick glance round to make sure they were unobserved and Steve had the gate open and beckoned Petey inside.

'What we doing?' asked Petey. He didn't like the turn events were taking at all. A bit of shoplifting or drunk and disorderly was one thing but breaking and entering was a much more serious crime, especially when it involved the house of their probation officer.

'Shut it,' hissed Steve, closing the gate softly behind him. Inside the fence was a concrete platform running the width of the narrow plot. Three steps led down to a tiny lawn which was bordered by flower beds and surrounded by rather battered looking fences. The house appeared empty, its windows blank, and there was no sign they had been seen from the adjoining properties.

'Go an' get that and bring it up here,' said Steve, pointing to the dustbin standing outside the back door. Petey swallowed nervously but obeyed, scurrying along the little path and seizing the bin. The lid slid off and rolled a few yards, the sound shockingly loud in the still morning.

'Watch wot you doing, you dozy bugger,' Steve snarled. 'Just leave it. Come on, hurry up.'

Petey struggled with the heavy bin, dragging it along the path.

'God, you are useless,' muttered Steve as he grabbed the handle at the back and swung the dustbin up the stairs. 'Might as well have turned up with a brass band, the racket you're making.'

Petey gave a final heave and dropped his side of the bin on the top step, stung by Steve's criticism.

'Would help if I knew what you was doing,' he said. 'Not just do this, do that an' shut up. If'n I'm so useless mebbe you should just get on with it yerself.'

'Oh no you don't, said Steve, grabbing him by the shoulder. 'You're part of this now and you don't weasel out so easily. Help me get it up by the fence.' Reluctantly, Petey lifted one side of the can, positioning it to Steve's satisfaction. 'Here,' said Steve. He handed over the tin of lighter fluid. 'Squeeze it round so it soaks all over the top. And make sure there's plenty. Don't want it going out when we've gone.'

Petey began to dribble the fuel into the dustbin whilst Steve surveyed the garden.

'Look at that,' he said, pointing to the bird table. The birds had retreated to the safety of nearby bushes, their faint calls and rustles betraying their presence. 'Should've put it down there. Maybe roasted a few of them little tweeters.'

Petey threw the can into the bin and stepped back, his face twisted in disgust. 'That's wrong,' he said. 'Don't think I want to be here no more.' He pulled at the gate but Steve was up the stairs in a flash, his foot in the way.

'Too late now,' he said, pushing Petey back towards the dustbin. 'Look what I've got here.' He pulled an empty plastic bag out of his pocket and lifted the lighter fuel tin out of the bin, closed the top spout using the side of the bag and slipped the whole thing in his pocket. 'So, that's your fingerprints on that. Any word from you and the cops get this to look at.'

Petey stood, frozen in horror. He was trapped by this cunning and malicious person, a false friend who would have no qualms about setting him up. He searched Steve's eyes for a glimpse of humour, the tiniest suggestion he was joking, and was met by a cold and malevolent stare. Petey had seen that stare before, in the face of Samuel Burton.

Bennie raced up the stairs, yelling for Alex all the way.

'Fire!' she shouted. 'There's a fire!'

'Well press the alarm and get the lads out of the class,' she replied, and began hammering on the doors to rouse any clandestine sleepers.

'No, not here – at your house,' Bennie gasped as she rounded the corner. 'Brigade just called it in.'

'Go on,' said Lauren. 'You get down there. I'll stay here.'

Alex looked from one to another, dazed by this awful news.

'Go *on*,' Lauren repeated, giving her a shove towards the stairs.

'Is okay,' said Bennie, stepping out of the way. 'We got this. You go home and find out what's happening.'

It was all over by the time Alex arrived, despite the fact it was only a five minute drive from the hostel. There was no sign of the fire brigade in the street but a small crowd of excited onlookers were jostling around the track leading up towards the rear of the terrace. She pulled up as close as she could to the entrance and hurried through the crowd, pushing her neighbours out of the way in her haste.

'Now then, Miss,' said a fireman, stepping in front of her and holding up his hand. 'You can't go over there. We need to make sure it's safe. Step back now, please.'

'It's my house!' said Alex, bobbing from side to side as she tried to see round him.

'Oh, sorry, Miss. Still, I must ask you to wait here and I'll ask the Chief to come over and have a word.'

He walked over to the firemen who were grouped around the charred remains of Alex's back fence. After a bit of whispering and pointing one of them ambled over towards her.

'Miss Hastings, is it?' said a large, broad shouldered man. 'It seems something started burning in your rubbish bin and it caught the fence. I don't suppose you would have any idea what might have started it? We often get bin fires from hot ash and such like.'

'It's summer!' Alex said. 'Why would I light the fire in July? And – is that my bin?' She pointed to the blackened lump on the top step. 'Well, it's not kept there. It was down by my back door when I left for work about an hour ago, so either it's grown legs or someone moved it.'

'Is there anyone else in your house who might have moved it or left something flammable in the bin?' the Chief asked, determined not to be put off his enquiries. In his experience no-one ever admitted to the sort of behaviour that caused a fire. 'Perhaps you had a bottle or something else made of glass at the top and the sun caused it to overheat?'

'I really don't think so,' said Alex. 'I try to recycle the glass if I can. And even if there was a jar or something, we always leave the bin in the shade, by the back door and with the lid on. Where is the lid?' she added looking round him.

'So you are saying the bin was moved and a fire started, possibly maliciously,' said the Chief. 'Can you think of any reason why someone might want to do that?'

The lingering smoke from her back fence was beginning to give Alex a headache and her eyes were burning from the fumes left by the fire.

'Look,' she said. 'I'm a probation officer. I've had to send all kinds of people back to prison over the past three years. I've supervised almost two hundred different clients. Take your pick.'

'There's no need to be like that,' said the fire chief. 'I'm trying to establish what happened and if this was set deliberately then that is a very serious turn of events. The police will need to be involved as there is always the chance this is a random incident, in which case there is a danger to the wider public, especially during a spell of weather as hot as this.'

Alex was sure he didn't mean it like that but it sounded as if he was more concerned about everyone else than he was about her. Fighting back tears she contemplated the wreck that had been her garden. The firemen had pumped gallons of water onto the fire and it had flowed across the top step and cascaded down into the flower beds and across the lawn. The grass, so carefully tended by Sue, was churned up into a muddy swamp and her precious bird table was lying on its side, the hangars and dishes scattered in the sooty mess.

She took a deep breath to steady her voice and said, 'I'm sorry, but I do think this was intentional. Will I be able to clear up or do I need to wait for the police?'

There was a shout from the group around the bin and the Chief hurried over, waving Alex back as she tried to follow.

'I think this was arson,' said one of the men. 'Here, smell that.'

The Chief leaned over the bin, which had finally finished smouldering. Mixed in with the scent of charred paper and burned plastic was a tang of something petrol based. He looked closely at the rim of the metal can and saw there were several places where the damage was more extensive, the soot and burn marks outlining faint splashes above the layer of charred debris.

'Burned from the top down,' said the fireman. 'Bottom layers are hardly touched and there's no glass in here, I checked.'

'Looks like she's telling the truth,' said the Chief gloomily. 'All right, get onto the police. We'd better mark it off.'

There was a shout from the tender and a young fireman waved from the window. 'Got another call,' he yelled. 'Fire in a field out by North Pethy!'

The Chief rolled his eyes and groaned. 'Tell 'um we got an arson here,' he said. 'Not ready to go out again yet.'

The fireman nodded and disappeared into his cab. 'Better start getting this packed up,' said the fire chief. 'Need to get back to the station as soon as we can. Gonna be one of them days.' He left his crew rolling hoses and packing their gear away, and walked over to where Alex waited impatiently. 'Looks as if you might be right,' he said. 'I'll call in the police and my investigator'll be down soon as I let him know. Meanwhile, 'fraid you can't touch nothing. We'll want the rubbish bin too, once the police have had a look.'

'Can I at least put my bird table back up?' Alex asked. 'It's not anywhere near the fence. Please?'

The table was a good way from the site of the fire and he took pity on her. 'Course,' he said gruffly. 'Hope your insurance covers this,' he added, waving his arm to encompass the wreckage of Alex's garden. Alex thought for a moment. She had no idea whether it did or not and the idea she might be able to claim for the damage had not occurred to her. 'Might be worth considering something else at the back mind,' the fire chief continued. 'Mebbe railings or bricks – even breeze blocks. Didn't spread next door and they got just blocks so should save you from another if someone's really got it in for you.'

The idea this might happen again had also not occurred to Alex, who was still trying to grasp the idea someone hated her enough to set fire to her fences. 'Well, yes, I'll think about that,' she said. Her voice was shaking and she suddenly felt quite dizzy.

'Hang on now,' said the fireman, grabbing her by the arm. 'You need to sit down. Been a shock, all this.' He led her over to a chair by the little table where she and her friends had sat talking, laughing and drinking wine just last night. Her head slumped forward and this time she could not hold back her tears.

Steve had run from the fire as soon as it took hold, scuttling down the path and hiding in the tunnel that ran under the main road. Here he had a good view of the whole thing and soon a group of curious onlookers joined him, milling around and chattering excitedly. Steve mingled with the crowd, able to step closer as the presence of so many others helped hide him. His heart leapt when Alex arrived and he watched her intently, willing her to break down. Despite the excitement the fire itself triggered inside him, he was bitterly disappointed when she disappeared into her garden with the fireman. He was sure she had been about to crack but now he could not be sure and it was far too risky trying to get a closer look.

He was concerned when the police put in an appearance and the rubbish bin was taken away by the fire brigade after they finished rolling up their hoses and packing everything away on the big, red tender. It meant they suspected the fire had been deliberate but there was no way they could pin it on him. He fingered the half-empty can in his pocket through the plastic bag and grinned. Let them try, he thought. He had the perfect fall-guy in Petey. Petey who had purchased the lighter fluid, carried the bin up the steps and left his finger-prints all over the whole scene. Yes, Petey had better behave himself now or he was in real trouble.

Chapter Twelve

Although she was desperate to get back to the hostel Alex was stuck at the house, fretting and increasingly upset by events. The police turned up and went through the debris, raking through the remains of her fence and trampling what was left of her lawn into a grassless morass. They had questions, most of them along the lines of, 'How do you know it didn't start by accident', with the implication the whole thing was somehow her own fault. When they finally left she had to go over to the garage to get more milk – they had drunk endless cups of tea and eaten all her biscuits – and stood in the forecourt, wondering whether she should go up to the supermarket and find something for dinner. Her plans to shop at lunch time had been derailed by events but she could not think of a single thing she wanted to eat.

A car horn just behind made her jump, and turning round she saw a familiar face peering through the windscreen of a rather disreputable looking van.

'Didn't expect to see you here,' said Ada, clambering down from the passenger seat. 'Thought you'd be at work.'

Tom stuck his head out of the driver's window. 'Sorry – didn't mean to startle you,' he said sheepishly. 'You alright? You's looking a bit pale.'

Alex tried a brave smile but it came out all crooked as her eyes began to water again.

'What's up, then?' demanded Ada, straight to the point as ever. 'Summat's not right. Not more trouble from them dozy bastards at work is it?'

'Now then, Ada,' said Tom. 'Let's not be talking like that. And 'ent none of our business anyway.'

Alex was startled to learn Ada and Tom knew about her troubles at the probation office. She'd not said anything outside the office or her home and always tried to be neutral in her conversations if she couldn't be positive about things.

'Don't look like that,' said Ada. 'Don't take no genius to work out things 'ent going well, what with you being moved from that day centre where you was doing so much good. The lads talk you know, and Brian, well he's just about the worst gossip on all the Levels.'

'No I 'ent!' came an indignant voice from the back of the van, and Brian emerged, struggling out from on top of a load of hay bales.

'Afternoon, Miss,' he added, brushing bits of straw off his clothes.

'Hello, Brian,' said Alex faintly. The whole day was descending into some sort of farce and she found her grip on reality sliding away.

'Got into they college,' Brian added and he gave a great, proud grin. 'Done the tests and everything. Then went into the paddock an' lots of 'em, they wasn't so sure round them animals but 'ent none of 'um so big as Pongo, so I didn't mind. Was a good laugh, seein' some of 'em.'

'That is wonderful news, Brian,' said Alex, and for the first time today she gave a genuine smile. Brian, a total no-hoper marked for a life of petty crime spent in and out of prison, was suddenly transforming himself into a young man with a future. This really was a miracle and she had no doubt who was responsible.

'You've done wonders, you two,' she said to Ada and Tom. 'Honestly, I wish I could send all my little reprobates to stay with you for six months.'

'Don't you dare,' said Ada briskly. 'These two is enough for me to be getting' on with.' She turned to Tom and said, 'Think there's some things you need to fetch from the market?'

There was a pause before Tom said, 'Oh, yes. Right you is, Ada. Reckon I'll stroll up an' have a look. Just park up over there an' we'll be off for, oh maybe half'n hour.' He gave Brian a nudge with his elbow, nodding towards the pavement. 'You wait over there, lad. Be with you in a moment.'

Without waiting for Alex, Ada headed towards the street. 'Which one's yours then?' she called over her shoulder.

'Hang on,' said Alex. 'I've got to get some milk. The police used it all.'

Ada gave her a stare. 'What you doin' with the police round?' she demanded.

Alex shook her head. 'In a minute,' she said, and hurried into the garage shop.

Over a cup of tea and some rather sad left-over biscuits, Alex found herself telling Ada everything. She had intended to point to the fence and make a bit of a joke about it but the sight of the desolation behind her house and the smell of the fire that lingered, an acrid pall over her kitchen and dining room, broke through her natural reticence and the whole story came pouring out.

Ada listened, making an occasional noise in sympathy but without asking any questions until Alex had finished.

'So,' she said, taking a sip of her tea and setting the cup down on the table. 'Assuming this is all personal – and certainly looks like it from what you is saying – the question seems to be is it 'cos of your work or 'cos of you an' your friend?'

Alex sat up in shock, aghast at Ada's words.

'Oh, don't you go givin' me that look,' grumbled Ada, reaching for her tea. 'I 'ent stupid, you know. Seen how you been since your friend from Bristol been around. Mary is it?'

'Margie,' said Alex faintly.

'That's right, Margie. Well, you's something of a changed woman, even though they 'ent tret you right up at the main office.' Ada jerked her chin in the direction of the town dismissively. 'Don't see no harm in none of it but even if I was so minded, 'ent none of my business. But some folk's not like that and might want to make mischief. On the other hand ...'

She paused to sort through the biscuits, selecting a chocolate wafer that she nibbled delicately before continuing. 'Yes, could just be stupid lads as found where you live and think they got a grudge over summat. That sound likely?'

There was the sound of a car horn outside on the road and Ada stood up, brushed some crumbs from her ample front and gathered up her shopping bag. At the front door she gave Alex's hand a squeeze.

'Don't you be fretting,' she said. 'Is nasty, that sort of thing, but you got a lot of friends round about, even if'n you don't realize it. Don't you try coping with all this on yer own neither. I'll get Tom to pop over tomorrow if that's alright. Have a look to see what he can do for the back.'

'Oh, no, really – there's no need ...' Alex protested.

'Don't worry,' said Ada, misunderstanding her concern. 'Brian be with me tomorrow so won't be tramping round yer garden. Will be just Tom.' With that she swept out of the front door and climbed into the front of the van, leaving Alex on the doorstep staring after her.

After a minute she closed the door and made her way out to the back. There was a pair of old gardening gloves on the windowsill and she pulled them on, gathered several bin bags and began the long and dirty job of clearing up. She had finished moving the last of the charred wood and was trying to scrape up the soot and melted debris left by the bin fire when Samuel trotted past on his way back to the hostel.

Her back was towards him and at first he only registered the signs of a recent fire but as she moved round the top step he realized who it was and his heart seemed to leap in his chest. Fortunately, his momentum kept him moving along the path

179

so when she did glance up he was just past her line of sight. Samuel slowed to a walking pace, acting casually as if he had a stitch in his side and as he bent over he sneaked another look at the forlorn little figure. He was suddenly filled with absolute fury. How could someone do such a thing? How dare they touch her or cause her pain? If he had the culprit in front of him at that moment Samuel would certainly have tried to kill them.

A woman was walking towards him and as he straightened up a look of alarm flitted across her face. Samuel realized he was snarling with rage, his face twisted and teeth bared. With a deep breath he tried to fold his face into a smile and nodded in her direction.

'Evening,' he said. She gave a squeak and hurried past, nodding in reply as she fled. 'Stupid cow,' muttered Samuel, then he dismissed her from his thoughts. Setting off on his run again, he was struck by the pleasing notion that at least he knew which Alex's house was now.

While Brian was out in the garden feeding the goats and fussing over the dogs, Ada told Tom about Alex's fire. Tom sat at the table and nodded thoughtfully, then walked to the door and stared out for a moment over the parched landscape.

'Been a lot of fires round about recent,' he said. 'That one last week, was a lad running off from there. Couldn't give much of a description but might recognize him again if I seen him. Think it might be one of her young hooligans then?'

Ada shook her head at him. ''Ent hooligans,' she said. 'Clients they called.'

'Don't care what you call 'um, setting fires is for hooligans,' said Tom. 'Takes a sick mind to do that, 'specially in this drought. And takes someone twisted inside to burn up a living creature like they done to them grass snakes. Something very wrong inside if'n they can do that. Person can torment an animal then they got it in them to do the same to a child. Don't like the look of all this, not one bit.'

Ada nodded, her hands busily working a lump of bread dough on the board by the window. 'Could be coincidence,' she said, but her voice lacked conviction.

'There was that tree burned up last month too,' said Tom thoughtfully. 'Takes hell of a lot to burn up a tree. Always going to have some grass fires and such in the summer, what with idiots larking about with fires and grockles just here for a day, leaving bottles an' fag ends around. But that bush with the snakes and now someone setting a bin alight – that's no accident.'

Ada thumped the dough around on the board, kneading enthusiastically until a thin sheen of sweat stood out on her face.

'Don't think is grockles did Alex's fence,' she said. 'That's someone as knows her and done it from spite. Want you to go over tomorrow, see what you can do for the back. Maybe a bit of a wall would be best. Give her some privacy and make it safe too.'

Tom grunted and headed for the garden. 'Reckon I could,' he said. 'Got a friend can get some blocks ...'

'No friend's blocks!' said Ada sharply. 'She's a probation officer so it got to be all legal.'

Tom sighed heavily but shrugged his shoulders as he ducked out of the door. He knew when he was beaten and fortunately he had a supply of breeze blocks in his shed, intended for a wall he never got round to finishing at his cottage. Gate would be a problem though, he thought. Wooden gate would just burn up if the arsonist came back. Needed to be iron rails if possible and that wasn't going to be cheap. As he helped Brian put the goats away for the night he turned the problem over in his mind.

Petey spent the evening trying to stay as far away from Steve as possible. He had run from the fire as soon as Steve flicked a lit match into the bin and kept on going. Desperate to establish some sort of alibi he had presented himself at the workshop, feigning a desire to join the team constructing the raft for the race in August. The supervisor was surprised to see him but gratified by any show of enthusiasm and soon Petey found himself hauling wood across the yard and holding timber steady as the more experienced workers measured and cut.

It was heavy, tedious work and by the time a break was called Petey was shaking with his efforts, covered in sweat and sawdust and heartily sick of the whole thing. Sitting in the shade of the workshop he examined his hands, wincing as he tugged at a splinter lodged in one finger. A shadow fell across his outstretched legs and he looked up, squinting into the bright sunlight.

'What are you doing here?' asked Ricky.

Petey glared up at him. 'Just havin' a rest afore I go back in. Is hot work,' he said. He looked enviously at Ricky's cigarette, burning unheeded in his hand. Petey rarely had enough money for tobacco and now every penny he had left from the meagre dole allowance was rattling around in Steve's pockets, along with that incriminating lighter fuel. Alex didn't smoke but Petey bet if she did she'd offer them around sometimes.

'Name?' asked Ricky. He consulted a handwritten list and shook his head. 'No, not on here. You're not officially part of the extended programme so I need you to leave the premises.' Without even looking at Petey properly, Ricky ducked into the workshop calling for the supervisor. Petey stared after him, stunned by what he'd just heard. What, he wondered, was the 'extended programme'? And why was an extra few hours in the workshop such a big deal anyway? Surely they *wanted* him to do something with his time. First the hostel threw him out and now this. The only person who wanted him around was Steve – and Petey didn't think he wanted to be around him.

'Why are you still here?' demanded Ricky from the workshop entrance. 'If you want to be included in some of the other programmes we need to meet and discuss this first. This is not a youth club where you can pick and choose what you attend. Speaking of which, you are scheduled to begin the

"Challenging Offending Behaviour" programme this week. I will be in touch with your supervising officer to make sure they have the details. Now, please go.'

He swept off, up the steps and through the door to the main office, leaving Petey feeling hurt, humiliated and extremely angry. After a moment he stood up rather shakily just as the supervisor looked out of the door.

'Sorry, lad,' he said. 'It's a bit of a new regime and I'm just getting used to all the rules and such. You're one of Alex's, right?'

Petey glared at him but managed a nod. He was not sure he could manage to speak, he was so angry.

'Look, I'll have a word with her and we'll put a recommendation on your file for you. Should be sorted by next week.'

'Don't bother,' Petey managed. 'Wouldn't come back anyhow. Is nothing but skivvying and I got better things to do.'

His better things turned out to be sulking by the canal, throwing stones at any fish unwise enough to surface and trying to ignore the growling from his empty stomach. Lounging in the entrance to the dining room before dinner he could smell Steve coming, a stale whiff of smoke and dirty clothes. Without looking round he shifted his position on the wall and sauntered over to Charlie, who was poring over a book, his lips moving silently as he read the close-packed print.

'Where's that to then?' he asked, leaning over his friend's shoulder.

Charlie looked up, annoyed at the interruption and slightly concerned about being mocked for reading.

'You's in my light,' he said, shifting round in his chair. Petey could sense Steve moving towards him across the room and pulled out the chair next to Charlie, sitting at the table and feigning interest in the book. Steve loomed over the pair, resting on one arm next to Petey and fixing him with a hard stare.

'Missed you this afternoon,' he said. 'Dunno where you went, rabbiting off like that. Something important was it?'

Charlie looked up from his reading and glared at him. 'Now you in my light too.' He sniffed and pulled a face. 'You don't smell too good. What you been up to?'

For a moment, Petey thought Steve was going to hit him but then he turned and hurried out of the room taking the stale scent with him. Charlie coughed and screwed up his nose.

'Could you smell that or was it just me?' he asked Petey. 'Nasty stink, like burning plastic or summat.' Before Petey could answer the door to the kitchen opened and two residents hauled out the cutlery trolley with a great clattering.

'Come on,' called one. 'Shift over – got to get them tables ready. An' put yer cups over there will yer?'

There was a slow movement of bodies as the residents shifted back towards the door. Suddenly there was the sound of raised voices as one of the residents walked off leaving cups, spoons and used tea bags scattered across the table where he'd been sitting.

''Ent mine and I don't see why I should have to clear it up,' he protested.

'Well, I ain't shifting it. Move it or you 'ent getting no dinner,' retorted the table-setter.

'You can't decide that – you's just the same as me,' the resident snapped and in seconds the room was filled with angry young men pushing and jeering at one another. Alex came through the front door just in time to see Lauren barrel her way into the middle of the fight and give a mighty yell. The shock of Lauren's arrival and the amazing volume of her shout startled them into immobility and she pushed the two groups apart, sending the setters back to the kitchen to fetch clean cutlery, ordering the rest into the television room and seizing the two protagonists by the arm made them shake hands before they cleared up the spilled mess on the floor.

'An' put them tables back an' pick up the chairs too,' she added. 'Oh, hello Alex. Didn't think you was coming back today. Everything alright?'

Alex looked at her indomitable friend and could not fight back a grin. 'Where's Bennie?' she asked. 'She's not left you on your own has she?'

'Course not,' said Bennie from the office. 'In here. Looking for cover this evening in case you was off any longer. I'll stay tonight but can't do more'n twenty four hours in a row 'cept at weekends according to the regs. Sent Lauren in there seeing as a lot of 'em is a bit scared of her and if she's to do any shifts on her own later we want to know she can handle it.'

'Course I can,' said Lauren.

Alex smiled and nodded. 'I've no doubt at all,' she said. 'We can't leave you alone without you being officially on the staff though. Either as relief staff or a student, so I'll get on to headquarters and talk to personnel about a temporary transfer tomorrow. You should go now – you've already covered a full shift.'

Lauren settled herself on a chair and folded her arms. 'Not until you tell what happened,' she said.

'Oh God,' said Alex, rubbing her eyes which were still smarting from the fumes. The noise level in the television room was rising again and the women glanced towards the hall.

'My turn,' said Bennie. 'You stay here and tell Lauren so she can get off. I'll go in to dinner and you can tell me afterwards.' She strode out of the door and the excited chatter stopped as soon as she crossed the hallway.

'Reckon I can learn a lot from you two,' murmured Lauren, 'given a chance. Now, what's this all about, this fire then?'

Tom arrived at Alex's house the next morning, timing it perfectly. Alex was in a hurry, worried about not keeping a presence in the hostel and still too distressed by events to ask many questions. Tom backed his van up, began to unload the breeze blocks, asked for a couple of buckets of water and set about his task calmly. Alex was so relieved to see him she pressed a key into his hand for the back door and was off to work before either Margie or Sue.

A few minutes later Margie appeared, strolling down the remains of the path to check him out. Tom set down the pile of blocks he was carrying and nodded to her.

'Mornin'.'

'Morning,' said Margie. They studied one another for a moment.

'Good of you,' said Margie finally.

Tom shrugged. 'No matter,' he said. 'Good friend is Alex, 'specially to Ada. Glad to be able to do summat back for her.' He looked round at the mess in the garden and shook his head. 'Don't know what some folk is thinking,' he said. 'Looks bad enough but could'a been a lot worse I guess. Solid wall should help keep 'um out, just in case they try coming back.'

Margie stared at him for a moment.

'Why would they come back?' she asked.

Tom suddenly felt uncomfortable. He'd hoped to turn up, build his wall and be home for supper. He'd not planned on much conversation and this woman in her prison officer shirt and trousers brought back some unpleasant memories from his youth.

'Just – if it was personal,' he said, keeping his head down and sorting the blocks into several piles. 'Or mebbe was just 'cos it was a wooden fence. Lots of houses, they got brick and such now. Not many would burn up like your'n did.'

Margie watched him as he worked for a few minutes. 'Do you want a tea or something?' she asked rather reluctantly.

Tom shook his head. 'No thanks – should get on.'

Relieved, Margie headed back into the house, unaware of the interest she had attracted from the jogger lurking on the tow path. Samuel watched the exchange with interest. He would have liked to hear what was being said but he recognized Tom from his trips past Ada's house. In fact he had once had an exchange of insults with Ada's son, Kevin, and he wasn't sure if Tom might recognize him, so he kept well back from the gap leading into Alex's garden.

He was puzzled by Margie's presence at the house. He knew Alex shared with Sue but this woman was not one of the probation officers. Yet here she was, wearing the uniform of the hated prison service and acting as if she belonged. He scowled as he turned away. He didn't like surprises and he didn't like anyone else getting in the way of what he hoped might be an interesting relationship with Alex. This stranger must go and as soon as possible.

As Samuel began his run back past the hostel and out along the canal path Tom looked up. Some instinct told him he was being watched and there was something familiar about the retreating figure. Perhaps this was the arsonist, he thought, but the man was taller than the figure he'd seen on the Levels. A sight fitter too, looking at him stride along. He hesitated, wondering whether he should say something to Margie but the back door was closed and she was nowhere in sight. Tom was always a bit nervous around strange houses and with a sigh he turned back to building the wall.

In her pink and fluffy room Rosalind was busy with the work rotas for the next month. She was finding it difficult to cover all the court sessions and for a moment she regretted packing Gordon off to Yeovil. No, she decided, he had to go. It would not be possible to enact the reforms needed to bring this old fashioned and inefficient service up to date with him in the office. He represented the old service, the 'guiding hand and support' model and the younger officers looked up to him. He had too much influence to be allowed to continue, so now he was Yeovil's problem. Rosalind hoped secretly he would find the endless commuting too much and do the decent thing by resigning. There were too many old-style officers filling posts that should be made available to younger, more open-minded recruits.

It was unfortunate that her only young recruit was Ricky Peddlar. He had shown promise as a student and proved his worth in the run up to taking charge at Highpoint but she was already having doubts about his ability to run the day centre effectively and she began to suspect he wasn't all that bright. That wasn't necessarily a bad thing. Rosalind didn't particularly like clever people, who had a tendency to ask too many questions, but a certain level of intelligence was an asset in the job.

She flipped through the court rota again, picking up her pen with a sigh. The door opened and Debbie slid inside without knocking.

'Can I help?' she asked, walking over to the desk.

Rosalind lifted the rotas off the desk and flapped them in the air. 'I really don't know how I can cover all of these with all the other commitments,' she said. 'Headquarters promised we could have another officer but now they say there's no-one available until the autumn. We're only one officer short officially and so their latest recruits are all going to other places.'

'Let me look,' said Debbie, leaning over her shoulder. 'Now, we've got Sue out on the road for most of the week but she's actually not covering more than one or two clients at a time. The problem with these visits is they eat up the time of an officer in a very inefficient manner.'

'Headquarters think it is a good idea, having one dedicated person,' said Rosalind irritably. 'The idea is to give a consistent provision over the whole area.'

'Of course it is,' said Debbie smoothly. 'I think it is an excellent idea – but it costs Highpoint the services of an experienced officer. Now, what if we make the case to headquarters that the time cost should be shared over the area? That way Sue's time is counted in all their statistics and we qualify for a new officer.'

Rosalind opened her mouth to argue and then stopped, pondered for a heartbeat and gave a tight little smile.

'You know, that might actually work,' she said. Debbie laid her hand on the senior's shoulder and Rosalind reached up to squeeze it absently. There was a knock at the office door and Debbie stepped back, standing up very straight as it opened to reveal Ricky looking decidedly scruffy.

'They said you wanted to see me?' he said, ignoring Debbie entirely.

'Please, take a seat,' said Rosalind, gesturing towards the hard chair. She waited until he had settled in front of her before continuing. 'I understand there are a few anomalies in the attendance records. Some clients seem to be in the wrong group and some not attending when they should be.'

Ricky leaned forward, almost touching the desk in his eagerness.

'Well, I don't want to speak ill of anyone,' he said. 'I must say, though, Alex was very lax about some of the records and she seems to have let clients join in the activities almost at will. A lot of them don't have a recommendation for enhanced contact so technically all they can do is come to the compulsory sessions and –.'

Rosalind cut him short with a wave of her hand.

'Yes, I am aware of how the system works,' she said. Ricky shot a puzzled glance at her. He was not used to being on the other side of Rosalind's displeasure. 'I will be addressing the optional attendance later with all the staff. However, there has been quite a dramatic drop-off in the core programme. Earlier this week only three clients came to the "tackling offending behaviour" session. Three – out of eleven!'

Ricky opened his mouth to speak but she cut across his excuses.

'You had ten for the first session with one in hospital, then … let me see … six for the second. It would appear they have decided they can attend those groups at will. Which, as we all know, is not the case.'

There was silence as Ricky struggled to find a response, but Rosalind was not finished. 'Some of our other groups seem to have mysteriously disappeared as well. The basic literacy group for example?' She tilted her head on one side and raised her eyebrows. Ricky shifted in the chair.

'Well, actually, Alex used to teach that one herself,' he said. 'Um, I think she's doing a class at the hostel now.'

'So the clients prefer to attend her sessions despite the fact they receive no credit towards their day centre orders,' said Rosalind. 'How strange. Unfortunately, it is strongly recommended all day centres offer such provision and we are due to be inspected at any time. I strongly suggest you arrange for a group to start this week and have lesson plans and the assessment schedule on my desk to look over by Friday.'

Ricky was aghast at the idea. 'We don't have a teacher,' he said.

'Surely that can be arranged through the local college or an agency?' said Rosalind sweetly. 'I believe Alex left her course outline as requested and so all you need to do is provide some clients.'

Ricky wasn't about to admit he hadn't bothered to look at the plans Alex had worked so hard to prepare. His vision of running the day centre had been one of supervising suitable staff who provided the type of courses and activities he thought should be on offer mixed in with a lot of praise and a fast track to senior grade. And no court duty, of course. Ricky hated court duty. He hadn't quite grasped the idea he would need to present recommendations to the magistrates or soon he would run out of people to come to his day centre.

He felt his heart rate begin to rise as a faint inkling of the enormity of his task began to seep into his consciousness.

'Well, you assured me you were up to the job and I have every faith in you,' said Rosalind, giving him a smile that seemed to drip insincerity.

'Thank you,' said Ricky miserably as he got up, realizing he had been dismissed. It seemed a long walk across the room to the door and he could not resist a glance at his old mentor as he opened it to leave the office. She had already dismissed him from her mind and was writing on the pad in front of her. His face burning with anger and humiliation, Ricky closed the door softly and marched back to his office.

Behind him, Debbie stepped forward again and leaned on the back of Rosalind's chair.

'Too harsh do you think?' Rosalind murmured, her eyes fixed on the notes she was making.

'Perhaps,' said Debbie. 'But it does no harm, reminding him who is in charge. And if he does make a mess of it you need to be able to show you took all the right steps to set him right.' She studied the paper in front of Rosalind, admiring the way the senior had reduced the meeting to a few succinct phrases, all of which showed the management's reasonableness. Rosalind signed the form, stamped it with the date and handed it to Debbie.

'File it away for me will you?' she said.

Debbie went to a steel cabinet in the corner, unlocked it with a key from her own bunch and placed the note in Ricky's new personnel folder before locking the drawer again carefully.

'Lunch?' she said hopefully.

Rosalind shook her head. 'Probably not wise,' she said. 'Dinner this evening though.'

Debbie smiled and nodded happily. 'I'll bring a bottle of the claret you like,' she said, before picking up her bag and heading out to the town.

Samuel stood in the middle of the upstairs room and contemplated the results of his hard work. At first it had been an obsessive desire to control and tidy his environment that drove him on but now he was beginning to think of the room as a useful space. One he might soon exploit for his own designs. The run had served to heighten his anger over the fence fire and to sharpen his anxiety about the strange woman who seemed to be so at home in Alex's house. As he jogged over the dusty tracks, jumping streams and avoiding the occasional vehicle, his mind sought out an explanation for the woman's presence but he could think of nothing that was acceptable to him. He knew the houses were small with only two rooms upstairs and he also knew Sue had been Alex's lodger since moving to Somerset so that would suggest ... The idea buzzed around in his head, was rejected furiously, yet kept reappearing, as relentless and irritating as the clouds of tiny flies that swarmed around him as he ran.

Now he stood in the dark space at the top of the cottage, scratching absently and waiting for an idea to form in his mind. She wasn't his type and he felt nothing but jealousy towards her, but the woman had to be removed from the scene as soon as possible. She was unlikely to be easily scared. No prison officer lasted long if they could be bullied or intimidated and her whole bearing, the way she walked, suggested self-confidence. Of course, he would expect Alex to have strong, clever friends but that was not enough to make him like this woman or tolerate her presence.

Samuel liked to perform his deeds in the home of his chosen woman. The thrill of being inside their safest place, of dominating them and their lives completely, was a major part of the pleasure but he didn't want to do that to Alex's home. A pity really as the fire meant there was a likely suspect just waiting to be caught, but Alex might decide life in Somerset was too much for her and he would lose her altogether. Much better to have this woman disappear quietly but permanently.

It could be practice, he thought. He had to work out how to get her out here, to the cottage, but once installed in the upstairs room he would have much more time. No wondering if the family were coming back or whether the neighbours had heard anything. There were several things he'd had in mind for a while now. This isolated little cottage offered him a chance to play.

It was a bigger job than Tom had expected and it was the end of the next week before he finished Alex's wall and installed a new iron railed gate complete with heavy-duty lock. Despite some pressure from Alex he refused to take any money for the work and insisted he'd had all the materials lying around at home. Alex had her doubts about the gate, which was obviously brand new, and, from the look of the keys, had never been locked, but faced with Tom's quiet insistence had accepted with a good grace. She did press a bottle of whisky into his hands as he left and was rewarded with a sudden smile of thanks.

'Feel better?' asked Margie as Alex came into the kitchen from the back door.

'God, yes,' said Alex. She hung one of the gate keys up on a hook beside the door and began fiddling with the other, trying to get it onto her key ring. 'I know it's stupid but I really felt horribly vulnerable with the old fence gone.'

'Not stupid at all. Here, give me that. You'll have yer fingernails off, messing like that.' With a quick twist she secured the key and handed it back. 'Even an old wood fence stops people looking in. Big space seems to scream an invitation to the bad boys, even if they don't know is your house. An' once you've had one fence burned don't ever feel safe behind another. Good job he done, that friend of yours,' she added.

Alex nodded in agreement. In the dining room Sue was humming tunelessly to something Jonny was playing on the stereo. It was the fourth time he's played the same song and it was beginning to get on Alex's nerves.

'Jonny! Play something else, please,' she yelled through the door. There was a pause before the sound of Bronski Beat belting out, 'I feel love' filled the house.

'Well, there go the last few illusions harboured by our neighbours,' Sue murmured as she swept into the kitchen in search of some clean wine glasses. Alex looked up, startled.

'What do you mean?' she asked. 'Is there a problem? It's just a record.'

Sue put the glasses down and sighed softly. 'Sorry, I shouldn't have said anything. This is our happy evening. Let's talk about it later.'

'No,' said Alex with a frown. 'Let's talk about it now.' They faced off across the little kitchen, an uncomfortable silence growing until Margie stepped between them.

'Mebbe we should eat first,' she suggested. 'Plenty of time to get talking later.'

Alex turned away, stung by Margie's disloyalty. Standing over the sink she clattered the pans together as all the frustration of the past month became focussed on the two people she had considered her closest friends. Margie laid her hand on her shoulder and Alex pulled away, not caring how unreasonable she was being.

'Let it go for a bit,' said Margie, undeterred. 'Been a bad few days and won't change nothing, waiting a little while.

Mind, that is a bit loud. I'll go ask him to turn it down a bit.' With a gentle squeeze on Alex's shoulder, she hurried through to the dining room where Jonny was about to treat them all to another rendering of his new favourite song.

'Enough,' she said sternly. 'We's about to eat and bit of music's all right in the background but this is loud enough to rattle me teeth. We got this last week,' she said, handing over an LP. 'Is amazing. Not heard anything like some of these songs before.'

Jonny took the record reluctantly and swapped the disk on the turntable, turning down the volume slightly. Then as the first notes of 'Graceland' filled the room he looked at Margie and nodded enthusiastically.

'See what you mean,' he said. There was a tap on the door and Lauren entered, looking a little frayed around the edges. Flinging herself onto the nearest dining chair she regaled the group with stories of her last shift at the hostel, one in which the art teacher loomed large.

'Honest,' she said. 'I thought some of the lads was weird but that Molly Brown, she makes 'um look almost normal. Came in today sayin' she couldn't possibly work in the room 'cos of the pictures there.'

Alex poked her head around the door with the main course and frowned. 'What about the pictures?' she asked. 'I chose them to help inspire the group.' Alex had been in court for most of the afternoon, arguing for a residential order on behalf of a new resident and had missed the class and Molly Brown's tantrum.

'Said they was lollipops and of "limited artistic merit",' said Lauren. 'Complained they was too much of a mix an' the colours clashed. Honest, coming from her …' Molly favoured rather long, flowing robes in orange and purple and could be heard approaching the office from some distance away as she always wore patent leather black and silver high heeled shoes that clacked loudly on the wooden floors.

'Oh,' said Alex. 'Well, I'll speak to her next week and see

what we can do. I thought it would be good to have a selection, sort of going through history.'

Maybe you should put them in chronological order?' suggested Sue, and Alex laughed, her ill humour forgotten.

'Better still, I'll get the lads to put them in chronological order,' she said. 'The first one to get it right gets their own box of tea bags.'

'Oh yes, meant to say,' said Lauren. 'Is about seven boxes on the trolley now. They just come back, all mysterious. No-one knows nothin' about them of course. So no need to buy more for weeks, I reckon.'

Alex gave a wide grin at this news. 'I knew it!' she said. 'They made me sweat a bit though. I thought they'd stop taking stuff last week.'

'They did,' said Lauren, helping herself to more chicken. 'They didn't put any back until today. Reckon they still got some stashed away but saves us having to keep refilling the jars every day.'

It hadn't taken long for the hostel to become 'us', Alex noted. She was impressed at how quickly Lauren had settled in to the role of relief warden. Unlike most of the casual staff she was available on a regular basis and so had a good idea of what was going on in a rapidly changing environment. Her years at the main office had also given her a sound knowledge of the law and she knew many of the residents from her previous role working the reception desk. She was, in many ways, the perfect member of staff and Alex had been grateful for her good humour and common sense during her own transition into a new role.

'Right, I'll need to be off soon,' said Lauren when the plates were empty and everyone was surreptitiously loosening their clothes. 'Will I be missing any pudding?'

'Only cake,' said Sue. 'Why do you have to leave? It's still early.'

'No such thing as "only" cake,' said Lauren. 'Can I take mine with me? I'm on duty over the weekend so will probably need a treat half way down Saturday.'

This was news to Alex, who dropped her fork and stared at Lauren.

'Who put you on for the weekend?' she demanded. 'I did the rota last week and ...' She screwed up her face trying to recall who was scheduled for the most unpopular of duties.

'Was supposed to be Melanie,' said Lauren, looking round for her bag. 'Only she rang through on Thursday, said she wasn't coming in no more. Bennie was in a state on account of your little problem with the fire so I said I'd step in.'

'Lauren, you've only been at the hostel a few days!' Alex said. 'It's far too soon for you to take the weekend shift.'

Lauren swivelled round and glared at her. 'I done six years in probation,' she said. 'Twice what you done actually. I know most of these lads and most of 'em know me. You saying I can't cope with 'em?'

'I know I couldn't do it,' said Sue, who was watching the stand-off with interest. 'You have to cook Sunday lunch. I suspect that would be beyond me.'

This raised a ripple of laughter around the table. Everyone had experienced Sue's attempts to cook on at least one occasion and no-one was eager to repeat the experience.

'She has a point though,' said Alex. 'It's always the most difficult part of the shift and ... well ... there's no proper kitchen help in ...' She was struggling to find a way to put her point tactfully but Lauren was having none of it.

'I know is a big kitchen,' she said, wiping her hands on her napkin. 'Industrial size almost. But you got chairs and a couple of stools. You think I can reach the stove at home without my special ladder? Anyway, most lads there is eager to help at the moment and a lot of them is monstrously tall.'

Alex knew it was no use arguing with Lauren when she'd made up her mind to do something.

'Just remember, I'm only a few minutes away,' she said as she waved her friend off into the twilight. 'Any problems you call me. It's not an admission of failure, especially on your first weekend shift. Promise?'

Lauren nodded and grinned as she hopped into her car. She had been worried Alex would step in and stop her and now she had a chance to really prove she could cut it in the hostel.

Back in the house Jonny was expressing his concern for his sister.

'I know she's set on doing this,' he said. 'God knows, I'm scared to try'n stop her sometimes but don't matter how smart she is or how well she knows the job, any one of them little sods could pick her up an' lock her in a cupboard and we'd never know about it. I don't know what Mum's gonna say when she finds out.'

'I don't think anyone could just pick up Lauren,' said Alex. 'She's pretty good at her job and if it comes to physical violence any warden is in trouble, male or female, no matter how big they are. The trick is never letting it get that far and Lauren's a past master at that. Besides, a lot of the lads know her and like her. It's not like she's a total stranger they're going to test out. Most of them already know better than to try.'

She made a good case, Alex thought as she climbed the stairs that night. She just hoped she had been right. The thought of Lauren on her own in the hostel, especially overnight, sat uneasily on her.

Chapter Thirteen

Sue was sleeping late, the result of a night spent talking and laughing long into the small hours and her desperately stressful weeks zigzagging across the county to attend pre-release meetings. Her language when the phone started to ring and did not stop was both colourful and inventive. Finally it fell silent and she poked her head out from under the covers, hoping to hear Alex's voice. Instead the phone started up again and this time it didn't stop until Sue dragged her aching head down the stairs to answer it.

'What?' she snapped. There was the sound of a bell ringing down the line accompanied by some heavy breathing. Oh great, thought Sue. A prank call from a weirdo on Saturday morning. 'Hello? Look, just piss off will you,' she snapped.

'You said to ring!' said Lauren sounding extremely aggrieved.

'What? Oh, sorry. I thought you were – never mind,' said Sue. 'Is there a problem? And what's that racket going on over there?'

'I need to ask Alex something,' Lauren said, raising her voice above the noise in the background.

'She's not here,' said Sue, who was now wide awake and beginning to worry about events at the hostel. 'Can I help? I can come down if you need me.'

'Well, I'll manage for the time being but could you get her to call soon as she's back?' Lauren hung up the phone without waiting for a reply, leaving Sue standing half-naked in the middle of the front room and screened inadequately by the net curtain. Hastily replacing the receiver she hurried upstairs and grabbed the nearest clothes, an eccentric mix of court blouse, suit jacket and jeans with fashionably ripped knees finished off by her trademark tiny sandals. Given Alex's improvements at the hostel she thought she could probably get some coffee there.

All was still and quiet as she pulled into the car park, deserted apart from Lauren's specially adapted car. Not sure whether this was a good or bad sign, Sue scurried through the front door and ran straight into Charlie. As he bounced off the opposite wall the ringing began again and Sue realized it was the fire bell.

'I told you to stay there!' Lauren yelled from the office.

'Sorry, Miss. Was not my fault,' yelled Charlie above the noise. He jostled Sue out of the way and pressed on the button for the alarm. A blissful silence fell on the building once more.

'I never done it,' said Charlie. 'Honest – was just coming down the stairs when it started. Now I bin stuck here an' is making my hand hurt.'

'I don't think you need to press quite so hard,' said Sue. 'Just enough pressure to keep it down. Hold on.' She rummaged in her pocket but found nothing useful. 'I'll take over and you go to the kitchen and get some cardboard – thick as you can find – and bring some scissors. And you'd better come back!'

Charlie shot off like a startled rabbit shaking his stiff hand as he went. He disappeared through the door to the dining room as Lauren materialized in the entrance to the office.

'What the hell you doin' here?' she demanded.

'Stopping the alarm and hopefully saving the hostel the cost of a false call out,' said Sue. 'What happened?'

Lauren scowled as she looked up at Sue. 'Some little sod decided would be funny to set off the alarm. Broke the glasses and scarpered – I heard the door go just as the bells went off. Now I got one lad upstairs and thought I had Charlie down here on the alarms whilst I look for the spares to fix 'em.'

'Ah,' said Sue. Her hand was beginning to cramp with the effort of holding down the button and she felt a bit more sympathy for Charlie. 'I don't know where they are kept,' she said. 'Have you looked in the drawers?'

Lauren threw a withering look over her shoulder as she headed back into the office. 'Never thought of that,' she said. Sue sighed and leaned harder on the fire button. Sometimes Lauren was a very difficult person to help.

Charlie returned, sliding on the floor in his haste and clutching some stout cardboard and a rather flimsy pair of scissors.

'Woah! Gently, Charlie,' said Sue, flinching as the blades stopped just short of her arm. 'Did no-one ever tell you not to run with scissors?'

'Sorry, Miss,' said Charlie. 'Is this alright?'

'It's fine,' she said, deftly changing places and taking the card. Somewhat reluctantly Charlie resumed his post and Sue began to trim the card to make a cover for the bell. Finally, she had a double thickness that seemed about the right size and motioned him to step away as she jammed it into the front of the box. There was an anxious moment as they stood looking at the makeshift repair before uttering a sigh of relief in unison.

'Great,' said Sue. 'I'll go and see if I can help Lauren.'

'What about Mike?' asked Charlie, glancing up the stairs.

'Mike? Who's Mike?' asked Sue.

'Is on the landing with the other alarm,' said Charlie.

Glasses, thought Sue. Lauren said *glasses*, plural. 'Bugger,' Sue muttered. She had hacked through the board recklessly and there wasn't enough left for a second repair. 'Go and get some more,' she said, waving the remains of the box lid at Charlie. 'I'll go and let Mike know help is on the way.'

Ten minutes later the three of them crowded into the office, where Lauren was balanced rather precariously on the desk and raking through the top drawer of the main cupboard.

'It's okay for now,' said Sue. 'Not legal though. If the brigade did call we'd be in real trouble without proper fire alarms. At least you managed to stop another call-out. That was well done.'

Charlie and Mike helped Lauren down from the desk and moved back to the door.

'Thanks to these two,' said Lauren. 'They was there in a flash. Thank you,' she added, throwing a smile to the two young men who were shuffling their feet and looking rather embarrassed.

'You need any help lookin'?' asked Mike.

'No, I know where they are kept,' said Alex, who had suddenly appeared behind them. The two lads jumped at her voice and edged to one side, allowing her to slide into the office. 'Still, you have been a great help from the sound of things. I'll make sure it goes on your records. Now, it is getting a bit crowded in here ...'

Charlie and Mike edged out of the room, but before they vanished Alex called them back. 'Get a cup of tea if you want,' she said. 'And here – have these to go with it.' She reached up to a shelf in the corner and took down a box of chocolate biscuits.

Oh, lush!' said Charlie. 'Thanks, Miss.' The two friends hurried off to the dining room, Charlie hugging the box possessively.

'Bennie's gonna be mad you done that,' said Lauren. 'Is up there to keep for a birthday or summat.'

'Well, I'm the warden now and anyway I'll replace them later. Those two just saved us a lot more than the cost of some biscuits and quite frankly I don't think a pat on the head is always adequate reward. Now, let me get to the safe and we'll fix these fire alarms properly.'

'We have a safe?' said Lauren.

'Oh, you'd be amazed and possibly appalled by what we've got in this place,' said Alex. 'Now, we can replace these but we don't have enough spares if it happens again so we need to make sure this stops now!'

Ricky Peddlar was having a miserable weekend. The meeting with Rosalind was as devastating as it was unexpected and he had retired to his room to sulk for most of the afternoon. It was completely unreasonable to expect him to teach the basic skills group and he had finally picked up the phone and started searching for a tutor to take on the task. Unfortunately, there was no-one available at such short notice and the private companies charged considerably more than his budget allowed. Had he bothered to read Alex's notes he would have known this before wasting an afternoon. She had run into the same problem, which was why she'd taken the class herself.

Faced with this ghastly prospect, Ricky had been forced to read through the lesson plans and outline provided but he was no teacher and the prospect of standing up in front of a group terrified him. When he realized there was no escaping the task he reluctantly dragged himself into the office on Saturday afternoon and began to put some lessons together.

As he shuffled papers around and chewed the top off his pen he brooded on his bad luck at having to work on his weekend. It was just not fair, he thought. First Gordon, the acting senior, had put him on twice-weekly court duties, excusing his actions by impugning the level of training Ricky had received. Well, he got what was coming to him when Ricky's training supervisor turned up as the new senior. But now, for some reason he couldn't fathom, that same supervisor was picking on him.

Of course, it was really all the fault of Alex Hastings. If she had done her job properly then there would have been a tutor in place and he would be enjoying a few beers with his friends instead of being stuck here. It was ridiculous not being able to afford someone to teach reading anyway. Who did these tutors think they were? It wasn't as if they were teaching anything difficult after all. Anyone could *read*. He turned back to the budget printout, scowling as he ran his finger across the paper. Where the hell had all the money gone anyway?

Despite the fact the meals at the hostel had shown some improvement since Alex's arrival Samuel still did not often eat there. The food might be a bit better but his companions' table manners had not improved and he disliked being in close proximity to a number of people. On Saturday he had gone down early and eaten as much toast as he could before the other residents began to trickle into the dining room. There had been a couple of biscuits left in a box on the trolley and after a moment's hesitation he had wrapped them in a clean handkerchief and slipped them into his pocket.

It wasn't stealing, he reasoned. They were put out for any resident to eat and he hadn't had any from the box. In truth he disliked the thought of communal food. You never knew who had touched it or whether they'd washed their hands but he needed bus fare to get him to the market at Taunton and he had been saving from his pitiful allowance for weeks. He should have enough for his purchase but nothing left for anything to eat during the day so the biscuits would have to suffice.

It was another warm day, the sun already hot enough to burn, and the bus journey sorely tried his patience. The vehicle was packed with shoppers and families all chattering and moving around, children squirming on their seats instead of sitting quietly as they should. He retreated to the top deck but found it full of young people laughing and pushing. Many of them were in pairs and behaving in an utterly shameless fashion. Despite the signs forbidding it some passengers were smoking, blowing the smoke out of the windows in a vain effort to hide their transgression.

Resisting the desire to shout at them, Samuel settled in a seat near the stairs, staring out of the window at the countryside below. He had not realized how exposed the landscape was from an elevated position. From his seat above the hedges he could see for miles across the fields, plot the course of the tiny waterways and even catch a glimpse of Glastonbury Tor in the distance as the bus wound its way round what felt like most of the county before finally turning and heading for Taunton. He made a note to check the times of the bus in future. It had a very limited timetable but the thought of being that exposed when he thought his movements and actions were hidden made him extremely uncomfortable.

Alighting in the main street in Taunton, Samuel had to stop himself scratching all over. The ride had made him feel grubby, tainted by the smell of his fellow passengers and their nearness. Taking a deep breath of the diesel-laden air he set off through the crowds trying to avoid physical contact with these strangers. Most of the stalls merited no more than a contemptuous glance. He hovered for a moment near the produce section, tempted by the display of fresh fruit that made his mouth water. Then a small child leaned forward and took an apple from the stall. Its mother snatched it away and put it back but Samuel turned away, disgusted at the thought of all the dirty hands that might have touched the goods.

Ignoring the growling in his stomach he hurried past the butcher's van where joints of meat hardened in the bright sunlight, on beyond the haberdashers who stood gossiping next to their displays of tablecloths and bright swatches of fabric. The air was thick with the scent of grease and onions from vans selling hot food and Samuel turned down the central aisle to avoid them.

He stopped abruptly as he spotted a familiar figure. Like a small battleship, resplendent in bright pink and powder blue, Rosalind glided through the crowds with Debbie trotting in her wake like a multicoloured tug boat. Samuel stepped back into the shelter of a stall offering bags, hold-alls and suitcases, pretending to examine the stitching on a faux army pack whilst all the time observing the pair.

Rosalind stopped at a table set off to one side. There was a notice on the front, though he could not make out what it said, but it was obviously a petition of some sort. As he watched, Rosalind exchanged a few words with the woman behind the table and then snapped her fingers at Debbie, who pulled a pen from her handbag. With a great flourish Rosalind signed the sheet on the table, handing the pen back to Debbie, who did the same. With a laugh that tinkled through the sound of the crowd the pair set off again and disappeared into the mass of people.

'You buyin' that or what?' asked the stall-holder. Samuel shook his head and put the pack back on the stall, hurrying over to the petition table. He had no real interest in Rosalind and what he'd seen so far had failed to impress him, but all information was good and this was a rare opportunity. Most officers were very precious about their home addresses, even Alex who, unusually for a probation officer, lived in the town.

'Would you like to sign?' asked the woman at the table hopefully. Samuel gave her a vague smile and picked up the form. Something to do with clearing the old canal into Taunton, he noted. Whilst he pretended to read the petition text his eyes scanned the rows of signatures, spotting Rosalind's almost at the bottom. A pen appeared in front of his eyes and he almost brushed it away before he remembered what he was supposed to be doing.

'Thank you,' he said insincerely, leaning over the table. He took his time, writing a false address in slow block capitals whilst repeating Rosalind's address silently to commit it to his memory. Handing back the pen, he turned away, drifting into the throng and disappearing, just another anonymous young man out for a stroll through the market on a Saturday. Keeping a sharp look out for the departed Rosalind and her lackey, Samuel made his way to the rear of the market.

Here were the unfashionable stalls, those selling live animals for the pot or bric-a-brac, second-hand clothes and rusted, useless tools. At the very back and too close to the wall of the cattle market for comfort was an old-fashioned knife grinder. The old man was sitting on the saddle of his machine which resembled an upturned bicycle. For a few pence he would put a fine edge on scissors, carving knives and worn-out, treasured penknives. To one side was a box containing a variety of blades, many of them salvaged and polished up with a fine edge. Samuel poked through the box careful to avoid seeming overly interested in his ultimate prize. At the bottom was a selection of fine old-fashioned straight-edged razors, all of them lovingly restored by the knife man.

'How much for this one?' Samuel asked pulling out one at random.

'Fifteen bob,' said the grinder. Samuel gritted his teeth, biting back his frustration. Did no-one in this God-forsaken place understand decimal currency? He dropped the razor back in the tin and shrugged.

'Just want one for my Grandad,' he said with a show of indifference. 'His is worn out and we're worried he'll cut himself.'

The grinder rose from his seat and started rummaging through the box.

'Well now, this is a fine example,' he said pulling out a black-handled razor. 'Good clean edge and newly riveted so is very strong. Give a good, clean shave this will.'

Samuel's heart beated faster as he looked at the blade sparkling in the sunlight. He reached out and took the razor, feeling the balance and testing the smoothness of the edge.

'Looks good,' he said. 'How much for this one then?'

'Just ten bob for you an' yer Grandad,' said the grinder, with a crooked smile. Samuel fished in his pocket and counted out the money whilst the seller wrapped the razor in some brown paper.

'There you go, lad. Nice to see some young folk lookin' out for their family.'

Samuel took the parcel and managed a sickly smile. The razor felt warm in his hand and he could hardly wait to get back to his cottage and try it out. It was a lot cheaper than he'd expected and he decided to treat himself to something for lunch before setting off for the return bus. As pleasurable as playing with his razor might be, there was just as much enjoyment in the anticipation. His eyes shone a bright, fierce blue as he worked his way back through the crowds.

Curfew at the hostel was 10pm, regardless of what day it was. This caused some considerable grumbling amongst the residents, especially on alternate Saturdays when most of them received their benefit cheques. The staff, on the other hand, were all in favour of keeping the restriction. It tended to put a brake on the sort of excess that had landed a number of the residents in the hostel in the first place and also meant they could get a reasonable night's sleep – at least in theory.

In practice, no-one ever slept properly whilst on night duty. The staff room was set at the end of the first-floor corridor and had a reinforced door, double locks, a safety chain and peephole as well as an independent telephone line. The window sported iron bars and inside was a private bathroom with shower and an alcove boasting a small television, kettle and mini fridge. A lot of thought had gone into making it as comfortable and safe as possible but that didn't alter the fact that the night warden was alone and twenty potentially dangerous men were just on the other side of the bedroom door. The hours were paid as a 'sleeping shift' but in truth they were far from restful. Alex had done night duty when she was a student and she hated it.

'You make the announcement,' she said. 'I'll come in about 10.45, after you've done the final check and you're ready to go up.'

Lauren pulled a face but she was already feeling the strain of the weekend and Alex's plan gave her a chance to go home and rest without having to admit she might have overtaxed her still-recovering health.

At exactly ten o'clock Lauren closed and locked the doors, making her way into the recreation room where the last frames of a pool tournament vied with football on the television for space and volume. She knew better than to try and break up the pool match directly. This was one of the rare situations where she allowed her size to dictate her actions.

Instead, she headed for the television set and switched it off. There was a stunned silence as the six lads who had settled down for some late-night viewing sat for a moment staring at the blank screen.

'Aw, come ON!' shouted one.

'Don't be tight,' said another.

'Yeah, even Marky let us watch of'n a Saturday,' Petey protested.

'I doubt that very much,' said Lauren. 'Seein' as *Mr Marks* has not been on duty over a weekend for longer than *you've* been a resident.'

The noise in the room diminished as the pool players turned to watch events with some interest.

'And you lot should put those down and listen. I've got an announcement and none of you can say you didn't hear what I said.'

There was some sniggering from around the table but Lauren fixed the culprits with a fierce stare.

'If'n you need me to explain what "announcement" means, I can use little words,' she said. 'Otherwise, listen so's I can explain what'll be the *consequences* if that there fire alarm goes off in the night.'

It was suddenly very quiet in the room. Assured of their full attention, Lauren continued.

'I don't get paid if I's up in the night for you lot. Not unless I'm up for at least an hour. So if there's an alarm, you will all have to go outside an' wait in the proper place. Which is in full view of that there road. I'll be telling the brigade they should check everything – every room an' every bin and anywhere else I can think of and you can be sure I'll be inside makin' them tea while you is all outside for at least my hour. Anyone got any questions?'

It seemed no-one had and it was a rather subdued group of individuals that trooped up the stairs a few minutes later. Lauren waited until the last of them had left before letting out a huge sigh of relief. Then she went back into the office to write up the day book and wait for Alex to arrive.

Ada peered wistfully out of her window at the empty pen in her back garden. It had taken her a long time to get used to Pongo, what with his size, his huge horns and not least his smell. Now the place seemed devoid of life without him.

'You sure he's fine?' she asked for the fourth time that evening. Tom looked up from his paper and nodded patiently.

'Checked all the fences m'self,' he said. 'Good and sturdy they is. Decent lock on the gate an' a full battery to be runnin' the 'lectric wires. Him an' Quinn, they's fine. Not going nowhere anyway, there's so much stuff for 'um to eat inside.'

Ada turned to look at him. 'Them's males,' she said. 'Always wanting what's out of reach, regardless of what's inside for 'um.'

Tom put his paper down with a sigh. 'I'll take you over tomorrow if'n will set yer mind to rest,' he said.

'Me too!' said Brian from the corner where he was working his way through a textbook on animal husbandry he'd borrowed from the local library.

'You only saw him yesterday,' Tom said.

Brian shrugged and returned to his book. 'Miss him, is all,' he muttered.

There was a clamouring outside the door and Ada opened it to let the dogs in. Tails wagging, they ran to Tom and then Brian before flopping on the tiled floor, tongues lolling as they panted in the heat.

'Fearful warm tonight,' said Tom. 'Too hot to sleep these past few days. Never thought I'd be sayin' it but we could really do with some decent rain. How's your tubs holdin' up, Ada?'

Ada flopped onto a chair by the table and fanned herself with a page from Tom's paper.

'More'n half empty,' she said. 'Used to get some water from that stream, end of the garden, but is dry now. Been nothing in there for a week. If'n it don't rain soon, don't know what I'll do. Is too much, luggin' it around in buckets from the sink an' anyway, don't like that smell from the tap water. Smells like swimming baths.'

'Could get a bit of hosepipe,' Brian said, setting his book aside. 'Would keep the veggies going 'til it rains and is easier to use. Just run it from the tap in here out the back door.'

Tom frowned at him. 'Hosepipe ban,' he said shortly. 'Came in couple a' weeks ago.'

Brian snorted in disgust. 'Who's to know, out here?' he said. 'Any road, is for townies with lawns and such, not folks growin' food. You's more like a farmer, Ada. Farmers 'ent got no hosepipe ban so shouldn't count for you.'

Ada was surprised at Brian's reasoning. He was certainly growing up, she thought. 'This is your doing,' she said to Tom. 'Don't you give me no innocent face neither. I heard this kind'a logic before from you – is a bad influence on the boy.'

Tom stood up and stretched, his long arms reaching almost to the ceiling. 'Don't you go blaming me,' he said cheerfully. 'Knows his own mind, don't you Brian? Though I must say, can't fault his reasoning.' He grinned at Ada who tried to look fierce in the face of his charm.

'Well, we better be off. See you tomorrow. You want I should bring a bit of hosepipe along?' He bent over and gave her a quick hug, then slipped through the door with Brian before Ada could react.

'Night,' came Brian's voice from the darkness.

'Night,' whispered Ada as she closed and bolted the door. She sat at the table for a moment, her eyes fixed on the two dogs. 'Well,' she said. 'He took his time.'

When the fire bell went off at three in the morning Alex sat bolt upright in the bed, the shock of the noise setting her heart pounding. Hurrying to the peephole in the door she peered through, hoping to catch a glimpse of whoever was responsible. In the dim glow of the emergency lights she saw doors open along the corridor as sleepy residents peered out into the gloom, but there was no sign of anyone trying to slip back inside. Right, she thought angrily, show time.

She hadn't bothered to undress, so sure was she of the night's events. Unlocking the door she flung it open and hurried down the hall banging on the few doors still closed.

'Out!' she shouted. 'Everyone up and outside. Now please gentlemen.'

There was a babble of protest, cut short when the first of the residents saw who they were dealing with. Moving swiftly she herded the first sleepy, tousled bunch out of their rooms and down the stairs.

'Assemble at the front,' she instructed. 'Line up by the front fence and keep the entrance clear for the fire brigade.' She deftly fielded several young men who tried to slip back inside their rooms.

'But Miss, I got no shoes!' one protested.

'Sorry,' she said firmly. 'Better than no feet though, which is what you'll be left with if there is a fire. Now out, as you are all of you.'

Moaning and grumbling, the residents made their way out of the building and across to the far side of the car park where they huddled together in the cool night air. Alex continued her checking of the rooms, making sure they were all empty. At the very end was the room occupied by Samuel Burton and she hesitated for an instant before knocking. The door opened immediately and she had the impression he had been standing behind it waiting. His face was expressionless but a tiny spark of bright blue betrayed his surprise at seeing her as it flickered in his eyes.

'I have to ask you to leave the hostel and join the other residents at the assembly point,' she said. For an instant she thought he was going to refuse but Samuel only nodded his head and stepped out of the room, turning down the corridor without a word. He was dressed, she noticed. Unlike a number of the other lads who were now gathered on the tarmac of the car park wearing only their boxers and T-shirts. Despite the warm night they were going to feel chilly soon as a little breeze blew from the east. Tough, she thought. They had been warned and they all knew the regulations.

The fire engine arrived with a great rush and noise of bells and flashing lights and Alex hurried down the stairs to meet them. A quick glance at the fire bells showed they were all still intact and so the alarm had to have been triggered by one of the detectors. As soon as the fire chief heard this he ordered Alex out and his men into the building to search for the source of the alarm.

Alex walked across to the group huddled in the corner of the yard. Some of them were already looking decidedly miserable but as she checked names against the hostel log she noted down anyone who was dressed, had their shoes on or looked in any other way ready for the evacuation. Apart from Samuel there were three lads who seemed better prepared – Petey, Steve and a new resident who shared the room with them.

She ran her eye down the list looking for his name. Mark, she thought. Oh, Mark *Anthony*. How unusual, especially for a young man who had ended up in a probation hostel. He was looking around nervously and his body language suggested he, unlike his room-mates, had realized he'd made a serious mistake. Alex fixed him with her best hard stare and after a moment he looked up at her, blushing furiously before dropping his head to stare at the lumpy surface of the car park. Got you, Alex thought. She would wait until the morning but Mark Anthony certainly knew who had set the alarms off and he was going to confirm her suspicions.

'You will all wait here until we get the all-clear from the fire brigade,' she said to the miserable little group. 'I need to do a check before you can come back in so it may be a few minutes.'

There was a bit of muttering as she headed back to the front door and she only just managed to hide a smile from them. Inside, the fire crews had found a sensor in one of the upper corridors with soot around the casing and there was a scorch mark on the ceiling.

'Hello there, Miss Hastings. Didn't expect to be seeing you again so soon,' said the fire chief. 'Look at this now. Looks like some joker with a lighter. Wouldn't leave burn marks with no cigarette.'

'Deliberate then?' Alex asked.

'No doubt about this 'un,' said the fire chief in disgust. 'Is another call-out to you. Getting to be expensive an' there'll be questions if it carries on. Can't be flying out here on all these false alarms when there's real emergencies needing us.'

Alex nodded her understanding. 'I'm keeping them out there as long as I can,' she said. 'I hope an hour or so in the dark might dampen their enthusiasm for this sort of thing a bit. If there's no other call on I don't suppose you could go through again, just to make sure?'

The fire chief hesitated, looking at his deputy. 'Nothing else so far,' said the fireman. 'Well, better to be sure,' said the chief and he sent his crew up the stairs again to look around a second time. 'Might take a while to get all the gear loaded back on the truck too,' he added, giving Alex a sly smile. 'Need to keep the area clear of civilians while we do that an' all.'

It was almost ninety minutes before the fire tender left and Alex opened the front door to allow the miserable residents back inside. Most hurried past in silence, eager to return to their beds but several gave her angry looks and she heard one mutter something that sounded like 'stupid bitch' as he headed up the stairs. Undisturbed by their hostility, she smiled as they trooped back up to their room, wishing them a good night as they went. Last in was Samuel, who seemed undisturbed by the night's events. He gave Alex a polite nod and the tiniest glimmer of a smile before making his way upstairs, leaving her to lock up and turn off the lights.

Although it was not yet five in the morning Alex went into the office and wrote up the incident in the day book. She was tired but didn't feel like using the staff bedroom and so finally she settled into the sole armchair in the office and dozed fitfully until woken by the morning sunlight creeping across the room.

Margie was up early and hummed her way around the narrow kitchen, tidying and putting away dishes and pans from the previous night before starting her preparations for breakfast. Alex had said she would be home in time for them to eat together before Margie's lunchtime shift at Shepton Mallet and she was planning something extra special. The supermarket had just started selling ready-made dough for pastries and Margie took a couple of cardboard tubes out of the fridge, peering at the instructions on the labels.

The oven was warming and the kettle boiling when Alex came through the door. Margie slipped the pastries in to cook on a baking tray and hurried to greet her.

'How was it?' she said, flinging her arms around Alex. 'Did they all kick off like you reckoned?'

'Well, they tried,' said Alex, sinking into a chair. 'Wow, I'm stiff. I think I'm getting too old to stay up all night. I know – there's a room for sleeping there but after the fire alarm went off and we got the little beasts back inside I didn't really want to be up there again. Something smells wonderful,' she added, looking towards the kitchen.

'You sit here an' I'll check on breakfast,' said Margie.

Alex leaned back in the chair and closed her eyes wearily. In truth, she felt as if she'd been run over by a truck and she was so tired her head was swimming. Only the desire to spend some time with Margie and the growling in her stomach stopped her from dozing off.

Margie reappeared with a pot of fresh coffee shortly followed by a plate heaped with chocolate croissants, cinnamon rolls and fresh raisin bread. They sat opposite one another and ate in companionable silence for a few minutes until Alex stopped and took a deep breath.

'This is possibly the most wonderful breakfast I've ever had,' she said, pouring herself another coffee. 'I could get used to this.'

'Is only 'cos I love you, so don't get to expect it,' Margie replied. Both of them froze, a heartbeat of silence rising between them. It was the first time either had used the word aloud. Alex looked up and their eyes met over the remains of breakfast. Then she reached out and took Margie's hand.

'I know,' she said softly. 'And I won't.' They sat at the table, smiling silly, giddy smiles, savouring the moment. The spell was broken by a hammering on the front door and Alex jumped to her feet, startled and alarmed.

'Oh no, I hope that's not more trouble at the hostel,' she said, hurrying to answer it. As she turned the handle there was another brief tattoo and as the door opened Jonny fell into the room, stumbling on the threshold and into Alex. Margie hurried to her friend's aid and together they managed to get him safely to the sofa.

'Oh my God, what's happened to you?' Alex said as she looked at his face. Both eyes were blackened and one was swollen shut. Blood trickled from a cut over his nose, which was twisted to one side, nostrils caked and bleeding. As he turned his head slowly to look at them with his open eye Alex realized his left ear seemed to be in the wrong place, the top of it hanging down almost to the lobe. Jonny tried to say something but all that came out was a hissing sound through a mass of pink bubbles.

'I'll call the police,' said Margie. 'An' you need to go to the hospital.'

'No,' Jonny managed, shaking his head and spattering blood onto the wall behind him. 'No p'lice.'

'Jonny, what happened?' Alex said, horrified at the sight of her friend.

'Is obvious what happened,' Margie snapped. 'Some evil bastard beat on him and pretty bad too.' She marched across to the phone and lifted the receiver.

'Nooo,' said Jonny. 'Not p'lice. Won't do no g'd. Just make it worse.'

'We need to get you seen to,' said Alex. 'Let us take you to the hospital. Come on Jonny, you're badly hurt. You need help.'

Jonny groaned and closed his eyes.

'Don't you fall asleep,' said Margie, replacing the receiver. 'Could have concussion from all that round yer head. Alex, you get a towel for supporting his neck.'

Alex hurried off, returning with several towels which they rolled up and placed around Jonny's neck and shoulders.

'You listen to me,' said Margie fiercely. 'Is only 'cos we don't say nothing that they get away with it. You don't report this an' they'll be out hunting some other poor bastard tonight an' it won't stop until they's caught and maybe they'll kill someone. Looks like they had a good try with you, an' you is going to the hospital whatever you say.'

'Maybe it *was* the police,' said Alex gloomily, looking down at Jonny's wrecked face.

'No,' Jonny whispered. 'Went past 'n left us though. Won't stop 'um. Just get pointed out an' on the record.'

'Where did this happen?' Margie asked. 'Was it in town?'

'Place out past Pethy,' Jonny mumbled. 'Was waitin' for us, I reckon. Thought it was quiet an' no-one bothered us. Was wrong.'

'How the hell did you get back here?' asked Alex.

'Long walk,' said Jonny. His eyes were starting to close again and Margie reached over and poked him in the ribs to wake him.

'Aaah,' he groaned, and tried to lift his arms protectively. Margie nudged Alex aside and pulled his shirt up to reveal a mass of bruising across his chest.

'That settles it,' she said, easing his top back over the injuries. 'Could well have some ribs broken too. We can argue 'bout the police as we go but you're on your way to the hospital. We'll go in my car – oh ...' She stopped and glanced at her watch. 'Got to leave in a few minutes or I'll be late for work. Alex ...'

'That's okay,' said Alex. 'You go get ready. I'll get Jonny into my car and take him round. Have you got a key? You never know how long we'll be waiting.'

'Shouldn't be *that* long,' said Margie, but she felt in her pocket and pulled out the front door key anyway. 'You try and get some sleep later,' she added as she headed up the stairs to change into her uniform. 'You're worn out after last night.'

'Tell me about it,' Alex muttered as she scrabbled in her bag for her car keys. It took a huge effort to get Jonny to his feet but finally she was able to manoeuvre him to the door. Margie clattered down the stairs again and together they helped him into the front seat of Alex's car. His eyes fluttered open and he peered around before groaning softly.

'Lauren said never get in your car,' he mouthed. 'Will be mad at me.'

'It's this or I'll go next door and borrow a wheelbarrow,' said Alex, sliding into the driver's seat and slamming the door.

'Yes please,' said Jonny.

Alex ignored him, setting off for the hospital with Margie following in her car. With a wave and a toot of the horn Margie peeled off at the entrance to the car park leaving Alex to wrestle Jonny into the emergency department.

Her shift ended at four on Sunday afternoon and Lauren decided to drop in to see Alex before heading home. She was feeling slightly guilty having let herself be persuaded to swap the night duty. It felt a bit like chickening out, although Alex had pointed out it was Lauren who had issued the ultimatum, Lauren who had to deal with the bad-tempered aftermath the next morning and Lauren who had to somehow get a Sunday dinner for thirteen young men on the table for lunch time.

'Rather you than me,' Alex had said as she left that morning, but Lauren still felt as if she had failed in some way. Knocking at the front door she noticed a dark splash on the step. She rubbed at it with her foot but whatever it was had dried in the sun. The door was opened by Sue, who blinked at her for a moment, looking flustered.

'Lauren,' she said. 'Ah – how did it go then?' Recovering some composure she smiled brightly but made no attempt to step aside and let her in.

'Was fine,' said Lauren shortly. Despite having spent the night at home she was tired and she ached all over from standing for so long.

'Alex in?' she asked, peering hopefully round Sue, who also looked round as if trying to spot her.

'I'm not … Actually it's not a very good time,' she managed. Lauren took a step back, hurt by her whole attitude.

'Oh. Well, I just want to talk a bit. Maybe you've got a cup of tea?'

Sue squirmed with embarrassment but refused to budge. 'Honestly, I'm sorry Lauren but it's a really bad time. I could get Alex to give you a call?'

Suddenly, Lauren heard Jonny's voice raised in protest from the back room.

'Wot's he doin' here?' she snapped, pushing Sue out of the way. 'Promised me he'd be home today on account of Mum bein' away an' not wantin' to leave the house empty too long. Said he'd be back afore I was off to work, though I never saw him.' She stormed through the front room and stopped abruptly when she saw her brother, his face black and swollen between the stitches.

''Lo, Sis,' he lisped, and she saw he was missing a tooth at the front. She collapsed onto a chair and stared at him for a moment.

'Well,' she said finally, her voice shaking just a little. 'What the hell you been up to now?'

Chapter Fourteen

The problem posed by Margie continued to exercise Samuel's imagination. He moved through the week, attending his workshop, signing on at the dole office and taking long runs out to the cottage on the Levels, but the whole time he was puzzling over how to get her out to his new base. He had no car and he could hardly haul her unconscious body onto the bus. The obvious solution was to stick to his usual pattern and ambush her in the house.

It would not be difficult, he thought. She worked regular night shifts and was often home on her own, sleeping and vulnerable during the day. One of her neighbours was out at work and the old couple on the other side went out often. Besides they were both a bit deaf and Samuel was confident he could keep any extraneous noise to a minimum. Despite all the advantages, however, he was extremely reluctant to invade Alex's house so he went back to the problem, worrying at it as he worked on the top room, turning it into somewhere he could enjoy the anticipated few hours with Margie.

He was surprised when one morning he jogged past one of the few buildings on his route and spotted two goats in the front garden. Slowing his steps he looked at them carefully, realizing with a start he had seen them before, on the land by the canal. The larger of the animals stopped his grazing and looked back over the fence, fixing him with his huge yellow eyes, and Samuel hurried on.

A tiny superstitious part inside his head was sure the goat had recognized him and the hard stare made him want to open the gate and do something violent. Taking deep breaths to calm his irrational anger he jogged on. No need to take any risks, he reasoned. Don't attract attention. Don't do anything that might bring the police out asking questions. He stopped abruptly as he rounded the bend and saw a familiar green van parked on the river bank. Sliding into the undergrowth he waited, watching and cursing softly at the two figures bent over the trap in the water.

'Looks better this time,' Brian said as he lifted the neck of the net out onto the side.

'Good catch today,' Tom agreed. Together they emptied the haul into a large cool box, leaving a couple of gudgeon to attract larger fish.

'Is we goin' to see Pongo now?' Brian asked as they heaved the box into the van.

Samuel stiffened when he heard this. Pongo, he thought. That was the name the old woman who had the goat used to call. If they came back along the road they would have to drive right past him.

Tom climbed into the driver's seat and shook his head. 'Leave him be to get a bit settled,' he said. 'Not good to keep turning up an' him not knowing if he's staying or coming back with us. Ada's hoping he'll get used to this an' earn his keep, so let him get on with it today.'

He pulled out onto the road and headed off towards his home, the van leaving a plume of dust trailing behind it and Samuel stepped out of his hiding place, checking in both directions before hurrying over to the net. The two tiny gudgeon circled endlessly and hopelessly within their confines, darting from one side to another as his shadow fell across the water. Samuel clenched his teeth in frustration thinking how close he had been to acquiring a decent lunch. Now he had nothing in his pockets and the cupboard in the cottage was bare.

Cursing his decision to dally in the hostel with a slice of toast he made his way to the cottage. There was still a lot to do but on some days he scarcely had the energy for his run, never mind the heavy work needed to get the room decent. Forcing his body onwards Samuel completed the run but he was shaking by the time he reached the side gate and for the first time in many months he sat down to rest inside, falling into a light doze in the sunlight that lit the kitchen.

Charlie knocked on the office door, peering in with a hopeful look on his face. Alex suppressed a sigh and motioned him towards a chair. She was still tired from the weekend and had spent what felt like a long twenty minutes on the phone to his tutor at the college. Charlie was doing very well in some areas but he really did not want to try a lot of the classes. As full participation was a condition of the course he was on the verge of being thrown out and Alex had needed all her powers of persuasion to win him a second chance.

'You can't pick and choose,' she said. 'You agreed to try everything – you never know when something will turn up that you never thought of but you really like.'

Charlie flopped back in the chair and stared at the ceiling.

'Stupid, some of it. An' there's cooking and stuff – is for girls.'

'You cook here,' said Alex, trying to keep the frustration out of her voice. 'Everyone should know how to cook.'

'That's different,' said Charlie. ''Ent like cooking for a job.'

Alex opened her mouth to point out nearly all the chefs in the country were men but decided it was a waste of time. The most pressing issue was to get him back to college in a positive frame of mind. She could work on all the other stuff later.

'So what *do* you like?' she said.

'Like the art,' said Charlie. 'Teacher 'ent so good as Mrs Brown, though we get more stuff to use. Proper easels an' all and we's doing some modelling this week.'

'Good,' said Alex, nodding her encouragement. 'And what else?'

'Like bein' outside,' said Charlie. 'Not the garden stuff though. Is too much like farm work and I 'ent doing *that*. Brickwork's okay but a bit boring. Wanted to try making patterns in my wall but the bloke, he said I done it all wrong. Said had to be just plain. Don't fancy doing that for the rest of my life neither.' He leaned back so far she thought the chair would topple over.

Fatigue, frustration and worry over Jonny combined in Alex's head and triggered an uncharacteristic burst of impatience.

'Art and working outside? Well, I'll see what I can do. Perhaps you fancy some work experience at the stonemason over in Pawlett? I'm sure he'd be happy to have a young assistant along to help with the heavy lifting.'

Charlie tilted his chair back again, the front legs hitting the floor with a loud bang. 'Reckon?' he said. 'Well, might be worth a try.' He unfolded his lanky frame, a broad grin on his face. 'Long as I don't have to do no more cooking.'

Alex glared at him. 'You will go back to the college and you will take part in all the activities and classes. *If* you do I will speak to your tutor next week and see what can be arranged.'

Charlie pulled a face from the doorway.

'You can't just do stuff you like,' Alex said. 'When you start work you get all the cruddy jobs and sometimes it feels as if you're just wasting your time but then as you learn about the job and how it all fits together you get to do the interesting things. That's how it works and if you're going to get a job and use your talent you have to get on with it!'

'What about you?' Charlie asked. 'You start on the naff stuff then?'

Alex laughed and nodded. 'What do you think weekend duty at the hostel is?'

Charlie laughed with her and with a quick wave trotted off upstairs to get his things. She watched him down the road as he headed off for the college. He was going to be late but she had promised to make a quick phone call to square things with the course leader. As she sat back at her desk she mused on his question. As a student she had done the mucky jobs, the unpopular shifts, working her way up to a qualified probation officer. But somehow it had all started to go wrong. From officer with a case load she had moved into the day centre and now she was doing a job normally covered in Somerset by a less qualified person. She fiddled with the pens on her desk, puzzling over how she had ended up in such a role. Still, she thought, as she lined up the day book and pad neatly, at least the only way for her now was up.

Jonny had escaped serious injury but his nose was broken and his ear had to be sewn back into place, a tricky and extremely painful procedure. Sue, who had by far the largest and most comfortable car, had driven him home on the Sunday evening with Lauren following behind. It was a sombre evening for them all and Lauren was relieved their mother was away at the other end of the county visiting her cousins. Jonny was still refusing to involve the police when they got him home but in the morning Lauren pitched in again.

'Shouldn't be letting them get away with this,' she said, delivering a large, sweet coffee to him in bed.

Jonny leaned forward for her to pile his pillows up before dropping back with a sigh. He took a sip from the beaker and pulled a face as the hot liquid hit the torn gums around his missing tooth. Several others were loose, he suspected, and his whole mouth throbbed in time to the thumping in his head.

'They don't do nothing,' he mumbled squeezing his eyes shut against the pain. The effort pulled at his stitches and he opened them again, squinting in the bright light. 'Friend of mine went to them and some of them didn't want to be in the same room. Said they might get AIDS and it was his own fault, way he walked and dressed up. Just gets your name on some list at the station. Once they got you tagged you're fair game for some of 'um.' He took another, more cautious sip and sighed.

'What happened anyway,' Lauren asked. 'You 'ent had no trouble like this before.'

'Was in the pub, small group of us sitting at the back. We had a few drinks, bit of a chat but nothin' loud. No-one paid us no mind until that bastard of a DJ got up an' started playing records. Pointed at people he knew, friends I guess, an' dedicated one song or 'nother to them. Then he points at us and says, "This is for the colourful gentlemen at the back" an' puts on Tom Robinson – you know, "Glad to Be Gay"?'

Lauren nodded and Jonny continued with his story. 'Everyone turned to look, of course, and a couple of big lads started singing along with it, pointing and waving their arms about. Decided was a good thing to maybe go somewhere else so we waited a bit, not to be too obvious, an' left. I'd had enough after that so others went off to find another pub but I was at the bus stop when someone jumped me.'

'Was it one of the big lads?' Lauren demanded. 'Did you get a look at who did it?'

'More than one,' said Jonny. 'Was at least three, maybe more.' His head sank back into the pillows and Lauren leaned over to catch the half-empty mug. 'Sorry, Sis,' he murmured and closed his eyes.

Lauren stood by the bed gazing down at her brother for a minute. Inside her a great shout of fury welled up and she turned and hurried away, anxious not to disturb him. She knew some of the local police were best avoided but there were some thoroughly decent ones too. How she wished her fiancée, Dave, was still based at Taunton but Dave was away on the three-month course for new detectives and not due back for several weeks. She washed the cups up and went into the front room still deep in thought. Finally, with a quick glance round the bedroom door to make sure Jonny was asleep, she lifted the phone and dialled a number.

Ricky's first attempt at a literacy class was an unmitigated disaster. His total lack of interest in the subject communicated itself to the group within a few minutes and they stopped paying attention, turning round in their chairs to talk, pulling faces at his back and after ten minutes folding the writing paper into wobbly planes they lobbed across the room. Ricky tried ignoring them, then attempted to stare them into silence and finally lost his temper and shouted. No-one jeered openly but the smug grins on the surrounding faces goaded him into red-faced fury. He ended the session after less than twenty minutes, sending the group out of the door on a tide of angry words. As the last young man slammed the door behind him, Ricky hurled the coloured flip-chart pens across the room and stormed off to sulk in his office.

At the reception desk Alison stood quietly, studying a list of internal phone numbers with great interest until Ricky was out of sight on the stairs. She had heard every angry word as well as being privy to the comments of the departing clients. Opening the main reception diary she made a note of the arrival and departure times for the literacy group, trying not to smile openly as she wrote.

Her caution was rewarded when Ricky materialized back at the door to the main stairs and stared at her suspiciously.

'I need the files for the basic skills lot,' he snapped, turning away without waiting for an answer.

'Of course, sir. At once, sir. Three bags full, sir,' muttered Alison without looking up from the diary.

'Even if others seem to fall a little short it is up to us to maintain our professional standards,' said Pauline from the office door.

Alison jumped, colouring red with embarrassment. 'I'm sorry, I didn't think anyone was there,' she said.

'Well, I heard what was said. Fortunately no-one else did but please bear that in mind in future,' said Pauline. 'I know there have been a number of changes recently and we are all a little stressed. We need to be patient and help one another if we can.'

Alison nodded but when the senior admin had gone back inside she scowled at the stairs, her resentment in being treated like a servant unabated. When she struggled up the stairs to Ricky's office he was sitting at his desk scribbling on a notepad, writing and crossing out. The paper was covered in doodles and odd words scored through she noticed.

'There you are. I was about to call to see where you'd got to,' he said. 'Put them there. I'll call when I'm finished.'

He really was a vile excuse for a human being, Alison thought as she headed back down the stairs. By the time she reached the lobby she was feeling the strain from the climb and she felt deep anger towards Ricky both for his boorish behaviour and on behalf of Lauren. It was Ricky's constant badgering that led to Lauren's fall as she struggled up and down the stairs trying to respond to his demands. Alison had been inclined to think it had been an accident at the time but after this morning she suspected he had indeed acted with malice towards her.

She had barely sat back down and caught her breath when the phone rang and she lifted the receiver to Ricky's voice demanding two sets of court papers. She rose, suppressing a sigh, and headed for the office but as she began to search through the cabinet Pauline stepped forward and held out her hand.

'I'll take them,' she said. Alison handed over the folders as Pauline added, 'Go back to reception. I'm calling a short meeting at lunchtime for everyone in the office but in the meantime I need you to stay at the desk.' Alison wondered how Pauline had known about the call but then Pauline knew everything that went on in the office. That was why she was such a good senior admin officer.

Ricky was surprised when Pauline stepped into his office after the curtest of knocks on the door.

'You asked for these,' she said, resisting the temptation to drop the folders in front of him. 'In future you will need to collect any papers you require yourself. We are short-handed in the office following Lauren's accident and I'm afraid we can no longer offer a dedicated assistant for the day centre.'

Ricky opened his mouth to protest but Pauline gave him no opportunity.

'I have reorganized the rotas to ensure we can cover the specialist work for the courts and our legally required paperwork. We are about to have a first-year officer join the team and they will need a dedicated assistant. As Alison has filled this role in the past she is the obvious choice, given the loss of Lauren's expertise.' She fixed Ricky with a stern look. 'Of course, I will try to accommodate any requests from you for help with reports and such like but routine paperwork and anything like teaching materials will have to be your responsibility for the time being.'

As she left, closing the door firmly behind her, Ricky threw the folders onto the floor in his fury. Court reports, client files and scribbled lesson plans all landed in a muddled heap and he kicked at them in frustration. After a few moments he bent down and began to throw them back onto the desk as the realization hit him that he was going to have sort out the mess himself.

He was in a thoroughly evil mood when the phone rang and Debbie informed him that Rosalind had scheduled a supervision session at the end of the week. Well, he thought, as he piled the files up and began to search for the paperwork he needed, he would just have to make sure Rosalind understood how hard some others were trying to sabotage him.

Steve had escaped official censure for the fire alarm incident as, despite Alex and Lauren's efforts, young Mark Anthony had remained steadfastly tight-lipped. He had a good line in denials and a fondness for answering questions with, 'Dunno', and finally Alex had sent him off with a stern warning. In appreciation of his silence Steve had invited Mark to accompany him on a trip around the market, pointing out the easiest stalls to lift from and introducing him to the 'five-finger discount'.

Mark was a fast learner and being an unfamiliar face was able to make several successful forays round the stalls before meeting up with Steve and Petey behind the Corn Exchange. The three of them walked over to the park and examined their haul but it contained very little to eat.

'What we doin' for dinner, then?' Petey asked anxiously. He had rather hoped to be included in the cooking rota for the week but Alex had struck all three of them from the list, one of the few punishments available to her without any firm evidence of wrong-doing. No hostel duty meant no midday meal and Petey, a habitual late riser, had missed breakfast that morning.

'I can get us something,' said Mark, rummaging in his pockets and pulling out a fistful of change. Petey's eyes widened as he took in the number of pound coins Mark held out casually.

'Where'd you get all that from?' asked Steve, casually holding out his hand.

Mark split up the money into roughly equal portions, handing it out to his new friends as if it were of no importance.

'My mum sends it,' he said. 'My father, he's a bit put out about all this but Mum's worried I'll not eat right or get into bad company or summat. She said if I had my own money then wouldn't need to steal.'

'Why'ja do it, then?' asked Petey, curling his fist around the coins and putting them away safe in his pocket.

Mark shrugged his shoulders, gazing over their heads at the market in the distance. 'Dunno. Somethin' to do I suppose. Bit of a buzz an' all.' He was feeling more confident after resisting the pressure to grass on his room-mates and they were more relaxed towards him. It was also gratifying to see how easily friendship could be bought when surrounded by the penniless.

The trio sauntered down a side street before emerging next to the fish and chip shop where the aroma of freshly cooked food drew them inside. Settling on a bench by the river they opened the paper wrapped packages and ate ravenously.

'So how come you got two names?' asked Steve, crumpling his papers and lobbing them in the direction of the bin. A passer-by glared at the three young men as the rubbish blew across the road and lodged in the railings over the water. Petey rose, screwing up his own wrappers, and hurried over to field the paper flapping in the breeze.

'Bit like having a servant,' remarked Mark, who was still picking at his chicken leg. 'My Dad works at the college. Not here – in Taunton. Teaches history and he's big on posh names. Thought if I had something a bit grand it might spur me on to great things. Mum never liked it though.' He rose from the bench and stretched. 'So what do you all do round here?'

Steve spat on the ground in disgust. 'Don't ask me,' he said. 'I'm not from round here. Just found meself stuck for a bit. I'd say ask *him*.' He jerked his thumb at Petey, who was busy stuffing the rubbish into the bin and trying to prevent it from blowing out again. 'He's not got much of a clue though. Ain't nothing much to do round here. You gotta make your own entertainment.'

'And what is it you make?' asked Mark, leaning forward eagerly.

Steve glanced over his shoulder at Petey and said, 'We ditch him an' I'll show yer.'

Another Tuesday workshop morning rolled around for Samuel and he dragged his tired body out of bed with reluctance. The shine had gone from the raft race and he was getting bored with the design process. Only the fact he was obliged to attend for the duration of his order kept him from turning off the tow path and heading for his cottage. There was a lot to do and yesterday he had slept most of the day away, waking with a start at the sound of a car passing on the road outside to find it was already time to leave for the hostel.

Despite his fatigue he forced his body into a trot and from the outside he appeared as fit and strong as ever. In his pockets were some early apples, a pear and several packets of biscuits from the breakfast table. Much to his surprise, fruit had started to appear on the menu at breakfast. Most residents ignored the new items and grumbled about the shortage of bacon and lack of pale, greasy sausages that had been the previous warden's choice. Samuel, who viewed most hostel food with disgust, was happy to relieve them of their fruit in exchange for his fried egg which always overdone and swimming in fat.

A pity they didn't offer boiled eggs, he thought. You were fairly sure whoever was cooking hadn't polluted a boiled egg and even if it was hard boiled it was still fairly edible. He toyed with the idea of suggesting it but decided against it. He had kept himself apart from hostel life for months and had no intention of engaging with the system at this point.

The riverbank was deserted and after a quick glance around Samuel ran up towards the new wall bordering Alex's house. As he slowed to a walk he looked over his shoulder before trying the latch on the new gate. Much to his surprise it lifted and the gate swung open a few inches. With his heart beating frantically with excitement he risked a glance into the tiny garden. It had been tidied up after the fire, the debris cleared away and a new metal rubbish bin stood by the back door. A shadow moved behind the glass panel in the back door and he closed the gate softly, hurrying away down the bank into the shelter of the underground tunnel.

'Alex?' Sue called, her eyes fixed on the back garden. 'Alex? Come here a minute.' She unlocked the back door and trotted down the path to the back gate, pulling it open and staring out in both directions. The path was deserted apart from a weary-looking woman pushing a baby away from town.

'What?' asked Alex from behind.

'Sorry. I thought I saw someone open the gate,' said Sue, still craning to see as far along as possible. 'We really should remember to lock up after we go out.'

Alex grunted and headed back inside. 'Why would anyone open our gate?' she asked.

'Why would anyone set fire to our fence?' Sue countered. 'And we must remember to use the lock. What's the point of having a good, solid wall if anyone can just open the damn gate?'

Alex sighed and reached for the key which was hung up on a hook by the back door. 'Here,' she said, handing it over to Sue. 'I'll get another one cut today or tomorrow so we've all got one.'

Sue took the key and added it to her considerable bunch. As she climbed into her car to begin another day of travelling across the Levels she considered Alex's last remark. It was the first time her friend had intimated Margie was becoming a permanent resident in the little house. She liked Margie and was happy for Alex but when they were together she sometimes felt awkward, out of place in what had been her own home. Perhaps, she thought, perhaps she should consider looking for a place of her own. Highpoint was her base, in theory, but it was right on one side of the area she had to cover and somewhere in the centre might cut down on the gruelling miles she covered every week.

In the workshop Samuel decided it was time to build a model of the raft. As he measured and cut the pieces of wood he considered Alex's lack of security. It was good for him, of course. Once through the back gate there was only a flimsy wooden door between him and the inside of the house but if he could gain access so easily so could anyone else. His concern for Alex caused his attention to wander and he knocked one of the pieces of his model off the table onto the floor. Reaching down with a curse his hand was caught under a boot that landed on the carefully crafted rudder assembly smashing the model piece and causing him to tumble from his chair.

'Oh, sorry, *boy*,' said the owner of the boot, who turned away with a sneer. Samuel sprang to his feet and hurled himself at the culprit, landing a blow on the back of his head and pushing him into one of the lathe tables. Sounds of the fight grabbed the attention of everyone in the workshop and it took the supervisor a few precious seconds to force his way through the excited throng. That was all the time Samuel needed to bounce his assailant's head off the metal surface before dropping him like a bag of bricks onto the floor.

He stepped back, shaking his injured hand and watching the crowd, ready to defend himself if anyone decided to join in. The supervisor stared at the man on the floor for a moment, then yelled at the rest of the group, sending them muttering back to their work stations.

'You, stand there an' don't move until I say,' he said, pointing to Samuel. Bending over the fallen man he checked for a pulse, straightening up when Samuel's opponent gave a groan and began to move.

'Help me get him up and into my office,' snapped the supervisor. 'QUIET the rest of you. Any more from you and everyone goes home and no-one gets credited with the session.'

Reluctantly, Samuel helped the injured man to his feet, trying not to breath the smell of body odour and alcohol that seeped from his clothes, and together they half-carried him into the area used as an office.

'Sit here for a few minutes,' said the supervisor. 'I want a word before you go home.' He beckoned at Samuel leading him through the workshop and outside into the sunshine.

'So,' he said lighting a cigarette. 'I can't let this pass, you know that don't you?'

Samuel stood absolutely still, a faint blue glitter in his eyes the only sign he was in the least concerned by events. The supervisor squinted at him through a faint haze of smoke.

'I know you didn't start it. Lad's a bully, always has been, an' he's been on your case since you got here but I won't allow fighting in my workshop. Whatever he done, you had no call to hit him like that. Lucky you didn't do some real damage.' He paused, waiting for Samuel to speak.

'It was hardly a fight,' said Samuel. 'He went straight down like the sack of shit he is.'

'You have personal issues, you leave 'em at the door,' said

the supervisor sternly. 'Now, you doing good here. One of the best workers an' your design is spot on. Don't want to lose you so I'm not making it official. But I'm not counting today off your order. You go home now an' come back Friday, do your session then with the other group. Go on, get out of here an' keep that temper of your'n in check.'

Samuel glared at him for a second, his eyes a brighter blue. Then he turned and walked away, uncurling his fists as he went. The supervisor watched to make sure he had left the premises before stamping out his cigarette and going back inside to deal with the rest of the group.

By Wednesday the worst of the bruising was coming out on Jonny's face and he could see out of both eyes, though one was still badly bloodshot. The ache in his head and around his ribs was starting to ease a little and he was able to get up and move around in short bursts.

'Need to get back to work,' he fretted that evening.

Lauren shook her head at him. 'No way you c'n go lookin' like that,' she said. 'Terrify the customers you would. An' what you going to tell yer boss then? Take a bit of explaining, all that. Not like you can get away with the old "cupboard door" story.'

Jonny had given the problem some thought. He was an assistant manager at the town's main supermarket, much valued for his ability to charm irate customers and deal with difficult shoppers. Looking like Boris Karloff in a horror movie, as Lauren had said rather heartlessly that morning, was unlikely to be much of an asset out on the shop floor.

'Thought I'd tell them I came off my bike,' he said. Jonny had an old but exceedingly powerful motorbike and had suffered a number of mishaps in the past. Recently, he'd started to take more care and had been free of broken limbs and torn ligaments for over a year.

'Well, could do I s'pose,' said Lauren. 'Maybe if'n you went face first into a post or summat. But you 'ent well enough yet. Need to rest up a bit like they said at the hospital.'

Jonny sighed in frustration. 'Don't want to lose my job,' he said. 'There's cut-backs coming soon and I need to be there, all reliable and visible.'

'You'll certainly be visible if you go in looking like that,' Lauren snapped. 'Do you more harm than good. You wait 'til Monday an' we'll see how you are.'

The doorbell chimed, cutting short Jonny's retort, and Lauren trotted through to the hall. There was a brief conversation and then she ushered Sergeant Willis, Dave's old mentor from the Highpoint police, into the room.

'Well now, Jonny,' he said with forced cheeriness. 'What you bin up to then?' He took off his cap and took a seat in one of the armchairs, trying not to stare at Jonny's face.

Lauren stepped back as her brother rounded on her angrily. 'I said no police,' he shouted. 'What part of that don't you get?'

'Now then, lad,' said Sergeant Willis, stepping between them. 'Lauren rang me and asked if'n I'd pop round more as a friend. Doesn't seem right, someone getting away with this sort of thing. Thought maybe we could do something about it.'

Jonny slumped back in the chair and glared at the pair of them. 'Like what?' he snapped. 'Didn't see who it was, didn't get a decent swing in so there's no marks on any of *them* an' after what happened to Kurt wouldn't trust your lot anyway.'

'What happened to Kurt?' asked Lauren. 'I thought you two … weren't friends any more.' She sneaked a glance at Willis, who was watching Jonny, sizing up his level of determination.

'Still see each other around,' said Jonny. 'He got jumped walking through town, month or so ago. Not so bad as this but someone made a bit of a mess of him. *He* went to the police – his mother made him go. Know what happened? Next week they're charging him with affray. So thanks, but no thanks.'

'You're obviously still upset,' said the Sergeant, rising and replacing his cap. 'I'll leave you to recover a bit but I will need a statement from you. And don't blame your sister. The hospital made a report too. They got to if they think is something illegal.'

Jonny glared at Lauren when she came back after seeing Willis out.

'Gee thanks, Sis,' he said. 'That's why I didn't want to go to the hospital neither.' He leaned back in the chair and closed his eyes and after a few minutes seemed to drop into a doze. Lauren sat for a bit longer, watching him with anxious eyes before leaving him to sleep. Maybe Alex would be able to talk some sense into him, she thought.

Chapter Fifteen

With Petey happily settled in the art class, Steve led his new friend away from the bus stop and out towards the area of the Levels where he and Petey had found the bunker. As they walked through the stubble he talked excitedly about the possibility of finding an unexploded bomb or perhaps some old shells left over from the war. Mark strolled along, his hands in his pockets, and listened, giving an occasional nod but not really paying much attention.

At the edge of the field the pair stopped and Steve pointed across the dusty field to where the grey, curved top of an old tank gun had once stood. 'Um,' said Mark, sitting down and yawning. 'There will be stuff around about, I expect, but I don't think will be easy to find. Look.' He waved his arm across the landscape. 'All harvested – right? Well, they use this bloody great heavy machine for that. And before that it's all churned up when they plough ready for sowing. Probably the whole dam' field's been driven over half a dozen times already this year. Anything in here'll have gone off by now.'

'Oh,' said Steve. His face fell as he looked out over all the surrounding fields of stubble. He had very much wanted to find something to blow up and now he felt like a fool in front of Mark.

'Don't need a bomb or such to make a big impact though,' said Mark. 'You got your stuff in there?' He nodded to the old bag Steve was carrying. 'Show us then.'

Steve crouched down and upended his bag. Lighter fluid, cotton wool, an empty beer bottle, the disposable lighter from the market and a box of non-safety matches fell out in a jumble. Mark picked through the collection, grunting at the cotton wool and holding the bottle up, one eyebrow raised.

'Makes a good little Molotov Cocktail,' said Steve with a grin. His eyes gleamed with excitement as he took the bottle, hefting it in his hand. 'Used a load like it down Brixton, during the riots. That was a great time yer know? Got a chance to have a real go at the coppers an' it was the black kids got blamed for most of it. Magic.'

Mark picked up the tin and shook it. 'Think you need a bit more'n that to make a decent bang,' he said. 'Called petrol bombs 'cos is mainly petrol in 'um you know.'

Steve glared at his companion and began to stuff the pile back into his bag. 'Can't be jogging around with a jerry can on the off chance,' he said. 'Figured I'd collect a few bottles and make 'em up when I'm ready.'

Mark leaned forwards and put a restraining hand on Steve's arm. 'Sorry,' he said. 'Was just joking, right?'

Steve hesitated and then relaxed, accepting the apology with a nod. 'Course,' he said. 'Now, let's go'n see if there's anything worth our time over there. There was a lot of wood and stuff round the bunker when we was out last time. Might make a decent little show.'

Together they picked their way around the few remaining hay bales, Steve stumbling occasionally on the rough ground. There was a good amount of wood left over from the old, cracked cover and a few pieces of heavier timbers that some curious youths had pulled out of the shelter. The pair built a wooden frame over the top of the bunker using the old beams and placed the smaller pieces of wood over the top. Then they gathered up piles of straw, bleached pale gold by the sun, and twisted small bundles which they lodged in the gaps of the ruined building and around the top. Finally, they made a long, loosely woven rope of straw and laid this along the ground, leading into the entrance of the old fortification.

As they soaked the wood around the improvised fuse with lighter fluid Mark had a quick look through the partially closed door. It was too dark to make out any details but there seemed to be a considerable amount of rubbish inside. Tilting his head to one side he caught a glimpse of some broken glass mixed in with old newspapers.

'What you doing that for?' Steve demanded. 'Come on, we're just about ready.' He laid the fuse over the edge, winding it around the pile of wood before stepping back to admire his handiwork. Mark wriggled off the top of the bunker and stood next to him, a sly grin on his face as Steve flicked the lighter and touched the flame to the straw.

There was a burst of flame as the lighter fluid caught, setting the straw ablaze. The fire rushed along the fuse, sparking and spitting until it reached the base of the bunker. Here the dry straw began to burn sending a growing pillar of smoke up into the clear blue sky and Steve crouched down watching greedily. The first pieces of wood began to smoulder, adding to the cloud of smoke, but then slowly the fire began to fade away as the last of the straw was consumed.

They waited a few minutes but it was soon clear the wood was not going to catch and Steve turned away and began to stamp back towards the road, disappointed and humiliated by his failure. Mark jogged up beside him, putting out an arm to slow his progress.

'Woah,' he said. 'Was just that straw don't burn hot enough to get the rest going. Burns real fierce when there's enough but takes a time to really catch.'

'How'd you know that?' asked Steve, still smarting over his failure.

'Seen fires in hayricks afore,' said Mark. 'Can't be put out when they get going and they smoulder on, comin' back again too. Had a couple near where I live an' they went on all night. No, we need summat to really get it going with a bang.'

'Petrol?' said Steve eagerly. 'Could use the beer bottle.' He stopped and began to rummage in his bag.

'Nah,' said Mark. 'Got a better idea. Come on, if'n we's quick we can get the bus over to Street an' I'll show you.' He headed for the road, Steve struggling across the stubble as he tried to keep up. Behind them the fire around the bunker continued to smoulder, glints of bright red appearing on the timbers as the breeze fanned it. Finally, it burned out, leaving only charred timbers for the farmer to find when he arrived to investigate.

Rosalind was not in a good mood on Thursday when Ricky arrived for his meeting. The long-postponed inspection date had finally been confirmed and her superiors at Taunton had informed her that the team at Highpoint would be up for examination for a full day, with special emphasis on new developments such as the day centre. She had a couple of weeks to get everything ready but as she would have been in post for several months by the time the inspectors arrived she could no longer lay the blame for all the shortcomings she saw in her team on the previous senior. Taunton had made it very clear on appointment that they expected her to turn Highpoint into a model of the new system in record time and she was determined to succeed, regardless of the cost to anyone else on her staff.

'He's late,' Debbie murmured from her desk in the corner of Rosalind's office.

'I know,' Rosalind snapped. 'I can tell the time.'

'I just think it shows a lack of respect towards you, considering all the help you've given him recently,' said Debbie.

'I think it might be a good idea if you went down to the office and spoke to Pauline about the arrangements,' said Rosalind. 'They will have to be on top of the paperwork for the inspectors and I want to set up a private area for them to work in. Perhaps you could look at Gordon's old room? It is large enough and quite convenient for the rest of the building.'

Debbie stood up and headed across the room, hurt by her exclusion, but before she could protest there was a knock on the door and Ricky walked in, red faced and slightly out of breath. Rosalind waved him towards the hard chair in front of her desk and waited for Debbie to leave. As the door closed behind her assistant she leaned forwards, resting her ample chin on her steepled hands. Ricky shifted uncomfortably on the chair, resisting the urge to speak first.

'Now, Ricky, I think we need to have a little chat,' said Rosalind, her voice dripping with false friendliness. She waited but he remained silent.

'Perhaps we could begin by discussing the basic skills sessions,' she continued, flipping open a folder in front of her. 'It says here you sent the group off after only twenty minutes. Is that true?'

'They weren't going to listen,' said Ricky. 'They sat there and started talking and there was nothing I could do ...'

'But it is your *job* to do something,' said Rosalind sweetly. 'The job you asked for as soon as I arrived. I obliged because I have great hopes for you but this sort of thing is not acceptable.'

Ricky tried to speak but she held up her hand and continued. 'Now, there has also been a problem with the workshop group I believe. Some bullying which led to a fight and consequent damage to work in progress.'

'That's nothing to do with me,' Ricky protested. 'I wasn't there and it's not my responsibility ...'

'Oh but it is,' said Rosalind. 'You are in overall charge of the day centre and all the sessions. Therefore you are responsible for ensuring everything runs smoothly, especially as the inspectors will be looking very closely at you and your provision in two weeks' time.' She slammed the file shut and Ricky jumped.

'So, I think we should write up the Monday session as a registration meeting. That will explain why they left so early. Of course, you will explain to the group they will not be credited with an attendance for this week. I expect to see a full turnout for the whole morning next week and you will ensure you manage to actually teach them something. Get them to write their life story perhaps. Then put a spelling list together from their efforts. Try using your imagination.'

Ricky nodded, sitting slumped in the chair.

'Now, your paperwork needs to be up to date, of course. Is that in hand?'

'Going to be a bit difficult without any clerical support now,' mumbled Ricky. Rosalind raised her eyebrows and tilted her head to one side.

'Go on,' she said.

'Pauline told me there's not enough staff to cover everyone and Alison will be working with the new officer. So I don't know how I'm expected to get everything typed up on my own.'

'I believe you still have clerical support for official records,' said Rosalind. 'Surely you can manage to dictate your notes for those?'

Ricky nodded again, sulking in the chair. 'It's really difficult, trying to get everything running properly,' he said angrily. 'I've been given an impossible situation. Half the damn clients seem to think they can do as they like. They turn up to things when they're not on the list or they don't turn up at all. I mean, I'm trying to get so useful stuff going but when Alex was here they were drinking in the day centre and playing computer games. Now they're all angry because I'm trying to do it properly!'

Rosalind gave a tight little smile. 'I will speak to Pauline and ensure you have the support you need for the inspection,' she said. 'Perhaps we can arrange for you to have one of the new computers as you need to prepare notes and lesson plans. You can use a computer I presume?'

Ricky's eyes gleamed greedily. He hadn't the faintest idea what a computer could do or even how to turn one on but it would be a very visible sign of status and he wasn't going to let the chance slip. Rosalind watched his expression closely, not fooled at all by his excited assurances.

'Well, every machine is different, so I'm told. I'll speak to headquarters and see if they can send a man down to run you through the basics.'

Ricky stood up and headed for the door, the humiliation of his dressing down forgotten in his eagerness to boast of his good fortune.

'Ricky!' Rosalind called as he reached the door. The young officer stopped and turned to look at her. 'Don't let me down.'

Alex was puzzling over the time sheets for her staff when Bennie came into the office on Thursday morning.

'Help me out here,' she said, pushing the papers across the desk. 'I've got to enter the hours for the last month so people get paid but I don't know what to do about that Saturday – you know, Lauren's first weekend shift.'

Bennie picked up the forms and frowned at them. 'What's the problem then?' she asked.

Alex pointed to the gap in the list. 'Lauren was on for Saturday through to Sunday lunch – not something I would have done so early in her time here by the way.' Bennie flushed at the criticism but held her tongue. 'Now, Lauren did a lot of the hours but I came in and replaced her for the night-time sleeping bit. We knew the little idiots would try to play her up and I wanted to stop all this fire alarm nonsense for good.'

'I don't see the problem,' said Bennie, pulling out her chair and sitting at the second desk.

Alex sighed, rubbing her eyes before picking up her pen again. 'So what do I put in the timesheet?' she asked. 'If I leave it blank then officially there was no-one here and staffing will be on us like a ton of bricks. If I put me down – well, I can't claim and it looks as if we didn't think she could do the job so personnel will be on the phone to ask why we're using someone we don't trust.'

Bennie nodded. 'So just put her in there and everyone's happy,' she said. 'It's not exactly a fortune and they have to pay someone for the shift so let's give it to Lauren.'

'I was thinking that was probably the best idea but ...' Alex stared at the papers again. 'Technically that's a false claim. And it's not as if it was a quiet night. I was talking to the blokes from the fire brigade for ages and the lads were out the front all that time. If I'd given it a bit more thought I'd have left Lauren upstairs doing the sleeping shift and I'd have been down here on a waking shift. Might even have caught the little swine in the act.'

Reluctantly, she filled the space with Lauren's name and signed the form. 'There. Done. I'll take it round to the office tomorrow before I come in to work. Can we get anything else ready that needs to go?'

She was interrupted by the phone and lifted the receiver to Mary, Charlie's tutor at the college, asking about the placement at the stonemason's yard. She had forgotten her hasty comments, never expecting Charlie would actually remember, let alone take it on himself to suggest it to the college. The tutor seemed quite enthusiastic, talking about the scope of opportunity and new visions for difficult young people and Alex had a hard time extricating herself from the conversation. In the end she found herself agreeing to attend a meeting at the mason's yard next Thursday, presumably to vouch for Charlie and help seal the deal.

'Just what I need,' she sighed as she pulled the hostel diary over towards her and wrote the appointment under the correct day. 'Bennie, you'll need to cover the literacy session next week. I'll be out in the morning,' she said. Bennie gave a groan but Alex knew she would be more than capable of handling the small group. They were coming along well actually. Most of them could read a simple tabloid newspaper and a couple of them had actually started looking at the few tattered books making up the hostel 'library'. One of the jobs on Alex's ever-expanding list was to look through the shelves and find some new titles, preferably books the lads would find interesting.

Bennie glanced at her watch and rose from her desk to do her sweep through the upper floors. There was still a problem with residents sneaking back inside during the day. Not only was it against the rules, there were some puzzling shortfalls in the kitchen and Alex was concerned that if residents could get in unseen they could also get out again at night. She could just imagine what the reaction would be in Highpoint if a client was caught breaking into a shop after curfew.

After doing a quick check round, Bennie looked in on the kitchen where Hazel was preparing lunch for the staff and a handful of residents who made up a work gang tidying up the garden.

'Strange thing, Alex,' she said on her return. 'Hazel says we've no mixed herbs left. There was a big bag I got from the market last week but this is all as is left.' She held up a sizable plastic bag, empty apart from a dusting of green at the bottom.

'Was that full?' asked Alex.

'Yep. Pound and a half there was. Now, why the hell would anyone take a load a' oregano?'

Alex blinked and suddenly burst out laughing. 'I don't believe this,' she said grinning broadly. 'It's my fault. We were talking about other addictions in the alcohol education sessions – you know there's a problem with glue as well as a fair amount of whizz and stuff around?' Bennie nodded, curious to see where this was going. 'Well, someone got on to stuff like mushrooms – a recipe for disaster if they were dumb enough to go looking for themselves – and I mentioned bay leaves.' Bennie frowned at her, puzzled.

'Bay leaves are part of the laurel family and one of the theories about the Oracle at Delphi is she was high as a kite on fumes from burning laurel leaves. Bay leaves, apparently, give a good high for some people though it only lasts a few minutes. I thought it was a funny story but now I'm wondering if someone isn't trying to get high on our mixed herbs!'

Lily was delighted by the impact Pongo and little Quinn were having on her garden. The pair settled into their new quarters and happily chomped their way round the border leaving an extra couple of yards level and ready for tilling. Tom spent a day constructing a shelter for the pair using some old pallets and the remains of a roll of damp-proofing plastic and the goats retreated to their sleeping area at night, munching contentedly on the straw Lily put down for bedding.

'Don't really need nothing down there,' advised Tom when he called to inspect his charges. 'Is so dry an' warm at night an' they'll only eat it. Make 'em fat and can give 'em terrible gas too. You want this all moved over the other side?' He pointed to the thick undergrowth crowding in on the left of Lily's garden.

'Would be lovely if you could,' she said, smiling at him. 'Maybe give it another couple of days if you think is enough for them to eat still?'

Tom paced along the side of the pen, looking closely at the ground as he went. 'Should be alright for a few days,' he conceded. 'Can bring Brian over at the weekend an' we'll have it set up for you in no time.'

'Can't believe the change in that lad,' said Lily. 'One day he's runnin' wild and leadin' my Charlie astray, next he's set to go to college. You done wonders, you an' Ada.'

Tom tried unsuccessfully to hide a proud grin. 'Well, is mainly Ada's doing,' he said. 'She allus said is good in everyone if you look hard enough.'

'I reckon Alex Hastings has it right,' said Lily. 'Said once was a matter of waiting and tryin' to keep them lads out of prison 'til they growed up a bit. Get 'em past their mid-twenties and find summat they like to do an' they leave their stupid years behind.'

'Or the love of a good woman,' said Tom. 'Seen a couple of 'em get a decent steady girlfriend an' they's set for life.'

Lily fixed him with a bright, fierce look. 'Speakin' of which,' she said. 'How's it going with you'n Ada? You still shufflin' your feet an' acting like a love-sick lad or you goin' to do something?'

Tom stared at her in surprise. He'd been so sure he'd kept his feelings hidden, but first Brian and now Lily had found him out.

'Don't rightly know what you mean,' he mumbled. To his horror he realized he was actually blushing.

Lily chuckled, enjoying his discomfort. 'Don't be soft,' she said. 'Plain as day, the way you looks at her. An' you 'ent never been one for doing stuff round the Levels, 'less it was for yer own benefit. Now suddenly you is everyone's helper, here and there fixing and lending and all that. Seems you found a good woman of your own.'

Tom was saved from having to answer by the arrival of Brian who swept round the corner of Lily's tiny drive in a cloud of white dust, bringing his bike to a halt by skidding round them and jumping off.

'Watchya,' he said cheerfully. Lily glared at him, waving her hand to disperse the cloud around her.

'Tom, you said was Ada's old place up the road,' Brian continued, ignoring Lily's displeasure.

'No business of ours,' said Tom firmly. 'Told you, is full of bad memories for her. She wants to let it fall down is up to her.'

'Is not that,' said Brian. 'Reckon maybe someone's in there. Thought I seen someone moving inside and looks like the path's a bit clear, trod down like. Perhaps would be worth having a look?'

Tom glanced across the hedges towards where Ada's cottage stood in the midst of its overgrown garden. 'You seen anything?' he asked Lily, who shook her head.

'No lights nor nothin' as I've seen,' she said. 'All quiet round here, 'cept when you comes barrelling along like a right hooligan,' she added, giving Brian a hard stare.

'Honest,' said Brian. 'Just a quick look.'

'No,' said Tom. 'And don't you go sneaking around neither. If'n I find out you been over there you's looking for somewhere else to live, you understand?' Brian nodded, crestfallen. 'Right. Now, we's back out here in a couple of days to move Pongo and Quinn. Come on, put that old bike of yours in the van and we'll be off.'

As the van rattled and jolted its way along the road Samuel waited, crouching behind the bushes that fringed the cottage. An unwary movement next to the windows had attracted the attention of the bloke on the bike and as soon as he realized he'd been seen he froze, poised ready to strike if the cyclist tried to get in. Although he was relieved when the potential intruder moved on, Samuel was not convinced he was safe. Moving swiftly but silently he gathered up anything that might point to his identity before checking the locks on the front door. Then he sidled out of the back, pulling the door closed behind him.

If they did come back he would have to start all over again, a prospect which filled him with anger, but at least they would not be able to tell who it was using the cottage. In the past Samuel would have shrugged off the delay, looked around and set up a new base but he was tired. The lack of decent food, the amount of exercise involved in running to and from the hostel most days and the strength of his compulsion, now a deep burning ache inside, combined to override his usual caution. He'd wait, he decided. Give it a few days and see if anyone came calling. If not he would go ahead with his plans. The thought made him smile, setting him buzzing with anticipation as he headed back along the back road to Highpoint.

The next morning was Samuel's first Friday workshop and he dragged himself into the probation office, tired and dispirited. He really didn't see why he was being punished for something that was not his fault and his enthusiasm for the whole stupid raft project was long gone. The months still remaining on his hostel order stretched before him and it was only the thought of seeing Alex that prevented him from heading into town to commit a stupid, petty offence that would get him locked up and wipe the probation commitment from his record.

To his surprise the supervisor greeted him warmly and offered him a coffee before he started work. His bench had been tidied, he noted. The half-finished model stood on his design drawings and all the tools he needed were laid out neatly.

'Give you a bit of a hand,' said the supervisor with a lop-sided grin. 'Nice looking model you got there. Can't wait to see how it does in the water.'

Samuel hadn't realized it was going to be a working model and he began to modify his plan, adding more detail to the rudder assembly and puzzling over the flotation tanks. He was fully absorbed in his work by the time the rest of the Friday group trickled in through the doors and they moved around him, giving the newcomer a few puzzled glances but leaving him alone.

Samuel looked up in surprise when the supervisor tapped him on the arm to tell him the morning session was finished. Once more he had become absorbed in the work, screening out all the sounds around him and the hours had sped by.

'Looking good,' said the supervisor, reaching out to lift the model from the wood clamps. Samuel held out his hand to stop him.

'Glue's still wet,' he said. 'It will need some waterproofing next week.'

The supervisor nodded his approval. 'Is a much better group, the Friday lot,' he said. 'Wondered if you'd like to transfer over permanent?'

Samuel considered this for a moment. Tuesday suited him better than Friday, breaking up the week and allowing him three long days at his cottage on the Levels. On the other hand, Tuesday workshop was becoming a bear pit. He loathed most of the other clients and they did their best to make his life as difficult and unpleasant as possible. The Friday group, on the other hand, had not bothered him at all. They even smelt less, he realized.

'If possible then it might be a good idea,' he agreed.

The supervisor smiled and nodded at him. 'To be honest I'm about to give the Tuesday lot a couple of right hard weeks and wouldn't be fair, having you in there too. Long as there's no fighting – deal?'

Samuel wanted to say it wasn't him who had started the fight and he resented the implication but at that moment a familiar car swept into the yard narrowly missing the bins and stopped, sinking down on its haunches as the suspension was switched off.

'Now, there's lucky,' said the supervisor. 'Come on lad – we can get Alex to sign you over and it'll all be official.'

Samuel followed him out into the bright sunlight, his face calm despite the racing of his heart. Damn the woman, he thought. What had she done to have this effect on him?

Alex, meanwhile, had hopped up the steps, almost tripping in her haste as she juggled the pile of papers and her pass key. She was still struggling as Samuel slid past the supervisor and caught the door, holding it open for her. Alex looked up and gave him a brief smile, lighting blue sparks in his eyes. Samuel stepped to one side just in time as Rosalind pushed past him from the day centre door, her eyes fixed on Alex, who was leaning on the reception desk waiting for someone to come out of the office.

'Alex,' said Rosalind, her voice silky smooth. 'How opportune.'

Alex turned, startled by the greeting. 'Oh, hello Rosalind. I was just dropping off the timesheets for the hostel.'

Rosalind brushed her words aside, bearing down on her with the menace of an attacking shark.

'I'm sure you have so many important things waiting for you,' she said. 'However, you still have responsibilities here.'

Alex opened her mouth to protest but Rosalind was in full flow and cut across her. 'There are certain standards you are expected to maintain even if you are only the hostel warden now. You are still considered a member of this team by headquarters and some of your recent actions fall far short of what we expect. Unauthorized use of petty cash, irregular staffing and that appalling incident where half-naked residents were forced out at night onto the pavement. I have had several phone calls about that.'

Samuel stood motionless in the corner, watching and absorbing every word. A slow, deep fury gathered inside as he listened. This travesty of a woman, this pink, fluffy, over-painted creature dared to criticize – to humiliate – someone as capable and admirable as Alex. The contrast between the two women could not be more marked. Alex seemed tiny next to the billowing bulk of the senior. She held her body rigid as Rosalind poured scorn on her record at the day centre, her approach to her clients and her insubordinate attitude towards anyone in authority. The office door opened and several members of the clerical staff peered out, horrified and fascinated by Rosalind's behaviour, but the abuse continued relentlessly.

Samuel stepped away from the corner, unable to stand it any longer, but he was saved by the appearance of Pauline, who marched into the lobby and cut across the flood of angry words.

'I believe you have the hostel figures for me,' she said to Alex, holding out her hand for the files. 'Rosalind, I understand you are expecting an important call from headquarters about the inspection. Shall I put them through to your office phone?'

Rosalind glared at Pauline but was unable to continue with her tirade in front of so many people. She turned on her heel and flounced away up the stairs leaving a cloud of face powder and the faintest waft of sweat behind her. Alex was white and shaking as she handed over the papers and Pauline took her arm and led her gently into the office. No-one paid Samuel any notice and he stood in the corner, his heart hammering as he tried to control his anger. He became aware of his hands, clenched so tightly into fists that the nails were digging painfully into the palms.

Taking a long, slow breath he uncoiled his fingers, wincing and shaking his hands. He waited for a couple of minutes before crossing the floor and tapping the bell on the reception counter. There was a brief pause before Alison opened the door to glare at him.

'What?' she snapped.

Samuel looked at her for an instant, a blur of images and memories running around in his mind. She had no idea, he thought. She spoke to him like that but a few months ago he had been inside her house, listening to her scream. If her husband had not arrived home early there would have been more screams but he had been forced to flee and was lucky to escape detection. She was unfinished business and he had been thinking of another little trip out to see her recently.

'Well? Do you want something or not?' Alison demanded. There was something vaguely familiar about Samuel. Something slightly unsettling that nagged at her, an itch inside her head.

Samuel saw the way she was studying him and let his body slump slightly, an imitation of the docile little probationers he so despised. It was unlikely she would recognize him he thought. Apart from the ski mask he had been dressed in shapeless and ill-fitting clothes that disguised his body shape. Even his shoes had been several sizes too large and stuffed with newspaper – the only reason the coppers got anywhere near him as he ran away.

'The supervisor wants to change my day at the workshop,' he said. 'He sent me over to speak to Alex about it.'

'Alex is a bit busy at the moment,' said Alison. 'I don't think she will have time to see anyone but if you give me the details I'll check with her for you.' She took a blank form from the counter and filled in the details Samuel gave her, then got him to sign it. He handed the paper back and went to sit down in the corner to wait.

'I think you'd better go back to the workshop now,' Alison said firmly. 'Alex won't be available for a while but I'll make sure she gets the details.'

Silently, Samuel rose and made his way across the yard. He didn't like being told what to do by anyone, especially someone he considered his inferior, but he appreciated

Alison's fierce protectiveness, her determination to defend Alex. Inside Samuel's head was a list of people who had wronged him in some way. People he had marked as prey, sometimes for something as trivial as sneezing too close to him at the bus stop.

For the first time he removed someone from his mental tally of victims. Alison was no longer in any danger from him. He would not be going out to repeat his visit, hopefully with a happier ending – for him, at any rate. Alison would never know it but those five minutes had saved her life.

As he walked back along the river he slowed near the gate to Alex's house. A rush of fury came over him as he recalled Rosalind's tirade and he stopped in the middle of the path, staring blankly at the back of the house. He still had no idea how to get Margie out to his cottage and despite puzzling over the problem for several weeks he was no nearer a solution. Now he was experiencing a change of heart. Margie was a source of resentment to him, the cause of enormous jealousy but he suspected she made Alex happy. Certainly, Alex had been more relaxed in the past few weeks despite the turmoil in her professional life. By contrast, Rosalind made Alex deeply unhappy. She was abusive, rude and thoughtless, a bully who represented everything he despised about a certain type of woman. If removing Margie was likely to add to Alex's unhappiness he reasoned, then getting rid of Rosalind could only be a good thing.

The thought of touching that puffy, damp flesh caused him to twist his mouth in disgust and the smell of her came back, adding to his distaste. For a moment revulsion fought with anger but the image of Alex's white face, the shock and hurt inflicted on her, filled his mind. He knew where Rosalind lived and she would be home all weekend. He had already noted the lack of a wedding ring but, even so, he was not going to rush into anything. Samuel was always very careful and he walked back to the hostel head down, planning his next move.

Chapter Sixteen

Jonny returned to work the next week, his bruises faded but still a stark reminder of his encounter with the unknown assailants. Not surprisingly he had declined an invitation to go out with the same group over the weekend and spent most of the time staring at the television, withdrawn and silent. Lauren hovered over him anxiously until, with uncharacteristic impatience, he snapped at her, sending her flying to her room close to tears.

'Won't even come here for the evening,' she reported on Friday. 'Says he's tired but all he done is sleep for the last week.'

'Shock,' said Sue. 'He took a nasty beating and it can dent your confidence. That injury to his ear is really bad and he's probably worried about going back to work too.'

'Why would that worry 'um?' demanded Lauren. 'Got a medical certificate an' all. Well, note from the hospital 'bout sitting down if he gets dizzy and stuff. One look at him an' is obvious he's not been skiving.'

'No, I mean – well ...' For once Sue was struggling to find the right words. Normally so articulate and occasionally overly forthright, she was finding the situation increasingly difficult.

Alex stuck her head round the kitchen door and called for table-setters and for a few minutes they were busily occupied getting the meal on the table, but when everyone was settled with full plates and glasses Lauren returned to the question.

'Don't see the problem with work,' she said in between bites of the pasta bake. 'Not like he started no fight. Anyway, he was goin' to tell 'um was the motorbike.'

Sue glanced up, then turned her attention to her food as Lauren fixed her with a stare. 'What?' asked Sue.

'Was gonna ask you the same,' said Lauren, setting her fork down beside her plate. Anything that could divert Lauren's attention from food was serious and it was obvious she was not going to let the subject drop.

'All right but I really don't want to get into this tonight,' said Sue miserably. 'There's – well, a feeling around town. Actually, round the area. A lot of stupid jokes and hostility and ...' She stopped and thought for a moment before continuing. 'I was in a meeting last week. There were people from all over the area, from probation but also from social services, education, special schools – you know the sort of thing. There were probably nearly a hundred people there, all supposed to be discussing how we can work together to improve provision for young people. I thought it was going to be a total waste of time, like most of these things.'

Alex nodded. 'I remember you coming home from that,' she said. 'You looked as if you'd been through a pretty unpleasant experience.'

'Yeah, I had – but not because it was the usual boring "management-speak" afternoon. We had some "workshops" where no-one actually seemed to learn anything and then the new careers lot talked about how wonderful the new provision was and how they were going to do everything all in one place – presumably all with the same half-trained idiots they've taken on recently.'

Lauren sighed impatiently. 'All very interesting an' depressing,' she said. 'Don't see what this got to do with Jonny, though.'

'Oh, it does,' said Sue. 'Well, then people got up and talked a bit about how they were changing things to meet this new way of doing the same old stuff, most of it very self-congratulatory but then one of the staff from a special school stood up.' Sue took a gulp from her wine to fortify herself before continuing. 'Now, you'd think someone who did a job like that would be a bit – well, open, accepting maybe. Well, he wasn't. He stood in front of all those people and boasted about how he'd just sacked one of his long serving teachers because he was gay.'

There was a sharp intake of breath from around the table but Sue, having finally started, was not to be silenced now. 'That's not the worst thing though. He said he'd do the same if he ever found any more of "those people" – that's exactly what he said – "*those people*" in his school. And then everyone got up and gave him a standing ovation. Almost everyone anyway.'

There were tears of anger in her eyes as she recalled her disbelief at what had happened. 'A few people didn't. Mary from the college – she sat there with her arms folded and then two men with her – I think they were from the college too – they got up and all three left. There were a couple of others I didn't recognize but the rest were just delighted with this little … little …'

'*Schmendrick?*' Alex suggested.

'I'm not sure what that is but it sounds about right,' said Sue.

'Weren't no-one from our lot there, was there?' Lauren asked anxiously.

'Rosalind couldn't make it, apparently, so she sent the odious Debbie,' said Sue angrily. '*She* was on her feet applauding with the rest of them.'

Margie reached over and poured Sue another glass of wine. 'Nothin' we can do about it,' she said. 'Just the way things is at the moment.'

'But surely 'taint legal?' Lauren protested. 'Can't just sack someone on account of that?'

'Actually, it is,' said Alex. 'There was a ruling in 1980 that means you don't have to do anything or come out at work or bring your significant other to the office party. If your boss finds out you are gay they can sack you. I believe the ruling said it is perfectly reasonable not to want to employ "those sort of people". So as long as you don't mind some people thinking you're a bigot you can do what you like.'

Lauren stared round the table in shock. 'But that's just wrong,' she said.

'Didn't say was right,' said Margie. 'Said it was the law.'

'An' I thought that Section 28 thing was bad,' said Lauren gloomily. 'No wonder Jonny di'nt want to go to the police.'

Later, in the kitchen, Alex and Margie cleared away and washed up, talking softly whilst Sue and Lauren listened to music in the living room.

'You goin' to do something about your senior then?' Margie asked as she stacked the plates neatly in the cupboard. Alex sighed and shook her head.

'I don't know,' she replied. 'It was all so sudden – I know she doesn't like me but I really was not expecting anything like that. And the stuff she knew – the damn alcohol education sessions! I guess you were all right after all. I can't deny her facts. It's just the way she interprets things and that's why she's there I suppose.' She tried to make a joke of the matter with a wry smile. 'There's a new sheriff in town and the management want her to change the way we work. I'm not happy with the way things are going so I'm in the way.'

Margie frowned at her. 'Don't matter about what she said or how she interprets stuff,' she said firmly. 'Can't be shouting at you in public like that. That is right unprofessional and out of order and I think yer union should know.'

'I don't think they'd be much help,' said Alex. 'I suppose I could ask someone but that's going to make things worse. At least it's only unofficial at the moment. If I call in the union it all goes on the record ...'

Margie slammed her tea towel down on the counter in frustration.

'Listen to yerself! You talking like she's right. You made a mistake with that course, right, but other than that you done nothing wrong. Don't let them get to you like this, you hear?'

Alex looked at her and smiled for the first time since her encounter with Rosalind.

'You're right. Thank you – I don't know what I'd do without you.'

Weekends at the hostel were hard for both staff and residents. On alternate weeks the arrival of the dole money for the majority of them meant one frantic evening out on the town and a difficult evening on the Saturday as tempers frayed and those who had indulged too liberally did what drunks do everywhere – eat kebabs, throw up, pick fights and talk rubbish to anyone who would listen. The non-dole weekend saw drifts of young men hanging around, bored and frustrated by having no money, nowhere to go and nothing to do. Both shifts had their downsides and neither was popular with the staff.

This was a non-dole Saturday and the only person up before breakfast was Samuel. Bennie, who was building up some leave time in lieu, pointed him towards the tea trolley, now liberally stocked and surprisingly tidy given its popularity.

'Won't be nothin' to eat for a half-hour maybe,' she said. 'Got to get the rota lads up first.'

'I can make a start if you like,' said Samuel.

Bennie stared at him, then tilted her head on one side. Samuel, in six months at the hostel, had never volunteered for anything before.

'If I can put a couple of eggs on to boil,' he said. 'Don't like them fried but no-one ever does boiled eggs here.'

Bennie hesitated for a moment before giving a nod. 'Seems fair,' she said. 'Just a couple of eggs then?'

Samuel tried a little smile but she was already turning away and on her way up the stairs to ruin the morning for the sleepers in Petey's room. Anxious to be finished and off as soon as the rest of the residents came downstairs, Samuel set to in the kitchen. The water urn was first, re-filled and set to boil whilst the industrial toaster warmed up. He removed and rinsed the beakers from the trolley before putting out clean spoons and put three eggs in a pan to boil. Then he began to feed bread into the ever-rolling maw of the toaster, fielding the finished slices with one hand whilst setting the frying pan to heat on the top of the stove. Thin strips of streaky bacon went under the grill and he was breaking eggs one-handed into the pan when Bennie reappeared, peering into the kitchen to check on his progress.

'You done this before?' she asked, watching his deft movements. Samuel froze, suddenly aware he had revealed something about himself through his actions. In truth he had fallen into a rhythm, working almost without thinking as he went through the familiar actions.

'Did a stint in one of the nicks,' he muttered, keeping his head down.

'Could pick up a job easy, 'specially if you showed 'em that,' said Bennie, nodding towards the frying pan where Samuel was just about to crack two eggs simultaneously on the side using one hand. The contents slid into the pan to cook and the shells landed neatly in the rubbish bin next to the stove.

Samuel cursed inwardly but ignored her, hoping she would go away. The arrival of the scheduled kitchen crew distracted her long enough for him to grab the boiled eggs and run them under the cold tap. Then he started setting the breakfast out on individual plates, ready for the new arrivals to serve. Normally it was sloshed on straight from the pans but despite his studied indifference to the other residents he could not bear to see his perfectly cooked food dumped onto plates, eggs broken and toast piled on top. There was a clatter of cutlery from the dining area and then the first knocks on the shutters.

'Someone come and open up!' he called, busy with the final service. Bennie appeared beside him along with Mark who gave the neat plates a startled look. The first couple of residents took their food with a muttered "Thanks", still too tired and half asleep to react to his unexpected appearance. Steve was next in the queue, however, and he looked at his plate and sniggered.

'Bit posh 'en it?' he said. 'Wot about a *serviette* then, eh? Maybe you should'a cut the crusts off the toast for us!' There was some subdued giggling from the next few lads in the line and Steve took this as encouragement.

'Wot about some sausage an' all – I bet you got some nice sausage tucked away back there.'

Samuel leaned over the counter and beckoned and before Bennie could react he upended the next plate over Steve's head.

'That's enough!' she shouted, pushing Steve back out of Samuel's reach. 'I said *enough*,' she repeated, pointing at Samuel. 'Mark and Petey, you take over serving. Samuel, please wait in the office. I'll be out in a minute.'

Hiding the pan with his body Samuel turned away from the serving hatch and scooped the boiled eggs out of the water, trying not to wince as the residual heat burned his hand. Dropping his own breakfast into the sweater he'd left on the counter he grabbed some toast from the machine before pushing his way past Petey and Mike, who slouched through the door to replace him. Head held high, Samuel marched into the office, ignoring the whispers from the dining room. He took a seat next to one of the desks, nibbling his toast as he watched the open doorway. A trickle of residents made their way downstairs, most barely dressed and still unwashed and he looked away in disgust.

Samuel wrapped the eggs more carefully in his sweater, stopping for a moment to examine his hand. The fingertips were bright red and there were signs of little blisters forming around the palm. He cursed softly, looking around for something to soothe the pain but there was no hand basin in the room and the first aid kit was slung on top of the cupboard behind the warden's desk. Very handy in an emergency, he thought, glaring up at the elusive green box.

Bennie hurried through the door, causing him to curl his fingers round the palm before sliding his hand under the sweater on his knee.

'Whew,' she said, dropping into her chair. 'Well that didn't go too well, did it? No good deed unpunished in this place.'

Samuel sat very still, his eyes focussed on a patch of sunlight reflecting off the desk. Tiny specks of dust glittered as they spun in the warmth but they did not evoke any sense of pleasure for him. Samuel saw air pollution where others smiled at tiny rainbows.

'You were doing me a favour,' said Bennie. 'And you were doing a very good job until – the incident shall we say. Why aren't you on the kitchen rota by the way?'

Samuel raised his eyes from the sunny patch and looked at her. There were black and red flashes across his vision from the brightness and he blinked several times.

'Peter Marks put me on cleaning,' he said evenly. 'I keep the upstairs bathroom clean and the hallway up there. And the laundry downstairs, seeing as no-one bothers to clean out the machines or wipe up after themselves.'

Bennie met his gaze and felt that tiny shiver of warning all good social workers develop. There was nothing on his record to raise any alarms but she knew instinctively this was a very dangerous young man.

'Of course,' she said evenly. It was rubbish, of course. Samuel simply cleaned the areas he used regularly for his own comfort but Bennie was not going to provoke him. She had every intention of handing the situation over to Alex at the first opportunity. 'It's a pity we can't have you on the kitchen list, though. You did really well this morning. So I think we'll forget about … the incident. As long as there's no repeats – understood?'

The faintest trace of a smile flickered over Samuel's face and Bennie had the uncomfortable sense he knew exactly what she was thinking. The sense of unease grew stronger as they sat in the office watching one another until there was the sound of breaking crockery from the kitchen.

'Oh bugger,' said Bennie. 'Go on now.' She waited for him to leave before heading to the dining room, where voices were being raised in protest and denial. After cleaning up the broken plates and getting them settled again she sat back down in the office, frowning over the day book. The fight should be entered, she thought, but it would seem poor repayment for Samuel's help with the breakfast and from what she had overheard he had been provoked. Of course, that let Steve off too but she had an idea about that. It was about time the kitchen had a good, deep clean and he was just the person.

Gazing out of the window as she waited for the last stragglers to finish their breakfast she pondered on what Samuel did all day – and where he went. She knew he was fit and he seemed to go running a lot but no-one could spend all day running, surely. She became aware of raised voices in the kitchen and with a weary sigh stood up and headed off again. It was going to be a long day and the enigma that was Samuel was forgotten.

A few months ago Samuel could have run all day but he was finding it harder each morning to get started and spent longer fighting the urge to stop for a rest along the way. Today was an easier day, starting with the town library where he consulted a selection of local maps before finding the one best suited to his needs. The place was empty so early in the morning and the woman on the desk was too busy reading the magazines that arrived in the early post to watch what he was doing. He pocketed the map, bade her a polite good day and walked out into the morning sunlight.

He had no need to steal the map. Samuel was in possession of a valid library ticket and could have borrowed any – or indeed all – of the maps had he chosen to do so. That left a trail, however. He didn't think anyone in the local police station would be smart enough to look up who had checked out maps of the area recently but he wasn't taking any chances. He would wipe it clean of any fingerprints and return it to the shelves once he'd finished and no-one would even know it was gone.

Seated under a tree, sheltered from the sun that was already hot enough to burn and from nosy passers-by, he unfolded the ungainly paper and traced a route from Highpoint out towards the Quantock Hills. A few miles to the west of the town was Cannington, site of Brian's future college. Peering at the small print he located Hagg's Hill running north out of the village towards the bay. Somewhere along there was Rosalind's house. Folding the map and tucking it into his bag, Samuel stood up, stretched carefully and set off across town, keeping to the side streets. It was slower but he was not going to be recognized by anyone living there. He wasn't in a hurry. He had food, water and he had all day. Doing a good job was more important than doing it quickly.

It took him an hour to locate the house, the last on the left next to a small wood. The location was perfect, almost too good to be true, with a clear view over the brow of the hill and nothing overlooking the small side garden. Samuel felt his pulse rate rise as he slid over the railed fence into the sheltering trees, moving carefully to ensure he had a good view of the house whilst staying out of sight.

It was very quiet under the canopy of trees and he listened for a minute to a dove calling in the branches above his head. There was no sign of life from the house though the curtains were drawn back, revealing frilly lace nets at the windows. He wondered idly which was the kitchen. What sort of a person had frilly curtains in the kitchen? They would trap grease and dust ... the thought of it made him squirm as he sat on a tree stump, eyes fixed on the sleeping house.

It is strange how the tiniest of events can have such a great impact on our lives. Samuel waited in vain, staring at the side door, scanning the windows for a flicker of movement. The few minutes he had spent in Bennie's office had delayed him just sufficiently to miss Rosalind's car as it swept down Hagg's Hill, turning right onto the main road and carrying her and Debbie off for a weekend in St Ives, where they owned a small fisherman's cottage.

It was not until he crawled through the wood to look at the other side of the house that he noticed the light was shining on the alarm box above the main door and realized the coast was clear, though he would have to rely on an external survey. Samuel was smart but he knew only enough about alarms to avoid them. Its presence did not worry him unduly. Few people set their alarm when they were in the house and the steady light confirmed his suspicion that Rosalind was not the sort of person to keep a dog. Dogs and alarms did not mix and there was no sign of her bringing a pet to work so that was one less thing to worry about.

Paying attention to the nearby road he completed his circuit of the house, noting the number of locks on each door, the size and location of the windows and which ones were not overlooked from the upper floor. Then he paced the distance from the trees to the house several times, listening to his footsteps and deciding on the swiftest and quietest route. Finally, he scouted out the hedge at the rear and checked the fences at the side of the property, just in case he needed to make a hasty exit.

The sun was high in the sky and he was tired and hungry by the time he had completed his rounds but Samuel was not disposed to hang around so close to his next target. He sipped some water from a bottle in his pack, shouldered the bag and slipped back onto the road. At the bottom of the hill he hesitated, debating whether to head for his cottage or find somewhere to rest. After a few moments he turned right towards the shadow of the Quantock Hills. It was a long walk but not as far as the trek east to the Levels. The road was empty of traffic, most tourists taking the motorway further south in their dash to Devon and Cornwall and most locals already out and on their way to the shops at Highpoint or the market at Taunton. Ignoring the ache in his head, Samuel strode down the road, confident he would find somewhere quiet and sheltered where he could rest.

Steve was in a foul mood when he eventually finished in the hostel kitchen. Forced to scrub the stoves and polish the sinks under Bennie's watchful eye, he had sulked and muttered his way through the morning until she finally gave up on his half-hearted efforts and kicked him loose. Grubby even by hostel standards, Steve took a few minutes to wash the grease from his hands and pull on a T-shirt that he had only worn twice before. Then he filled his pockets with matches, a lighter and some crumpled paper before opening his cupboard and retrieving a box of firelighters from the bottom where they nestled up against the bag containing the incriminating can of lighter fluid. This he stuffed up his shirt, an awkward and very obvious lump across his chest. Fortunately for him, Bennie was busy doing the noon hand-over with the relief warden when he reached the bottom of the stairs and he was able to escape without being noticed.

There was no-one waiting for him, of course. His fair-weather friends had left as soon as breakfast was done, setting off without him and leaving him to slave away in the kitchen alone. His anger fuelled the craving inside and as he walked along the road every house, every driveway seemed to offer him temptation. Dustbins packed with combustibles stood next to wooden fences, piles of wood and old cars awaiting collection or repair filled the front yards and nylon clothes fluttered from plastic lines round the back, glimpsed through the gaps between houses. He hesitated at one house, drawn by the sight of a rabbit hutch down the side path but the door opened and a girl stepped out, a bowl filled with lettuce and grains in her hands and he moved on reluctantly.

After half a mile the houses began to thin out until they stopped entirely and he was walking through open country-side. Steve hated the countryside. It was big and empty and utterly devoid of anything of interest. He marched on, still reciting his woes inside his head, until he reached a small building site. More interesting, he thought. The site was a short cul-de-sac set out on the open land. There was nothing around it but trees and grass – and the tiny midges that tormented Steve every time he ventured outside.

A dozen houses were in the process of construction, several only marked by ditches and foundations but some of them part-built, though without doors or windows. The outline of a road was laid out too, the white surface a scab on the lush green that surrounded the site. Steve looked around and wondered who would want to live in such a bleak, featureless place, an island of raw brick and tarmac overlaying a swamp.

He was about to move on in search of something better when he detected the faint scent of tar in the air. Sniffing loudly he tracked the smell to a locked shed at the rear of the final plot. The smell was strong as he tugged at the door but it was made from solid wood and fastened with a heavy padlock. In frustration he kicked at the door and felt it give a little but the lock held. Gritting his teeth against the pain in his foot he kicked again and this time a small gap opened at the bottom by the frame. For a few moments he considered chucking a firelighter inside but the odds on him getting it close enough to the tar were so small it was not worth the effort. Besides, if he came back with the right tools he could get inside. The thought of the burning power from a bucket of pitch made his head swim with excitement. All he needed was a little patience and the right target. And a hacksaw, of course.

Turning his back on the siren song of the unobtainable tar, Steve wandered around the deserted site, kicking his way through the lower floors of half-finished houses and toying with the idea of a little graffiti. He decided against the latter, not wanting to alert the builders to his interest in the site and there wasn't enough finished to make it worth setting a fire. He decided to move on, especially as the sun was high overhead and turning his exposed skin bright pink.

Steve tramped along a dusty pathway, across the fields and away from the building site. The air was still in the midday heat and in the distance Glastonbury Tor seemed to shimmer, a bright point on the horizon glittering in the light. After hopping over tiny, dried-up streams Steve finally came up against a wider canal still flowing endlessly from the wetlands towards the sea. The path met a narrow road that crossed the water by a bridge but Steve was too tired to go any further. Seeking the shady side of the canal he leaned against the crumbling brickwork and worked the aging, ratty trainers off his swollen feet.

With a sigh of contentment he plunged his legs almost knee-deep into the water and sat on the bank, wriggling his toes in the coolness. For a few minutes all thoughts of fires faded away and he was transported back to his childhood, to long days in the park with his Nan, fishing for 'tiddlers' in the little streams and the rare treat of an ice-cream on a hot day. Steve bit his lip as he gazed into the rippling water. He missed his Nan, gone some five years now. Had he thought about it a bit more he might have realized her death coincided with his first spell in a young offender's institution. From then on his life had been one arrest after another, until he found himself out on the Levels in Somerset, friendless and adrift. But Steve was not one for reflection and instead he sat with his feet in the water, brooding on how unfair life was.

The weekend dragged for Jonny too. Still visibly bruised, and with two black eyes fading to a dirty green colour, he had no desire to parade his humiliation around the bars and clubs of the county. Not being a great sports fan, and never having got into the habit of reading, he was reduced to lying out in the sunshine in the small garden at the back of his mother's house in a vain attempt to tan out the worst marks on his face. Saturday evening found him nursing a bottle of cheap wine followed by several shots from the (medicinal) brandy bottle and on Sunday the resulting headache kept him in bed for most of the day. By Monday he was actually looking forward to returning to work.

Despite having taken the precaution of wearing dark glasses to hide the worst of his injuries, his appearance caused quite a reaction when he walked into the staff room just before 8.30 in the morning. Several of the younger female staff members fluttered around him making soft sounds of sympathy whilst the other junior mangers stared and began to make uneasy jokes.

'Look like you had a run-in with Frank Bruno,' said his fellow assistant manager.

Jonny smiled nervously and tried to shrug off the attention. 'Just a bit of a knock on the bike,' he said.

'You run into a street lamp or what?' joked the assistant manager. 'Thought you had to wear a helmet now? How you got your ear all torn up if you was wearing a helmet?'

Jonny's hand went to the torn ear, instinctively touching the line of black stitches still clearly visible across the side of his head. He grinned and tried to shrug off the question. 'Don't remember rightly,' he said. 'Was knocked out, so maybe happened gettin' the thing off my head.'

'Ooh, if some bloke from the ambulance pulled *my* ear off after an accident I'd bloody sue 'um,' said the assistant manager.

'I don't think that is likely to happen,' said the manager appearing in the doorway and frowning at Jonny. 'And I would remind you to moderate your language. You are in a position of responsibility and whilst you are at work you represent this store. Mr Anderson, would you come to my office please?'

Jonny glanced round the staff room but everyone was suddenly very busy and unable to meet his eye. With a sigh he followed his boss down the corridor and into a large and well-appointed room.

'I have a letter from the hospital ...' he began, but the manager ignored the proffered envelope and waved him towards a chair.

'You need to fill in one of these self-certification forms as well,' he said, shoving it and a pen across the desk. As Jonny wrote on the form, he continued, 'I appreciate your loyalty to the company, Mr Anderson.' He stared hard at Jonny's face.

'From the look of you it would have been easy for you to take another week off.'

'It's coming up to holiday time,' said Jonny. 'I know we're going to be short-staffed this month so ...'

The manager waved a hand at him once more. 'Yes, well, as I said, I appreciate your loyalty. However, I cannot use you out on the shop floor looking like that. I hope you can appreciate my position. You are my best customer service man and you have been missed but I fear you might be less than reassuring at present.'

Jonny reached into his inside pocket and pulled out his dark glasses but before he could put them on the manager banged on the desk in frustration.

'No, no, *no*!' he said. 'You look as if you have stepped out of a gangster film! No, I think you will be most usefully employed supervising the warehouse for the next few days.'

Jonny left the room, depressed and strangely humiliated. He hated working in the warehouse, where all the least able juniors and young trainees from government schemes were placed. The work was dirty, cold and tedious in the extreme. The last time he had been sent there he'd spent most of a day trying to catch three young workers whose idea of improving productivity was to hide behind the packing cases and eat chocolate covered cereal from the broken boxes.

Half-way through the afternoon he received a summons to the manager's office and ambled down the hallway, hands in the pockets of a borrowed overall, wondering what the old fool wanted this time. He stopped in the doorway, shocked by the sight of an unfamiliar young policeman sitting opposite the desk. The manager half stood to greet him, then dropped back into his seat and waved impatiently for him to close the door. Jonny sidled over to one side, eying the pair nervously. Whilst the young constable gave him a smile and an encouraging nod the manager was now glaring at him and suddenly Jonny had a very, very bad feeling about all of this.

'Mr Anderson,' the manager rumbled deep in his chest. 'I have just had a rather enlightening chat with PC ... er ...'

Sloane, sir,' the policeman supplied helpfully.

'Yes, PC Sloane. It seems your explanation for the injuries you suffered last week was not strictly accurate. In fact PC ... Sloane here has come to ask for your assistance in identifying the young man who is alleged to have attacked you outside a public house of rather dubious repute.'

'If I might add something here?' said the PC. He looked rather like an eager puppy, thought Jonny. A puppy who was about to piss all over him. With a sinking heart he listened as the policeman outlined events from two nights ago when another young man had been targeted at the same bus stop and kicked senseless. On this occasion, however, a passing motorist had stopped and intervened, possibly saving the victim's life as he was still in hospital in a very serious condition.

'We would like you to come down to the station this evening and see if you can identify any of the men from the pub that evening,' said the PC. 'This would give us a chance to pick them all up. We will arrange an identity parade if you let me know when is convenient for you. Here – this is my badge number and you can leave a message on this number.' He stood up and leaned over the desk to shake hands with the manager. 'Thank you for taking the time to see me,' he said cheerfully, smiling at Jonny.

'Well,' said the manager as the door closed behind the young policeman. 'It would seem you have not been strictly truthful in relation to your "accident". Have you anything to say in defence of this deceit?'

Jonny looked at the man's smug, self-satisfied face and felt a rush of loathing. 'I don't know what the problem is,' he said angrily. 'You've got a letter from the hospital saying I needed to rest for at least a week 'cause I had concussion. I don't see what business is of you or anyone else here how it happened.'

'Well, I disagree,' said the manager. 'I think it is extremely important and a grave breach of trust. Given the circumstances of your recent absence, and the fact you have falsely represented yourself to me for the last two years, I have no

alternative but to terminate your employment with immediate effect.'

Jonny sat in the chair, frozen with shock. Despite all the
rumours running through the fledgling community, despite
the recent experiences of some of his friends, he had still not
expected this. He was a *manager*. He had some status at
work. This sort of thing didn't happen to people like him …
Then the realization struck him. Of course it happened, and
only to people like him.

'You can't do that,' he said softly.

'Oh, I can,' said the manager. 'I can claim that you are an
undesirable type of person and I can dismiss you for that. Or
I can dismiss you for falsifying your self-certification form.
The law is clearly on my side, whichever reason I choose.
Now, bearing in mind the fact you will almost certainly need
to request a reference from me in the near future, which
option would you prefer?'

Jonny watched as a self-satisfied smile spread across the
man's face, too angry to reply.

'Well, I think we both know which option is less damaging,'
said the manager. 'Now, I believe you have a set of keys?'

Silently, Jonny rose from the chair in front of the desk. He
removed the ring from his pocket, unclipped the shop keys
and dropped them on the desk. Then he took off the overall and laid it over the chair. The manager watched him, his
glasses glinting in the neon light.

'I will have your P45 prepared and sent to you,' he said
as Jonny opened the office door. 'I assume you still live with
your mother?'

Jonny gritted his teeth but managed to keep silent as he
closed the door behind him. Walking down the hallway to his
locker he heard whispers from the staff room.

'What's happened?' asked one voice.

"E's sacked Jonny,' came the reply.

'Oh,' said the first voice. 'What he do that for, then?'

There was the sound of whispering and a snigger. 'No – you
reckon?' said someone and the staff room door opened fur-

ther as several of his colleagues – ex colleagues he reminded himself fiercely – peered out at him. He had a strong desire to turn round and stamp his feet at them, sure they would break and run like the two-faced little cowards they were. Instead he took his meagre belongings from the locker, propped it open with the key on the shelf and left the building, his head held high.

Chapter Seventeen

It was the first week of July on the Levels and the heat wave showed no signs of letting up. Ada opened all the windows in her cottage in a vain effort to generate a through breeze but that required some movement in the air outside the house and the sun blazed down, hot and heavy, on the still countryside. Desperate to escape the heat of the kitchen, she and Tom had taken to eating outside and spent their evenings in the shade of the cottage, gazing out over the dry and dusty land. Despite her initial misgivings Ada had accepted Tom's help rigging a hose pipe from the kitchen tap and her salad garden had so far survived the fierce heat, a small oasis of green in an increasingly parched landscape.

'One thing about Pongo being gone,' mused Tom on Monday evening. 'Couldn't sit out fer long with him just over there.'

'How's he doin', then?' Ada asked, She missed the old goat despite the smell.

'Oh, champion,' said Tom. 'Him an' young Quinn, they doing a right good job. Dead pleased is yer friend Lily. Says she knows a couple o' people would be interested in 'em if you wants to hire 'em out later.' He took a swig from a luke-warm bottle of beer and pulled a face. 'Be able to get a fridge from yer goat money soon. Wouldn't need to touch nothing from that compensation. Would improve this here no end,' he added waggling the bottle at her.

'You want a fridge, you go buy one,' said Ada. 'Never had one before an' don't see the need at my age.'

'Never had no goats nor no hosepipe afore but is happy you got 'em now,' said Tom.

'Strange talk from you,' Ada snapped. 'Not like you an' your sort is much for possessions anyway. Tie you down, stuff does. Gets you all tangled up in bills for this an' running costs for that and afore you know it you's in debt an' no way out.'

Tom stared at her, the bottle half-way to his lips. 'What you mean,' he said lowering his drink to the table. 'What you mean, "my sort?"'

'Travelling folk,' said Ada with a touch of defiance. 'Is what you was born to and I know how hard is to walk away from what you knows best. I seen you sometimes, staring out like you was wondering what was over the next hill. Can hear it callin' you sometimes.'

'Is that what all this'n about?' asked Tom. 'You think I've a hankering to be off again, leavin' all this behind?'

Ada folded her arms and refused to look at him.

'Oh you great daft woman – is the best I bin in my life, even when I had Bella and, yes, course I miss her. But was you I saw first when I was no taller than this table an' I always carried a torch for you Ada. If'n I thought I had any chance I'd ask you to wed in a heartbeat.' He stopped abruptly, con-scious of blurting out his deepest secrets to this frustrating, irritating woman whom he loved so much.

'Well, anyway,' he mumbled, lifting his beer again. 'I 'ent hankering fer no more travelling. Them days is over.'

Ada rubbed at her face, looking away from him. 'Some-thing in my eye,' she murmured. Tom watched her, amused and touched by her reaction.

'So was you plannin' on ever asking anything?' she said when she'd finished wiping her eyes dry.

Tom sighed and scratched his head, unsure of his ground now they were actually having the conversation he had imagined so often.

'Was,' he said finally. 'Until that cheque come in.'

'What the hell's that cheque got to do with anything?' asked Ada.

'Well, you's a wealthy woman now,' said Tom, shifting uncomfortably on his seat. 'Lot of blokes as would look twice at you now, just on account of that. Didn't want you thinking I was after yer money ...' His voice trailed off as he realized how feeble it sounded.

'Oh you girt old fool!' said Ada. 'I never thought that of you!'

They looked at one another and suddenly began to laugh.

'So, would you think about it then?' Tom asked.

''Bout what?' Ada demanded. 'Woman likes to be asked proper, you know.'

Tom groaned. 'Oh, come on, Ada. I 'ent got the legs for that now!'

'Here,' said Ada dropping a cushion from one of the chairs onto the floor. 'Now – what was it you was wanting to ask?'

Slowly and carefully, Tom got down on one knee.

The first week in July limped by, too hot for people to work in their glassed-in offices but too early for the annual holidays. Schoolchildren sat inside classrooms, chewed their pens and stared out of the windows longingly, and the pall of chemicals from the giant plastics factory seemed to sink lower every day, forcing women to gather their washing from the lines and close the doors against the stink.

Alex was starting to get a feel for the hostel and slowly slipped into something resembling a routine, broken only by occasional bursts of artistic temperament on the part of Molly Brown, the art teacher, and even less frequent summons to the main office in town. Mornings were spent checking the day book and paperwork and supervising and helping with the domestic side of running the place. Afternoons were for court reports, assessing residents' progress, planning provision and activities and meetings with other services. Early evenings and (very) occasional weekends gave the opportunity to get to know the residents and stamp her authority on the set-up.

Despite the perceived demotion in her status within probation, Alex found she was welcomed with enthusiasm by some of the other service providers. Alex had built quite a reputation over her time in Somerset and for a lot of people it was a positive thing. Mary from the college was one such person. When Alex dragged herself somewhat reluctantly to the meeting between the college tutors and the stonemasons she was surprised and impressed by the woman's energy and enthusiasm. After some hard bargaining and Alex's endorsement of Charlie's character they reached an agreement allowing him two weeks' trial with the possibility of a training placement if he did well.

Driving back to the hostel Alex realized she was smiling. The unexpected success, coming after what felt like a whole long list of failures, had reminded her why she had chosen the job in the first place. It didn't matter what the management got up to, how they tried to belittle her and undermine her confidence. She could still reach out to a lost hope like Charlie and help him turn his life around. It was shaping up to be a good end to the week that had begun so badly.

Lauren had arrived at the hostel on Monday distraught over Jonny. It had taken Alex and Bennie most of the afternoon and endless cups of tea to calm her down and the story left Alex feeling sad, angry and apprehensive in equal measures. At home, Sue had tried to be reassuring.

'It's appalling, I know,' she said. 'Still, they're not going to try anything with you or Margie.' From the corner Margie looked up from her book and snorted.

'Can do what they like at the moment,' she said. 'Still, there's a lot of bullying but if'n you hang on they gets bored. Or moved on somewhere else.'

'Look how fast they're moving everyone around,' said Sue. 'Rosalind'll be gone soon and you'll still be here, doing what you do best. Which is a bloody good job!'

The loyalty of her friends gave Alex heart, not just Sue and Margie but the way everyone in the office had rallied round her after Friday's incident with Rosalind. She tried to put her concerns aside and focussed on how she could make the hostel a better place – safer, more productive and a more positive environment for residents and staff.

One problem she faced almost weekly was finding suitable people for the weekend. Despite several memos to headquarters the 28-hour duty with a sleeping shift in the middle remained the pattern and takers for such a long and arduous session were few. Lauren was still willing to do many of the weekends but she had cried off on Wednesday, too concerned about her brother to leave him alone on a Saturday night.

'He 'ent right,' she said. 'This hit him real hard an' I don't know what he'll be up to on his own. Mum's still away so is down to me to watch him.'

Alex had every sympathy with her friend but it left her facing a gaping hole in her rota for the next week and even students were hard to find. With the end of the college year many had left the area or gone on holiday and the handful who were left were not attracted by the miserly pay on offer. Finally, and with considerable reluctance, Alex had accepted an aspiring first year, a young man who hoped to go on to university to train as a probation officer. He was raw, inexperienced and over-confident but he was all she could get.

On Thursday morning he had arrived late for his induction and seemed more interested in the pool table than the hostel regulations. Alex stressed the importance of the curfew and took him through the routine used to ensure everyone was inside and in bed by ten but when he left she shook her head, not sure he had taken any of it seriously.

'Don't you fret,' said Bennie. 'I'll be popping in over Saturday, 'specially as is dole weekend. That lad'l learn fast enough is not all about chatting an' making friends. What's he called?'

'Andy,' said Alex. 'Are you sure about this? I can always take the weekend myself.'

'You got too much on at the moment,' said Bennie firmly. 'Got to start delegating a bit or you'll be worn out and good for no-one nor nothin' by end of the summer. Got anything planned?'

Alex realized she had nothing planned. In fact, she and Margie had done nothing with their precious days off for weeks.

'You know, I might go up onto the Quantocks,' she said. 'I used to drive up and walk on Sunday afternoon when I arrived but it seems ages since I've been back.'

'Good idea,' said Bennie, nodding with approval. 'Do you the world of good and they say it might be sunny over the weekend.' They grinned at one another, the thought of rain now a distant memory.

'It has been very hot recently,' said Alex.

'You watch out for fires while you's up there,' said Bennie. 'Folks don't learn an' is the start of grockle season so is a load of visitors tramping about, dropping their fag ends and leavin' bottles lying. Too easy to start something in this weather but the very devil to put 'um out.'

Alex may not have had plans for the weekend but both Samuel and Steve had. Samuel used his free days to make final preparations for the visit to Hagg's Hill. A set of old and anonymous clothes were wrapped in a bin bag at the bottom of his cupboard. He had picked up a pair of worn sneakers in a second-hand shop and put them through the washing machine in the hostel basement, taking care not to touch them unless he was wearing a pair of the thin cotton gloves he had stored in a bag under his pillow. He had taken to slipping the razor in with his wash kit, reasoning that it was likely to be overlooked if anyone happened to search his room. There was no way to disguise the heavy parcel tape or his knitted ski mask, currently hidden amongst his clean underwear, but Alex wasn't one for snap searches. Just one more thing he appreciated about her.

Steve's preparations were less careful and considerably simpler. Hanging around the yard until everyone had left the workshop for a break on Monday he nipped inside and filched a hacksaw from the peg board. With this slipped into his pocket he had everything he needed for his weekend. Despite sharing a room with them he was still not on speaking terms with Petey or Mark and spent most of his evenings in front of the television set. Never the most popular resident, no-one tried to involve him in any of the activities during the evening and Steve's resentment towards the whole area smouldered as his impatience for the weekend grew.

Samuel had already decided Friday was the best time for his visit. The workshop session finished mid-afternoon and he made his way back to the hostel, eager to establish his presence early on. Stopping by the office he signed in and complained of a headache, telling Bennie he was not feeling well.

'I'll probably just sleep it off if I can,' he said. 'Don't save me any dinner.'

Bennie was busy finishing off a list of instructions for Andy and barely looked at him. 'I'll put a note in the book,' she said. 'Do you want the relief warden to look in, check you's alright?'

'No,' said Samuel, barely suppressing a grin at the sound of 'relief warden'. 'I will be fine. I'll come down if it gets any worse.'

'Probably been too long in the sun,' said Bennie to Alex, who had been arranging for their most competent and compliant helpers in the kitchen over the long shift.

'Mmm,' mused Alex, not entirely convinced. 'Did you offer him anything for it? No, it's okay – I'll pop up in a few minutes and check he's settled.'

She sat down and began running through the instructions until Andy arrived, flushed from the effort of cycling from the train station through the early weekend traffic.

'It's crazy out there!' he said, wheeling a very nice looking sports bike through the front door and leaning it up against the wall.

'Beginning of the holiday season,' said Alex. 'And a word of advice – I wouldn't leave that out there. You might like to lock it up in the garage out the back but I'd use a padlock too. I think most of the lads here can open the door without any trouble.'

A look of alarm flitted across Andy's face and he took the proffered key and hurried out to the rear of the building, wheeling his new bike to safety.

'Well, if that's any indication, he's not terribly experienced. And hasn't quite grasped the nature of our hostel,' Alex murmured.

Running through the list took the last bit of Alex's working day and drove any thought of Samuel from her mind. It was only when she got home she remembered, and was tempted to phone, but Bennie would be gone and she really didn't think it was a good idea sending Andy up to wake Samuel. In the end she let it go, sinking gratefully into an evening of good company and a few glasses of wine.

The arrival of a new member of staff was always disruptive and Andy's tenure began on a rocky note. Despite Alex's arrangements the evening meal was late as he failed to round up the kitchen crew, and soon hungry residents gathered by the closed hatch, banging on the shutters and chanting. Rather than sending them back to the tables and intervening in the kitchen himself Andy chose to impose his authority on the crowd by shouting and pushing them away from the shutters. Bennie, who had been lurking in the car park, waited for a few minutes but as the noise grew she went back inside and somewhat reluctantly restored order.

Amusing as he might have found this on a normal day, Samuel lay upstairs seething with frustration. He dared not try slipping out of the front door with everyone milling around in the hall and now Bennie was staying late he didn't dare leave through the side window. She was quite capable of popping up to check on him and, unlike Alex, more than willing to poke around his room. His caution was repaid when, a few minutes after quiet was restored downstairs, there was a knock on his door and she stepped inside.

'I brought you some aspirin,' she said, placing a beaker of tea and two tablets on the table next to his bed.

Samuel rolled over and opened one eye, faking a pain in his head.

'Thank you,' he groaned. 'What time is it?'

'You've not been asleep long,' said Bennie, stepping back towards the door. 'I'm about to go off duty.'

Samuel made a non-committal grunting noise and raised his head from the pillow. In the light that leaked round the curtains he could see her studying him from across the room.

'Thanks,' he said again. Push off you nosy cow, he thought. Why don't you just go? Finally, Bennie opened the door and slipped out. She stood in the hallway for a moment, not entirely satisfied Samuel was really ill but there was no sound of movement from within and finally she headed down the stairs and outside into a beautiful evening.

Samuel waited for five minutes, listening for the faintest sound before he slipped out of bed and gathered his things together. Boots, fresh clothes, cotton gloves, tape, mask and his lovely open-faced razor, all packed neatly in a small army pack. The corridor was deserted when he opened the door and crept along the hall to the side window. Slipping through, he left the latch raised a fraction so he could get back in when he returned. After his own, very special, beautiful evening.

The big flaw in his plan was he had nothing to eat – in fact he had eaten very little since his toast at breakfast. Wary of dropping anything in the house he had left his dole money hidden in a drawer at the hostel and besides, he didn't want to be seen by anyone in a shop who might identify him later, destroying his perfect alibi. As he set off along the back streets and footpaths out of town his excitement began to mount and all thought of food was pushed aside. At last, he was back to doing what he did so well, what he was born to do. The fact his actions would remove a problem for Alex, setting her free from this odious woman, made the plan sweeter still and he was smiling in anticipation by the time he reached Cannington.

It was only a few weeks past the summer solstice and the sun was several hours from setting, so he made his way, slightly breathless after his run, up the hill and slid into the darkness of the wood overlooking Rosalind's house. A glance at the driveway showed a large silver car pulled up by the front door. He had hoped to arrive before she got home but the unexpected events at the hostel had delayed him. Still, he had all night before him and it was better to change into his other clothes outside the house, using the time to observe and make sure he had not missed anything important.

Pulling on the gloves he began to dress for the night. Once he was ready he stepped softly up to the perimeter of the trees, keeping just beneath the shadows, and watched for a few minutes. Rosalind was not one of those people who saw the need to draw her curtains until it was dark outside and as dusk crept over the house she turned on the lamp in her front room, sitting in full view and sipping something from a cup. Her eyes were vacant as she stared out into the garden but Samuel took a step backwards just in case.

After a short while Rosalind glanced at her watch and rose from the chair, heading for the kitchen where presumably she would be occupied with making her evening meal. When a light went on at the side of the house Samuel pulled the mask over his head and picked up the tape and his razor. His heart beat fast and loud and there was a faint buzzing in his ears and he darted across the lawn and stood for a moment under the window he had identified as the best entry point. Then there was the sound of a door opening at the back and he froze in place. Tuneless humming was followed by the sound of a bag dropping into a bin before the door clicked closed again. It seemed his luck was holding for there was no sound to indicate a lock being turned. The silly bitch had left the door unlocked for him.

He waited a few minutes longer but finally could no longer contain his impatience. Tingling with anticipation he turned the corner, ducking below the level of the window as he reached for the door handle. It turned smoothly and he pushed the door open, stepping in behind Rosalind who was leaning over the sink.

'What the bloody hell ...' she began, but got no further as Samuel swung his fist, knocking her to the floor. She collapsed onto the floor with all the grace of a sack of potatoes and lay on the tiles moaning softly.

Samuel leaned over her, grasping her hands to bind her wrists with a length of parcel tape. When she tried to struggle free he hit her again, knocking her out this time. Ripping lengths from the roll of tape he covered her eyes and sealed her mouth, stepping back to admire his work. Slipping round the corner he flicked at the curtains, sealing the interior of the room from view. He was truly excited now, eager to begin, but he forced himself to stand for a moment, breathing deeply to restore some calm. He wanted to savour this evening. No need to rush. He must be careful to make no mistakes that might cut short his pleasure.

There was something both fascinating and repulsive about Rosalind's house. He was aware of a peculiar, musky odour composed of stale cooking smells, talcum powder and a large bunch of roses drooping in a vase on the sideboard. A faint shiver of disgust ran up his spine and he hesitated before returning to the kitchen.

His eyes were brilliant sparks of icy blue as he looked down at the woman slumped helpless and blind on the floor. Reaching down he grabbed her by the arms, straining to drag the considerable weight through to the living room. She was coming round again and tried to pull away feebly so he let her drop heavily onto the tiles.

'Keep still or I'll move you a piece at a time,' he hissed into her ear and to reinforce his point he took the razor from his pocket, laying the open blade against her face. She flinched, giving a sob deep in her throat and he considered cutting her, just to show he was not joking. He didn't see the frying pan coming until the force threw him aside across the kitchen where he landed heavily against a sharp corner.

'Get away from her, you bastard!' shrieked Debbie, raising the pan, a cast iron French skillet, and hitting him again. Samuel raised his arms to protect his head and felt something crack in his wrist. Rolling over, sliding on the tiles in a bid to escape, he managed to dodge the next blow and was out of the back door and running over the hill towards the open land and the sea before Debbie could stop him.

Debbie locked the door before kneeling over Rosalind.

'Lie still,' she said. 'It's okay – it's okay, he's gone. You're safe now. Just lie still and I'll try to get this stuff off.'

As gently as she could, Debbie peeled the tape from Rosalind's mouth. The senior screamed as it came free, a delayed reaction to her ordeal.

'My eyes!' she cried, and Debbie picked at the tape. 'Do my hands – here – I'll get the rest myself. Just undo my hands and call the police!'

Debbie sat on the floor, shaking as the full horror of what had happened hit her. Then she reached into a drawer and pulled out a pair of scissors, freeing Rosalind's wrists.

'Oh God, oh God, oh God,' Debbie sobbed.

Rosalind peeled the last of the tape from her face, stripping most of her make-up and one false eyelash with it.

'Just call for help,' she said. 'He could still be out there!'

Debbie hauled herself up and staggered into the front room to make the call. When she returned, Rosalind was still on the floor, though she was sitting up, leaning against one of the cupboards.

'Here,' said Debbie, placing a cushion behind her head. 'They're on their way, with an ambulance. They said not to touch anything ...'

'Bit late for that now,' said Rosalind gruffly.

'Are you okay? No, that's a stupid thing to say. I mean – how are you? Can I get anything for you?' Debbie asked.

Rosalind shook her head, flinching as the pain from Samuel's punches began to seep through the fuzziness in her head.

'You've just saved my life,' she said with a rather shaky smile. 'I think that's enough for one night.'

Debbie sat on the floor next to her and reached over, pulling Rosalind's head onto her shoulder and wrapping her arms around her.

'It's over,' she said. 'It's all done and help's on the way. They'll get the little shit. Just rest now.' She rocked Rosalind gently as they waited for the police, both of them weeping with fright and relief at their narrow escape.

Samuel's head was spinning as he stumbled out of the kitchen and all he could think of was to get as far away as possible. Running until he was out of sight of the house, he finally lurched, gasping and shaking, into another patch of woodland. As he fought to recover his breath he realized he had left his pack in the woods. The pack with his real clothes and his real shoes, items that could be traced back to him. Reaching into his pocket he felt the handle of his precious razor but in his haste he had dropped the roll of parcel tape. He tore the mask off his head with a curse, falling back against the rough bark of a tree. Only then was he aware of a stabbing pain in the centre of his neck.

Reaching round carefully he poked at the sore area. The fingers of his white gloves came away spotted with blood. The corner of the kitchen, he recalled, had been tiled and he had landed on it with considerable force. He tried moving his head and shrugging his shoulders, wincing as a wave of nausea had him grabbing at a branch for support. He felt round the wound again. It was just above the vertebrae, below his skull. He was lucky he wasn't paralyzed, he thought. Exploring the side of his head he encountered several large swellings, one close to his forehead that threatened to affect his vision.

He was badly hurt, he realized. He had to get somewhere to rest and make plans. The hostel was out – even if he could get back inside without being seen it would be obvious he'd been up to something in the morning. No, the only safe place was his cottage. Miles away, on the other side of town, it offered almost unobtainable safety. Gritting his teeth, Samuel forced himself to stand up, spurred on by the faint sounds of sirens from just over the hill behind him. Slowly and painfully he began the long journey to his sanctuary.

Steve woke early on the Saturday, eager to begin the day. Ignoring the grumbles of his room-mates he pulled open the curtains and rummaged around the floor, searching for some reasonably clean clothes, all the time whistling merrily. As he left the room Petey stumbled out of bed and dragged the curtains back over, mumbling angrily, but Steve was already heading through the door to the dining room, eager to grab some breakfast and be off.

In the kitchen Andy was struggling with the demands of cooking for more than a dozen residents. He had been up for an hour, having experienced a disturbed and rather uncomfortable night, and he was not at his best. The tea urn was cold and there was no milk in the fridge so Steve went to the front door and collected the bottles, opening one to drink straight from it. The others were left on the side as he wandered over to the kitchen and poked his head in hopefully.

'Ah, good – come on,' said Andy.

Steve shook his head. 'Oh no, I ain't on today. Look on the rota. I ain't doing no other lazy bugger's shift.'

Andy glared at him but was handicapped by not yet knowing the names of most of his charges. As far as he was concerned anyone around should help out but Steve had already gone back out taking a packet of biscuits with him.

'They'll be down soon so you'd better get this urn on sharpish,' called Steve from a table in the dining room. Andy was saved from total humiliation by the arrival of Bennie, who swept in, set the water boiling, checked the rota on the back of the kitchen door and disappeared upstairs, returning with two dishevelled and sleepy helpers.

'There you go,' she said, pushing the kitchen crew through the door before opening the fridge and putting the milk away. 'Menu's in the folder in the office,' she added over her shoulder on the way back out again. 'Steve – use a cup and don't you dare put that bottle back in the fridge now you've been spitting all over it!'

Andy glared at him on the way to the office. This job was way too much hard work for the money and he wouldn't be doing it again. Not knowing the residents or the hostel, he failed to keep count of who was in and no-one thought it odd when Samuel failed to show up for breakfast. He was often out for the whole day, returning just before curfew and most of the lads preferred it when he wasn't around anyway.

When the hatch finally opened, Steve grabbed a plate of eggs with several slices of toast and retired to a corner to wolf his food down. He had a busy day planned and needed a decent breakfast to keep him going. As soon as he'd finished he walked off leaving the plates on the table surrounded by crumbs, the half-empty milk bottle abandoned. Other lads followed suit and as soon as they finished serving, the kitchen lads grabbed their own food and retired to the dining room, leaving Andy to deal with the washing up.

Despite his shouts no-one answered to the names he called from the cleaning rota, the guilty parties sneaking back upstairs to grab an extra hour in bed. By the time he realized no-one was coming to help, the kitchen crew had disappeared and he stood in the dining room surrounded by discarded food and dirty crocks, seething with impotent anger.

Steve hurried up the stairs, grabbed a carrier bag from his locker and left, slamming the door behind him. He still had some money left from his dole, having shunned the pub the night before, and he waited until the Glastonbury bus pulled up at the stop, climbing aboard and buying a ticket out to the edge of the Levels. It was another lovely day without a cloud in the sky and he gazed out over the parched fields, many of them full of stubble for much of the wheat was already harvested.

He got off at the junction to the new road that led to the new houses. Approaching the close carefully he was relieved to see it was deserted and the shed was still locked with a single padlock. Pulling the stolen hacksaw from his carrier, Steve worked at the lock until it came free and the door swung open. In the corner was the object of his desires, a huge electric pitch barrel. The intoxicating aroma filled the small space and he sniffed deeply, his head swimming with the fumes. Casting around he found an old paint tin and collected some sticks which he set ready as the pot heated up.

When the black, sticky tar was soft but not liquid he dipped his sticks into it, coating each with several layers and laying them aside to set. After a moment's thought he went outside and pushed his way through the site's surrounding hedge into a newly harvested field where he gathered an armful of straw left by the baler. Twisting this into several thick bundles he made some straw and pitch torches to add to his sticks.

When they were all dry he put them in the paint can and unplugged the heater. It would be wonderful, he thought, to see that go up but the consequences were likely to be extremely serious, possibly leading to a major investigation and Steve preferred to avoid that level of police scrutiny. Perhaps when he was finally leaving to go home, he thought.

Steve closed the door behind him and secured it with the cut padlock before setting off across the fields. He could see his target in the distance, almost hidden behind a stand of low trees. It was not an easy hike, over rough ground with stubble catching at his ankles and brambles and nettles tangling around his legs. He made a detour round the field where he and Petey had encountered the adders, which forced him to wade through several streams, though they were reduced to a trickle of water and several inches of slippery, sticky mud. Several times Steve stopped, resting in one of the shrinking patches of shade, until finally he pushed through the final obstacle and reached the giant hayrick.

The collected straw from half a dozen fields was piled up in bales to make a traditional stack. It towered over Steve, who stood before it, sniffing the warm, dusty smell of the straw. Reaching out with one hand he brushed the surface, feeling the stalks crackle under his fingers. It was perfect – dry and loosely packed with tiny gaps between the bales.

With shaking hands Steve emptied his carrier bag onto the packed earth. Starting with the firelighters he chose three spots where there were wider spaces, pushing them into place, then he added the pitch-coated sticks and then the stubble. Finally, he squirted each area with the remains of his lighter fluid, shoving the can into the stack before stepping back to take a last look at the mass of hay.

The first straw bundle smouldered but did not light and it took him several attempts before a tell-tale blue flame bloomed around one of the treated areas. He stepped back, watching anxiously as the fire flickered and threatened to go out in the gentle breeze but then it reached inside and caught one of the pitch-covered sticks. A dark trickle of smoke began to rise from the side of the stack as the heat inside ignited first the wood and then the surrounding straw.

Steve stepped forwards to examine the third set of incendiaries, concerned he might burn one side away and the hayrick would topple over without catching properly. There was no sensation of heat as he put his hand on the area and he fumbled in his pocket for the lighter once more. The left side was more resistant to his attempts and he had several goes at lighting the straw and wood. He was so intent on finishing the task properly he failed to notice smoke rising from the second place until there was a loud 'whoosh' and flames shot out from between the bales towards him. Stumbling backwards, he just escaped a second small explosion as the third site erupted in flames.

Sparks shot from the burning haystack, striking Steve on his face and burning holes in his clothes. Torn between fear and awe at the sight, Steve hesitated, then turned and ran as fast as he could away from the fire. He stopped half way to the edge of the field to marvel at the ferocity of the blaze. Thick black smoke poured from the massive haystack and where the fire touched the ground the stubble began to catch light. As the little flames began to creep across the field towards him Steve retreated further, aware suddenly of the stinging on his face. Raising his hands to touch the sore sports he encountered only dust where his eyebrows should have been and he flinched as he brushed over a rash of small burns on his forehead and cheeks. He'd never been injured before but then he'd never set a fire as large as this before, and it was large – and growing with every minute.

As more of the haystack caught alight the fire found its voice, a dull roar that grew louder as the flames rose upwards and outwards. Despite his distance, Steve could feel the heat rolling towards him and he moved back again, retreating towards the little stream that bordered one side of the field. He stood for a minute, admiring his handiwork but suddenly he felt something run across his foot. He glanced down just in time to see a rat scrabbled over his shoes and disappear down the side of the stream. Steve shuddered, kicking futilely in the direction of the animal but the rat was gone, fleeing ahead of the spreading blaze.

Steve coughed as the breeze stiffened for a moment, blowing the thick smoke towards him. His eyes began to water and he decided it was probably time to emulate the rat and leave the vicinity. The hayrick was well alight now, growling and roaring as the fire burrowed deeper into the tightly baled straw. It threw off sparks, burning bits of hay and a tremendous wave of heat as unchecked it began to extend its boundaries.

Soon more animals began to flee before the flames but Steve was away and watching from the main road by then. When the fire brigade finally arrived it was obvious they could do little to contain the blaze, let alone put it out. He hid behind the hedge, hugging himself with glee as the firemen discussed what they could do so far from the water mains, with all but the biggest rivers drying up.

'Might have to try'n keep it away from people's houses an' wait,' said one man gloomily.

'What about that patch, just aside of it, though?' asked another. 'Is peat bog, that. Dry as dust on top an' for good way down too. If that catches it could run on underground 'til winter.'

'Better make sure it don't catch then,' said the fire chief, coming round the side of the engine. 'Want you two back in Highpoint to refill the tanker and get on to Taunton. Tell 'um what we got here. Tell 'um we need everyone they got and every drop of water too. Meantime we should try an' cut a fire break, try to keep it away from the peat.' He spat in disgust, glaring at the fire. 'This is as bad as I've ever seen. We find the little bastard as did this, I'll string 'um up myself!'

Chapter Eighteen

It was dawn on Saturday morning by the time Samuel finished his long, hard trek across the countryside to the cottage on the Levels. A lesser man would have given up long before he reached his destination but Samuel was driven by a desperate urge to survive, to win through, and despite the buzzing in his ears and the increasing heaviness of his body he had forced himself onwards. The journey took him much longer than usual for he had to follow small unlit tracks round villages and a longer diversion to avoid Highpoint. Coupled with his injuries, he had been close to exhaustion when he finally stumbled over the threshold of the cottage, his head spinning.

There was nothing to eat in the cottage but he found a bottle of water and sipped it slowly, fighting waves of nausea. Finally, he'd dragged his aching body upstairs to the shiny clean bedroom and collapsed on the empty bed. It was not how he had imagined using this space but he was too tired to care. As the sun rose over the surrounding countryside Samuel fell into a deep sleep.

Tom and Brian were driving to Lily's house to check on the goats when they saw the smoke rising from Steve's fire.

'Now that don't look too good,' observed Tom as he pulled the van over and got out to see what was happening. 'Not so far away neither. Here, you got better eyes'n me lad. Pop over there a way and tell us what's goin' on.'

Brian hopped out of the van, clambered over the fence and trotted in the direction of the fire. As he got closer he could smell the smoke, now a heavy black pall over the area. In the distance were the figures of the firemen, tiny against the huge fire. He squinted against the fumes, watching for a moment before hurrying back to Tom.

'Looks like the big hayrick on old Potter's field,' he said. 'Is the fire brigade there but seems they's digging out stuff. Don't see no water out there.'

'That's 'cos is no water,' said Tom grimly. 'They's trying to keep it off the peat and drive it back aways, maybe in range of a tanker if they can get one out here. Don't look too good if they don't get a hand on this'n soon.'

Brian looked over his shoulder along the road and then back towards the fire.

'Don't think is likely to reach Pongo an' Quinn?' he asked.

Tom frowned as he watched the direction of the smoke.

''Ent likely,' he said. 'Still, don't like the idea of leavin' 'em. Bit too close for comfort and round here fire can take off an' you got no chance of escaping it. Should go an' check Lily's alright too,' he added, giving Brian a reproachful look.

'Course,' said Brian, unabashed by the implied reproach. They clambered back into the van and drove along the lane a short way, Tom pulling up just past Lily's drive.

'Hop out an' check she's in,' said Tom. Brian slid out of the door and trotted towards the house, stopping on the way to greet the two goats.

'Yo – Lily?' he called.

'Who's that, then?' was the reply and Lily opened a top window, peering down on the young man.

'Come to check you is alright,' Brian shouted. 'On account of there's a girt big fire over Potter's field.'

'I noticed that,' said Lily dryly. 'Been watching to see which way is moving. Afternoon, Tom,' she added.

'Lily,' said Tom politely. 'Now lad, you go up the lane a bit an' see if is moving this way. Don't get too close mind. Don't want you doin' nothing stupid or Ada'll have my hide.'

Brian glanced at the goats anxiously.

'I'll not let nothin' happen to them two,' said Tom. 'Look, they 'ent worried yet. Animals got a feel for danger, 'specially fire. They get a smell of the smoke and they'll let us know. Off with you now.' He gave a gentle shove and Brian set off down the drive and left along the road towards the fish nets and Ada's old home.

Although he could smell the fire as he got closer it didn't seem to be moving towards Lily's place and the wind, what there was of it, was blowing off to the left. Bad news for the firemen in their struggle to keep it away from the peat workings but a piece of luck for Lily – and the goats. He stopped a couple of fields away and watched for a minute before turning to go back. Something caught his attention and he turned back to stare at Ada's old cottage. The gate was ajar, out to the back.

He was sure Tom had said it was all locked up and he knew it had been closed the last time they drove past. The old house and its grim history held a horrid fascination for Brian and he could not resist staring whenever they called in at the fishing trap. Definitely open now though, he thought. No storms or even much wind to push it in the past week or so, which meant only one thing. Someone – some stranger – had been trespassing. Brian began to step across the road when he recalled Tom's warning not to interfere. The desire to have a quick look around tugged at him and he was torn between loyalty to Tom and a searing curiosity. Just as loyalty won he saw a flicker at the top window and realized the house was now occupied. He was over the road in seconds, pushing open the rotten front gate and heading for the back door.

Samuel saw him coming from the top window and made a dive for the stairs. Woken by the distant commotion and a thundering headache, he had been observing the fire for a while before Brian appeared. The window was thick with grime and he was confident he would not be seen but a fit of dizziness overcame him and he almost fell back onto the bed. Grabbing at the windowsill his arm brushed against the dirty glass leaving a streak in the grime.

As Brian pushed his way in through the back Samuel wrenched the front door open and was off across the field, running as fast as he could to get past the fire and away to safety. Brian heard the groaning of the front door and pushed past the kitchen table into the front room, but was too late to get a good look at the intruder. He considered going after him but the fire was blazing now, flames shooting high into the air, and he decided to check around the cottage, make it secure and get back to Lily's. Despite Tom's confidence he was concerned about the goats and hoped to persuade him to move them as a precaution.

In the distance Samuel was struggling. It was more than twenty-four hours since he had eaten anything and he had been bordering on malnourishment for some time. His vision refused to clear and he was giddy, made more unsteady on his feet by the smoke that drifted around him from the fire. In addition, though he didn't know it, there was a small but growing bleed in his head at the place where Debbie had hit him with the frying pan. The pressure was building slowly, made worse by his sudden activity and the frantic beating of his heart as he fled.

There was a shout from nearby as the firemen spotted him. Several waved their arms to warn him away but one brave young man started off towards him, hoping to catch the arsonist responsible for the growing disaster. He was called back by the fire chief who was desperate for every pair of hands in his effort to contain the fire and Samuel scrambled behind a hedge, almost fell into a narrow drainage channel and forged on, disappearing from view.

After fighting over stubble and through heavy undergrowth the wide expanse of the flower meadows offered him a chance to put some distance between himself and any pursuit and Samuel lengthened his stride, trying to ignore the sickness in his stomach. His vision dimmed periodically and as he ran under the shade of a willow he looked forward, hoping to spot a familiar landmark. In that moment of inattention he put his foot into the middle of an adder's nest.

Maddened by fear the snakes roiled around Samuel's feet, striking again and again at his legs. Many of the bites met his shoes or were deflected by his trousers but some hit his exposed ankles. Samuel stumbled away, treading on several snakes that turned and bit him furiously. He tried to kick them away but the spinning in his head finally overcame him. He fell, first onto his knees and then face down into the nest.

Alex and Margie sat in the shelter of a rocky outcrop eating cold chicken with their fingers and savouring the warmth of the sun on their legs.

'Why don't we do this every weekend?' Alex asked, leaning back on the stone.

'Can't afford the chicken,' said Margie.

'No, I mean – oh, you're teasing me aren't you.'

'Might be,' said Margie with a grin. 'Might be, might not. What you think?'

Alex returned the smile and shook her head. 'I know, I'm too serious most of the time.'

'Serious is good, 'specially for work but wouldn't do you no harm to relax a bit more,' said Margie. 'Coming up here's a right good idea. Gets you away from all that.' She gestured across the landscape laid out below them. The heat caused the view to shimmer, a lake of green and gold with the stark blue of an unclouded sky above them.

'It looks pretty wonderful from up here, though,' said Alex. 'It's such a beautiful part of the world.'

'Shame about some of the people, though,' said Margie.

'Not fair,' said Alex. She was feeling very relaxed and correspondingly magnanimous. 'It's the same wherever you go. Most people are fine but a few stinkers cloud your view of things.'

'Speaking of view,' said Margie, leaning forwards. 'Look down there, way across towards Glasto. You see anything?'

Alex peered in the direction she indicated, screwing her eyes up against the glare. 'Hard to see in this,' she grumbled and began to rummage in her bag for some dark glasses. 'Right – where – oh my god!' As she turned back, a plume of smoke rose into the air in the distance. The two women leaned forwards, peering down onto the Levels, trying to make sense of what they saw.

'Wild fire, I reckon,' said Margie. 'Though maybe not, seein' that black in the smoke. Wild fire burns white and grey first. Black – is perhaps oil or petrol so unless 'tis a car or summat then could have been set.'

'Surely not,' said Alex. 'What sort of an idiot would start a fire in a heat wave like this?'

'Most of 'em from my experience,' said Margie, staring at the fire. 'Looks like the brigade's there now. Wonder what they goin' to do for water? Levels, they be dryin' up in this. Lots of empty streams and not much piped water way out there. Wonder what's burning.'

'There's those ghastly little estates they're plonking down all around,' said Alex. 'Maybe it's one of them.'

Margie gave a little laugh. 'Don't think is one of them. Pity, mind.'

They sat for a few minutes more watching the fire grow but the relaxed mood was broken and they packed up the remains of their picnic and set off back down the hills to the car park.

'You got anyone as likes to set fires, then?' Margie asked casually as they began the drive home.

'Oh, don't let it be one of mine,' Alex groaned. 'That would be the end for me.'

'Can't blame you if you's not on duty,' said Margie. They drove in silence for a few minutes, the inside of the car flickering as they passed through leafy tunnels of trees that broke the sunlight into bands of light and shade.

'They can you know,' said Alex finally. 'If I didn't spot the signs. And besides, I put whoever is in charge over the weekend on the rota so it's my responsibility. What seems doubly unfair as I have to take someone on the list from headquarters and they never seem to have anyone even moderately competent available. Can you imagine the trouble we're in if it is one of ours? Rosalind will go ballistic, especially as the damn inspectors are finally coming next week!'

As they rounded the bend out of the woods and started down the hill the pall of smoke was clearly visible, spreading out across the landscape ahead of them.

Steve crouched in the hedge, not daring to move as the firemen set up their control centre a few yards away. The breeze stiffened and began to blow the smoke towards them, prompting a flurry of activity as the men rushed to dig a new ditch between the creeping fire and the road. Hunched over in misery, his face and hands stinging and his eyes watering, Steve struggled not to cough. There were a few minutes of relief as the fickle wind changed direction again but then the smoke was back and Steve could no longer fight the burning in his throat.

A hand reached through the hedge and seized him by the shoulder, pulling him roughly through the branches out onto the road. Covering his face with his hands, Steve cowered on the tarmac as the firemen surrounded him, towering over his hunched body.

'Look what we got!' said one to the fire chief, who was hurrying over to see what the commotion was about.

Tilting Steve's head up, the chief peered at his face. 'Interesting collection of burns you've got there lad. Care to tell us how this happened then?'

Steve glared at him, jerking his head back and hunching over again.

'I ain't got nothing to say.'

'Fine by me,' said the fire chief. 'Much better you tell it to the police. Keep an eye on him 'til they gets here. Don't want this one slippin' away. Tell you what though,' he said, turning back to look down at the young man, 'we got them evidence bags in my truck. Take a couple of 'em and wrap his hands up. Reckon the crime scene blokes might want to test him and don't want no smart solicitor claiming was from after the fire or picked up round about.'

Steve struggled as two hefty firemen hauled him to his feet and dragged him none too gently over to the fire engine.

'You can't do this!' he shouted. 'Can't just keep us here – I got rights!'

The fire chief swung round to face him, his face an angry mask.

'So does all as live an' work out here,' he said. 'And all the animals too. So you sit there an' keep yer mouth shut, an' you better pray this don't spread 'cos if it does you looking at a long time inside.'

'You don't know it was me!' Steve yelled at his retreating form. 'Can't prove nothing!'

'Maybe I can't but we know was you an' there's some right clever coppers on their way to prove it,' said the chief as he walked away.

When Brian got back to Lily's cottage Tom had the back of the van open and was trying to load Pongo.

'Here now, give us a hand,' he said, wrestling with the animal.

'You doin' it wrong,' said Brian. 'Got to take him by the horns, like this, see. Then you just leads him in all gentle.' Pongo stopped struggling and meekly followed Brian up the ramp and into the van's interior.

'Well now,' said Tom in admiration. 'Still, how'm I supposed to do that with Quinn? Got no horns!'

Brian gave Pongo's nose a stroke and attached his halter to the side of the van before sliding out and walking over to the little companion goat.

'Quinn 'ent no trouble,' he said, slipping a rope over his head. Quinn trotted after him into the van without a murmur. Tom shook his head and said to Lily, 'Never seen nothin' like that afore. A marvel with goats that lad is.'

Lily smiled, a rather tight-lipped smile as she glanced anxiously at the burning fields.

'Think maybe you better come along with us,' said Tom. 'You got anything you want to bring? Don't think will reach this far but all that smoke's gettin' a bit strong.'

'Well – I need to close my windows,' said Lily. 'Can't have that getting in and ruining everything. And there's my chickens – oh dear ...' Her eyes began to fill with tears as she watched the firemen scurrying around the blaze.

'Tell you what,' said Tom. 'I'll take the chickens now and drop 'em off at Ada's. You go back in and close up an' collect what you want to take. Brian'll wait here, make sure you're alright and I'll be back for you both.'

'I can drive the van,' said Brian.

'Mebbe you can but you ain't,' said Tom sharply.

'Makes more sense,' said Brian. 'I's better with Pongo an' seems to me if'n we need to go is better we goes fast. Take you an age to get 'um both out and tethered.' He held out his hand for the keys.

Tom hesitated but the sight of Lily struggling to be brave in the face of possible disaster won through his stubbornness.

'You drive careful,' he said sternly. 'Don't be flying round no corners. Will be some panicky people around on account of this an' I don't expect to see no scratches in my paintwork neither.'

'Couldn't find no paint to scratch in all them dents,' said Brian, seizing the keys from Tom's outstretched hand. 'Don't worry,' he added, as he swung himself into the driving seat. 'Wouldn't do nothin' as might hurt Pongo now would I?'

'Cheeky little ...' mumbled Tom. He turned to Lily and gestured towards the house. 'Now then, let's get them chickens o' yours in boxes and see what else you might want. Ada'll look after yer, no worries. You go in and close up an' I'll see to them birds.'

The fire burned hot and hard, through the haystack and across the stubble until it finally reached the dry edges of the peat cuttings. Here was a rich source of fuel and the fire growled hungrily as it settled in to feast. For three days and nights the combined fire brigades of the county struggled, first to contain the blaze and then, inch by painful inch, to drive it back on itself over the scorched earth. Even after the flames were out, the land itself continued to smoulder as areas of peat burned underground. The smoke drifted over the ruined landscape as teams of men in breathing gear toiled under the burning sun to dig out the red-hot earth and finally extinguish the fire.

On the fourth morning they found Samuel, still lain across the remains of the adders' nest. His face was horribly swollen and dried blood was smeared across the side of his head. The fire had spared him but the effect of the adders combined with the smoke and the injury to his head had been enough to finish him off. He had regained consciousness a few minutes after his fall but found himself unable to move, even when the last of the snakes slithered over his neck and escaped the threatening fire.

Paralysed by the multiple bites, his vision fading as the blood seeped out of the wound inside his head, his one fear was surviving long enough for the fire to reach him. Samuel had destroyed the lives of many women in his short time on earth. Perhaps it would have been some small consolation had they known he died as helpless and afraid as they had.

The grim discovery sent the overworked crime scene team rushing to the site. The body had been spared the attentions of the local wildlife, most of which had fled before the fire, but the flies had got at him and he was already past the stage of rigor mortis and into what the police surgeon referred to as 'the runny bit'.

When he arrived at the mortuary a quick look at the body revealed he had suffered a blow to the head as well as the wound at the back of his neck. Compounded by the smoke inhalation and the adder bites the coroner was at a loss as to actual cause of death. Then news of the attack on Rosalind filtered through from Highpoint and the police at Street began to wonder if their bloated corpse might be the same man.

He had nothing to identify him in his pockets apart from the razor but a search of the wood behind Rosalind's garden uncovered Samuel's pack with his everyday clothes. Alex rang the station to report him missing on Monday morning and on Wednesday she was dismayed to receive a visit from Sergeant Willis, who had some rather uncomfortable questions for her and her staff. He placed several evidence bags containing a dark shirt and a pair of running shoes on the desk in front of them.

Both Alex and Bennie recognized the clothes at once. Samuel had been the neatest dresser in the hostel, even including the staff. Bennie vouched for the fact they matched what he had been wearing on the Friday evening, the last time she saw him. Then Sergeant Willis took out a third bag, this one containing the razor. Alex looked it for a moment, reached out and touched the plastic. It crackled under the fingers and she jerked her hand away.

'Did you find any parcel tape?' she asked.

'Why do you want to know that?' Willis said, taking out his notebook again.

'A few months ago,' she said softly. 'My assistant Alison – a man broke in with a mask on and a razor like this, remember?'

'Oh, now you reminding me, I do recall,' said Willis. 'Was nasty that – but we put away that lad as was a flasher for it.'

Alex nodded glumly. 'I did have my doubts at the time but I never could prove anything. I ...' She stopped as Bennie kicked her on the knee under the desk.

'Didn't see much of Samuel,' said Bennie smoothly. 'Came here with not much of a record – certainly nothin' serious. Just always a repeat offender so they stuck him here, see if the routine might sort 'um out. Weren't no trouble, always clean an' a bit keen on his fitness. Most days he was out runnin' and was training for the raft race.'

'Has there been another break-in?' Alex asked anxiously.

'I can't say,' said the sergeant, scribbling furiously. 'Still making enquiries on that score. Well, now we got to see what killed him afore we untangle all this. Glad I'm on this side of the job today I tell yer. Between us, he might have been a good looking lad once but he ain't any more.'

'Why the hell did you do that?' demanded Alex after the sergeant had left. She rolled up the leg of her jeans and peered at the knee.

'You was about to put yerself right in it,' said Bennie. 'Saying you thought maybe he was mixed up in that stuff with Alison an' you not reporting any of it – what d'you think they'd make of that up at headquarters then?'

'That wasn't what I meant,' Alex protested, rubbing her shin.

'Don't matter,' said Bennie. 'That's what they can make of it so my advice is just keep quiet and let the coppers do their job, their way. No good'll come of fiddling about now. Let it lie, that's what I says.'

Before Alex could reply the phone rang. It was Debbie, back in the office and dealing with Rosalind's appointments as if she were the senior.

'You're due to have supervision this week,' she said.

Alex frowned, both at the thought of a supervision session with Rosalind and because she had thought the inspection team were due in on that day. Surely Rosalind wanted to keep her as far away from them as possible unless they started asking awkward questions. The way she felt at the moment she certainly had some awkward answers for them.

'The inspection has been put off again,' Debbie continued, correctly interpreting her silence. 'However, given the delays and the additional time we have now had to prepare, it is important we have everything up to date. Your supervision is overdue by several weeks so I've booked you in for Friday at three.' The phone went down before Alex could reply.

'Damn, damn, damn!' said Alex, dropping the receiver. 'The bloody arrogance of the bitch!'

'Rosalind or Debbie?' asked Bennie without looking up from the file she was reading.

'Debbie,' said Alex. 'Though if I'm being honest, both I guess. Hello – who's that?' The front door slammed and both women rose from their desks, relaxing again as Lauren barrelled into the room.

'You heard then?' she said, leaning on Alex's desk.

'Heard what?' Alex asked.

''Bout Friday night,' said Lauren. 'Seems someone was up at Rosalind's house, top of Hagg's Hill over Cannington way. Broke in an' had her trussed up like a chicken when Debbie come in and whacked him over the head with one of them posh French frying pans. Knocked him clear across the room and he took off over the hills. From what I hear, could be the same bloke as broke into Alison's!'

'Debbie?' said Alex, confused by this strange story. 'What was Debbie doing at Rosalind's house?'

'Who knows,' said Lauren dismissively. 'Maybe they was having dinner together. You know they's close friends.' She was much more interested in the identity of the assailant and rumours of Samuel's disappearance were circling round the day centre groups and setting off a fever of speculation. Alex fielded Lauren's questions as best she could but all the time she was turning the puzzle over in her mind.

'Don't know, don't care,' said Sue that evening. 'Bennie's right – if it turns out that Samuel was the one in Rosalind's house you really need to stay out of the whole ghastly mess. There'll be all sorts of questions flying around anyway without you putting yourself forward as the one most likely to blame.' She took another mouthful of her chicken salad and chewed thoughtfully. 'I don't think it's a good idea, poking around in her domestic arrangements anyway, especially considering the climate of opinion around here.'

'Well, I suppose she's entitled to her privacy,' said Alex rather grudgingly. 'If I want to keep my private life to myself I guess she should have the same consideration.'

Sue put down her fork and stared at her friend, a pitying look on her face. 'You are kidding, right?'

'What do you mean?' Alex asked.

Sue laughed and shook her head in mock dismay. 'As soon as Margie arrived on the scene I got *so* much sympathy at work,' she said. 'Everyone was asking if I was okay and inviting me into the office for coffee. Don't tell me you didn't notice?'

'I thought that was because of your move into the court duty,' mumbled Alex. 'Do you mean they all think ...' She felt herself flush with the embarrassment of this news.

'Don't worry,' said Sue. 'I disabused them of that idea, though I'm not sure they believe me. Anyway, I don't care what people think so it doesn't bother me at all. Actually I think it gives me a bit of mystique.'

'That's easy for you,' said Alex. 'It's a bit different for some of us. Look at Jonny.'

The smile faded from Sue's face and she nodded, more serious again. 'You're right. I'm sorry – still, whilst it would be a hoot if they were – shall we say more than friends? – I don't think you'll find any allies in that direction.'

Alex managed a smile, wanting to apologize for her rudeness but still dismayed by the idea her private life was public knowledge around the office.

Having spent a comfortable few days with Ada, Lily returned to her home once the fire brigade gave the all-clear. They were old friends with few secrets and it had taken all of half an hour for Lily to weasel the story of Tom's proposal out of her.

'So what'd you say?' Lily asked.

Ada gave a small, secretive smile and then nodded her head. 'Well, don't think many is comin' knocking, not at my time of life. He's a decent man and handy around the house so ...'

'Oh Ada, go on! You don't marry 'um if they's good around the house, you give 'um lunch and a peck on the cheek. Don't you play the hard-hearted madam with me. You always been soft on Tom and he's always been soft on you.'

'Perhaps,' said Ada, but her eyes were sparkling and finally she couldn't hide her joy. 'Seemed about time and he asked right proper, down on one knee and everything.'

Lily laughed at the thought of Tom kneeling to ask Ada to marry him.

'Took him longer to get up again after,' Ada continued. 'Right stiff in one leg he is. Had to give 'um a hand.'

'When's it goin' to be? Summer wedding is always nice,' said Lily. She was already plotting to be a maid of honour, or at least a matron.

Ada shook her head. 'Not time now, what with Tom's folks bein' out on the circuit with the fairs. Thought maybe September time would be good. They's all here for the grand fair and autumn wedding seems about right, seein' as we's in our later years.'

Tom and Brian accompanied Lily on her return and without them she readily admitted she would not have coped with the damage left by the smoke. Everything had to be taken out of the little house, scrubbed clean and left to dry in the sunlight that still beat down on the Levels. Tom collected baskets of curtains and bedding, transporting it to Ada's house where it was washed, dried and returned, fragrant with the scent of wild flowers and fresh air. Brian, who had no fear of heights, climbed an old ladder and rocked about at the top cleaning the soot from the window panes and frames and Tom filled endless buckets of water from the canal to remove the layer of ash and dust that covered every plant in Lily's garden.

It was Friday morning before Brian was satisfied the land was clear enough for the goats and Ada went over in the van to help celebrate their arrival and Lily's return to her home. Standing by the front gate she stared down the road towards the old cottage, just visible on the bend. She was saddened to see the state it was in but had never been able to summon the courage to visit her old family home.

Frank, her first husband, had died there, the victim of a vicious man who was bent on revenge. She had been spared the details of Frank's end but knew his killer had kept the body in the house because parts of it had been discovered by the police. She shivered at the thought of the place and wondered what she was going to do with it. It was registered under her maiden name and no-one had tried to get any rates for it in years but she felt a responsibility towards the old place. There were plenty of people desperate for somewhere to live and the bulk of the building was sound enough.

'What you brooding over?' Tom asked, stepping up behind and putting his arms around her.

'Just wondering about my old house,' she said.

'Fancy me getting wed, not just to a rich woman but one with two houses,' teased Tom.

'Don't,' she said, still looking along the road. 'Sometimes I thinks maybe is a curse on the place. Nothin' good happened there for most of my life an' I was glad to leave it soon as I got the chance.'

'We should go there,' said Tom. 'No, I mean it, Ada. I'll come along and we'll go in together, see what's there. Ain't having you afeared of some old house and it's sitting over here, causing you worry.'

Ada pulled away from him, wrapping her arms around her body.

'Don't know as I can,' she said.

'Well, we'll bring Brian along,' said Tom. 'No, don't you give me that look Ada. He's been in, chasin' that squatter out when we was moving Lily so *he* ain't afeared of it. 'Sides, he's been desperate to see inside proper like. After all he done, helping Lily and all, would be a bit of a treat for him.'

Ada wasn't sure the idea of the deserted cottage fitted with her notion of a treat but she knew when she was beaten. Together, the little group walked the short distance down the road, where Ada stood for a moment, hand on the sagging gate, before she pulled back her shoulders and strode up to the front door, the picture of defiance.

'Is locked,' said Brian from behind her. 'Closed it all up when I was here.'

Ada glared at him. 'So how the hell we going to get inside then?'

'Is open round back,' he said cheerfully, pushing the remains of the side gate open and stepping through. The back of the building was considerably neater than the front for both of the previous occupants had concentrated their efforts on those aspects hidden from the road. The windows had been cleaned as had the paintwork, though the fire had laid its sooty hand on this building too.

Ada stepped into the kitchen and was almost overcome by a flood of memories. The old iron grate was still in place and had been used and cleaned recently from the look of it. A familiar table was placed by the rear window overlooking the canal and there was a soot-spotted cloth laid across it. A few plain plates were stacked on the pine dresser and when she opened the cupboard she found one perfect blue and white meat platter at the back.

'Was a wedding present,' she said, lifting it out and gazing at the painted figures. 'Fancy this still bein' here. Forgot all about it, I did, after my mother passed.'

She put the plate gently on the table, smiling at the memory it evoked. They moved through to the front and here the extent of the cottage's neglect was much more obvious. Brian stepped through the grime on the floor heading for the stairs leading to the bedrooms.

'Stairs is clear,' he said in response to Tom's protest. 'Was upstairs I saw summat moving an' all.'

Tom turned to Ada, who was frozen in the middle of the room.

'You go up if you want,' she said. 'I'm goin' back to the kitchen.'

After a moment's hesitation Tom climbed the stairs to find Brian in the doorway of the rear bedroom, staring at the bloodstains on the cover of the bed in the otherwise pristine room.

'Ah,' said Tom, taking in the scene. For once Brian was at a loss for words as he pointed to the ski mask lying on one corner of the bed.

'Think we need to get the police out here,' said Tom. 'Should'a listened to Ada. She's right – nothing good happens here. S'like there's a curse on this place.'

Chapter Nineteen

Samuel's death and the arrest of Steve for arson shocked the hostel, residents and staff alike. When the police arrived to search the rooms most of the lads gathered downstairs, hanging around the pool table until Alex chased them out into the sunshine. Samuel's room revealed nothing of interest and little of his personality apart from an almost obsessive drive for order. The space was cleaned, dusted and his minimal possessions were put away neatly, even his shirts hung by colour. He had no form of identity, no photographs and no letters apart from two from his most recent court appearances. Samuel died an enigma, unknown and unmourned.

The cause of his death raised some concerns, for if the blow to the head and subsequent brain damage had killed him then the police would be forced to charge Debbie. Once they had taken statements from Rosalind and Debbie it was obvious she had acted in self-defence and everyone agreed no jury would ever convict her, even if it came to court. Due process, however, dictated she still could be charged and this would probably be the end of her career.

'You saved my life,' Rosalind said at least three times every day. 'You were so brave – I can't imagine what would have happened if you'd not been there.'

The attack had left both women deeply shaken and although they kept up an appearance of confidence and professionalism there were times when both wanted to lock themselves in their rooms and weep. Neither felt safe after dark anymore and Rosalind finally gave in to Debbie's arguments, allowing her to move into the house on Hagg's Hill.

'Just for a while,' she said. 'It looks quite natural, not wanting to be alone after something like that.'

They still drove their own cars to work and kept a formal distance from one another in public, guarding their privacy fiercely. There was a great deal of sympathy for the pair, both in Highpoint and the wider community, and the general feeling was that it would be an outrage to charge Debbie, considering the circumstances. The tension remained, however, and both Debbie and Rosalind began to feel the strain over the next week. Finally, the coroner put them out of their misery by ruling in all probability the adders had caused Samuel's death.

'I've reports of almost twenty bites on the body,' he said. 'Now, one bite or even a couple would not prove fatal to the average adult but twenty would certainly kill. Especially as the deceased was running, causing the poison to circulate rapidly. Add to this the impact of smoke inhalation and I have no doubt in my mind this was either an accidental death or possibly misadventure.' With this statement there were only two possible outcomes for the pending inquest and Debbie was able to breath a little easier.

Alex gathered her papers ready for the supervision session, unaware she was walking into a maelstrom. The police had been back almost every day, to search Steve's room and take away his hoard of stolen items from the market, to check the files for the two young men and then to interview Steve's room-mates. His fondness for setting fires was quickly established when Petey, sweating with fear, blurted out the story of the lighter fluid. Desperate to explain how his prints got onto the can he went into as much detail as he could, implicating Steve in a series of fires whilst trying to present himself as an innocent victim. He even took off his shirt, the better to show the scar on his neck from the first fire.

They had less luck with Mark, who arrived in the office with a man in a very expensive looking grey suit in tow.

'This is my solicitor,' he said casually, and then spent the next half hour chanting, 'No comment ... No comment,' until the police gave up in disgust.

'Not much we can tie him in with anyway,' said Sergeant Willis gloomily. 'Like to know where he got the money for all the gas and firelighters and so on though.'

Alex was sympathetic but equally helpless. She had received a strongly worded letter from the same solicitor that morning, complaining about Mark's treatment at the hostel, the 'unnecessary and unwarranted' interviewing of his client and informing her there would be a formal complaint made to probation headquarters.

'What the hell do they expect?' asked Willis. 'They don't want him mixing with criminals then they should'a done a better job raising the little toe rag!'

Alex raised a weary smile at this. 'There's one thing I've learned over the past few years,' she said. 'If we get a Kevin or a Darren then they're going to be trouble but if we get a Mark Anthony then the parents are going to be trouble.'

'Yer not wrong there,' said Sergeant Willis as he rose to leave. He stopped at the door and looked back at her. 'You take care of yerself now. Had a rough time recently, what with the fire an' all this – and other stuff besides. You just watch yerself. You does a good job and I reckon we need people like you.' He nodded and was gone before Alex could reply.

She recalled his words as she pushed open the door to the Highpoint office and walked up to the counter. Alison was on reception and greeted her like a friend, much to her surprise.

'You got time for a coffee?' Alison asked. Alex glanced at her watch and shook her head.

'Sorry. I'm due upstairs in a couple of minutes. Maybe afterwards if you're still here?'

'Oh, we'll be here,' said Alison. 'Lots to do still, ready for this ever-changing inspection date. I'll be so glad when it's finally over. Good luck,' she added as Alex headed up the stairs. Never a good omen, Alex thought as she knocked on Rosalind's door.

It was opened by the ubiquitous Debbie. Much to Alex's surprise, Debbie gestured for her to enter and then left the office, closing the door behind her. Rosalind sat behind the desk, leaning slightly forwards and watching Alex with bright, hard eyes. She looked disturbingly like a rather portly praying mantis. A portly *pink* praying mantis, Alex thought as she walked across to the chair. Rosalind waited until Alex was seated and then held out her hand for the files. In silence, Alex sat and waited as her senior flicked through the papers, occasionally stopping to scribble something on a pad next to her on the desk.

The minutes crept by and the chair was hard and uncomfortable but Alex forced herself to sit motionless, her eyes unfocussed and staring blankly at the wall behind Rosalind's head. Still no picture of Barbie, she thought, looking at the empty space. Finally, Rosalind admitted defeat, slapping the files closed and pushing them roughly across the table.

'You seem to be keeping up with the administration of the hostel at least,' she said grudgingly.

'Thank you,' said Alex, reaching out to take the folders. Quick as a snake striking, Rosalind put her hand on the files.

'Perhaps we can use this time to explore some wider concerns,' she said, giving her insincere smile.

Alex felt a great sense of weariness wash over her.

'I don't have any wider concerns, thank you, Rosalind.'

The smile vanished in an instant and Rosalind moved back in her chair, her eyes hard and cold.

'You may not but I certainly do,' she snapped. 'Let us begin with the way you dress.'

Before Alex could react to this statement Rosalind forged ahead.

'Of course, this is an expression of your unorthodox lifestyle and it is too late to prevent the ugly rumours and gossip permeating my office. However, I will not have this sort of thing tainting the name of the service far and wide. It is bad enough your unprofessional approach to your duties has caused a considerable amount of trouble both in the day centre and with certain clients. I appreciate you have not benefitted from proper and appropriate supervision during your time here but as a supposedly experienced officer I expected far more from you.'

Alex tried to speak but Rosalind was in full flow.

'It is no coincidence, I feel, that the atrocities perpetrated over the last week are all down to your clients. Men you are supposedly supervising! That is the most fundamental requirement of your job and you have failed miserably.'

'As to your personal life, I understand you have chosen to live in town where your actions are most visible and you hold political meetings advocating anarchy at the weekends ...'

This was too much for Alex.

'That's nonsense!' she protested. 'I don't know what you are talking about – '

'You and your – housemate – Sue were overheard discussing your Friday night activities a few weeks ago,' said Rosalind smoothly. 'You referred to a meeting at your house of the Anarchists' League of Highpoint.'

She leaned back in her chair, radiating smugness.

Alex was lost for words, searching her memory for some explanation. Then came a moment of inspiration and she couldn't suppress a grin.

'I'm glad you find this amusing,' said Rosalind.

'No, I don't,' said Alex. 'What you heard – it was a joke! We have friends round on Friday nights but we never know who's coming or what we'll eat – or even if we'll eat some weeks. It just sort of happens so we sometimes call it "The Anarchist League". How stupid has someone got to be to take that seriously!'

Rosalind flushed and Alex suddenly realized she had made a bad mistake. Before she could remedy the situation the senior launched another attack.

'Not everyone can be as *clever* as you are,' she said. Somehow she managed to make the word 'clever' an insult. 'It is yet another example of your inability to consider your actions in the context of your position. I fear there is very little for you here in the future, given your past record and present attitude. However, if you wish to stay you will need to make some changes. In future I do not expect you to intimate in any way – *any way whatever* – that you are in a non-traditional relationship. By this I mean by what you say, what you do, what you wear, how you behave in public and by omission. Have I made myself clear?'

Alex sat, frozen in the chair. The words 'non-traditional relationship' rolled around in her head and all she could think was Rosalind didn't even have the guts to say 'lesbian'.

'You can't do that,' she managed finally.

'Oh, I can,' said Rosalind. 'I have enough in your file to ensure you never work as a probation officer again. I would suggest you find yourself another post as soon as possible. You are, of course, at liberty to take this up with headquarters but they countersign any reference I give so I wouldn't bother if I were you.'

Debbie was standing outside the door as Alex left, her rosebud mouth pulled up into a smirk of triumph. Alex stopped, wanting to say something, but then turned and walked away down the stairs. What was the point anyway?

Alex spent a week reading the probation bulletins and was surprised to see one area in the north of England advertising for half a dozen members of staff. It seemed she was not the only officer at odds with the system but she was not ready to quit just yet. That would be too much like letting Rosalind win. Personnel at headquarters were most obliging when she requested leave to attend an interview and she was gratified to receive an acceptance a couple of days later. Rosalind had kept her word and given her an acceptable reference, it seemed.

'Probably just wants rid of me,' she confided to Margie the evening the letter arrived.

'Could stay and fight it,' Margie suggested.

Alex sighed and shook her head. 'I went to see my assistant chief on Monday,' she said. 'I thought if they would just back me up I could move internally – maybe go to Taunton or somewhere. But he told me I must have been mistaken.' Alex's lips twisted into a bitter smile as she recalled this final humiliation. 'He told me they had a policy about "that sort of thing" so obviously it couldn't have happened.' She clenched her fists in anger, adding, 'Of course, a policy is only as good as the monitoring and I suspect this one has wandered off into the countryside somewhere. So it's not as if I can come out, say to hell with them all and dare them to do something, because I think they probably will. I need to go – before I'm pushed and I can't get a job anywhere.'

Margie took Alex's hand and stroked it gently. 'We just got to wait and see how it all goes,' she said. 'Been bad afore, got better. There's lots of people as would step up to help you an' most folks don't really care that much.'

Alex smiled, grateful for the support, but looking around her it seemed folks *did* care. She had to hope her new employers were a little less 'caring' and maybe she could get by.

They were about to settle down for a quiet evening when there was a call from Lauren. Alex took it rather reluctantly, drained of any energy to go out and help if there was a problem at the hostel but Lauren's words filled her with sadness.

'Is Jonny,' she said. 'Him and Kurt is going away. Said they's off to Amsterdam 'cos is nothing left here. Jonny won't go out 'cept it's dark on account of his face and Kurt jumps like a scared rabbit the whole time. I tried to talk to 'um but they's fixed on it now. What'm I gonna do without him?'

Alex replaced the receiver and felt tears fill her eyes. She understood what was driving the pair. Life was getting harder every day and sometimes she thought quite seriously about leaving for somewhere she could live, work and walk down the street in safety.

Later that evening the phone rang once more and Alex recognized her mother's voice.

'Hello dear. How are things going with your move?'

Alex had been forced to tell her family of her plans – though not the reason behind them – when her interview date clashed with a family visit. She had been waiting for her parents to come back for more details ever since. There was a thoughtful pause when Alex outlined her new job before her mother replied.

'You should contact your Aunt Julie. She lives up there – well, you should know that. We used to go for holidays when you were little.'

Alex had forgotten all about Aunt Julie – mad Aunt Julie as her brothers called her. An artist of some note, she resided in a grand Edwardian house on a cliff facing the North Sea. Family holidays had always been fun, she recalled. And cold – especially when she and her siblings had ventured into the water.

'I think you might find you have quite a lot in common,' her mother continued. 'You know she was sent down from Oxford, don't you?'

Alex could recall something being whispered about this scandalous event but no-one had ever told her exactly what had happened. There was a touch of humour in her mother's voice as she relayed the story.

'She was brilliant, of course. And very popular with everyone. She was invited to one of those fancy dress themed balls they have, in her third year. Well, the subject was architecture – so impractical but you know what students are like. Anyway, your aunt took it on herself to go as Radcliffe Hall.'

Alex tried but could not suppress a giggle. 'You're kidding,' she said.

'Sadly I am not. The authorities did not think it was so funny,' her mother continued. 'The colleges took quite a dim view of ... that sort of thing ... in the fifties. So she came home in disgrace.'

Alex put down the phone feeling much better about the move. She suspected Aunt Julie might be quite a lot of fun.

As soon as Alex decided to find another job everything started to go wonderfully at work. Mark Anthony's father agreed to have him moved to a different hostel on the far side of the county, Steve was sent to Pucklechurch to await trial and Petey received a formal caution but was allowed to return to the hostel where he spent his days attending classes and trying to inveigle himself into the good books of Molly Brown through the art sessions. Charlie came back from his college placement a couple of weeks later, a huge grin on his face, and handed Alex a letter from his tutor. Alex opened it, trying to rouse some enthusiasm but feeling as if it was all rather a waste of time.

'Go on,' said Charlie. 'Is good news – but will need yer help if'n is to work out.'

Story of my life, Alex thought, skimming the note. When she had finished she blinked, looked up at Charlie and then read it again, more carefully this time. Charlie, it seemed, was one of the best lads the stonemason had ever had at the yard. Not only was he strong, willing and exceptionally hard working, he also had a natural ability to carve and an eye for a decent design. In fact he was so good the mason had taken the liberty of showing some of Charlie's work to two friends of his. These men were equally impressed and had got in touch with the college to discuss taking Charlie on as an apprentice.

This was all heart-warming stuff and the sort of thing Alex dreamed about for her charges but it was the final paragraph that left her struck dumb. They were offering him an apprenticeship as a sculptor, working with them on the restoration of Wells Cathedral.

'So can I go an' do it?'

Alex took a deep breath, laying the letter down on the desk in front of her. 'You know it's seven years don't you?' she said.

Charlie nodded.

'Seven years of doing the "naff stuff". Not much money and having to go to college every week too.'

Charlie grinned, still nodding.

'I'll have to see who can take your order for the next year and get the court to agree to release you from your residency requirement,' she continued. Charlie's smile slipped a bit.

'Don't think they'll say no, does you?' he asked anxiously.

'I would hope not,' said Alex. 'This really is such an amazing opportunity.' She felt a little of the old spark inside of her. 'Leave it with me, Charlie. I'll see what I can do.'

'Thanks! Girt magic en't it?' And he was gone, leaving her to muse on the fact that if he made it through the training then his work – the carvings made by one of her lost boys – would be studied and admired by generations of visitors to the cathedral. Charlie, at least, would leave something beautiful behind him.

When she told Bennie after suppertime her assistant tried once more to persuade her to stay.

'No-one ever done as much as you. Place is running smooth now and most lads is knuckling down an' getting somewhere.'

Privately, Alex thought a lot of this was due to the double shock of Samuel's death and Steve's incarceration but she was pleased none the less.

'No, I'm never going to be able to do my job here,' she said. 'You can do just as well – probably better seeing as you're not under the same level of observation. I hope they have the sense to make you warden.'

Bennie gave a little smile. 'Won't have a lot of choice, unless they bring bloody Peter Marks back. Running low on probation officers they are, way they treating 'em'.

Alex was grateful for the quiet support offered by Bennie. Over the past weeks it had seemed as if people were avoiding her. Never a great socialite, she had still enjoyed a number of friendships with her co-workers and there had been regular invitations to dinner, skittles matches or drinks out at Highpoint's numerous pubs. Now the phone was silent and the 'Anarchist' evenings were no more than a meal on Friday evening for her, Margie and Sue.

'Maybe they think it's catching,' she said to Margie one night.

'More like running scared,' was the reply. 'Inspection was a bit of a nightmare by all accounts and no-one wants to be seen as bein' out of line. Folks is scared for their jobs, an' scared folks is easy to bully.'

Even Sue, her closest and oldest friend, seemed a bit distant and preoccupied and this, more than anything else, hurt her. When Alex announced she had found another post at the far end of the country Sue had congratulated her with a tight smile and carried on eating her dinner.

Alex didn't know how to broach the subject and so the silences grew between them. Margie was another matter, a different but equally thorny problem. She had already moved once, coming to Highpoint from Bristol. Much as she longed to, Alex didn't know if she could ask her to leave another job on her say-so. The days ticked past, nothing was said and each of the trio suffered agonies of uncertainty over the future.

Finally, Sue took up the matter with Margie.

'I don't know if you're moving or staying,' she said. 'And please don't take this the wrong way but should I be looking for somewhere else to live?'

Margie let out a huge sigh of relief.

'Was wondering if we'd get to moving day and still all be sittin' here staring at a pile of boxes,' she said. 'Depends on if Alex wants me along. Would take a while to find something but ...'

'I thought Shepton Mallet was your perfect job?' said Sue.

'Reckon I'd rather have any old job an' be with Alex than one as is perfect but without,' said Margie.

'You must tell her,' said Sue. 'I know Alex and she's eating up inside not knowing.'

Margie smiled at Sue. 'You'm right. I'll tell her tonight. Will be stayin' around for a bit though. What about you? Were talkin' about getting a place of yer own, while back.'

Sue pulled a face. 'Hmm. Well, I don't know I can manage it, the way things are at the moment. Might have to rent somewhere and see how it goes.' She looked around the room, sad at the thought of leaving somewhere she had been so happy. 'Damn Rosalind!' she snapped. 'Why did she have to come here and ruin everything?'

'Maybe you should buy this place,' said Margie thoughtfully. 'Alex'll need to sell an' you could have me as a lodger for a while, give you time to sort out someone else?'

Sue looked at her and suddenly smiled. 'That's the best idea I've heard in ages,' she said.

The week before Alex left she took the last of her accumulated holiday and spent most of it sorting, packing and discarding, and on the Tuesday evening Margie came home to find her standing in the middle of the front room surrounded by boxes, in tears.

'What now?' Margie asked, reaching out to give her a hug.

'There was a call, about ten minutes ago,' Alex snuffled.

'Don't you listen,' said Margie fiercely. 'Is some ignorant, stupid people in this world and ...'

'No, not that sort of call,' said Alex. 'It was – I'm not sure who it was but they sounded familiar. It's someone from one of the other offices I think. Anyway, they wanted to say goodbye and they said they were sorry.'

'Sorry you leaving?' asked Margie.

Alex shook her head. 'No. They said they were sorry they couldn't come to see me in person. They didn't want me to think too badly of them for being scared.'

They sat in the growing darkness, holding hands, both of them wondering how they had come to their present situation. Finally, Margie shook herself and stood up stretching and leaning over to pull the curtains shut.

'Come on, no point brooding. You got to get up north an' find somewhere nice for us to live so you need looking after afore your long journey.'

Pauline was not a person who tolerated fools gladly and in her opinion the service she loved and, despite all the tinkering from above, continued to believe in was being run by fools. She watched as the management allowed an idiot in the form of Garry, Rosalind's predecessor, to cut a swathe through the provision. She tried to protect the younger officers from the worst excesses of new workloads and unreasonable demands. She had stood up to Rosalind about under-staffing and fought to keep control of her office but there was little she could do for Alex but sympathize.

When she heard of Rosalind's 'suggestion' that officers and staff would be best advised not to have any contact with Alex before her departure she was quietly furious. She would not allow her staff to disobey the management in the office but outside was another matter. Quietly and efficiently she made plans, gathered friends and allies and put her own money and time into ensuring those who genuinely wanted to would be able to say their goodbyes.

A brown envelope circulated the office with a card inside and those who knew and respected Alex slipped money inside. There were more than even Pauline had expected, from all tiers of the service. Even Bert the evening caretaker and Hazel the cleaner at the hostel put in to the collection. Pauline cornered Margie one day, stopping her outside the house on her way in from work. Together they mulled over the thorny problem of a suitable gift until Margie hit on an original idea.

'I'm not sure we can do that,' said Pauline. 'And I'm sure we shouldn't be encouraging that sort of behaviour.'

'Come on,' said Margie. 'You got to use what you got an' we got a lot of willing hands with the right expertise. I can get a key for yer if'n you can organize the rest.'

Despite her misgivings Pauline had to admit the idea was attractive and finally agreed.

'I'll drive her to yours on Friday,' she said. 'What time you want her there?'

Alex had been dreading the last Friday night in her old home and so took a lot less persuading than she usually did to go out for the evening.

'Surprise,' said Margie, when pressed on their destination. 'Promise you'll like it though.'

Alex settled back in the passenger seat, disappointed Sue was not home yet.

'It doesn't seem right, having our last Friday without her,' she said sadly.

'I told her where we going,' said Margie. 'She's planning on joining us a bit later.' She drove up the road, anxious to get Alex away before Sue arrived, weaving through the residential streets until pulling up outside Pauline's house. Alex peered out of the window, taking in the unusual number of cars parked outside.

'Isn't that Tom's van?' she asked, pointing across the road.

'Maybe. Come on – they expecting you,' said Margie.

The front door swung open and Pauline hurried down the path, arms wide open in welcome.

'Come in!' she said, leading a stunned Alex into the hall. Friends and colleagues crowded round her, hugging and shaking her hand, pulling her through to the back where the conservatory opened out onto rolling lawns. Tables set with food and bottles of wine lined the walls and there was a pile of cards and small gifts waiting for her. Alex looked around the room, spotting so many familiar faces. Most of the serving officers were there, even Margaret who had seemed so remote when she arrived nearly four years ago. Gordon, still exiled to Yeovil, raised a glass in her direction. Bennie whispered in her ear, 'Was terrible hard, keeping this a secret!'

Surrounded by so much affection, Alex struggled not to cry. Someone placed a glass in her hand, someone else started the record player going and the evening was in full swing.

'I'm really sorry I'll miss your wedding,' Alex said to Ada.

'Never mind. You go an' make a decent life, you and your friend,' said Ada. ''Sides, if we can't settle on a house won't be no wedding.'

Tom appeared at her side and gave Ada an affectionate squeeze.

'Would be more sense in using my place,' he said. 'Is bigger and got mains electrics an' a telephone an' all.'

Ada glared at him. 'What'm I gonna do with a telephone?' she asked. ''Ent no-one I know got one so who's I gonna call? Anyway,' she said, turning to Alex, 'you know what he ain't got? Asparagus bed, that's what. Takes six years to grow it on to eating an' that's next year. Think I is leaving my asparagus?' She tried to look fierce but the way she stood, leaning slightly against Tom's strong frame, suggested they would find a way round the problem.

After an hour someone called Alex's name and she ambled back inside. The whole crowd gathered round her and from the grin on some of their faces she surmised this was the embarrassing part of the night. Toasts, good wishes for the future – stuff like that.

'We all wanted to get you something you would use every day, something to remember us by,' said Pauline. 'Well, we hope you like it.'

The crowd parted, opening a path to the front door where Sue stood, twirling a set of car keys round one finger. Alex walked over and gave her a quick hug before she noticed the keys belonged to her car.

'What ...?'

Sue grabbed her hand, almost pulling her down the steps to where the old Citroën was parked in the drive. The car was spotless, gleaming and rust free. Alex stared at it for a moment and then noticed something protruding from the roof.

'That's ... I don't have a radio,' she said, peering through the front windows.

'You do now,' said Sue gleefully. 'And it's got a cassette player too.'

'How the hell did you manage this?' Alex demanded.

'Well, said Pauline, leading her back inside. 'The hostel lads wanted to help too. It seems the same skills used to remove car radios can be used to fit them. They were out the back cleaning and polishing all evening.'

Alex looked around at her friends and colleagues, so many of them willing to risk their own position to show their support for her. Margie was right, she thought as she walked into the kitchen to thank Pauline. Things got bad and then they got better again.

It was late on Sunday morning when Alex set off from Highpoint. She drove along the smaller roads, wanting to see the countryside one last time and in the golden light of autumn it seemed to her it had never looked so beautiful. When she reached the road leading into Bath she pulled over into a lay-by and stepped out, looking back one last time. A gentle breeze blew but there was a hint of the cold to come as it began to pull the first leaves from the trees. There was a flurry overhead and as she looked up a great cloud of birds swept across the sky, crying and wheeling as one, heading south for the Levels and their winter home.

Standing by the boundary stone between counties Alex remembered the good and the bad, friends and enemies, all she had failed at and all the lives she had helped to heal. She didn't expect the future to be better, though she hoped it couldn't get any worse. She just wanted it to be different. Sliding back into the driver's seat she opened a cassette box, given her by Margie as she was leaving. The sounds of 'California Dreaming' washed round the car and Alex grinned as she pulled away back onto the road. Going in the wrong direction for that, she thought, but there are a lot of roads to choose from. She had Aunt Julie waiting to greet her, she had a job and hopefully she would soon have Margie by her side too. Humming along to the music she headed north.